BARNABAS
BOPWRIGHT
SAVES THE CITY

Praise for
The Dubious Gift of Dragon's Blood

"Freeman does a great job of building an unfamiliar environment without overwhelming the reader with superfluous details...VERDICT: From swoon-worthy romances to epic dragon fights, this has a little bit of everything for readers to enjoy."—*School Library Journal*

"Sixteen-year-old Crispin Haugen is chosen to be the Dragon Groom who will mate with the Dragon Queen in order to maintain the Five...Further complicating matters is the growing attraction between Crispin and the Prime Magistrate's handsome and devout pupil Davix. The recurring emphasis on personal agency and consent is a pleasant surprise, especially as it is applied to both intimate relationships and the chosen-one trope."—*Kirkus Reviews*

By the Author

The Dubious Gift of Dragon's Blood

Three Left Turns to Nowhere
(with Jeffrey Ricker and 'Nathan Burgoine)

Barnabas Bopwright Saves the City

BARNABAS BOPWRIGHT SAVES THE CITY

by

J. Marshall Freeman

2022

ISBN 13: 978-1-63679-152-4

THIS TRADE PAPERBACK ORIGINAL IS PUBLISHED BY
BOLD STROKES BOOKS, INC.
P.O. BOX 249
VALLEY FALLS, NY 12185

FIRST EDITION: MAY 2022

CREDITS
EDITORS: JERRY L. WHEELER AND STACIA SEAMAN
PRODUCTION DESIGN: STACIA SEAMAN
COVER DESIGN BY INKSPIRAL DESIGN

Acknowledgments

This book has a long history. It began life as my first novel (that wasn't X-Men fanfiction), twice as long and not yet sure what it was. I put the manuscript aside in frustration and moved on to my next novel, only to have Barnabas and his friends rise one night from drawer oblivion and proclaim, "You're not done with us yet."

To the dozens of eyes that have danced across these pages in their several incarnations, I give thanks.

Thanks, too, to Bold Strokes Books for the dedication you have shown me and all your authors. Your passion, organization, and hard work have made these early years of my writing career possible. Sandy Lowe, Ruth Sternglantz, Jerry Wheeler, and Stacia Seaman—thank you for meeting my anxiety and stubbornness with grace and enthusiasm.

This is a book about changing the world, or at least our own little corner of it. It is inspired by the audacity of young activists who are not going to let the adults bury our heads in the sand while the world burns.

To Béla, who wanders with me in the Witch's wood
and never forgets to bring the pebbles.

And to Matt W. Cook and A. M. Matte,
who dance the full moon jig with me
around the bubbling cauldron.

PART I

THURSDAY

CHAPTER 1

It was the best city in the world, and Barnabas Bopwright loved it with all his heart. He loved the beautiful discordant symphony of sirens, jackhammers, and gut-deep subway rumbles. He loved the smell of hot chili chestnuts rising from the vendors' carts, and he loved the crowds marching down the sidewalks with their steaming cups of KonaBoom coffee, past majestic towers that kissed the sky.

Barnabas had lived in the City for all of his fifteen years and five months. He had ridden the subway alone since he was twelve, and he knew that whole underground labyrinth by heart. He could tell you to take the Green Line to the Manhammer Audiodome. He knew which end of the platform to stand on if you took the Purple Line to the Jumble Market. And if you were going to River's Edge Park on a Sunday morning to see the skaters perform their sickest moves, he knew it was better to get off at Caramello Station and walk back through the marina than to do the obvious and exit at River's Edge Station. Barnabas Bopwright wasn't some suburban weekend faker; he was a true child of the City that Lawrence Glorvanious built.

On a Thursday morning in early May, Barnabas was woken by an incoming TxtChat message from his best friend and possibly girlfriend, Deni Jiver:

AGirlNamedDeni: We have a real camera!!!!!

He thumbed his reply:

barnabusToNowhere: Where from?

AGirlNamedDeni: Just get to school. Don't be late. You're probably still in bed.

barnabusToNowhere: Wrong. Already dressed and half out the door.

Barnabas shrugged the pillow off his head and squinted at the golden glow coming from behind his bedroom curtains. *Okay, sunny day, let's do this!*

As he reached into the pile of clothes beside his bed for something clean enough to wear to school, he caught sight of his new poster on the wall: a photograph of a lone mountaineer peering out from the summit of a mountain. Barnabas could only imagine the sense of triumph, climbing alone to the top of the world, proving to everyone you were a success after all. He looked at the man's broad, tanned shoulders and the powerful muscles of his hairy legs and wondered if he could ever be that heroic. He picked up a T-shirt from the pile, gave the pits a sniff test, and hurried down the hall to the bathroom.

Deni's news about the camera was a relief. The special guest at that morning's school assembly was Arthur Tuppletaub, the mayor. As videographer for the Journalism Club, Barnabas was responsible for making the footage look good, and the only camera he had was a five-year-old smartphone. And at that moment, it buzzed.

AGirlNamedDeni: You better be on the subway already.

He texted back a thumbs-up. His mother was standing at the front door, simultaneously texting and wrestling a chunky gold earring into place as he headed for the kitchen.

"Oh, Barney-lamb!" she exclaimed, planting a quick kiss on the top of his head while scrolling through her messages. "I ordered you and Sam a build-your-own pad Thai for dinner."

"But, Mom, I thought it was family dinner night."

She bit her lip. "I know, I know, but I've *just* been appointed to the board of a new charity." She turned a no-nonsense corporate smile in Barnabas's direction. "It's a *wonderful* organization! We're raising money to send *party kits* to people in refugee camps. Balloons, games, decorations for Hawaiian-themed prom nights—"

"But don't they mostly need, you know, food and medicine?"

His mother clucked her tongue and adjusted her suit jacket in the hall mirror. "That's what *everyone* does. If you want to get donors for a start-up charity, you have to *differentiate* yourself!" She looked back down at him. "Did I kiss you yet?"

"Yes," he muttered sourly, turning away as she left the apartment. Sam, his stepfather, was at the kitchen table with one of his indigenous musical instruments, examining the horn and sinew that made up its body and strings. He put it aside and brought a plate of eggs and toast to the table for Barnabas.

"Sorry about family dinner," Sam said. "But we'll have a good time. Just us men, right?"

Barnabas winced.

Sam handed him a folded bundle of orange cloth. "And you might want to wear this. It's a bit chilly out." Barnabas unfolded it to find a sweatshirt from Agranda Latté's latest tour—swag from the radio station where Sam worked. Barnabas cringed. The idea of walking into school in a pop-diva shirt was mortifying.

He knew he should be nicer to Sam, but the man still seemed like an odd limb grafted awkwardly to the body of their family. Maybe it was just too many changes too fast. Within months of his mom marrying Sam, they had both lost their jobs. The family was forced to sell their big uptown condo and move into this cramped apartment. Sam went from professor of world music at the university to afternoon DJ at a crappy top 40 radio station. But he never complained or took out his frustration on them.

Barnabas pulled on the sweatshirt and managed a smile. "Thanks, it's great."

As he dug into his breakfast, his phone buzzed again.

AGirlNamedDeni: Cal and I will meet you by the elevators at 8:50.

Barnabas checked the time: 8:12.

barnabusToNowhere> yup np. Wait what. CAL?!

Chapter 2

By the time he'd brushed his teeth, packed his school bag, and made it to the door, it was already 8:17. He was just tying his shoes in the front hall when he saw a courier package with his name on it sitting on the mail shelf.

"Sam! What's this package?"

Sam called from the kitchen, "Oh, I forgot. It came for you while you were in the shower."

Late as he was, Barnabas couldn't resist tearing it open. The packing slip showed the sender address in Japan. *Thelonius!* He tossed aside the packaging and paperwork and, ripping away the bubble wrap, found a surprisingly heavy device about the size and shape of a baseball, made of shiny blue plastic.

He stared at it for a second before stuffing it into his backpack and running out the door. Barnabas took the elevator down thirty-five storeys from his family's apartment and stepped into the endless rolling boil of the City. No matter how depressed or angry he felt when he woke up, joining the electric thrill of the morning crowds always brought him to life.

He descended into Kiletko Station, where he took a southbound Red Line subway to Rebbertrue Station and followed the shuffling crowd up an escalator to the Yellow Line. The Yellow Line, which ran parallel with the river, was the first to have the flashy new subway trains, with their elegant, angled windows and state-of-the-art 3D info screens. The Wi-Fi on the Yellow Line was top-notch, and the recorded station announcements were narrated by a mystery woman with a deep voice Barnabas found incredibly sexy. She always sounded a little condescending, on the verge of laughter. "Deerlick Station is next. Deerlick." The second time she said it, she separated the words—Deer Lick—as if she was saying, "Did you all *hear* that? What does that even *mean?*"

He took out his phone, put in his earbuds, and initiated a

VidChat with his half-brother, Thelonius Bopwright. Thelonius was living in Tokyo with his Japanese mother, teaching English. When they vidchatted, the phone screen seemed to Barnabas like a strange *Alice in Wonderland* mirror. First of all, night and day were reversed. As Barnabas headed for school, Thelonius was getting ready to go to bed. But more than that, everything on the far side of the screen looked vaguely familiar but was oddly different. For instance, when he answered the call, Thelonius was munching on something that looked like a pepperoni stick but could have been made of seaweed.

"Did you get it?" Thelonius asked. "Tracking says you got it."

"Yes, this morning. What is it?"

"It's called a diaboriku. They're already really popular here. Give me your best guess what it does."

"Di-a-bo-ri-ku," Barnabas repeated carefully. "Can you give me a hint?" He took the blue sphere from his bag and examined it critically. On one side was a small glass circle, like a camera lens, with a larger lens on the opposite side. Clustered between were three rubbery green buttons and one red one.

Thelonius gave him a smug smile. "Put on your Junior Sherlock cap, Buster!"

"Don't call me Buster. And I'm not part of your stupid Sherlock club." He pushed the buttons on the device. Lights flashed and an annoying beep sounded, but nothing happened.

"Deductive logic is not stupid," Thelonius say, "Start by reading the instructions."

"They're in Japanese!"

Thelonius laughed, and Barnabas was going hurl some choice brotherly curse when he realized the subway had reached its terminus, Admiral Crumhorn Station. He put the diaboriku back in his bag.

"Got to go, Lony."

"Don't call me till you figure it out, Buster!"

Crumhorn Station had been built for old-fashioned rail traffic years before the first subway tunnels existed. When he walked through its cavernous spaces, Barnabas liked to imagine it was a hundred years ago, and he was Mayor Lawrence Glorvanious himself, dropping into the gentlemen's lounge or the elegant restaurants, or maybe checking in at the swanky hotel. All of these were gone now, but the majestic central hall remained. Its hand-carved columns rose high into the air, holding aloft the great domed ceiling of stained glass. While everyone else marched along, noses down in their phones, Barnabas turned his eyes upward, lost in his city's history. And that's why he didn't see the kid coming.

The collision was sudden and jarring, and Barnabas and the

little human missile both found themselves on their butts on the hard floor. The kid was maybe twelve, with unkempt, dirty blond hair and astonishingly wide eyes. He was wearing khaki coveralls way too roomy for his skinny body.

"I'm sorry! Oh, Father Glory, I'm sorry!" the kid shouted, running to help Barnabas up as he looked all around nervously.

"It's fine. I'm okay."

The boy stared for another second before he turned and hurried away.

Barnabas noticed a colourful sheet of folded paper on the ground. "Hey, buddy!" he called. "You dropped something." As the kid reversed course, Barnabas picked it up and unfolded it. It was an old subway map from before everyone used the transit app. When he opened the second fold, something about the familiar map caught his eye, something… different.

A shadow fell across Barnabas, and a large, calloused hand unceremoniously snatched the paper away. Barnabas looked up to see a man dressed in a worn one-piece khaki coverall—the same kind the kid was wearing. He wore a toolbelt and heavy boots grey with dust. His sweaty, shaved head reflected the red neon sign of the nearby KonaBoom Koffeeshop: "Hot and fresh, every day." The man was old— maybe forty or fifty—but he looked strong. His black eyes, piercing as a crow's, bored into Barnabas.

"Thank you," he said coldly as he refolded the map and snapped at the terrified kid, "Can't I trust you with *anything*?" He grabbed him roughly by the arm, and they disappeared into the thick flow of the commuter crowd. Were they father and son? Barnabas thought maybe he should follow to make the sure the boy was okay. He also wanted to take another look at that subway map.

"A northbound Green Line train has arrived on track five," said a PA announcement that echoed across the vast hall. "All aboard."

Barnabas cursed under his breath. It was too late to reach the train now, and taking the next one would make him six minutes late for school. But that was okay. His homeroom teacher would just be taking attendance before leading the class to the assembly with Mayor Tuppletaub. The only real problem was Deni, who was going to interview the mayor onstage. If her videographer didn't show up on time, she would be devastated. In his head, he could hear her say the word with high dramatic fervour: "DEVASTATED!"

He thought again about the man, the kid, the map. *Well*, he thought, *I have a few minutes to kill*. So, he tightened his backpack and went after the mysterious pair.

CHAPTER 3

The Junior Sherlocks were an informal group of nerd adventurers Thelonius had founded with a subset of his D&D buddies in high school. It was their self-appointed mission to solve the mysteries of the universe, great and small. For instance, why did the physics teacher, Mr. Meyers, change into a red track suit and fishing hat at the end of every school day, and who were the other three identically dressed men who always picked him up at 3:30 in a beaten-up blue Chevy?

Barnabas had made fun of his big brother for this pastime, but, truth be told, he didn't consider himself smart enough to be a Junior Sherlock. Yet here he was in detective mode, trailing suspects through Admiral Crumhorn Station at rush hour.

Spotting the man and boy standing behind a photo booth, Barnabas pushed sideways against the flow of the crowd, earning himself a string of curses from angry commuters. He scuttled low and tucked himself behind a garbage can opposite the photo booth. Peering around the garbage can, Barnabas saw the miserable kid, eyes resolutely on the ground as the man lectured him.

"You are an undiluted idiot, Galt-Stomper! You know that map is a restricted document beyond the Frontier, and yet you toss it away like a candy wrapper."

"I'm sorry, Mr. Glower," the kid murmured, and Barnabas thought, *so not father and child.* Barnabas's phone vibrated aggressively in his front pants pocket, and he reached in awkwardly to grab it.

AGirlNamedDeni: Camera is here. Where ru?!

"And I'm losing a full day of collecting!" Glower went on. He pulled up his sleeve to check a heavy watch. "No more delays. Let's get oriented."

The kid with the weird name—what the hell was a Galt-Stomper?—started poring over the map. "Look! We're at Admiral Crumhorn, and we have to go all the way *there* to Minimus Junction and—"

"I know where we're going! Put that map away."

With a forlorn expression, Galt-Stomper folded the map and pushed it into the back pocket of his coveralls. Glower moved them closer to the stream of commuters, until they were standing right above the crouching Barnabas. The map in Galt-Stomper's back pocket was mostly hanging out. *What did Glower mean it was a restricted document?* He craned his neck to see if he could read anything on the folded paper.

Glower said, "Let's go," and the pair lurched forward, vanishing into the crowd. Barnabas found himself staring in shock at his own outstretched hand. He was holding the map. For a frozen second, he squatted there, amazed at what he'd done. Then he jumped to his feet, waving the paper in the air and shouting, "Hey! You dropped your document!"

But they were already gone. And he had the mysterious map. Excitement overcame guilt as he crouched back down and began unfolding the well-worn paper. His phone buzzed.

AGirlNamedDeni: BARNABAS?!!!!!!!

barnabusToNowhere: there in 5

"A northbound Green Line train has arrived on track six. All aboard," said the PA, and Barnabas cringed. He'd never catch it. He was now at least fifteen minutes late for school, not to mention a thief.

He opened the next fold of the map. The different colour-coded subway lines were as familiar to him as his nose in the mirror, but then he saw the oddity that had caught his attention before. In the lower right-hand corner was Admiral Crumhorn Station from where Yellow, Green, and Purple lines shot out at different angles like limbs of a rainbow tree. He knew as well as he knew his own name that Crumhorn was the final stop for all of them, but on this map, another line continued beyond the terminus, disappearing under the last unopened fold of paper. Although the line seemed to be a continuation of the Yellow Line, the colour changed to blue after Crumhorn. No, not blue. The line that emerged on the other side of his favourite station was *aqua*! As he had learned in art class, aqua was not blue or green. It was a mystical colour associated with the primordial sea, with the unknown.

With a sense of thrill and foreboding, he opened the last fold of the map and saw another subway line, an Aqua Line that followed a strange, nonsensical path, first west, but then veering north to the edge of the City, continuing beyond the Tower District.

The PA crackled once like it was clearing its throat before the announcement rang out: "A northbound Green Line train is approaching on track five. Please make your way to track five."

There was no more time to spend contemplating this mystery. Barnabas folded up the map, stuffed it in his bag beside his books, his lunch, and the diaboriku, and ran to meet his train.

Chapter 4

As soon as the Green Line train pulled from the station, Barnabas made his way to the very end of the car and squatted by the back window. For a second, he wondered if maybe he'd imagined the altered map, but when he unfolded it, there was the Aqua Line. Whereas all the other lines in the system ran relatively straight, the Aqua meandered drunkenly as if it couldn't quite make up its mind where it was headed. It crossed other lines, but there were no interchange stations. And the names of the Aqua Line stations were *madness!* Some were just numbers, although not in order. Others had names like Final Process, Drum, Lesser Holding, Cracks, and Doomlock. Down in one corner, text in a tiny font read, "All Praise to Father Glory."

Is this a joke? he wondered. But Glower and Galt-Stomper had seemed deadly serious. He exited the train at Blesskind Station thinking how his life was filling up with mysteries—first the diaboriku and now this alternate map. Maybe the Junior Sherlocks worked freelance and he could hire one.

But now all that mattered now was getting to school before Deni had a heart attack. He bolted up the stairs to street level and ran down the sidewalk, bursting through the doors of a mid-size office building and not slowing until his finger hit the up button beside the elevator doors with well-practiced precision.

The Sky High School of Youthful Enthusiasm occupied the top four floors of the building, which also housed a P.R. firm, several lawyers' offices, and two rival dating app companies. There were just 127 students at the school, ranging in age from twelve to eighteen, but it was an exceptionally engaged group. After regular classes ended each day, almost all the students stayed for extracurricular activities. There were debates and model world governments, music-making of all types from medieval to hip-hop, gaming and game design, visual arts, theatre arts, and video production. Sports activities were rare, partly because the school's mission was "to make a brighter future by igniting the creative spirit," and partly because a school in a narrow office building had no place for a gym.

Barnabas burst out of the elevator, almost colliding with Deni, who stood there, quivering with fury.

"Nine twenty!" she hissed through gritted teeth.

"Nine sixteen!" he countered.

She gave his sweatshirt a look of disgust. "Agranda Latté? Really? You're trying to kill me." She turned to the boy standing to her right. "Calvin, camera!"

Cal Kabaway was new to the school, having only recently moved to the City. It wasn't clear to Barnabas why anyone would bother showing up for the last two months of school instead of just starting in September, but the handsome boy with the black curls and warm brown skin had immediately made an impression. He was always well-dressed and confident, and though he wasn't all that tall—maybe five-eight to Barnabas's five-five—he walked around with a sarcastic smirk that made Barnabas feel looked down on. Cal handed Barnabas his camera, already mounted on a sturdy tripod. It was an enviable piece of gear—a ProVizaleer XV, midnight blue and shiny silver, styled more like a sports car than a video camera.

"Calvin is part of the Journalism Club now," Deni announced. At five-ten, she was the tallest of the trio.

Why? Barnabas wanted to ask. *Because he can afford a fancy camera?* Up to that point, he and Deni had been the only members, and he felt a stab of jealousy.

"Here's the plan," she said. "Did either of you see the clips of Ingrid Arngrod interviewing Senator Bolvine?" Cal and Barnabas looked at each other in confusion. "She got him to admit rigging an election back when he was in high school. She destroyed his career in five minutes!" Deni said this last bit with a hungry grin.

"And that's what you want to do to Mayor Tuppletaub?" Barnabas asked, suddenly wary of the whole enterprise.

"We're late. Let's go!"

They followed her to the auditorium, which doubled as the school cafeteria. As they walked, Cal explained to Barnabas how to use the camera in his annoyingly charming Caribbean accent. Barnabas tried to simultaneously look like he already knew this information and to memorize every single detail.

They found the doors of the auditorium blocked by an intimidating man they had never seen before. His heavily muscled physique seemed ready to burst out of his shiny, shark-grey suit. He wore dark glasses, and his blond hair was styled in a bowl cut that looked a little ridiculous, not that you would dare say to his thick-jawed face. This tough guy was obviously part of the mayor's security. The name tag on his lapel read "B. Klevver."

"Who are you?" Klevver challenged them.

Deni threw her shoulders back and looked the man in the eye. "We're the Journalism Club. Will you please stand aside?"

Klevver looked like he was about to demand ID or handcuff them, but after a tense few seconds, he moved away from the doors. Deni pulled them open and waved the boys in.

The assembly had already begun. A teacher near the door turned to them and brought a finger to her lips, but Deni had no time for authorities other than herself—she was in directing mode. Deni walked halfway down the centre aisle and showed Barnabas where to set up, whispering instructions to him about how to frame the image. Cal, meanwhile, connected a shotgun microphone to the camera and walked to the edge of the stage with it, unspooling a long cable as he went.

Up on stage, Mary Rolan-Gong, principal of the school, was grinning and making announcements. On chairs at the back of the stage sat the mayor, alongside a sharply dressed advisor who was whispering in his ear.

Ms. Rolan-Gong turned her perpetual enthusiasm up a notch and said, "Before I introduce our very special guest, the senior choir has a special performance for us all. This is a song that used to be a staple of civic gatherings, but has not been heard in many, many years. Please stand for the City's anthem!"

The whole room got to its feet in bemused unison as seven students and the music teacher, all in matching school sweatshirts, moved to the front. Barnabas started filming. With gusto and pep, the choir sang:

> *Hail to the future, sprung from the land,*
> *Hail to the roads built by spirit and hand,*
> *A world where our children can prosper and play,*
> *In this fair, golden City rising skyward today.*

The loud cheers for the cheesy song were mostly sarcastic, but Barnabas was glad to have another bit of the past brought back to life.

"And now," said the principal, her enthusiasm climbing to yet another level, "it's my privilege to welcome to our school, His Honour, the mayor of our City, Arthur Tuppletaub."

CHAPTER 5

The mayor's advisor was still whispering last-minute instructions in his ear even as he stood up. Mayor Tuppletaub was a strange creature: a big round head on a long, angular body. Maybe this mismatch made him top-heavy because he practically tumbled to the front of the stage, grabbing at the mic stand like a novice swimmer reaches for the edge of the pool.

"Hello!" he shouted over the applause. "Sit down! Sit! Gosh, it's the leaders of tomorrow all in one room! I'd better get on your good sides now." He flashed his trademark smile, which opened up across his soft, childish face like the ground opens in an earthquake.

Ms. Rolan-Gong, still holding her mic, laughed brightly and made a one-handed clap. She said, "Mr. Mayor, I know this is a busy time for you with the election just three weeks away. We're so grateful you could fit us into your schedule."

"No, no, I'm delighted to be here. It's important our youth understand the *awesome*, one-of-a-kind City they live in and learn how it all works! So that it continues to be the best…just the *best* City in the whole world!"

He himself led the applause on this one. Barnabas panned around the room, capturing footage of the appreciative audience, though various students tried to ruin the shot by waving into the camera and picking their noses. He turned the lens back to the stage. He had never really thought of the mayor as an actual person before, just a media creation made of video clips and sound bites. But now Barnabas was the one making that footage. This electronic relationship with Tuppletaub felt weirdly intimate.

The lights dimmed, and an onscreen presentation began. The mayor provided his own narration, inserting himself into the history of the City that they all knew from civics class. The first image was Lawrence Glorvanious, mayor of the City in the days before world wars and radio, looking dapper in his top hat, smoking a cigar, and standing beside his architects and engineers—also in top hats, also smoking cigars—to examine the scale model of the new downtown. This image was followed by a slide of Mayor Tuppletaub beside the same model in the municipal museum. The slides continued to alternate between the great mayor and the not-so-great mayor, currently polling at a nail-biting forty-nine percent as the election drew near.

The mayor said, "My administration has worked hard to maintain and build upon the visionary, uh, *vision* of Lawrence Glorvanious, whose vision of the City, more than a hundred years ago, has made us the envy of the world!"

Deni had snuck up behind Barnabas. "Maybe that's what his advisor was telling him before," she whispered in his ear. "'Say *vision* a lot.'"

A teacher turned around and whispered, "Sit down, Ms. Jiver."

Deni ignored this. "I'm going to try and really shake him up with my questions. Be sure you get his reactions on camera." She returned to her aisle seat, pulling out her phone to read through her notes one last time.

The presentation continued with a cool 3D animation Barnabas had never seen before about the growth of the Tower District. The signature buildings—Delphic Tower, the Jezebel, the Reaktion, Neverlander, Greatest Hiltz, and the Honey Pot—rose like blades of grass as a year counter clocked forward through the twentieth century and into the twenty-first.

The animation ended with a dramatic pull back to reveal the whole City, the river in the foreground and the towers standing in the back like the tall cousins in a family portrait. The sun glinted off the City's stadium, the Manhammer Audiodome, and then began to set behind the skyline. The music swelled, and up onstage, the mayor almost sang his narration. "In good times and, uh, not-so-good times, it is the people of this great metropolis that have worked together to take what is already great and grow it into…into an even greaterer future!"

"And now, Mr. Mayor," Ms. Rolan-Gong said brightly as the lights came up and the applause died down, "one of the City's up-and-coming reporters would like to ask you a few questions. Here's Deni Jiver from our Journalism Club!" Barnabas swung the camera around to follow Deni as she walked up the stairs onto the stage. He noticed for the first time how professionally she was dressed. Her long, honey-coloured hair was neatly clipped on top of her head, and she wore a slick jacket over a shiny shirt, her dark jeans tucked into black boots. Appreciating the looks of his old friend was still new to Barnabas.

Soon, Deni and Mayor Tuppletaub were seated opposite each other on two chairs, each with a handheld mic, and Barnabas framed them in a nice two-shot. Despite being so well put together, Deni looked kind of terrified. Her first questions were softballs: Why did the mayor go into politics? What did he want to accomplish if he was re-elected? Her voice was low enough that someone at the back yelled, "Speak up!" Then Deni found her confidence. She cleared her throat and looked the mayor in the eye. "Your main rival in next week's election, Kasha DaSouza, says that this City gets rich off the exploitation of its workers. She says that demands for fair wages have gone unanswered by your administration."

Barnabas zoomed in on the mayor's face, but the reaction wasn't shock or annoyance or the panicked twist of his pumpkin face that Deni might have been hoping for. He just nodded and smiled. "Well, I wouldn't go so far as to call Ms. DaSouza a rival. Her polling numbers aren't keeping me up at night."

Barnabas tried to think calming thoughts at Deni, but already her eyebrows were knit together and her voice rising higher. "Actually, there is strong grassroots support for her positions. For instance, with the price of housing continuing to, um, escalate year on year," Deni looked down at her notes, flipping through several screens before popping back up to finish her sentence, "how is the average steam worker or sanitary collector supposed to raise a family?"

The mayor leaned back in his chair as Barnabas had seen him do on talk shows, quintessentially relaxed. Deni, in contrast, looked coiled and uncomfortable.

"Listen, Ms. Jiver. I admire your passion, but the truth is that compared to any other metropolis the size of the City, we have a higher standard of living, including for our City workers, less unemployment, cleaner air, lower crime rates. When he founded this City, Lawrence Glorvanious built a great system, and a long line of mayors, including myself, have worked hard to adapt it to the times." Tuppletaub turned and found the camera, looking straight into it. Barnabas, pinned by the man's eyes in his display, felt invaded. "Is everything perfect? Of course not. And I am grateful to passionate voices like Kasha's for keeping us on our toes."

"Sure," Deni said, like she was about to contradict him, but she couldn't seem to find the words. Barnabas's heart sank. *Come on, Deni! Don't let him win!*

The mayor took the opportunity to carry right on with his agenda. "Did you know that we're increasingly using steam power to cool buildings in addition to heating them? Trigeneration, it's called!"

"What about subways?" Barnabas heard himself shout. Deni was so surprised, she dropped her phone with a loud clatter. Barnabas felt every eye in the room on him, Deni's the widest. Calvin swung the shotgun mic around to pick up his voice.

The mayor blinked a few times, caught off guard. "Subways? Um, there aren't any plans for more…um, for development of any new—"

Barnabas seemed to have lost control of his mouth. "There aren't any, uh, *secret* subways? You know, that the public doesn't use? Or know about?"

Mayor Tuppletaub's jolly, dimpled demeanour abruptly grew stony. He stared at Barnabas as if trying to see inside his head. "No," he said, his voice a little husky. "There aren't any secret subways."

Holding the mic against her chest, looking somewhere between furious and ready to cry, Deni shouted at him from the stage. "What are you talking about, Barnabas? *I'm* doing the interview!"

The mayor recovered his poise and smiled sympathetically at Deni. "No, it's fine. Good question, son. I'm afraid we don't work like that. New projects only go forward after rigorous economic and environmental assessment." He laughed. "Heck, I wish I could suddenly stand up in a council meeting and say, 'Tada! Here's a new subway!' or 'A new park, out of thin air!' I'd be the most popular mayor in history."

Ms. Rolan-Gong, smile bright as ever, glided forward and took away Deni's microphone. "Well, thank you, Ms. Jiver. And thank you *so much*, Mayor Arthur Tuppletaub for coming to our little school and being such a, gosh, *inspiration* for our students."

The mayor acknowledged the applause with a beaming smile, but when his gaze fell on Barnabas, the smile faltered. The security man, Mr. Klevver, climbed the steps to the stage, and the mayor extended a skinny finger, pointing out Barnabas to him.

CHAPTER 6

Barnabas stood at his locker as students and teachers streamed past on their way back to class. He peered out from behind the open door, watching for Deni, but also for the mayor and his spooky security man. He wasn't sure which encounter would be more nerve-racking.

Why did the mayor look so upset anyway? Barnabas was now pretty convinced the map was a fake, or just some strange, unrealized proposal. How could the City hide an entire subway line? He decided he would show Deni the map. She'd figure out what it was.

Deni and Cal finally appeared as the last of the students headed for second period. Cal ran straight to his camera, checking it for scratches or fleas or whatever. Deni's approach was slower, and she gave Barnabas a cold, flat stare the whole way down the hall.

"If," she said as she closed the distance between them, "you had any *brilliant* ideas for more interview questions, you could have shared them with me before we started."

"I know…"

"…instead of…"

"I know, sorry."

"…like a total…I mean, *secret subways?*"

Barnabas decided *not* to show Deni the map. It was a safer bet to just shift the blame.

"I was trying to help," he said with as much innocent concern as he could muster. "You were a little lost."

Deni's face immediately changed from fearsome to pitiable. She fell back against the bank of lockers and slowly slid down to the floor. "I know. I sucked." She sighed heavily.

Barnabas sat down beside her. "No, you didn't. It's just the mayor's a total pro at the interview thing. You should have seen how he worked the camera."

"I thought you looked very professional," Cal blurted out, standing above them. "And very pretty."

Barnabas stared up at him, annoyed. What was with Cal? Especially what was up with the way he was looking at Deni? Did he like her? Like her *like that*? Barnabas expected Deni to make some caustic reply to Cal's mush, but she smiled at him gratefully. Their eyes locked like they were sharing a super-special moment of mutual understanding. Barnabas writhed in confusion.

What did Barnabas and Deni mean to each other, anyway? He cringed at the memory of a cold day in November, more than a year earlier, when he'd asked Deni to a movie. They had been going to movies together for years, but in his head, this time was different. When she met him in the lobby of her apartment, she sniffed the air and shot him a bemused look.

"Are you wearing *cologne*?" Her laugh felt like a long shard of glass plunging into his stomach. "Is this a *date*, Barnabas?" And it sort of was. The character of their friendship changed then, and at a summer party on a riverboat, they kissed with awkward excitement under a hazy half-moon.

But nothing had ever been definitive or declared. They weren't like other *official* couples who made out publicly and were rumoured to do more. And yet her sudden interest in this newly arrived boy felt like a betrayal.

"We better get to class," Cal said, checking his fancy watch.

Deni shook her head. "No, I got us permission notes. I said we needed to download our footage after the assembly. And thank God. I'm a wreck." She reached up a hand to Cal, and he pulled her to her feet, practically into his arms. Barnabas decided he *would* show Deni the map. Maybe sharing this secret would make her turn her attention back his way.

"Listen," he said. "I have something in my locker you need to see."

Deni spun around, eyes full of excitement. "No! I have something to show *you!*" Her depression apparently forgotten, she ran to her locker and, with great care, pulled out a large, square paper bag.

"Check out what I found at the Jumble Market!" she said. In the bag was an old vinyl record album. *The Brownbag Bopwright Trio, Live at the Blistered Lip* read the cover over a Picasso painting of a group of blocky musicians. Barnabas vaguely remembered having seen this rare album before. His father had a small army of ardent fans around the world, passionate music lovers who all had favourite Brownbag Bopwright saxophone solos. They talked about his tone like wine connoisseurs, calling it "warm as old leather," "sweet and blue." Deni had learned her love of jazz from one of her moms, Mom-Amy, who had been thrilled when she found out Barnabas was the son of the minor living legend.

Deni carefully extracted the album from his hands like he couldn't be trusted with it. "I'll play it for you later, okay?"

"I don't really know anything about jazz," Barnabas mumbled. He thought of the last time he'd seen his dad—a quick lunch at a crappy pizza joint back in March. It had been a spontaneous visit, exhilarating but over so fast that Barnabas spent the next week wondering if it had been a dream.

Cal said, "I want to hear it, Deni!" and Barnabas gave him a withering look.

"So, what did you want to show me?" Deni asked.

Barnabas's uncase grew as he walked back to his locker. He knew Deni would be thrilled by the map. She would have all kinds of theories about what it meant, about what huge conspiracy might lie behind its existence. Having failed to destroy Mayor Tuppletaub in the interview, she'd see the mystery of the map as her next ticket to fame. He could imagine her on the evening news, all poised and serious, or hosting a documentary on the mysteries of the Aqua Line. "And now, we're arriving at the thrilling Doomlock Station!" she would say to the camera with breathless intensity. *Does Deni think she can just go running after Calvin AND steal my discovery?*

He decided *not* to show her the map. Then he remembered he did have something else to show off. He reached into his backpack, hanging from a hook in his locker.

"Voilà!" he said, pulling out the diaboriku. "My brother sent this to me from Japan. I have no idea what it does."

"Is it a camera maybe?" Cal said.

Deni shook her head. "Why would anyone need a camera like this? It wouldn't be any better than your phone."

"Maybe," Barnabas said, "it's a kind of medical scanner."

Deni rolled her eyes. "The Festival of Ridiculous Theories continues."

"No, you know," he insisted, "it could tell if your friend was a zombie. Or your mom had been replaced by an alien!"

"Stop, please!" she said, wincing at all the stupidity. Barnabas, sick of humiliation, decided he would make the diaboriku work. How hard could it be? Furrowing his brow, he tried various combinations of buttons: red, green1, green3, green2—nothing. Red, green2, green1, green3—nothing. Green1, red, green3, green2—nothing! Consistent, unimpressive nothing.

Deni plucked the diaboriku from his hands. "Let Cal try. He can figure anything out." The compliment clearly buoyed Cal's spirits, and he took the little sphere and began to pace up and down the hall, fingers poking and prodding the big rubber buttons. Barnabas glared at the lithe figure in the brilliant white T-shirt he was sure had cost a fortune.

Deni checked her phone for messages while Barnabas tried to source the weird smell in his locker. Just as he located the half-rotten sandwich at the back of the shelf, he heard a gasp from Calvin, followed a scant second later by a high-pitched scream from Deni.

Barnabas spun around in time to see a monster rising up above them, huge, grotesque, and poised to attack.

CHAPTER 7

It was a horror straight out of a science fiction dystopia, a human-hunting robot so large, its head grazed the ceiling. Midnight blue with shiny silver streaks, it had a single cold, glistening eye whose pupil contracted and dilated as it turned its malevolent gaze on them. It stood on three legs, hissing and chirruping, each appendage tipped with a terrible, pointed claw. Barnabas dropped to the ground as the beast reared up on two of its back legs and swung the front leg at him.

Cal ran, and the monster followed him. Deni screamed again, and this inspired Cal to make a U-turn and run to her rescue. But the monster turned with him and bore down on Deni as she tried to squeeze herself into her locker. Then Cal tripped on his own feet, dropped the diaboriku, and the monster vanished. The mysterious device rolled quietly across the floor, coming to a stop near Barnabas's feet.

Barnabas felt like reality had backflipped in front of him. The sound of three kids panting like dogs on a hot summer day was the only noise in the hall. Deni stuck her head out from her locker, her hair loose from its clip, staring at the spot where the creature had stood.

Cal's hand was shaking as he pointed at the fallen diaboriku. "Wh-what the hell is that thing?" Barnabas didn't understand what he meant at first, but then he did. Had the little sphere from the other side of the planet caused this creature to appear in their midst? Had it maybe opened a doorway into another universe?

Barnabas picked it up cautiously. "I don't know. I thought it was just a toy."

Deni extricated herself from her locker. "Words," she gasped. "There were words above the creature's eye. 'Province' or something."

Barnabas noticed Cal's camera, standing serenely on its tripod, right where they had left it. Suddenly he understood. "ProVizaleer. That's what it said."

Cal wiped his sweaty brow with the back of his sleeve. "But that's the name of my camera." They all stared at the black camera with its shiny lens, standing on three legs, just like the monster had.

Deni again took the diaboriku from Barnabas and handed it to Cal. "Do it again. Stand in the same place and push the same buttons." He pushed the sequence of buttons and, with an innocuous beep, the monster returned. It stood just down the hall, twitching and growling as before. But now that they weren't terrified for their lives, they saw a high definition, if somewhat distorted, 3D projection. It looked solid, except where its limbs intersected the nearby lockers. When you knew what it was, you could see the monster was a fake.

Barnabas said, "Oh my God, the diaboriku takes whatever you point it at and *monsterizes* it."

Cal let go of the big red button, and the camera-monster vanished.

Deni grabbed Cal's arm. "Do another one. Do the fire extinguisher!"

Cal crossed to the bright red canister hanging near the staircase and punched in the sequence again. A great red robot was instantly looming above them. It was tall and cylindrical, waving its long, black, serrated appendage menacingly, ferocious clangs emanating from its hissing insides. Barnabas now understood the two lenses. The small one read the source, and the big one projected the transformation.

Cal smiled. "That's pretty damn good. Well, the surround sound could use some work."

Annoyed, Barnabas grabbed the diaboriku back from him, and the robot vanished. "Now you're the expert? A minute ago, you were crapping your shorts like the rest of us." He stuffed the device into the pocket of his sweatshirt.

Deni checked the mirror in her locker, re-clipping her hair before closing the door with a bang. "I can take absolutely no more stress. We'll lock up the camera in the office, then I want a hot chocolate at KonaBoom."

As they climbed to the twelfth floor, Barnabas stayed a few steps back and watched Deni and Cal flirting. They laughed together and bumped into each other not quite by accident, intimate in a way that made them look cooler and more grown up than him.

They reached the twelfth-floor landing, and Cal and Deni turned right toward the office, but Barnabas stayed where he was. He put down his backpack and leaned over the rail, staring down into the abyss, hypnotized by the repeating pattern of stairs and railings that shrank as it receded, floor by floor. He imagined himself tumbling like Alice down the rabbit hole.

A door opened below, and the stairway was abruptly filled with a noisy, laughing group of adults in stylish clothes. The procession was led by Principal Rolan-Gong, grinning and pointing out art hung on the wall of the landing.

The principal walked past Barnabas, followed by a bald man with rimless glasses talking to a woman in a hairstyle that must have taken three hours and a team of engineers to assemble.

"I'm supporting him because he can push my plan through council," the man said. "All those green protestors are costing me a fortune."

She nodded. "Well, if Tuppletaub wants my name on the youth shelter, he owes me that zoning change."

"Seems fair!" said a man behind them. They were all heading down the hall and disappearing into the teachers' lounge.

The long stairway parade ended with the mayor, in smiling conversation with an elderly woman who hung off his skinny arm. When he noticed Barnabas, his smile died and he pulled out his phone, making a short call as he disappeared into the lounge.

Deni and Cal had reappeared, and Barnabas asked her, "Who were they?"

"The richest parents in the school. They're having a fundraising breakfast for the mayor. Champagne, orange juice, and tax write-offs. Now, come on, boys, it's time for my hot chocolate."

The last thing Barnabas wanted was to sit at a tiny café table and watch Deni and Cal stare into each other's souls. "You go ahead," he said. "I'm gonna chill here."

Deni squinted at him. "Are you depressed?"

"What? No!"

"I have a *great* therapist if you need."

"I don't, and I'm not depressed."

"If you say so," she said with a shrug. "Come on, Cal." As they disappeared from view, Barnabas heard them sharing a little laugh, and he felt utterly abandoned despite the fact that he was the one who refused her invitation.

Did he even want Deni as a girlfriend? She was still his best friend, but sometimes he felt stupid and poor around her. He definitely found her attractive. There was one sweater she wore, and the curve of her breasts in it reverberated in his memory. But there were other tantalizing images he hoarded. Billy Baker, for instance, who had permanently changed into shorts on April first, no matter how warm or cold it was on any given day. Barnabas's first glimpse of those long, hairy legs sticking out from under Billy's desk had made him lose his place as he was presenting a report on the Silk Road. What was *that* about? He wasn't gay—I present to the court Deni's breasts in evidence—but he wasn't straight either, that much was becoming clear.

The sound of self-satisfied laughter wafted through the air like expensive perfume. Barnabas slipped down the hall and pressed his ear to the brightly painted door of the teacher's lounge. His mom would have killed to be in there. "Contacts are everything," she liked to tell him. "That's why we send you to a school we can't afford."

His thoughts were interrupted when a meaty hand dropped onto his shoulder.

"Hello, little cameraman," Mr. B. Klevver hissed in his ear.

CHAPTER 8

"Come with me, please," said Klevver, his politeness at odds with the way he was dragging Barnabas down the hall by the arm.

"Let go of me!"

"Easy, cameraman. I just need five minutes of your time. A little longer if you don't co-operate."

Klevver spun Barnabas around and walked him backward like they were dancing a tango, until Barnabas found himself backed against the railing of the stairwell. Klevver grinned a wide grin that might make flowers wilt. In the periphery of Barnabas's vision, he saw the man's fist clenching and unclenching.

"Okay, then," Klevver said, his tone a study in nonchalance. "I have a list of questions His Honour, Mayor Tuppletaub, would like answered. You can do that, can't you?"

Barnabas nodded, too scared to speak.

"Good boy." Klevver cleared his throat. "Why did you ask the mayor about secret subways?"

Barnabas shook his head and tried to speak. "I-I don't know… Just…needed to ask something. M-made it up."

The security man started to chew, apparently on some gum he'd been storing in his cheek like a hamster. "Have you ever been on a secret subway, that is if there was such a thing? Which there isn't, by the way."

"No. I was never on anything like that."

"Never," the man repeated, cords of tension twitching in his jaw as he pulverized the wad of gum.

"No."

"Is one of your parents a…" He uncoiled his fist and reached into the breast pocket of his jacket, pulling out a scrap of paper. "Here we go. Is one of your parents or anyone in your family a deputized Guild Council Interlocutor?"

"Guild Council what?"

Klevver was wearing silvered sunglasses, but Barnabas could swear he saw the man's eyes narrow. "You heard me," he growled and leaned closer to Barnabas, grabbing a handful of Agranda Latté's face and some of the skin underneath. "Guild. Council. In-ter-loc-u-tor."

"I don't even know what that—" But he didn't get to finish the sentence. Like a construction crane, Klevver lifted him into the air. He was heaved up and over the railing. *I'm dead*, Barnabas thought, *and I'm only fifteen!* But he didn't fall. Klevver was holding him by the ankles.

Squirming and spiraling his arms, Barnabas looked up from his inverted perspective and saw the security man leaning over the railing. His dark glasses were hanging half off, his eyes insane blue marbles, and he was screaming, "*Tell me, you little snot.*"

The sweatshirt bunched up around his chest, and Barnabas watched in shock as the diaboriku slipped loose from the pocket and fell past his head. He grabbed for the device, but the toy hit the landing below and started bouncing down the stairs. Above him, Klevver was red in the face, out of control. "You stinking little monkey! You slug! Who do you think you're trying to fool, you jacked-up little—"

"Klevver!" shouted a familiar voice. Barnabas, heart pounding, eyes blurred with tears, turned his upside-down head and saw upside-down Mayor Tuppletaub running down the hall. "What the hell do you think you're doing, you idiot? There's an election in three weeks. I can't have my staff murdering children at a time like this."

Klevver looked startled as if coming back to himself from a great distance. "Sorry," he mumbled, like a shamed little child. "I lost my temper again, didn't I? I just didn't want to disappoint you."

"Pull him up! Quickly, quickly," Tuppletaub hissed, peering back down the hall toward the staff lounge. Klevver hauled Barnabas over the smooth railing and dropped him unceremoniously on the floor beside his backpack. The two men were right above him, but Barnabas was too stunned to even crawl away.

"What were you thinking?" Tuppletaub yelled, pulling at his sparse hair. "I'm surprised I didn't find you applying electroshock to his eyelids."

"That's actually really effective."

"Shut up!" Mayor Tuppletaub reached a hand down to Barnabas, who took it gratefully. "Are you okay?"

"Yeah, okay…yes," Barnabas murmured as Tuppletaub pulled him to his feet.

But the moment he was standing, the mayor grabbed him by the shoulders and continued the interrogation. "Listen, boy. There are things you do not want to be involved in. How do you know about secret subways? What have you seen?"

Barnabas's heart was pounding. He was about to confess to stealing the map, but a moment of clarity cut through his panic. If he admitted to seeing the map, he'd have no way of claiming ignorance. He had to make up a simple, innocent story and stick to it. "I-I was at Crumhorn Station, and I overheard some, uh, I guess they were transit officials or something."

"Saying what exactly?"

"Nothing. Just like, 'You don't want to get caught using the *secret subway*.' Something like that."

The mayor stared him in the eye, trying to make him crack under the pressure. Barnabas held his gaze until Tuppletaub said, "And that's all they said?"

Barnabas nodded.

Still holding his shoulders, the mayor leaned in close enough that Barnabas could smell his bitter coffee breath. "Well, you listen to me. There are *no* secret subways. Anyone who says there are gets in big trouble. Sometimes they disappear and are *never heard of again*." The round, angry face filled Barnabas's field of vision, and he felt a pathetic moan escape his lips. "Have I made myself clear?"

"What is going on?" said a concerned, fluty voice. Barnabas, Mayor Tuppletaub, and Mr. Klevver all turned simultaneously to find Principal Rolan-Gong watching them.

Tuppletaub instantly let go of Barnabas's shoulders, and only then did Barnabas realize just how hard Tuppletaub had been digging his fingers into his flesh. "Ah, Madam Principal!" said the mayor, instantly jovial. "I was just reminding this young man about the importance of journalistic ethics."

"Oh. It seemed like you and your associate were…" She looked around, but Klevver had vanished again, like a thief in the night.

The mayor shook his head as if it was all a sad misunderstanding. "I'm afraid this child, Mr.….?"

"Bopwright," she answered.

"Mr. Bopwright needs to learn that being a journalist is no excuse for rudeness and impropriety. He practically threatened me, as if I was hiding important state secrets. It was almost amusing."

The principal gasped. "Mr. Bopwright, I'm surprised at you. The mayor is an honoured guest at our school." Barnabas felt his face burning red. Ms. Rolan-Gong turned to Tuppletaub. "I'm so sorry, Mr. Mayor. I think perhaps today's clickbait media is not the best example for our students to follow. All those paparazzi and leaked videos. *Intimate* videos! Perhaps we need to re-think the need for a Journalism Club."

Tuppletaub smiled and waved away her concern. "Oh, please, don't let it trouble you. I'm used to worse. You should look at the online comments whenever I give an interview. Complete lack of civility."

"Nonetheless, Mr. Bopwright, you are suspended for three days."

"But—"

"Are you able to let yourself in at home, or do you need to be picked up?"

"No, but I…" Barnabas could barely speak in his hurt and outrage. For a second, he thought about bringing the principal to his locker and showing her the secret subway map. But he was just a kid. No one would believe him, not when it was his word against the mayor's. And if he did reveal the map, he might just disappear in the night, never to be heard from again. Tuppletaub would say some sad words on television about another "troubled youth" and get away with it.

The principal papered over her stern face with fresh smiles. "Your Honour, if you would come back down the hall for a quick group photo…" She led the mayor away, giving Barnabas one more dirty look over her shoulder. "And you leave my school this minute, Mr. Bopwright."

Barnabas felt run over, wrung out, closer to crying than he had in years. He rubbed at the sore skin on his chest and shoulders and felt sorry for himself. They had no right to treat him like that.

A growing cacophony of voices and footsteps rose up the stairwell. Classes were changing from second to third period. Barnabas pulled himself to his feet, straightening his clothes when he suddenly cried out loud, "The diaboriku!"

CHAPTER 9

The stairwell was busy with students hurrying to third period. Some greeted Barnabas as he raced past them, pulling on his backpack, but he didn't answer. *Where is it? Where?*

Finally, he spotted the little sphere sitting placidly on the tenth-floor landing, its big glass eye looking up at all the hubbub. Barnabas sighed with relief and headed for it. But then one last student, late for class, ran past him, and as she passed, the heel of her shoe grazed the diaboriku. Almost languidly, it rolled toward the stairs.

"No!" Barnabas screamed, but the toy didn't care. It tipped off the edge and began bouncing downward, ricocheting off the wall of the next landing to continue its descent. Barnabas ran down the stairs in desperate pursuit, but the diaboriku was accelerating as it fell. Barnabas ran, peering down into the stairwell flight after flight, hoping to catch a glimpse of it. He stopped for a few seconds around the fifth floor, breathing hard, and in the echoes from below, he could hear its retreating bounce, and then nothing. He started running again, taking the stairs two at a time, the palm of his hand rubbed raw on the plastic bannister.

Barnabas emerged into a short utility hallway on the first floor where the recycling bins were stored. The diaboriku sat against the emergency exit. Hands braced on his knees, Barnabas tried to get his wind back. But at the very moment he straightened up, the heavy steel door opened to reveal Orlando, the building custodian, silhouetted by morning sunlight. With a lazy roll, the diaboriku slipped between Orlando's feet into the alley beyond.

"Barnabas?" the man said in surprise as the boy squeezed past him in the narrow door frame.

By the time he got clear of the door, Barnabas could just see the toy at the end of the alley, rolling across the sidewalk between the feet of pedestrians before dropping off the curb onto Blesskind Avenue. He raced down the alley and jumped up on a concrete planter box, shielding his eyes from the sun to search the chaos of the road for the proverbial needle in the haystack. He caught a final glimpse of the diaboriku, already two blocks away as it vanished between a mail truck and a tour bus, heading downhill toward the Tower District.

Barnabas had no idea how long he stood among the weeds in the planter box, numbed by misery and regret, blinking back tears. It might have been five minutes later or fifteen when the man spoke.

"It seems you've lost something."

Barnabas looked down at him. Actually, given the man's height, Barnabas was almost eye to eye with him, even though the man was down on the sidewalk. It was Mr. Glower, the strange bald guy in the khaki coveralls from Crumhorn Station.

"Yeah," Barnabas said, finding it hard to get his voice to work. "I lost my…uh…it's this round thing. Rolled down the street." His voice choked a bit as he added, "It's from my brother."

"Mmm," replied Glower, nodding. He cracked his knuckles, and his black crow eyes studied Barnabas's face. Glower didn't seem to remember him, much less connect him to the loss of the map.

To their right, the door of the building burst open, and the mayor marched out onto the sidewalk, yelling into his phone. "Don't lecture me. I've been trapped at this ridiculous school for hours."

The mayor's advisor followed, ear glued to her own phone. "His Honour is already outside. Bring the car around immediately."

Barnabas jumped down from the planter box and ducked behind it before the mayor could spot him. A limo pulled up to the curb, and the mayor opened the back door, still shouting into his phone.

"Well, you won't complain when you see the donations I just got." Then the mayor spotted Glower, and his face went white. From his hiding place, Barnabas watched Glower give the mayor a curt nod. Tuppletaub climbed hastily into the limo, leaving the door open. Glower walked toward the waiting car, but halfway there, he turned and looked down at the bit of Barnabas's face he could see behind the planter.

"Sometimes things return to you," he said, "but usually, they are gone for good, and then you have to decide what to do with that terrible, burning hole in your heart. Some say a wise man accepts his sorry lot. But there is another way. You can seek revenge for what was done to you. Life is really about deciding which sort of man you are."

Having delivered this dark sermon, Glower followed the mayor into the limo, closing the door behind him. A moment later, the car was in motion and disappearing around the corner.

Barnabas stood slowly, brushing the dust off his clothes. He contemplated everything he had just learned. Mayor Tuppletaub knew

Glower. Therefore, the mayor probably for sure knew about the secret subway. His head close to exploding, Barnabas turned and headed back to the building. He needed to collect some textbooks to get him through his suspension. But standing at the door was Mr. Klevver, with a crocodile's grin on his pale, hard face.

CHAPTER 10

"Hello, little cameraman," Klevver said, cracking his knuckles methodically. It sounded like dry kindling snapping in the forest.

Barnabas's voice cracked too as he called back. "The mayor told you to leave me alone."

"Oh sure, there's things His Honour has to say *out loud*. I mean, he's an e-lec-ted o-ffi-cial." Klevver enunciated the words with knife-point precision. "But it's my job to do what he *really* wants." He grinned and started across the sidewalk toward Barnabas, moving his hand under his jacket.

Barnabas jumped off the planter and hit the sidewalk running. He didn't look back, just focussed on getting down into Blesskind Station. As he turned to descend the stairs, he saw Klevver running after him with an efficient stride, his grin greasy and hungry.

Despite his desperate flight, Barnabas's mind was as sharp and clear. Unless the train was already at the station and he could dive through the closing doors just before Klevver, he'd end up stuck on the platform, an easy target for the mayor's enforcer. No, he had to act unpredictably. When he reached the bottom of the stairs, he didn't turn right toward the turnstiles but kept barrelling straight across the lobby up the staircase that led to Blesskind Avenue's west side. He emerged cautiously onto the street and looked all around, but Klevver was nowhere to be seen.

Ducking into the doorway of a closed restaurant, Barnabas pulled out his phone and started to call 911, but before he could punch the final number, he stopped. If he was an enemy of the mayor, why would the police help him? After all, Ms. Rolan-Gong had known Barnabas for years, and even she had immediately sided with Tuppletaub. He needed to get home, but he would get there by an unpredictable route. He ran two blocks to Haverstall Road and caught a westbound trolley to Haverstall Station, where he transferred to the southbound Purple Line.

With rush hour over, the train was half empty, a startling change after the chaos of his morning commute. He opened his backpack and pulled out the secret map. He considered leaving it on the seat beside him to become someone else's problem. The flimsy, crumpled scrap was no longer just an oddity. It was a foggy glimpse into something big and important, something too weighty for Barnabas's narrow shoulders. But wasn't uncovering secrets a kind of power? Maybe that was the real reason Thelonius became a Junior Sherlock.

The Purple Line subway pulled into Admiral Crumhorn Station, and Barnabas put the map away, exiting the train skittish as a rabbit in an open field. He hurried to the Yellow Line, where trains were waiting on both sides of the platform, a normal situation here at the terminus station. But there was no choice. A transit crew was putting up out-of-service barriers in front of every door of the train on platform six, though the doors remained open.

"The train on platform six is out of service," confirmed the announcement.

Barnabas watched a transit worker walking through one of the train's cars, checking the corners and under each seat, before emerging back onto the platform and announcing, "All clear." Another worker answered, "Check," and tapped on the tablet he was holding. It seemed like a lot of fuss, but maybe this was normal after rush hour.

Barnabas moved into the train on platform seven and took one of the many available seats. A station announcement sounded: "The westbound Yellow Line train on Platform seven will depart in one minute. All aboard."

He felt a moment of triumph. He had escaped Klevver, but with that behind him, he began to grow nervous about his parents. What would they say about his suspension?

A tall black man with a dusty mohawk, wearing dirty blue coveralls and mud-stained boots, entered through the nearest subway door. He was tall, easily six-five. A thick rope trailed out behind him onto the platform, and when he whistled and gave the rope a tug, the biggest dog Barnabas had ever seen followed him into the car. It was all muscle and drool and wore a harness filled with hand tools, scraps of metal, and coiled lengths of piping. The man, humming a tune in a low mellifluous voice, passed Barnabas, and the dog growled low at him, breath hot and meaty.

Then a uniformed woman, almost as tall as the guy with the mohawk, entered the subway car. Barnabas had never seen her sleek, spotless, blue uniform before. Kind of old-fashioned, it consisted of a long jacket with padded shoulders, trousers that narrowed dramatically below the knee to fit snugly into her shiny black boots, and a high peaked hat in matching blue.

No, Barnabas realized with a shock. Not blue...*aqua*. Like she had leaped from the folds of his map, this woman had something to do with the Aqua Line. The secret subway.

"Denizen, stop!" the Aqua Guard called with no-nonsense authority. "You can't bring your dog on a City train. Show me your travel documents."

The man handed over a small stack of papers. "It's my first time here," he said. "Got to fix a Valley-City water bridge. And Marigold's always with me on the job." He patted the animal's monstrous flank.

The guard reached into her shoulder bag and removed what looked like a policeman's ticket book. "I'm going to have cite you for this." She began writing in the book.

"I didn't know," the man said, his eyes filling with panic as she tore off the red page from her ticket book and handed it him.

Through the open door, Barnabas heard the transit worker with the tablet yelling, "You all clear on car sixteen or what?"

Way down at the end of the platform, the guy who had been checking the cars stepped out an open door and yelled back, "All clear!"

The guy with the tablet unclipped a walkie-talkie from his belt, "Outbound train Aqua-Oscar-Romeo thirteen clear to cross the Frontier," he told the walkie.

"Hold it," the Aqua Guard yelled, stepping out of the subway. "Let this denizen on board." Barnabas watched her lead the unhappy mohawk guy and his giant dog from platform seven to platform six. The guy with the tablet pulled one of the barriers aside so man and dog could board the out-of-service train.

Barnabas got up, peering from the shadows by the open door at these Aqua characters. He was about to lose them, lose his chance to solve this mystery that had already endangered his life. He heard the familiar chimes that preceded the closing doors, and he sprinted across the platform, not even thinking whether he was noticed. He dived through the doors of the train on platform six, and they closed just behind him.

He rose slowly from the dusty floor and peered around. The only passengers he could see were mohawk man and his dog, but they were down at the far end of the car, and the man was thoroughly absorbed in the red ticket he was holding. Barnabas crouched behind a bank of seats and braced himself for the subway to move west. When it unexpectedly rolled east, he lost his balance and fell to the floor.

Wait, he thought. *Where are we going?*

CHAPTER 11

B arnabas raised himself up to peer out the window. The train was not moving back along the Yellow Line where it was supposed to go, but into unknown territory. The familiar platform of Admiral Crumhorn Station with its warm ochre wall tiles disappeared as the train entered the tunnel slowly, making a wide, screeching turn to the left. The lights in the car dimmed to a sickly yellow, like yogurt gone bad.

The train arrived a few seconds later at another platform, and Barnabas figured they must still be within the mammoth structure of Admiral Crumhorn Station. People were on the platform, and he ducked down to consider his next move. When the doors opened, he would march out confidently, switch to the westbound platform and catch a train back to the normal world of the Yellow Line. "Sorry, I fell asleep," he'd say if anyone challenged him.

What do you know about secret subways? Mayor Tuppletaub screamed in his head, and he suddenly lost his nerve.

Parked down at the end of the car was a tall red machine with big rubber wheels and several robotic arms outfitted with nozzles and brushes, some kind of cleaning rig by the look of it. It completely filled the gap between the wall and the empty operator's booth, and Barnabas knew there was a two-person bench behind it. After a quick look back at the man and his dog, Barnabas jumped onto the machine's big rubber wheel and squeezed himself between the chassis and the wall, tumbling forward onto the bench. It was a perfect little cave where he was invisible to anyone in the subway or on the platform. Even better, if he peered between two of the machine's appendages, he could see the whole car.

No sooner had he tucked himself back in than the subway began a series of shocking transformations. Loud motors growled, and metal scraped on metal. Large panels outside lowered over the big glass windows and the subway doors, leaving only narrow slits of thick, scratched glass to peer through. Half of the seats folded into the floor and various racks and hooks rose up in their place. The graceful lines of the Yellow Line train vanished, turning the elegant vehicle into something resembling a long, heavy tank. There was no doubt now he was on the secret subway. He was on the Aqua Line!

The overhead lights came back on at full brightness as the newly reinforced doors with their tiny porthole windows scraped open. The people on the platform boarded the subway. These new passengers on the secret side of Crumhorn were as tall as mohawk man and the Aqua Guard, everyone at least six feet tall, and a few as big as basketball players. Some of these giants wore business clothes and carried leather briefcases, while most dressed in coveralls of various colours, with dented hardhats on their head and muddy construction boots on their feet. Some pushed large, wheeled machines bristling with blades and hoses, or carts filled with bundles of piping and coils of electrical wire. And there were more of the giant dogs on thick leashes, their harnesses full of gear.

The passengers secured the machines and carts in place with lengths of woven strap that spooled down from the ceiling, and then secured themselves into the seats with harnesses pulled from the wall behind them.

A tall woman with thickly muscled arms was securing a wheeled bin that looked to be a soup of oil filled with thick bolts. She called to the mohawk man, "What's with the red ticket, Derlik?"

"Oh, hulloo, Dana. I was reg-slapped by an Aqua. Said I couldn't bring Marigold cross the Frontier. Are they gonna throw me in Doomlock?"

Dana, grunting as she pulled her seatbelt tight, said, "Jagged life. Talk to your guild advocate as soon as you get home."

Doomlock. Barnabas knew that ominous name. He pulled out his Aqua Line map and spotted the station about halfway between Crumhorn and the serpentine line's terminus.

A station announcement rang out, the voice male and stern. "The outbound Aqua Line train will depart in one minute."

Barnabas stared at the open door nearest him. *I should get up,* he thought. *I should exit right now before this goes too far.*

He peered out the train's open door and saw the guard in aqua walking purposefully down the platform, hunting for infractions. Barnabas sat back down.

The door chimes rang like the bells of fate, but just before they closed, one more person leaped through the doors like a bounding rabbit. His landing was clean and elegant, and he slid across the floor on one knee.

"Huzzahs and ovations, ladies and gentlemen," he said in a loud, smoky voice. "Falstep is here!"

Chapter 12

Everyone in the car seemed excited to see him. Some laughed, some even applauded. He stood to his full height which, unlike everyone else on the train, was about the same as Barnabas's. He bowed.

"Thank you, thank you," the little man said. Veins stood out on his red nose, and age lines clustered around his sparkling eyes and mobile mouth. He slicked back his stringy, greying hair with both hands and walked toward an empty seat with a determined stride. He suddenly tripped, flipping a full turn in mid-air and landing on his ass. Laughter rang out. Even miserable Derlik couldn't help but smile. Barnabas figured this Falstep for some kind of circus clown, though he wasn't sure why this clown was so famous.

The lights dimmed again when the train began to move, and Falstep hurried to strap himself in. Only when the subway began picking up speed did Barnabas understand the need for all the security harnesses. The first curve was wide and easy, but the train was still accelerating, its angle of descent steepening. The clatter and bang of wheels on track grew louder, and the next curve raised up a screech at track level. Everything in the car rattled and jostled, and a couple of slick bolts flew from the oil bucket, skittering across the floor like dice.

Barnabas, in his little cave behind the machine, had to brace himself against the wall and dig his heels into the smooth vinyl of the seat to keep from flying free like the bolts. The noise grew ever louder, and he gritted his teeth, hoping the ride would be over soon.

The train abruptly levelled out and burst into the next station. The driver slammed on the brakes with such a heavy hand, the wheels squealed in protest and sparks flew up outside the windows. Barnabas was pressed back against the seats and then thrown violently forward into the side of the machine as the train jerked to a final stop. He rubbed his bruised forehead.

The lights in the car went back up to full brightness as the door chimes sounded and the heavy doors scraped open. A blast of wet heat entered, and dark, smelly mud oozed into the subway car from the platform. *What kind of disgusting subway station is this?* Barnabas wondered. He couldn't see any station sign through the thick steam on the platform.

"Extreme heat," the announcer warned. "Remember to adjust your Q clamps before leaving the train."

Dana called to Derlik. "Hey, since you're free, want to join me on tunnel expansion for your shift?"

Derlik nodded.

"Okay, let's get off here and backtrack through the blast path." They all undid their harnesses and gathered at the door, Derlik shortening up Marigold's leash. Dana grabbed a flashlight from her belt and shone it into the obscuring steam of the platform.

Weird and scary as this station was, Barnabas decided he'd slip out after them. If he got a return train right away, he might make it home before Sam. The thought of walking in and seeing his stepfather sitting there with disappointed eyes was more than Barnabas could bear today. He slid quietly out of his hiding place and climbed down off the rubber wheel to the floor. No one seemed to notice him except Falstep the clown, who quirked an eyebrow and frowned, and Marigold, who growled low, showing teeth as long as a human finger.

But before any of them exited, the thick steam disgorged a trio of terrifying figures dressed in thick, green coveralls, three-fingered gloves, and boots built up so high, they had to bend just to enter the car. Once inside, they raised their heads. They had no faces, just grey metal helmets that enclosed their entire heads. Valves on their necks opened and closed with a sibilant hiss. Their eyes were invisible behind thick black lenses that protruded from the helmets.

Worse, two of the helmeted figures had enormous dogs of their own, straining on thick steel chains. As soon as they saw Marigold, they barked ferociously, a sound that made Barnabas's head ring. When the new dogs showed their polished triangles of razor-sharp metal teeth, Barnabas scrambled back into his cave.

Five giants and three animals squared off in the doorway, the two groups glaring at each other. Were they going to fight? If so, it would be a terrible one. Everyone in the car was watching.

Dana was the one who broke the silence. "Come on, denizens, let us pass. We need to get to work." But the giants in their unearthly robot suits didn't move.

The woman gritted her teeth. "Gricklickers!" She put a hand on Derlik's shoulder and said, "Come on, it's not worth it." She led them down the car to the next set of doors, but before they exited, she shouted, "Clouding Guild doesn't run the Council. The Father didn't give the Valley to you alone." They exited into the steam.

Taking their seats, the helmeted people reached for latches at their throats. Three sharp hisses of released air, and they lifted off the helmets to reveal two men and a woman, all with short-cropped, sweat-streaked hair, and glistening faces. Barnabas thought they looked very pleased with themselves—bullies, confident in their cruelty, like Mr. Klevver.

As the trio pulled on their seat belts and harnesses, Falstep sauntered down the car to stand directly in front of them, hands on hips.

"Y'know," the clown said, "you Clouders gotta learn to lighten up. Come on up to the circus and, you know, let off a bit of *steam*!" He did a little dance step and finished with a flourish. "Steam! S'a joke! Man, I waste my best material on the terminally humourless."

The faces of the Clouders darkened in anger. "The Father is sickened by your triviality, clown," said one with a long scar down his face. "Your weakness weakens us all."

The clown turned back to them. He touched his forehead and bowed slightly. "And the blessings of the Mother on you, denizen," he said.

He looked around as if for applause, but the other residents of the car were looking away in nervous embarrassment. For just a moment, Falstep stared in Barnabas's direction. He winked before turning and skipping away to the far end of the subway car.

CHAPTER 13

Huddled in his little alcove, Barnabas hung on for dear life as the train skidded and sparked through the tunnel, travelling ever downward. He thought about the stolen map. Now he understood why there were no transfer stations where the Aqua Line crossed the other lines. This subway had to be hundreds of feet below the regular ones. How long would the escalator have to be to get the passengers back to the surface? Or maybe these passengers never went above ground.

When the train shrieked into the next station and jerked to a halt, the doors remained shut. The lights in the car didn't come on this time, and Barnabas heard his fellow passengers shifting, coughing nervously. Outside, a voice said, "Secure to arrive," and the doors slid open.

This time, the view through the open doors was not mud and steam. Everything at this station was black tile and polished chrome. The platform signs read "Doomlock." A group of four guards entered the subway car, approaching a woman at the far end. When she stood shakily, Barnabas saw her hands were shackled. The guards led her out onto the platform, and as she passed the nearest door, Barnabas could hear her plaintive voice.

"Father Glory, hear your humble child. Grant me the endurance of body and mind to build your Holy City." Her voice grew in desperation. "Mother Mercy! Kiss the head of your humble child and bring her close to your breast." As they led her away, her voice and the sound of their boots on the concrete faded. Barnabas held his breath, trying more than ever to remain utterly undetectable.

"Secure to depart," said the platform voice, and the doors slid closed.

The train screeched and rattled as it plunged into the depths. The lights hadn't come back on after Doomlock, but with each sudden turn, sparks flashed in the tunnel around them. In those momentary flashes, Barnabas could see the subway car and its occupants, including the clown, who was sitting way down at the end. The next time the sparks flashed, Falstep was closer, halfway down the car, his big nose in striking profile. Darkness again for maybe ten seconds, then the train took a tight curve and sparks again lit up the car. The clown was nowhere to be seen.

The overhead lights came on abruptly, blindingly bright, and Falstep was right outside Barnabas's hiding place, standing on the machine's rubber wheel. He reached out a bony hand and, with surprising strength for someone his size, pulled Barnabas out of his safe cave. He dragged him by his shirtfront to a nearby seat and strapped him in.

"I didn't mean to be here!" Barnabas screamed uselessly into the clatter and roar. "I'm really sorry. Please let me go home!"

"Shut it, kid. We'll worry about getting you home later." Falstep's voice was a scratchy old vinyl record, his breath a thousand cigars. "Here, you'll need to wear this." He pulled a red rubber ball out of his chequered jacket and stuck it unceremoniously onto Barnabas's nose, pulling the elastic strap over his head. "Keep that on. And if anyone says anything to you—*anything*—you answer, 'raspberry soda,' got it?"

"What?" He reached up to remove the red clown nose, and Falstep slapped his hand.

"Leave it! What's your name?"

"I'm Barnabas Bopwright...*ow!*" The clown slapped the top of his head.

"What did I say to say?"

"R-raspberry soda?"

"Good. And where do you live?"

"Raspberry soda."

"Perfect. Follow my lead and we might just keep you out of Doomlock." The image of that dread subway stop where the woman had been led off in shackles filled his chest with cold terror. He looked at Falstep and nodded.

The train's descent levelled again, and they burst out of the darkness. Barnabas twisted in his seat to look out the narrow slat of the window. For maybe ten seconds, they were outside, under the sunshine, passing through dry scrubland. Then they were inside again under artificial light. The train was slowing, its brakes shrieking mass murder, until finally, when the noise couldn't be any louder, the train gave a final shudder and came to a decisive, steaming halt.

CHAPTER 14

The subway doors opened.

Falstep unbuckled his harness and jumped from his seat. He pulled a soft tweed cap out of his jacket pocket and plonked it down on his head before unbuckling Barnabas's harness and pulling him to his feet. "We gotta get going."

"Where to? Where are we?"

"You mean 'raspberry soda.' I'll answer questions later. Come on."

Hugging his backpack to his chest with both arms, Barnabas followed Falstep out onto the platform. Giants were all around them, rolling machines and carts from the subway down ramps to the floor of what looked like an enormous shipping yard. Heavy-duty conveyor belts, like an airport luggage carousel on steroids, travelled right and left and up and down in every direction, carrying bundled construction material, sealed shipping containers, large inscrutable machines, barrels full of smoking chemicals, and cages with huge dogs and other animals inside.

Concrete walkways ran between the conveyor belts, and Falstep weaved an energetic course along them, dodging around people and machines, occasionally hopping up and over benches and other obstacles. Terrified of getting lost in this chaos, Barnabas hurried to keep up. The noise was deafening.

Falstep came to a halt so suddenly, Barnabas crashed into him.

"Dung," the clown said, barely audible over the noise of the conveyor belts grinding away beside and above them. Barnabas looked up to see three Aqua Guards walking their way.

"Put on your backpack and follow!" Falstep shouted, and Barnabas almost screamed in surprise as he jumped up onto one of the moving belts. Falstep skipped across a large, moving palette filled with cinder blocks, and hopped down onto a walkway on the other side. Barnabas scrambled up onto the edge of the belt, but by the time he found the nerve to cross, the nice stable cinder blocks were gone, replaced by a line of long troughs, the first filled with bubbling tar and the next with greasy, black gravel. He stole a glance to his left and saw the guards maybe fifteen feet away.

"Now, now!" yelled Falstep, standing on the far side. Barnabas looked down. Passing by now on the conveyor belt was a bin of scrap metal junk—engine parts, old copper tubing, and dented lengths of ductwork. Barnabas jumped in and scrambled over the shifting pile, losing his balance as he reached the far side, almost falling back before Falstep grabbed his arm and heaved him up.

"Move it," he yelled, leading them down a spiral staircase to a lower level. They ducked under a set of big, grimy pipes too low for any of the tall people to follow and popped up on a different walkway on the far side.

"That's it," Falstep said, grinning and panting hard, a hand on Barnabas's shoulder. "They'll never find us."

"Uh…" Barnabas grunted and pointed over Falstep's shoulder. Another Aqua Guard was fast approaching, waving at them.

Falstep's smile died. "Remember," he hissed into Barnabas's ear, "raspberry soda."

"Denizen Falstep?" said the guard.

Falstep pulled a small hand mirror out of his breast pocket and checked himself. "Yup. I appear to be me." He crossed his eyes, puffed out his cheeks, and adjusted his hat.

The guard laughed, but then looked around as if smiling was against the rules. "You just came off the train?"

"Yeah, a bit of circus business in the City." He reached again into his checked jacket and pulled out a piece of paper with a red seal on it. "Transit permission, everything in order."

The guard waved it away. "That won't be necessary. We heard reports from a couple of passengers of a possible penetration of the Frontier. Did you see anyone unusual?"

"No, nothing I can think of. Some mook from Forming got reg-slapped trying to take his dog topside."

The guard seemed to notice Barnabas for the first time. "Who is this with you?"

Barnabas couldn't breathe. His leg began twitching.

Falstep spun on his heel as if he had forgotten Barnabas was there. "This? This is a lump of useless that thinks he has what it takes to be a clown. Like it's something just anyone can aspire to." He gave Barnabas a sharp whack on the head with his palm.

"What's your name, young denizen?"

Barnabas, his head stinging, said, "R-raspberry soda."

Falstep rolled his eyes and muttered, "Here we go…"

"And is your residency registered through Pastoral Park?"

"Raspberry, uh, soda?"

Falstep pushed him aside. "Don't waste your time, officer. He's the kid of one of the stagehands. Only he's a bit…" Falstep whistled drunkenly and let his head loll around on his neck. "Can't even open curtains on cue. So, what do they do? They give him to *me*. As if being skull-cracked means you're clown material." He shrugged in elaborate frustration. Barnabas suddenly understood Falstep's plan. He did his own imitation of the cross-eyed face, and Falstep shook his head in mock disgust.

The guard seemed unsure what to do next, so he took the transit documents from Falstep after all and gave them a cursory glance before handing them back. "Have a good day, denizen," he said. "I got my family tickets for the circus's new show."

"Great, Officer. I'll give the kiddies some special balloons."

The guard walked away, and Falstep let out a long, hissing breath. "Hoo-boy. You did real good, kid. Come on, Wickram's supposed to be meeting us in the parking lot. The sooner you're safely in Pastoral Park, the better." He pulled a half-smoked cigar out of his jacket pocket and lit it with a wooden match. Barnabas stumbled after him as they went down a walkway and out through a black metal door. They walked under the bright sunshine across a wide parking area filled with heavy trucks, coming and going in a cloud of diesel.

Barnabas had questions. "Um, raspberry soda…"

Falstep shook his head and laughed. "You can speak English now, kid."

"Right, sorry. Where are we, and who are you exactly?"

"This is the main transfer station," the clown said, "and I'm Falstep. Falstep Fruntovuvver. Son of the late, great Onestep Fruntovuvver, Principal Clown of Tragidenko's Circus of Humanity."

Barnabas, still trying to make sense of *main transfer station*, asked, "Who? You or your father?"

"Who what?"

"Is Principal Clown?"

"Both. He were, I are." He straightened the clown nose on Barnabas's face. Falstep Fruntovuvver, Barnabas noted, didn't have one himself.

He led them across the parking lot, dodging around moving trucks. Barnabas, hurrying again to keep up, said, "I'm Barnabas Bopwright. Are we going to your circus?"

"Wickram's probably all the way at the back, or late as usual. This way."

Barnabas looked back at the giant bulk of the transfer station as they walked away. He didn't want to meet any more Aqua Guards, but wasn't it a bad idea to get farther from the subway? He had wanted to get home quietly, not get in more trouble with his mom and Sam than he already was, but it was time to call for help. He pulled his phone from his pocket and was alarmed to find no signal. He held the phone in the air, pointing it in different directions. *What the hell?*

Falstep had already walked ahead, making Barnabas run again. "Listen," he said when he caught up, "thanks for trying to keep me out of trouble, but I'm just going to get on the next train back to Admiral Crumhorn Station."

"No train till next Tuesday. Tuesdays and Thursdays only."

Barnabas had never heard of a subway with a schedule like that. "Then if I can just get some signal, I'll call home and tell my stepdad to come and get me."

"From the City? How's he gonna do that?"

"He has a car. He doesn't use it much but..." Barnabas grabbed the clown's arm and pulled him to a halt. "Wait! What do you mean 'from the City'?"

"Huh? Where do you think you are?" Falstep asked, staring at Barnabas like he really *was* the addle-brained son of a frustrated stagehand. "You think you're still in the City?"

"I'm not? But we were on a City subway. How far away...? I mean, which way...?"

Falstep looked delighted. Without taking his eyes off Barnabas's face, he pointed right and up. Something was wrong. Something was weird. Barnabas turned in the direction of Falstep's hand. From this part of the parking lot, the transfer station was no longer blocking the view. Barnabas could see the subway tracks running out from behind it, passing through the landscape of low, scrubby plants and then disappearing through an arched portal into the base of a huge wall of rock and earth. Barnabas looked slowly up the face of this mammoth cliff, rough and unadorned except for a few plants struggling to hang on to narrow outcroppings. Higher and higher his gaze climbed until he had to tilt his body backward to see.

And on the top of this wall, right up against the edge of the cliff, was a long line of beautiful skyscrapers glinting in the morning sun. He knew those towers. They were all the skyscrapers of the Tower District—the Jezebel, Greatest Hiltz, Delphic Tower, and the rest—but he was seeing them from an angle he'd never seen before. He was looking at them *from behind*, teetering on the edge of a giant cliff that shouldn't even exist.

Barnabas's mind, already wobbling, started to spin like a top. "That's...that's impossible."

CHAPTER 15

Falstep took off his hat and turned to stare up at the towers. "It's quite a spectacle, all right."

Barnabas's confusion turned to anger, because obviously he was being tricked. "This can't be true. If the City was sitting on the edge of a cliff, people would be talking about it."

"Oh, *people*." Falstep laughed. "People believe whatever you tell them. They have more *important* things to talk about, like the price of smoked raisins or how their favourite movie star waxes her armpits."

Barnabas turned back to stare up at the towers, at the birds flying around the peaks, so far away they looked like fruit flies. And in the already spectacularly strange picture, he noticed more strangeness. "There are no windows! None of the buildings have windows on this side!"

The clown yawned loudly. "Wouldn't do to have them see the Valley." He extended an open palm and spun on his heel. "We don't exist. None of this does. Hey, there's the cart. Come on."

This time, Falstep didn't hurry. He sauntered, relighting his cigar with lazy panache. At the edge of the parking lot was a single, ancient oak tree protected by a short chain link fence. Parked in its shade, at odds with all the heavy diesel trucks, was a sturdy, old-fashioned, four-wheeled cart. In the back was an open flatbed with wooden rails, and up front, a driver's bench. Two grey mules were hitched to the cart, chewing placidly on the weeds at their feet.

Falstep knocked on the back of the cart. "Hey, hey, fanfares and confetti, I'm back."

A gangly figure jumped down from the lower branches of the oak tree. He was wearing dusty jeans and an embroidered denim shift. Shoulder-length straight brown hair flowed from under his floppy hat, framing his brown skin, hazel eyes, and jutting jaw. Despite the kid's height, Barnabas could see he was around his own age.

The kid pushed back his hat and grinned. "Yeah, I could smell the fine aroma of burning stinkweed!" He hopped over the fence, which only came up to his waist, and suddenly spotted Barnabas. "Hey, who's that?"

"He was hiding on the train," Falstep said as the boy gawped. "Let's get out of here. You can ask your questions when we get on the road."

The boy gave the mules a quick, affectionate pat as he took his place on the driver's bench and picked up the reins.

Falstep climbed up beside him, then turned around. "Hey, Platypus, hop in the back."

"It's Barnabas." He looked up again at the utter strangeness of the City on the cliff and wondered how he could get back there. He thought of the Aqua Guard and Doomlock, and realized it was too dangerous to wander around this unknown place alone. He had no choice but to go with this strange pair. He threw his backpack into the cart and climbed in clumsily after it. Around him on the floor was a pile of red fabric, shot through with sequins, several dented cans of paint with hand-written labels, including "Momo's darkest blue," "Faerie green," and "Don't Use This," and an old acoustic guitar, covered in a colourful collage of band stickers.

"Yeah, sit anywhere, Barnabas," said the kid. "I'm Wickram. *Mother Mercy*, you live in the City? You are *so* lucky."

Barnabas sat down on the fabric. "I didn't mean to come here," he said. "I got on the wrong subway."

"Yeah, I bet. Who would want to leave the City? Do you have the new DigiPlayah SmartMedia Centre?"

"Uh, no, but some of my friends do."

"I want one of those so bad. There's nothing down here in the Valley except stones and dust and factories. Nice nose, by the way." He laughed and reached back to squeeze the red foam ball. "Honk!" Embarrassed, Barnabas pulled it off and stuck it in his pocket.

Someone started shouting until the three of them turned to look. It was another tall kid with pasty, freckled skin and curly orange hair. "Hey, circus," he shouted as he marched through the parking lot, pushing a big wooden crate on a hydraulic trolley. Barnabas saw Wickram's eyes narrow in anger.

"Clouding fitsker," Falstep murmured, but he didn't seem as annoyed as Wickram.

"Hey, circus," the kid shouted again. "If you keep jugglin' your balls, you'll go blind."

Wickram gritted his teeth and breathed hard through his nose, looking anywhere but at the kid.

A burly woman with a greyer version of the same orange hair

stuck her head out of a truck parked just ahead. "Kallus! Don't talk to those libertines. Get over here with the cargo." The kid glared one more time at Wickram as he disappeared behind the truck.

"Can we hit the flippin' road?" Falstep said.

Wickram shook off his funk and saluted. "Absolutely. Yah, mules." He gave the reins a shake, and the cart jerked into motion, tipping Barnabas off the pile of material onto the floor.

CHAPTER 16

"D id you get me something in the City?" Wickram asked as he steered them out of the parking lot onto a busy, smoothly paved, four lane road.

Falstep gave him a half smile. "Well, let's just say you were on my mind."

"I bet it's a harmonica. Hey, Barn. Can I call you Barn? Do you have those Grumpton Homing Shoes? The ones that point you to the KidLiquid treasure stations?"

"Uh, I did. But the OS was a mess. A bunch of little kids got lost in a bad part of town, so they shut down the network."

They were clip-clopping down the road, the slowest vehicle in traffic. Big trucks had to swing wide around them to pass. Barnabas moved to the back of the cart to look up at the City. *His* City. It felt like it had just been stolen from him, the whole story of his life rewritten.

Wickram continued to talk like the world was still normal. "Hey, Barn, you ever been to the Manhammer Audiodome?"

Barnabas nodded vaguely. He stood, balancing himself on the railing behind the driver's bench. "The cliff doesn't look very stable. What if a building falls off?"

Wickram shrugged. "Hasn't happened yet, but all kinds of things fall off all the time. That's why we have the Tumbles. Look at the base of the cliff." He handed Barnabas a pair of binoculars from under his seat. Through the lenses, Barnabas could see a long chain-link fence in front of the cliff, extending in both directions as far as the eye could see.

Every few seconds something fell into the Valley. First, three car tires went over edge, bouncing off outcroppings and tree roots on their way down. Farther along the cliff face, a stuffed giraffe spun end over end like it had leaped in despair when some kid stopped loving it. Everything that hit the dry ground behind the fence, from a record collection to a refrigerator, sent up a plume of dust.

"Excellent, right?" Wickram said, turning around again. "There's only one guy brave enough to walk around in the Tumbles, and that's—"

"Hey, *Platypus*," Falstep yelled. "Sit your butt down before someone sees you." He gave Wickram a whack on the shoulder. "Where's your brains? We got to keep him secret until they organize papers for him. We almost got busted by an Aqua at the station."

The cart was now passing an enormous factory. Barnabas watched huge metal bins being hoisted to the top of the building, where they tipped their contents of heavy rock into a smoking mouth that belched flame with each load. On the other side of the road, tall men and women in heavy work clothes and hardhats supervised giant forklifts stacking enormous piles of gleaming girders. The clang and grind were deafening, the exhaust fumes choking, but clown, kid, and mules just plodded along oblivious.

"What is this place?" Barnabas called over the din.

Wickram yelled back, "Forming works. They make the City's building materials."

Tucked in the space between two huge towers was a small church, complete with a dirty rose window and a spire decorated with two outsized devotional statues. One was a grim-looking businessman in an old-fashioned suit and tie, round opaque glasses, and a walrus moustache. Clutched in his upraised hand were three lightning bolts, like he was the Zeus of Wall Street. Opposite him was a statue of a beautiful woman standing on a base of clouds, long hair framing her calm face. She held her arms out in front of her, as if offering a big hug to those who entered her church.

"And who are they?"

"Father Glory and Mother Mercy." Barnabas knew these names. They had been on his secret map, and muttered by Galt-Stomper, the prisoner at Doomlock Station, and by Wickram when they met.

They passed two more giant worksites, each with its own small church, before the noise finally diminished, and Barnabas asked the question he really meant. "What is *all* of this? What's the story of the Valley?"

Wickram grabbed Falstep's shoulder. "Can we do the 'Guts and Glory' show for him?"

"Leave me be. I just got home."

"Fine I'll do it myself. Barn, hand me my guitar and take the reins."

While Wickram tuned up on the driver's bench, Barnabas stared at the collection of leather strips connecting his hands to the mules' heads. "Should I really be backseat driving like this?"

Wickram played a big chord. "Don't worry, the mules know where they're going. So, this is a show the council contracted us to do. We take it around to schools in all the different guilds." Wickram began strumming the guitar with big sweeps of his long fingers and making trumpet noises with his mouth. He thumped a beat on the floorboards with one heel.

"Long ago," he began to the accompaniment of his guitar orchestra, "the City was but a low and dirty town. But there was a man with a dream who saw a chance to build a modern Rome on the shores of the mighty river."

The story wasn't as unfamiliar as Barnabas thought. He said, "Lawrence Glorvanious. He was the one with the dream."

Falstep gave him pitying look. "Oh, we all know about the *great mayor*. But what you City folk don't know…you City folk with your colour televisions and-and plastic underwear suits—"

Wickram turned around and said, "He means streamcorders and omnifloat memory access. He's old."

"Shut it, punk. Just play, and I'll sing. You have a voice like a crow."

"Excellent!" Wickram said, finger-picking a rhythmic accompaniment.

Falstep's singing voice was high, strong, and clear, and his hands cut through the air to emphasize his words.

> *Long ago in a marketplace,*
> *A man stood up with a solemn face.*
> *Said, "I'll lead you to a land of grace—*
> *We'll build the Holy City in the sky."*

> *Choosing only the tall and strong,*
> *He led his bright and devoted throng*
> *On a journey perilous and long—*
> *To build the Holy City in the sky.*

"But if it wasn't Lawrence Glorvanious," Barnabas asked between verses, "who led the people here?"

"Father Glory, of course," Wickram answered as he executed a long descending run and Falstep began the second verse.

> *With trees to cut and swamps to drain,*
> *They built the Valley in the snow and rain,*
> *For the cliff-top City's earthly gain—*
> *And to build the Holy City in the sky.*

Bringing iron from deep in the ground,
Dredging water till they nearly drowned,
Through generations glory bound—
They built the Holy City in the sky.

"Then we get the kids to name all the work guilds," Wickram explained, bringing the beat down to a low, insistent pulse. "Furrowing—who mines ore from the earth, Forming—who makes the building materials, Coursing—who pumps and purifies the water, Sorting—who processes waste, and Clouding—who runs the steamworks."

Barnabas was starting to understand. "And that's how the City—my City—really runs?"

But Wickram didn't answer. Hunching over his guitar and banging his feet on the floorboards, he made the beat louder and louder. He and Falstep started nodding like metalheads before singing together.

In fire forged is the girder beam!
Blazing flame creates the steam!
And in every heart, there burns a dream—
To build the Holy City in the sky!

Falstep stopped abruptly, leaving Wickram to do the big finale alone. "We build the Holy City in the sky!"

"Hey, Platypus," Falstep said, "take a left on Commercial Street!"

Barnabas stared at the reins in confusion, but Wickram grabbed them and turned the cart. "I thought we were in a rush," Wickram said.

"Man's gotta quench his thirst. Won't be but a second."

CHAPTER 17

The cart turned into a street filled with noise and colour. It was like an outdoor shopping mall, with neon signs advertising boots, caps, hoops, and whirlytoys. The stores all seemed to be on the second and third floors of the brightly painted brick buildings, the ground floors occupied by bars and restaurants—mainly bars. Even now, in the middle of the day, the looming buildings and smoke-filled sky made it feel like twilight, and the electric lights glittered and shone.

"Just keep driving," Falstep said as he jumped off the cart and started running toward a tavern called Maizy's Tasties. "I'll catch up to you at the end of the street!"

Although Barnabas could still hear the grind of the factories, the pounding music of Commercial Street, blasting from speakers on every utility poll, all but drowned it out. It was weird music, old-fashioned and contemporary at once. Tubas and banjoes in three-quarter time, but fast, with a driving electronic beat.

"Ugh," Wickram said, sticking out his tongue in disgust. "I hate dub-polka!"

Valley folk were inside the bars and restaurants, laughing loudly over their food and drink, playing darts, and singing along to house bands. Parents were leading their kids up the stairs to clothing shops, and the kids were laughing and chasing each other over bridges that crossed the street overhead. And every few minutes, Barnabas caught sight of Falstep draining a pint of beer or knocking back a shot before slamming some coins down and running to the next establishment.

Raising his voice above the hubbub, Barnabas said, "Why is everyone out partying in the middle of the day?"

"The Valley never sleeps. With three shifts of workers, it's always someone's time to blow off steam."

An amplified voice, thin and tinny, reached their ears. "Reject the wanton and the crass! Turn your back on temptation and embrace the simplicity of the working life the Father has bequeathed to you."

Barnabas saw two familiar figures standing on the sidewalk in front of a gaming parlour where people tossed balls through hoops and shot arrows at targets. It was the orange-haired mother and son from the parking lot, the woman preaching to the passing crowd through a megaphone.

"It is with the exertion of your muscles, not with intoxicants and vulgar music that you will find true freedom. Reject this street of vice and visit your local church."

The son held up a large white sign with crisp black letters that read, "Remember, the Father is always watching."

Through clenched teeth, Wickram muttered, "Why does Clouding have to spoil everyone's fun?"

"Clouding? The steam people?" Barnabas asked, and at that moment, the woman and her son spotted their cart.

"When the circus came to the Valley," she proclaimed, "it presaged the decline we see all around us. Intoxication! Fornication! Reject these shallow libertines. Only those with dirty hands will build the Father's heavenly City."

Wickram was practically vibrating with anger. He shook the reins. "Yah, mules, let's go!"

But then the orange-haired kid broke away from his mother and began running beside the cart, shouting, "And send those sad-ass horses off to the slaughterhouse."

"They're mules, you ignorant carrot," Wickram told him, gripping the reins until the tendons in his arms and hands looked like steel cables.

"Then you can pull the cart yourself, circus freak. Eat your oats and crap on the road."

"Yeah?" Wickram snapped, turning to yell down at the kid. "Well, my turds honour the Father better than any prayer you fart out your steamhole."

The kid's face turned as orange as his hair. "You'll pay for that, circus freak."

"Make me!" Wickram jumped from his seat, landing on the kid. In a moment, they were rolling on the asphalt, fists flailing, grunting and shouting insults.

"Wickram!" Barnabas yelled, scrambling onto the driver's bench and grabbing the reins.

"Stop them," a passerby called. "Someone call the Aqua Guard."

"No!" Barnabas yelled back, and people looked his way. He reached into his pocket for the clown nose and pulled it on.

A wail from the road: "Owwwwwww!" Barnabas turned around to see the orange-haired boy being hoisted to his feet by his freckled ear.

"Ow! Ma, let go!" the kid squealed with embarrassment. "The libertine started it."

Barnabas suddenly remembered how to stop horses and, he guessed, mules. He pulled back on the reins and, to his great relief, the car slowed and stopped. As the preacher woman dragged her son back to their spot, Barnabas jumped from the cart and ran to Wickram. The boy was breathing hard, his clothes dusty and his hair a wild mop. One of his knuckles was cut, and a thin trickle of blood dripped down from his hairline.

"You're lucky your mom's here to save you, steam punk," he shouted. "Don't mess with the Circus of Humanity."

"Wickram, come on. Someone's calling the Aqua Guard. They shouldn't see me, right?"

As if a switch had been thrown, Wickram's hard fury softened. He even smiled. "Oh yeah, good point, Barn. Let's go."

They climbed onto the cart, Barnabas crouching in the back again, and continued on their way. At the end of Commercial Street, as Wickram turned left onto the main road, Falstep leaped into the back of the cart, panting, shiny with sweat under his peaked cap.

"Feeling better?" Wickram asked.

Falstep, standing with wobbly dignity, belched loudly. "You have no idea how stressful it is going to the City." His lids were drooping, and as he sat down, he bounced off Barnabas and rolled onto the floor. "Think I'll take…a little…nap."

None of this seemed to bother Wickram, who just kept driving. He pulled out a canteen and handed it back to Barnabas. "Water?"

Barnabas, throat parched from the dusty road, took the canteen and drank. "Thanks." He checked his phone again. Still no signal. "Hey, Wickram, is there anywhere my phone will work?"

"Is it the RoamFone Ultimate? With gigawave two-way GPS?"

"Um, not the Ultimate. Just the first gen."

"Still cool. Yeah, there's just one place in the Valley you can get a signal, and we're going there."

"Great, thanks." It was three o'clock. He had a plan, but he needed to reach Deni before she left school.

They passed through a miserable landscape of oil-soaked scrubland and towering scrap heaps. The sight made Barnabas feel lost and sad. Wickram crossed his right leg over his left and hung the reins on his toes. He picked up his guitar and started playing a haunting melody that echoed all the sadness Barnabas was feeling and somehow made it bearable. They climbed out of a dry ravine, and suddenly a green hill rose before them, topped with a forested plateau.

As the cart climbed the switchback road, their surroundings grew increasingly lush with berry bushes and wildflowers, and Wickram's tune shifted into a major key. The buzzing of insects and the insistent chirruping of birds drowned out the sounds of the factories behind them. The road levelled out, and they entered a lane bordered by tall beech trees. Barnabas felt himself relax, maybe for the first time since he'd woken up that morning.

"You're really good," he said. "I mean on the guitar."

Wickram gave him a sceptical look. "You play an instrument?"

"No. Mom didn't want me to end up like... Um, my dad's a musician. And my stepdad used to teach music at a university, so I know what's good when I hear it."

Wickram spat out onto the road. "Whatever. It's not like it's any use. I mean, if I was up in the City in a real band, and I was performing at the Manhammer Audiodome in front of ten thousand people..." He windmilled his right arm and brought it down to strum a power chord. His eyes shone like he could see this dream concert happening.

A big sign arched over the road, with stars, moons, and swirling capital letters cut from copper: "Welcome to Pastoral Park. Home of Tragidenko's Circus of Humanity!!"

Barnabas got goose bumps. "You know what, Wickram? In my whole life, I've never been to the circus."

"Really?" He yawned. "I've never been anywhere else."

CHAPTER 18

The mule cart emerged from under the canopy of trees into a wide sunlit square, bordered by flower beds bursting with pansies and hyacinths. Scattered through the square were vividly painted statues of clowns, acrobats, and horses.

But what put a smile on Barnabas's face was the enormous circus tent. It was easily five storeys tall and fat as a cupcake, with the same promise of sweet delight. The huge expanse of canvas was painted in swirling bands of red and gold and festooned with silver flags that snapped in the breeze. Painted on the central panel was a great eye, staring out across the world, a single blue tear hanging from its corner.

"That's amazing," he said.

Wickram couldn't suppress his pride. "Yeah, it's not bad."

The cart followed a road around the tent. A gate stood open, and as they passed through it, the peaceful scene changed in an instant. Three people in purple coveralls crossed their path, carrying enormous bundles of palm fronds and peacock feathers. A scrambled jangling of bells sounded to their right, and three bicycles flew by, ridden by figures with their hair in enormous curlers.

"Something's up," Wickram said. "Everyone's in an utter stumblestorm."

The cart wove between wooden buildings with signs like Canvas Workshop and Ropes and Rigging. Through the open doors, Barnabas could see a flurry of activity. Voices called out: "I need three number fours and a wrapped fall-net." And, "I don't care if it's not finished. Stow it in the travel trunk."

As they passed a long building called Wardrobe, a woman with a bright tangle of red hair and enormous, black-rimmed glasses ran out, spilling needles, measuring tapes, and spools of thread from her apron of many pockets.

"Wickram, stop!"

He pulled back on the reins.

"You stole my fabric," she said, leaping aboard the cart and rolling the unconscious Falstep off the pile of material, which she bundled into her arms.

"Hey, it's not my fault if you left it in the cart."

"I have to finish four jerseys in two hours." She noticed Barnabas sitting in the front. "Who's this?"

"Kid from Furrowing. Wants to perform Ikarian games." She looked doubtful, so Barnabas nodded. Wickram said, "What's happening? Everyone's running around like the tent's on fire."

"Performance tonight. Get yourself to the Big Top now. The maestro is about to address the company."

"A performance? The new show doesn't open for a month." But she was already jumping from the cart and running back to her workshop.

They'd only just gotten under way when they were stopped again, this time by a man with a weather-worn face and an undisciplined crest of frizzy grey hair stuck through with stray bits of straw.

"You didn't sign out my cart, boy," the old man growled. "Or my mules."

"Don't get your guts corkscrewed, Whistlewort. I was just picking up Falstep at the station."

Whistlewort peered into the back of the cart and shook his head. "You shouldn't let him drink like that! What would your father say?"

"I don't know, I never listen to him."

"And who the Holy Couple are you?" Whistlewort wheezed, squinting at Barnabas like he was under a microscopic.

"Um, I'm from Frowning. I want to do uncaring games."

"Ikarian games, you mean? Then it's funny you're wearing a clown nose, don't ya think?" Blushing, Barnabas pulled off the sweaty red nose. Whistlewort banged the side of the cart near Falstep's head. "Hey, Head Clown!"

Falstep muttered, "Did I miss my cue?"

"Get to the Big Top," Whistlewort told the two boys. "I'll sober him up and make sure he's ready to perform."

Wickram threw his arms out in a helpless shrug. "This is mule dung! Who the hell are we performing for?"

The old man's eyes were like two blazing pistols. "Clouding Guild!"

Wickram drew in a sharp breath.

Whistlewort rode the cart away with Falstep, and Barnabas stumbled to keep up with Wickram, who was powering grimly up the dirt road on his long legs, guitar strapped to his back. They walked by another workshop. Inside, men and women were cutting wood, drilling, sanding, and nailing. Barnabas noticed they were all using hand tools like the kind he had seen in the Crumhorn Museum. Something occurred to him.

"There's no electricity here," he said.

"Nope," Wickram answered. "Pastoral Park—it's boring and dark."

"But rest of the Valley has power."

"The circus has purity of vision," Wickram said with evident sarcasm. "But even out there in the rest of the Valley, we got none of your internet or cell phone stuff."

"How do you know about them then?"

"I do my research. I want to live in the City some day."

The carpenters as well as workers from all the other buildings began filing out into the street. Every resident of Pastoral Park was heading for the huge circus tent, which loomed ahead of them, shining in the sun.

Another boy around Barnabas's age emerged from an alley and began walking beside them, and Barnabas couldn't take his eyes off him. His tight red-brown curls were tied into a bun on top of his head, showing off his light brown, freckled face with its wide flat nose and big, smiling eyes. He wore pants with a zebra stripe and a V-neck smock shirt in a rich peach colour. A heavy bag on one shoulder bent him a little to one side.

"Can you believe this, Wickram?" he asked. "We're killing our deadlines for firksome Clouding." He nodded toward Barnabas. "Who's this guy?"

"This is Barnabas. He's from Coursing. Brilliant on the mini trampoline. Built his own rig when he was only seven."

The boy put a hand on each of Barnabas's shoulders and brought him to a stop in the middle of the path, turning him back and forth while he looked him up and down. Barnabas felt like it was his turn to talk, but he couldn't get his mouth to work.

"Mini-trampoline, Wickram? I doubt it. Anyway, welcome, Barnabas, whatever your *real* story is. I'm Garlip, design apprentice."

Barnabas glanced down into Garlip's big bag, which was stuffed with sketch books, crayons, and other art supplies. He got his tongue in order long enough to say, "Hey," which seemed to amuse Garlip. The boy gave him a wink, turned and ran ahead, climbing a short set of wooden steps into a side entrance of the Big Top.

"Did you hear that, Barn? He called me a liar!" Before Barnabas could respond, Wickram's hand shot up and waved. "Hey, Mom!"

She was sitting quietly on a low crate beside the wooden stairway and hearing him, jumped to her feet with a smile. Barnabas didn't think she looked old enough to be the mother of a teenager. But when they got closer, he could see the shallow wrinkles in her brown face and the strands of grey in her long, straight black hair. She was noticeably shorter than the other members of the community, bringing the total to three of the number of non-giants Barnabas had seen in the Valley. Himself included.

Her smile dropped as they got closer. "Look at you," she said with a trace of an Indian accent as she reached up to touch Wickram's bruised cheek. "I send you on a simple errand, and you get into another fight? What am I to do with you, Pickle?"

"It wasn't anything, Mom." Wickram's voice was petulant, but he looked at the ground, embarrassed. "I just slipped in a pile of stupid." She pushed back his hair and clucked her tongue at the cut on his temple.

"Make sure you clean that before rehearsal starts." She sighed and caressed his hair tenderly for a moment before Wickram pulled back from her. "And where is Falstep? Did you meet him at the station?"

"Yeah, sure. But when we got back, he didn't feel well."

"I know what *that* means." His mother rolled her eyes. "Honestly, I'd feel more secure if you were being watched over by a hungry bear." She took a deep breath and let it out slowly. "Now, introduce me to your friend. Hello, I am Sanjani. You are the boy from Forming Guild who wants to learn trapeze? We did not expect you until next week."

"No, Mom, he's from the City. He has the RoamFone first gen."

Sanjani's mouth dropped open, and she put a hand to her chest as if she suddenly couldn't breathe.

"I'm Barnabas Bopwright," Barnabas said, trying not to be freaked out by her reaction. He held out his hand for her to shake, and she grabbed it protectively in both of hers. Her big, warm eyes were wet as she looked deep into his, and Barnabas wanted to pull away in embarrassment like Wickram had.

Sanjani looked around anxiously and lowered her voice. "Does anyone else know he's here, Pickle?"

"No, we kept him on the hush-hush. 'Step put a clown nose on him, so he'd look like he was from Pastoral Park."

She bit her lip. "We'll need a plan. And papers. Wickram, go inside. I'll help your friend." Wickram started to climb the steps into the tent.

"Wickram, wait," Barnabas said, running after him. "I have to make that call, remember? It's really important. You said I could get a signal somewhere."

"Oh yeah, I forgot." He yelled, "Mom! Barnabas has to pee. He'll be right back." They ran around the huge circus tent until they were standing where no one could see them. Wickram pointed straight up. "You have to get up there."

Barnabas squinted into the sun. "Where?"

"There. The peak of the Big Top."

CHAPTER 19

Barnabas stared up the side of the Big Top toward its distant summit. "You're kidding."

"No, you'll definitely get a signal. Just hang on tight. It gets really windy up there."

Wickram didn't seem to think this plan was self-evidently insane. Barnabas's mouth was suddenly dry. "Am I allowed to do that? Just climb up the tent?"

"No, of course not, but everyone's inside now. You won't get caught."

"Your mom…"

"Just find her when you get back down." He pointed at one of the struts holding up the tent wall. "See? There's little ladder rungs."

Barnabas almost dropped the plan, but he needed to reach Deni or he was screwed. He pulled the straps of his backpack until they were as tight as his nervous stomach and began to climb. The rungs of the ladder were barely large enough for his feet and dug painfully into his hands.

He looked down at Wickram, who cringed. "I guess really you should have a safety harness. Or a net." Then his face brightened. "Oh well. No stakes, no prizes, right? Okay, got to head into this mystery rehearsal situation. Catch you later."

"No stakes, no prizes," Barnabas said to himself and began to climb faster. The vertical portion of the ladder was about two storeys of climbing, then the ladder tilted to follow the angled slope of the tent. He passed an air vent cut into the canvas and heard a riot of sound from below. Peering through, he saw a traditional circus ring surrounded by benches set in semicircles around the ring. A hundred or more people were clustered together in little meetings, everyone shouting and pointing. A knot of musicians sat to one side, all practicing different parts. Garlip was in conference with, Barnabas figured, the other designers. Acrobats, clowns, and jugglers had all carved out a bit of space for themselves, stretching, trying out moves.

A sudden wind grabbed at him, and he remembered he was high in the air on an urgent mission. He hurried upward to the pinnacle of the tent, where he sat on a narrow platform, wrapping both arms around the central flagpole. The huge silver flag overhead slapped at itself in the wind. To his right was the still-incomprehensible sight of the great cliff, and sitting on top of it, the City—his home.

Around him was the Valley, an industrial wasteland. Open-pit mines scarred the landscape like pockmarks. Huge factories belched smoke into the sky. Heavy trucks ground their way along the grid of roads, and fat pipelines criss-crossed the dry earth. In sharp contrast, directly below him, Pastoral Park was a green haven, changing from manicured parkland to dense forest as it neared the cliff.

Keeping one hand on the flagpole, Barnabas shrugged his backpack off his left shoulder and reached inside for his phone. *Signal! Sweet signal!* He almost cried with relief. But he only had a few minutes to reach Deni before she left school. He pushed the FastCommand button and called out loudly, "Dial Deni, speaker on!"

He tucked the phone into his shirt pocket and hugged the flagpole. The wind was picking up, and the platform on top of the tent began to sway like a ship in the swell.

"Barnabas!" Deni screamed from his shirt pocket. "Where are you?"

Barnabas had been so focussed on reaching her, he'd forgotten to decide how much of the truth to tell. "Ms. Rolan-Gong suspended me."

"Oh my God. What did you do?"

He ran the whole sequence of events through his head: Klevver hanging him over the stairwell, Mayor Tuppletaub interrogating him, the diaboriku, running from Klevver, the Aqua train…

"I-I wanted to see if I could get a better interview with the mayor, so I snuck into that meeting with the parents and started asking him questions."

"You idiot. I'm the reporter. Stick to camera work and leave the heavy journalism to me, okay?"

"I know that now."

"No wonder Rolan-Gong was pissed. You interrupted her sales pitch to the rich parents. Do you need me to bring you anything from school?"

"That's why I'm calling. I'm kind of not going to be home."

Deni didn't respond, and Barnabas could practically hear her mind turning. A loud cheer erupted from down below in the tent, and he wished he could be inside watching the rehearsal. "But you don't want your mom and stepdad to know where you are, right?" Sometimes her intuition was scarily accurate.

"Just for a while, Deni."

"How long?"

He remembered what Falstep had said about the train schedule. "I'll be back next Tuesday."

"Five days..." Deni said. Barnabas could feel her growing excitement. "Okay, I can imitate Mom-Morgan on the phone, at least good enough to fool your mom. I'll say you're staying in our guest bedroom during your suspension and editing the footage from this morning's assembly. I'll spin something about how Mom-Amy is using the project to tutor us on journalism and fostering a progressive agenda."

"That's genius. My mom loves your parents. She said they're good role models or whatever."

Deni was talking faster and faster, warming to the brilliance of her plan. "I'll drop by your place to pick up some clothes. I'll totally sell the whole narrative."

Despite the fact that he was high in the air, swaying wildly in the wind, Barnabas smiled. He knew Deni would be able to make all these crazy schemes work. "You're brilliant. And then I'll be back at school next Tuesday, and no one will ever find out. You totally saved me."

She asked the question in a voice so calculatingly casual, she almost sounded bored. "And...when did he get in touch with you?"

"Who?"

"I know what's going on," Deni shouted. "You don't have to pretend."

"Barnabas?" called a distant voice, almost inaudible under the wind.

He looked down and saw Wickram's mother, Sanjani, circling the tent, looking for him. "Deni," he said, "I have to go."

She ignored him. "It's your father, isn't it? I mean your *real* father. He came and took you away this morning, right?"

"My father? No." If Sanjani looked up, she'd see him, then who knows what trouble he'd be in. "Deni, I have to hang up." Carefully he let go of the flagpole and got on his hands and knees, stretching one foot back to find the first ladder rung.

"*Don't you dare*," she snapped at him in sudden fury. "If I'm going to help you, the least you can do is be honest with me." As quickly as he dared, Barnabas began to climb down.

Deni's voice ached with reverence. "Oh my God, Brownbag Bopwright. I grew up listening to his Village Vanguard bootlegs. Mom-Amy used to play me 'Midnight Sun' as a lullaby. The way he could arpeggiate a diminished chord…" She moaned like it actually hurt to contemplate something that beautiful.

Deni's voice dropped out for a second as Barnabas left signal range. He stopped his descent. "Look, Deni, I can't talk. She…*He's* waiting for me. In a big vintage Cadillac."

"Oh wow, you're *SO lucky*. Where is he taking you? New York? New Orleans? Paris? Is he going to bring you down to some waterfront dive where the jazz is so pure, you could light it like kerosene?"

"Barnabas? Are you here?" Sanjani called from below.

"Crap…"

"What's wrong?"

"Uh, they just called our flight. Final boarding." He started climbing backward again.

"Go! Go!" she said, her voice cutting in and out. "I'll cover for you here. *Barnabas, listen.* This is *incredibly* important."

He stopped. "What?"

"When you're on an epic journey," she told him solemnly, "remember to enjoy the ride."

CHAPTER 20

Barnabas didn't bother with the last few rungs and jumped to the ground, landing with a muffled thump on the soft grass. As if to congratulate him for a job well done, a trumpet inside the tent played a triumphant fanfare. He walked around the perimeter of the Big Top until he found Sanjani.

"Hi," he said, and the woman whirled around.

"Oh, Barnabas, there you are. I was getting worried."

Her excessive concern for him was making him nervous. "I guess we were just walking in circles around the tent, looking for each other."

"Yes, I suppose. All right, follow me." Sanjani headed back to the road, and he fell into step beside her. "So, when did you come through the forest?"

He found the question strange, like she was asking if he was an elf or something. "I didn't come through a forest. I came on the subway."

Sanjani stopped and looked him in the eye. "You mean you got through the Frontier without papers? How is that possible?"

"It was sort of an accident."

"Well, you were very lucky not to get caught."

Coming down the road toward them was the old man, Whistlewort. He was leading a magnificent white horse with a long flowing mane that gleamed like the curl on a wave. Behind them, a little shaky but at least mobile, was Falstep.

"Whistlewort, dear one," Sanjani called. She pointedly ignored Falstep. "We were just coming to find you." The man stopped and scowled at them, but this didn't seem to bother Sanjani. "This is Barnabas. He's from the City. Came through on the train."

"Ha! Ikarian games, my ass," Whistlewort said, crossing his arms on his chest. "On the train? That was damn foolish!"

"I didn't plan it."

Sanjani put a reassuring hand on his shoulder. "No one blames you, dear." Although Whistlewort looked like he did. "So, we'll need to take steps to keep him safe."

Whistlewort pointed Falstep at the Big Top. "The maestro's just starting rehearsal. Get in there and keep drinking water." He handed Falstep a canteen and gave him a shove in the right direction. Whistlewort looked Barnabas up and down, like he was trying to figure out how to dismantle him. The horse snuffled and pawed at the ground.

Sanjani said, "First of all, he'll need identity papers."

"I can whip those up pretty fast, good enough to fool any Aqua who don't look too close." He pulled a short knife out of his pocket and began twirling it absently in his hands. "But I'm thinkin' long-term. Been quite a while since we had to plead the case of a defector."

"I'm sure we can find him a place in the circus." She turned to Barnabas, her eyes moist again. "We'll be like a new family to you, dear child, I promise. And in a year or so, we'll take you before the Guild Council—"

"The Guild Council ain't friendly to us these days," Whistlewort said, twirling the knife.

Barnabas was following this conversation with growing agitation. "Excuse me," he said, but they didn't seem to hear him.

"Dimitri is trying to change that," Sanjani insisted.

"Dimitri, you'll forgive me, is a dog who keeps gettin' beat and goes on waggin' his tail regardless."

"Excuse me," Barnabas said, loud enough to get their attention. "Hi, sorry, I think there's a misunderstanding here. I don't want to stay in the Valley."

They stared at him for several uncomfortable seconds. "Then why the hell didja come here in the first place?" Whistlewort barked.

Sanjani looked confused. "Really, dear? You don't want to stay? You didn't come here to…get away?"

"I'm sorry. The Valley looks really interesting, but I have to get back to my family. I have school and stuff."

She looked back at Whistlewort. "He's hoping to go home again. What can we do?"

Hoping? Barnabas thought, alarmed.

Whistlewort tapped the point of his knife against one callused fingertip. "Well, identity papers are the least of it. He'll need a plausible story, an exit plan…And I never forged travel documents before. That's not gonna be easy."

"Thank you, my friend," Sanjani said, although Barnabas hadn't heard the old man promise anything. Whistlewort disappeared around the back of the tent with the amazing horse, and Sanjani clapped her hands, a bright smile spreading across her face. "So, Barnabas, are you ready to see the Circus of Humanity in action?"

CHAPTER 21

Barnabas knew how big the Big Top was—he'd just climbed it. Somehow it was even bigger inside, a whole world of its own. Two broad wooden poles rose from the floor to hold up the canvas roof. Platforms for the trapeze artists were built around these, and even higher catwalks were hung for the gas lamps, which filled the tent with a bright, warm light. On the ground between the two poles was the circus ring, demarcated by a short wooden circle glistening with glittering red paint. Behind it, a series of tall black curtains separated the performance area from the backstage.

Performers were pulling costumes from rolling racks and dressing with little regard for modesty. Barnabas tried not to stare at all the toned, muscular bodies squeezing themselves into skin-tight costumes. Meanwhile, the bandleader dictated changes to the musicians, and carpenters and painters swarmed over every surface like ants, splashing colour onto sets and securing railings to the audience risers. Barnabas spotted Garlip wrapping a tentpole in silver streamers. The boy saw him, smiled, and winked, and Barnabas felt his face go hot.

A group of performers in silver and orange rolled in through the Big Top's main entrance on a series of amazing green bicycles like art deco grasshoppers. The first two were a middle-aged man and woman, followed by a little boy on the smallest bike in the group, and finally by two teenage girls, obviously twins. Spotting Barnabas in the audience, the twins jumped off their bikes and ran up to greet him.

"Hi!" said one of the girls. "I'm Hulo and this is—"

"Bulo," said the other. "We heard you came from the City. That's flamtasmic. We have to rehearse now—"

"But have dinner with us tonight before the show."

Barnabas was startled that they already knew about him and just nodded dumbly. Hulo and Bulo jumped back on their bikes and followed the other members of what must have been their family through a gap in the backstage curtain.

Wickram emerged from the same gap and ran up the aisle to sit beside Barnabas. He was dressed all in black with his hair tied back in a ponytail.

"Hey, Barn. You make your phone call?"

"Yeah, thanks. This…" He gestured around the Big Top. "It's amazing!"

From an entrance to the right of the ring, Whistlewort entered with the white horse. He handed the reins to a beautiful Chinese girl who jumped up from her floor stretches to greet him. She moved with the fluidity of a ballet dancer, her long black hair flowing behind her like the train of a ball gown.

Wickram was staring at her, his eyes like pools of melted ice cream. "That's Graviddy. She's my girlfriend."

Like she had caught a lucky updraft, Graviddy swung effortlessly onto the horse. She gave the majestic beast a small nudge with her knees, and they cantered off across the ring, other performers hopping out of her way.

"She does horse tricks?"

"No, the horse is just for flair. Graviddy's a silks artist. The best."

Barnabas wasn't sure what that was. "And what do you do? Play guitar in the band?"

"Nope, I'm a stagehand." He pointed across the ring. "See that curtain? The red one, just to the left of the big black one in the middle? That's my curtain. I have to pull it aside for a bunch of entrances and exits and then make sure it gets back into position."

"That's it?"

In a flash, Wickram went from happy to furious. "You don't think stagehands are important? How do you think all the curtains move, and the props and apparatuses get where they have to go? Magic?"

Barnabas raised his hands in surrender. "No, no, that's not what I meant. It's just…you seem really creative, and I thought maybe you'd be doing music, or drawing sets or—"

"Well, I'm proud of my work. The stagehands are like a family. We watch out for each other, and we do everything so perfect, no one even has to remember we exist."

Barnabas was trying to pull together an apology when another remarkable creature swept in through the centre stage curtain and strode to the middle of the ring. He was big in every direction—tall as well as wide—and all but engulfed in a long coat of coloured patches. A floppy purple hat sat precariously on the mountaintop of his long, tangled hair, which reached down to his shoulders to form a continuum with his beard, itself long enough that the end was tied with a ribbon. Together, mane and beard formed a thundercloud of hair, auburn where it wasn't shot through with bolts of white. The eyes in the centre of this cloud were black pools, but they were charged, bright as lightning.

"Who…?" Barnabas said, startled to see Wickram crouched down behind the bench, like he was playing hide-and-seek.

"That," he said in a whisper, "is Maestro Dimitri Tragidenko!"

CHAPTER 22

"Attention!" called Maestro Dimitri Tragidenko. "Attention is desired and required." From behind every curtain, members of the troupe emerged. Up on every ladder and across every rigging strut, work stopped. Five or six trapdoors opened in the floor, and all the clowns, including Falstep, peeked out. Wickram got up and went to stand with a group of men and women in black clothing who must have been his stage crew "family."

"My darlings, my darlings," the maestro said to the assembled circus. "You have made many beautiful things full of love. I am humbled." His voice was exotically accented, rising and falling in a full-bodied sing-song, and the company hung on every word. "We don't yet precisely know what is this show we are making, yes? But tonight, despite all this yessing-and-noing, this guessing-not-knowing, we must put on a polished performance." He rocked back and forth from toes to heels, turning slowly to look at everyone with his warm, piercing eyes. He threw a fat finger in the air. "So! Tonight, we are seeing how far we have travelled on this sea of confusion to reach the shores of *truth*."

Barnabas started to applaud, but no one else did. He shoved his hands under his armpits.

Tragidenko smiled at him and gave a little bow before continuing. "Here is the running order."

The woman beside the maestro, her head shaved shiny clean, read from a piece of paper on her clipboard. "The Aerial Darios, the Spinning Finn Family, Graviddy, Forest tableau, Clown Wars, Tumble Times, and the Opening of the Heavens."

The maestro nodded. "If your act is not included, do not despair. We still have a month until the real opening. So, as our time is precious, we will run straight through, pausing only if mortal danger presents itself." He clapped twice, and the company moved purposefully to their starting positions.

Wickram pulled aside his red curtain and waved at Barnabas to join him. Barnabas ran down and entered the backstage world of the circus.

"I thought maybe you'd like to watch the rehearsal from here."

Barnabas nodded enthusiastically.

"But tonight, you'll have to be in the audience."

The backstage was as big as the audience side, all lit in tiny pools by candle and kerosene lamp. Performers were still trying out little bits of choreography while wardrobe people crouched beside them, sewing on feathers and repairing seams. Giant set pieces were being wheeled into place. Masks, hoops, juggling clubs, teeter-totters, and torches were laid out on tables, waiting for their moment in the spotlight. A jungle of ropes hung down from the dark, like a giant puppet master was somewhere above getting ready to bring the whole show to life.

Wickram was testing his curtain, giving the rope a few short tugs if a pulley stuck. An older man in stagehand black stepped up to Wickram and tapped him on the shoulder.

"Okay, you're here," the man said. "That's a start."

Wickram looked uncharacteristically sheepish. "Yeah, Nivvin, I'm here."

"But are you awake? That's the question."

"Yeah, of course I'm—"

"You only have four cues, right? Just four things in a row to get right. Now, I'm thinking that's more than you've managed in the last three weeks. But I'm also thinking you're a smart kid who knows better than to mess up a dress rehearsal for such an important show. Am I right?"

Wickram straightened his spine and shouted, "*Yessir*."

"Good, 'cause I'm watching."

Nivvin walked away, making minute adjustments to sets and props as he went. Wickram was red with embarrassment and staring at the floor, so Barnabas wandered away to watch a man dressed head to toe in green feathers playing a mandolin and singing a dirty song for his friends' amusement.

"Hey," Wickram said, taking him by the arm and bringing him back to the red curtain. "We're about to start. You gotta stay by me or you'll get in someone's way."

"Five minutes," called the woman with the shaved head. "The call is five minutes." The chatter backstage stopped. It was only a rehearsal, but the atmosphere was electric, like the moments before a summer storm.

Wickram gave Barnabas a stool to sit on and showed him where he could peek through the curtains to watch the stage. The bald woman yelled, "Places," and the house lights dimmed.

Chapter 23

As Barnabas watched aerialists, cyclists, and clowns fly, tumble, and sail across the ring, he had a sudden memory of standing in the wings of the Malibar Theatre, seeing his father perform on the famous stage. He remembered feeling privileged, like his special vantage point was proof of his father's love. Had his mother been there beside him? He was very young then, so she must have been. But he only remembered seeing his father and applauding loudly along with the enthusiastic audience after each of his solos.

Wickram opened his curtain, and half a dozen tumblers did backflips past him on their way offstage. A couple of them turned their heads to check out Barnabas. In the audience, front row centre, Maestro Tragidenko gestured broadly and whispered notes to the bald woman, who wrote down every word, her face as calm as his was expressive.

Then Graviddy appeared, riding the white horse around the ring. Long bands of material were being lowered from the catwalk, and Graviddy stood in the stirrups, reaching for them.

"No!" Tragidenko called from his seat. "You must rest your shoulder, my dear. Save it for tonight."

Graviddy sat and pulled back on the reins. She tossed her head like she was offended, but her voice remained calm. "Yes, Dimitri." She did an elegant dismount from the horse, and it ran to a waiting handler as Graviddy walked gracefully toward Wickram's curtain.

"Barn," Wickram whispered. "Don't mention the girlfriend thing. She doesn't really, um, know about that." He pulled the curtain, and Graviddy sailed through the opening, radiating confidence. She turned and looked Barnabas in the eye, and he felt his stomach flip over.

A fast set change. Painted trees were rolled onstage, lights flashed, and music swelled. A veritable army of nymphs and faeries rose from the trapdoors, engulfed in smoke. And just as suddenly, Maestro Tragidenko was beside them, the very definition of larger than life, emanating a subtle aroma of wood smoke, sweat, and flowers. Barnabas drew back into the shadows.

Tragidenko put a huge hand on Wickram's shoulder and pulled him closer, gesticulating at the stage and whispering. "There! There! Imagine a solo guitar playing! Flying arpeggios of *light* and *mystery*. A sound which grows and ebbs like waves. Perhaps a flute enters and sings a countermelody, something like only you can compose for it, yes?"

Wickram stiffened, his jaw growing tight. "I don't think so," he said in a low growl. "Will you go away? I'm working here." He pulled the cord to open his curtain, and an acrobat in a deer's head mask passed them, pirouetting onto the stage.

Tragidenko leaned closer, putting his arm right around the boy's shoulders. "But, yes. Yes. You hear what the band plays now? They are good people, but their music, it is senti*mental*, not worthy of the spectacle. It needs subtlety, grace, and a core of iron. You could raise up the hearts of the audience, Wickram. If I were like you, young and talented—"

Wickram threw off Tragidenko's arm and turned on him, eyes full of fury. "But you're *not*. You keep thinking you know me, but you don't. You don't care what *I* want out of *my* life. What *I* think." Barnabas gasped in shock.

Tragidenko raised his hands and looked for guidance from above—from God or the spotlight operator. "He doesn't *want* this," the maestro said, raising his voice. Everyone backstage turned and stared. Even the performers onstage were giving little sideways looks, and the clarinet player missed a cue. Tragidenko, his eyes like the craters of twin volcanoes, brought his face close to Wickram's. "You want to be musician, to be *artist*. But when you get a chance to make music for something *majestic*, for something bigger than your own little *playacting*, you are too singular, too important."

"Something *majestic*," Wickram imitated with derision. "Meaning something *you* want."

From somewhere behind them, Nivvin shouted, "Wickram!"

But Wickram's engine was now fully revved up, and nothing could slow him down. "Maybe I'll just walk out of here and go work in the foundries at Forming! Then who will you have to manipulate?"

Tragidenko laughed, a dark laugh that made the end of his beard swing like a pendulum. "Oh, excellent. You in the foundries. A poignant image. Will you bring your mother along to serve you cold drinks when the furnaces grow too hot?"

"Wickram! Wake up," called Nivvin, but it was too late. A group of nymphs was struggling to pull aside Wickram's curtain so they could get offstage. "Crump!" Nivvin yelled and ran over to pull the curtain himself.

Wickram froze in disbelief. Tragidenko, for his part, seemed to shrink into himself. His furious eyes grew soft and ashamed. Sheepishly, he murmured to Nivvin, "My fault. I interrupted the boy—"

Life flowed back into Wickram, who shouted, "No! It's my fault. You were right about me, Nivvin—I'm useless. I quit. I resign my position in the circus." He turned and ran, disappearing into the darkness at the back of the tent.

The show had ground to a complete halt. Tragidenko pulled at his beard with both hands, squeezing his eyes closed, his whole-body shuddering. Everyone was silent. Finally, the maestro opened his eyes, shook himself like a wet dog, and strode into the ring.

"All right, all right," he called. "Technical difficulty. Let us take that exit as read. Please set up for next scene—the Clown Wars!"

With Wickram gone, Barnabas felt like he had no right to be backstage. He followed Wickram's path into the darkness, trying not to trip over anything. Deep in the shadows, he could see a thin square of light in the wall of the tent. He pulled the canvas flap aside, shading his eyes against the glare of the sun, and stepped down into a meadow behind the Big Top. Following a sniffling sound around a big boulder, he found Wickram sitting on the grass with his back against the rock.

Barnabas approached cautiously. "You okay?"

Wickram wiped at his eyes with his sleeve. "No. I utterly flat-stomped it." He shook his head. "Four flippin' cues. I couldn't even get four cues right."

"Well, Tragidenko distracted you," Barnabas said, sitting down beside him.

"That old goat. He rashes me like nettles. I can't think straight when he starts talking like that."

"How can you afford to talk to the head of the circus that way? What if he fires you? Throws you out?"

Wickram laughed, harsh and brittle. "I wish. He can't throw me out, Barn." He took a shuddery breath. "He's my father."

Chapter 24

"Wickram?" Sanjani called, coming across the meadow toward them.

"Balderdung," Wickram said. "I gotta go, Barn. I'm glad you came to visit us lowly Valley folk." He shot to his feet and ran off in the opposite direction of Sanjani's approach.

Barnabas expected Sanjani to be angry when she reached the boulder, but she just sighed and leaned against it, catching a bit of late-afternoon sunshine on her face.

"So, Barnabas," she said with a weary half-smile. "Now you've met the whole family."

"Do you want me to run after him?"

"No, he'll be fine. What I really want is for my husband and son to stop being so pig-headed with each other." She ruffled his hair and then pulled back her hand. "Sorry, it's been a while since I've been able to reach Wickram's head, and I guess I miss it. You must be hungry. We're having an early dinner before the show. Come."

As they walked, Sanjani pointed out features of the community such as the library and the bathhouse. On the wall of one large building was an amazing mural of the Valley and the City.

"A talented young designer named Garlip painted it," Sanjani told him.

"Oh, I met him. Beautiful. The mural, I mean."

The building turned out to be the community dining hall. Inside, staff was getting ready for dinner, setting out condiments, plates, and baskets of cutlery on large wooden tables. By the time the rehearsal was over and the population of Pastoral Park flowed into the dining hall, the smell of spices filled the air, and each table held gleefully mismatched plates and cutlery and small vases of spring flowers in all the colours of the rainbow.

"Thumbbutter," Sanjani called to a teen girl with a strong, muscled physique and short dark-blond hair. "This is Barnabas. Can he sit with you and the other students?"

"Sure, Sanjani. So, you're the kid from the City. That's utter cracked. Welcome." Barnabas saw others staring at him too and realized that news of his identity had spread across the whole circus community. Thumbutter led him to a table full of teens by the back wall.

"I doubt we'll see Wickram tonight, so you can have his place," she said. "Hey, everyone, this is Barnabas. Barnabas, this is Soonie, Mooney, Beaney, and Moe. That's Hulo and Bulo."

Hulo said, "We already met."

"Before the rehearsal," said Bulo.

Thumbutter ignored the interruption. "This is Dromadop, and he's Garlip. He's not a performer."

"You say that like an insult. We also met," said Garlip. "Come sit beside me, Barnabas." And he did, their thighs touching in the tight space.

Someone slid in silently on his other side. "And I'm Graviddy."

"Oh yeah," Barnabas said, flustered by the almost otherworldly poise of the girl. "You're Wickram's—" He caught himself. "Wickram told me all about you." This caused a small wave of eye rolls and snorts around the table. "Is your, um, shoulder okay? The maestro said—"

"I'm just recovering from a strain. He needs me to be at my best for Clouding Guild."

"She's the star," said Thumbutter, and Barnabas expected the others to laugh again, but no one did.

Waiters brought bowls of food to the table, and the kids began passing them around and filling their plates.

Garlip said, "I heard you climbed on top of a train to get down to the Valley. I heard that you did it on a dare." He sounded thrilled.

Barnabas's eyes went wide. "No! I didn't mean to come down here at all." He proceeded to tell the story, his narrow escape from a killer, running onto the train. This led to a side lecture about what it was like to ride a subway, which, in turn, led to him providing half-remembered statistics on the population of the City, and finally, a short treatise on how supermarkets worked. Somehow, despite all the talking, he managed to eat two portions of the delicious food.

"The City is *full* of killers," Thumbutter said knowingly.

Barnabas, offended on behalf of his city, was about to correct her when the loud conversations in the room suddenly dampened to urgent whispers.

"What's happening?" Barnabas asked, and Garlip turned him around to see the group entering the dining hall.

"Clouding Guild," he whispered.

There were maybe eight of the Clouders, dressed in simple grey ponchos and black pants. Whistlewort and other older members of Pastoral Park were showing the group to their tables when the dining hall door opened again, and in walked Maestro Tragidenko with a woman. She wasn't that tall by Valley standards, but wide and strong and serious, like she had been carved from a single stump of hundred-year-old oak. Tragidenko, in a wide-lapelled pinstripe suit and gold bowtie, was all smiles, but she was scowling, surveying the hall with grave mistrust like she was assessing the danger to her people and readying herself to order a sudden retreat.

"That's Carminn," Garlip told Barnabas. "The Speaker of Clouding Guild."

"There's no kids," Barnabas said. "I figured they'd bring their kids to see the circus."

Garlip shook his head. "No, of course not. They wouldn't expose them to our kind of sacrilege."

"Gonna be a reaaallllly fun show," Hulo muttered.

"Utterly," Bulo agreed.

Tragidenko's bald assistant rose to tell the performers to make their way to the Big Top. Everyone began shuffling out, with Beaney, the youngest of the kids and the only one Barnabas's height, balancing a rubber ball on the end of his nose like a trained seal. Garlip, Hulo, Bulo, and Barnabas stopped at the door to look back at the Clouders, who were seated around two tables with the elders of Pastoral Park.

Bulo said, "First person who catches one of them smiling gets five farthings."

"I'll take that action," Hulo said. "Falstep will get them laughing."

The visitors from Clouding Guild had begun to pray in unison, their heads lowered. "O, Father Glory, who sets us to work for our bread, give us the strength to build your Holy City."

Barnabas was surprised to see Garlip was also reciting the prayer under his breath. Then Garlip caught Barnabas looking and stopped, crossing his eyes and sticking out his tongue at him.

"Let's go entertain the servants of God," he said, leading them from the dining hall.

CHAPTER 25

Barnabas had grown just as nervous as the rest of Pastoral Park about the show, and sitting by himself in the stands, waiting for the curtain was unbearable. Nivvin was teaching someone Wickram's curtain cues, and that just made Barnabas sad. He left his backpack on his seat and ran out through the tent's main entrance.

Out in the parking lot stood a small bus and a big truck that must have belonged to the Clouders. He heard someone singing and circled around the Big Top to investigate. Behind it, at the edge of the woods, stood a collection of brightly painted cottages, some no bigger than a garden shed. The singer was inside one, doing warm-up exercises, her voice climbing higher and higher with each cycle. "Mi-ay-ee-ahhhhhh, oh-may-yoo!"

Then he heard another voice from another cottage. It was Wickram. "Come on, just one drink."

"Do not touch my hooch," Falstep said from inside. "Make yourself useful and hand me the thin brush and the blue paint."

Barnabas considered knocking on the door and joining them, but maybe that was wrong to do before a show. He decided to go ninja and take a peek. Bracing his foot on a decorative moulding below the window, he pulled himself up until he could peer inside.

The single room was a mess of makeup, costumes, and wigs. Falstep was seated in front of a big mirror surrounded by bright kerosene lamps, putting on his clown face. At the back of the cottage was a small bed with a pile of well-thumbed books on the nightstand, and on a shelf above, a collection of half-empty liquor bottles.

Falstep took the brush from Wickram and painted a blue tear on his white face, an echo of the big weeping eye on the Big Top. Wickram, too tall for the room, sat down on the unmade bed and reached up for a brown bottle from the shelf. He took a long swig and burped.

"Hey!" Falstep said, eyeing him in the mirror. "What'd I say about my hooch?"

Wickram shot him back a smile full of innocent mischief and put the bottle back in place. Somewhere behind Barnabas, the opera singer started up again. "Mi-ay-ee-ahhhhhh, oh-may-yoo!"

"Blue wig," Falstep ordered, and Wickram brought it to him. "Blue is for *serious* clowning."

His wig in place, Falstep took a black and white picture of another clown down from the wall and spoke to it. "What do you think, Onestep? Do I got the clown mojo tonight?"

"Your dad's dead, 'Step. And even if he wasn't, why would you care what he thinks? You're a genius." Wickram's words were slurry around the edges.

A quiet voice behind Barnabas said, "Is everyone in the City a spy, or just you?"

Startled, Barnabas lost his grip and tumbled off his perch, landing on his feet and falling backward against someone. Barnabas turned to find Garlip grinning at him and bringing a finger to his lips.

"Shhhhh," he said.

Barnabas smiled back, returned the gesture, and the two hurried away.

"I didn't mean to spy," Barnabas explained as they circled back around the Big Top.

"Don't worry. You're curious. It's cute."

Cute. "Does Wickram drink a lot?"

Garlip shrugged, making his hair bun jiggle. "When he's sad. Wait, quiet!" He pulled them into a shadow as Graviddy stepped out of the Big Top through a flap, all dressed and made up for the show. She was beautiful, almost otherworldly—not someone humans could talk to, just maybe build a temple to. Then, without warning, she lurched sideways and vomited into a bush. Barnabas almost ran forward to help her, but Garlip held him back. Matter-of-factly, Graviddy wiped her mouth with a handkerchief and slipped back inside the tent.

"She does that before every show," Garlip said. "It's weirdly impressive."

"Is Wickram really her boyfriend?"

"You should ask fewer questions about Wickram and more about me. I'm really interesting." He booped Barnabas on the nose with an ink-stained index finger and followed Graviddy through the tent flap.

CHAPTER 26

B arnabas got back to his seat just as the band took their places to the right of the ring. They played a comedy tango with a wheezy clarinet weaving over a woozy beat. The small audience was made up of Pastoral Park residents who weren't actually involved in the show, and they clapped along with pleasure. Barnabas was just getting into the song when Whistlewort and Sanjani arrived, leading the delegation from Clouding into the Big Top. The Speaker, Carminn, entered first, peering into every corner of the tent, like sin might be hiding in the shadows. Most of the group looked just as stern, but Barnabas noticed one guy, the youngest by far, who was mesmerized by the sights and sounds in the tent, trying unsuccessfully to hold back his smile.

A long drumroll began, and the lights dimmed. A cymbal crashed as a curtain parted at the back of the ring, and Maestro Dimitri Tragidenko swept onto the stage. He was dressed in a long, shining great coat of purple satin, with an orange top hat balanced rakishly on his unruly mane of hair. The maestro's eyes sparkled, and his smile shone forth from the centre of his beard like the sun breaking through storm clouds.

"Ladies and gentlemen, honoured guests. Welcome to a night of laughter, tears, and adventure. This is the show of shows. The imagination made manifest. *The utter flamtasmic!* Welcome to Tragidenko's Circus of Humanity!"

Barnabas and the audience from Pastoral Park clapped loudly, but the lack of applause from the Clouding contingent seemed to suck the energy out of their efforts. Barnabas tried to enjoy the show as much as he had during rehearsal, but the scowling Clouders were a heavy grey cloud that extinguished all wonder and fun. Nothing amused or excited them—not the tumblers, not the aerialists, no fire trick or startling act of balance.

Falstep and his clowns burst into the ring on mismatched bicycles, crashing into one another and flying over handlebars into each other's arms. Falstep's bicycle flew apart in mid-jump and, still holding the handlebars, he let his momentum carry him into the audience. He ran all the way up the steps to the Clouding group and gave the handlebars to the young Clouder, who laughed out loud. His elders shot him a dirty look.

"And for our next assault on the senses," he said, "I need a brave volunteer." When he reached his hand out to Carminn, the Speaker crossed her arms over her chest, and the others all followed suit including, reluctantly, the young Clouder. There was a look of panic under Falstep's manic smile. He gave a squeak and ran back down the aisle as if he were being chased by a swarm of bees.

The only time the magic returned was when Graviddy performed. As she rode in on the white horse and circled the ring, Barnabas was again shaken by her beauty. She raised her arms to the heavens, and the heavens answered with long lengths of white silk. Catching hold of them, she sailed from the horse's back into the air. It all looked so effortless, so perfect. And when she was high over the ring, wrapped in her silks, she suddenly let go and spun downward, catching herself just above the stage.

A male dancer twirled out from behind the curtain and caught her hand. Running and leaping with the grace and power of a gazelle, he circled the ring, pulling Graviddy along as she hung from the silk by one wrapped ankle. As the man ran faster and faster, the connection between them grew strained, until suddenly they broke apart and Graviddy flew into the air, spinning off into the darkness at the top of the tent. The dancer stood alone in the ring, panting heavily, his arm stretched heavenward as he looked up with longing. Barnabas too longed for the angel to descend again into the lonely human realm.

The spotlights went out, leaving little afterglows in his eyes, and the house lights came up for intermission. Barnabas turned around and looked at the Clouding contingent. They were leaning toward Carminn, foreheads creased, conferring quietly but with emphatic hand gestures. Carminn scowled and nodded slowly. Performers were peering through cracks in the curtain, watching these deliberations.

In fact, the only one not following the conference was the young Clouder, who Barnabas figured was maybe twenty years old. He was walking around the perimeter of the ring, staring at the lights and colours in wonder, humming the last song under his breath.

The deliberations seemed to be over. Carminn stood. "Sensash!" she shouted at the young Clouder, who ran back up the aisle to her as if tugged by a leash. Carminn led the Clouding contingent up the aisle and through the exit. The curtain at the back of the ring shot aside, and

Maestro Tragidenko hurried out after them, followed by the whole of the circus. Barnabas emerged in time to see the Clouders climbing into their bus, all except Carminn, who was making her way to the big truck.

"Wait, please!" called Tragidenko, running to catch her. "The show, it is only half over."

"Oh, it's over for us," she replied, climbing into the driver's seat and slamming the heavy door. Her vehicle looked like a cross between a pickup truck and a whale shark, its huge grill like a set of shining steel teeth.

"But did you not understand our performance? It is a celebration of human power, of the creative potential of community. Working together just like we all do in the Valley—like you do in your steamworks—to honour Father Glory."

She looked down on him from her open window. "You know what I saw? Vanity. Frivolous nonsense instead of decent, holy work." She started up the powerful engine, which broke the stillness of the evening.

"You are not understanding the metaphor!" Tragidenko shouted over the noise.

Banks of headlights on the front of the truck blazed into life, pinning the circus troupe in a harsh, accusing glare.

Carminn leaned out her open window. "If it were up to me, this place would be torn to the ground, and you'd all be sent to work in the mines. Learn to get your hands dirty."

She threw the vehicle into reverse and did a three-point turn, kicking up more dust than seemed necessary. The bus with the rest of the Clouders followed her down the road in its own cloud of black diesel fumes. From the grimy back window, the young Clouder, Sensash, stared at them forlornly.

"Wait!" Tragidenko yelled after them. "We have prepared a reception after the show! With elderberry wine and ginger scones!" He spun on his heel and spat on the ground. "Bah." He dropped his scowling face to his chest.

No one spoke. Sanjani stepped from the crowd and put her arm around his waist, and after a minute, he raised his head, looking more weary than angry. "Well, we tried." He gave them a little smile. "You, my beautiful children, were sublime. You respected your audience even when they did not respect you. I am so, so proud."

"Yeah, sure," said a quiet voice behind Barnabas. He turned around and saw Falstep, sitting on the ground, utterly dejected. No one else seemed to have heard him.

"What will we do now?" asked one of the trapeze artists.

The maestro wiped his brow. "Now, we will sit together with

friends, drink some wine, and remind ourselves that tomorrow the great curtain of life rises again. Good night, my darlings." Singly or in groups, the company separated and headed off into the night.

Barnabas alone didn't have a destination, until Sanjani approached and put a hand on his shoulder. "Come, young man. You have had a very long day."

PART II

FRIDAY

CHAPTER 27

Barnabas couldn't remember where the dream had started. He could hear Mayor Tuppletaub on stage, telling knock-knock jokes as Deni shouted camera directions. But Barnabas couldn't find Cal's camera. "It's up in the office!" she screamed. "Hurry!" So he ran up the stairs, climbing flight after flight, till he was drenched in sweat. Mr. Klevver was waiting for him at the top. Before Barnabas could save himself, Klevver grabbed him and hurled him over the railing into the bottomless stairwell. By some miracle, he was able to catch the railing and hang there by one small, inadequate hand.

"Help!"

The stairwell was now packed with familiar faces—all his classmates and teachers, his parents, Thelonius—everyone staring, no one coming to his aid.

"Don't worry, dear!" his mother called. "If you fall, I'll start a charity for you."

Klevver started shaking the railing, and Barnabas struggled to hang on. But it wasn't just the railing. The walls and floors bucked and waved, and an ominous rumble grew ever louder.

"Stop," Barnabas cried. "You'll bring down the whole building."

And that's exactly what happened. The ceiling cracked, the floor gave way, and Barnabas tumbled into the abyss, surrounded by all the contents of the school. Desks, whiteboards, wall maps, a hundred papier mâché volcanoes from the freshmen and a hundred aspirational collages from the seniors, disappearing into the void. *And all the King's horses and all the King's men could never put Humpty together again...*

❖

His eyes snapped open, and he took a minute to orient himself. It was morning, and he was in Wickram's bed. He had been so tired after the performance, he could barely remember Sanjani leading him up a long hill and then up the stairs to the dark bedroom. The minute he'd hit the pillow, he'd immediately passed out. Now, in the bright light of morning, he took in his surroundings. Wickram's small room was a veritable palace of music and City culture. Every square inch of wall was covered in band posters, pages torn from old movie magazines, and tourism photos of the Tower District and the Manhammer Audiodome.

Around the narrow, wooden bed were various musical instruments, including Wickram's guitar, a button accordion, and several wooden recorders. Barnabas's jeans were neatly hung over the back of a chair. On the seat were a faded T-shirt from the band Big Mouth Grouper which Wickram had obviously outgrown, clean socks, and a pair of strangely cut boxers that must have been the style here in the Valley.

Dressed in someone else's clothes, Barnabas descended the stairs and found Sanjani at the kitchen table, leafing through a pile of old photographs, writing notes on the backs with pencil. The main floor was a single, bright room painted in a happy yellow. The only decoration was an old-time circus poster in a gold frame.

"Good morning, Barnabas," Sanjani said with a smile and indicated a pile of buttered toast, jams, a bowl of fruit, and slices of dried sausage laid out on the table. "Please help yourself. Excuse my rudeness, but I'm preparing a presentation on the circus for the Valley archives."

"Thanks. Where's Wickram?" Barnabas asked as he filled his plate.

"He didn't make it home last night. He'll be here soon to pick up his books before school. You should join him. You met most of the students at dinner last night."

"Um, yeah, maybe."

The front door opened, and Dimitri Tragidenko burst in. He was built to occupy larger spaces like the Big Top. Here in the little cottage, he looked like a doll scaled too big for the dollhouse.

Sighing, Sanjani rose and went to him, helping him off with his big purple coat. "Finally, someone is home."

"Forgive me, dearest. I was in the Big Top. Many exciting plans for tonight's rehearsal."

"And your son probably slept at the clown dorm. Luckily I had Barnabas for company."

The maestro turned his burning eyes on him, and Barnabas felt like a bug under a scientist's magnifying lens. "Ah, the boy from the City. Friends are always welcome. You are my son's great friend, I hope. You will be a good influence?"

Barnabas just smiled awkwardly, and then scooched out of the way as Tragidenko dropped heavily into the chair beside him. The maestro filled his own plate with everything left on the table except one of the apples and began to devour it all with noisy gusto.

"I loved the show last night," Barnabas said when the silence had gone on too long for comfort. "I'm sorry about the Clouders."

Tragidenko gave a guttural growl and crushed his toast in agitation. "These Clouding maniacs with their heartless dogma will convince the Guild to throw us out!"

Sanjani blew crumbs off the photo she was labelling and put it aside. "You have to stop worrying, my love. Clouding doesn't control the Guild. Not yet, anyway. And everyone else loves the circus." She picked up a piece of walnut from his plate and brought it to his lips. He snapped it up like a dog. Sanjani giggled, and a deep laugh rumbled out of Tragidenko. Barnabas tried to will himself invisible.

"You are right, my darling, as usual. Enough of my glooming." He stood and walked to the door, taking a striped fedora from a hook on the wall and plopping it on his head. "With great appreciation for your nourishment of body and soul, I depart to discuss lighting cues." But even as he reached for the doorknob, Wickram flung the door open from outside. Father and son locked eyes for a tense moment, and then Wickram pushed past and ran up the stairs.

Tragidenko shrugged at Sanjani and left, shaking his head and muttering. Almost immediately, Wickram bounded back down the stairs with his schoolbooks under his arm and said, "Come on, Barn."

"Let me make you some breakfast," Sanjani said.

Wickram circled the table on the way to the door and grabbed the remaining apple. "I'm good."

"I guess I'm going to school," Barnabas called over his shoulder as he ran after Wickram. "Thanks for everything, Sanjani."

CHAPTER 28

Sanjani snuck over to the kitchen window to watch the boys as they vanished down the road. She knew if Wickram caught her, he would shout something like, "I'm too big to be carried off by eagles, Mom!"

She lifted the full watering can out of the sink with two hands and carried it to the back door. It was true. She didn't need to worry so much about her son when Barnabas posed the real danger. They would have to handle the situation very carefully. She had been delighted in those five minutes when she imagined Barnabas was going to join the circus. It would have been nice to have someone around who needed her in a way her own son no longer did, someone who understood what it meant to be a newcomer. As much as this was her community and had been for eighteen years, she was still "the girl from the City" to the older members.

She stood in the back door, looking down on her tiny garden, and tumbled down the cliff of memory.

She stood before the door of the apartment, looking for the courage to move. The little bag had been hastily packed with more sentiment than practicality, but she thought she had everything she needed. What did a person really need, after all? Acceptance, safety, love.

She glanced over her shoulder at her parents' bedroom door. They were still asleep, though not for much longer. "To be in bed after the sun has risen is to throw away the day's opportunity." That was one of the many maxims her father had shouted into her ears since she was young. He should have shouted them at her little sister, too, but Kareena was somehow exempt from these rules. Kareena, their baby, would stay in bed for hours without repercussion. Only Sanjani had to be perfect.

A floorboard creaked beneath her feet, and she gasped. She could not afford this paralysis. She unlocked the deadbolt with painful slowness and reached for the doorknob. The bruising on her wrist had grown darker overnight. She pulled open the door, and then she and her bag were through and into the hall. She lost control of the heavy door and it banged behind her, but she was running for the stairwell now. It had to be the stairs, because waiting for the elevator, begging it to hurry, knowing the apartment door was about to fly open and he would be upon her in his undershirt, his uncombed hair, and all of his betrayed fury, was simply out of the question.

Only when she was on the subway, and many stops stood between her and her father, only when she emerged into a neighbourhood where no one would think to look for her, did she breathe free. What now? She would walk the streets like a normal person. She was only seventeen but already felt very grown-up. She would walk the streets and look in the shop windows. She would read the paper in the library, scanning the classifieds for a job, for an apartment. Her future belonged to her.

It was a beautiful late September day, and the early morning chill was gone by eleven o'clock. She enjoyed lunch in a pretty café, but the bill, when it came, shocked her. She had taken money from her mother's purse, the only thing that truly made her feel guilty, but she had to make it last. Still, today was a day to celebrate, so a little extravagance was called for.

Many hours later, with sore feet and her hunger returning, she sat on a bench in River's Edge Park, watching the lazy brown river pass below as the sun began to set. The day dimmed more quickly than she was ready for. Dusk flowed into the park like an inky presence, filling the spaces under the trees with the first pangs of doubt. The wind picked up, and soon she was cold. The only thing she had to eat was a pack of soup crackers that she had slipped into her bag at the restaurant.

Now was the time to find a phone booth and call her best friend. Dorothy was not exactly expecting her call, but Sanjani had hinted that someday she might need her help. But then a voice in her head said, "And what if Dorothy panics and tells? Or what if her mother doesn't believe your story and calls your parents just as you're settling in for the night in Dorothy's room?" She imagined herself in pyjamas, hair damp from the shower, helpless as the bedroom door opened to reveal her father, an invincible, implacable giant.

So, she didn't phone. She stood, picked up her bag, and walked. And soon she was crying.

The group of men was still far away. They were mere suggestions of danger, rough smudges that moved vaguely in her direction, whose shouts and intentions were still unclear. She walked away from them, trying to appear confident and certain of her path. But soon it was certain they were following, and the only direction she could go was deeper into the groves of the park.

Before long, their shouts turned from teasing to threats, and they were running after her, incomprehensible silhouettes, monstrous and impervious to reason. Their pounding footsteps seemed to come from all directions. Jumping over a short fence, she left the path to run through the underbrush. Branches cut her arms and face, and more than once she tripped and landed painfully, bruising her knees, ripping her tights. But she stood again, running deeper into the woods.

It was terribly dark now. Surely too dark for the men to find her, yet she knew she wasn't safe. She found herself in a garden of giant boulders which stood, cold and silent, like a herd of stone cattle. She listened with all her concentration for the sound of footsteps and snapping branches, but she only heard her own breathing.

And then she did hear something, something like a voice which wasn't a voice, saying words which were almost just sounds, almost just the wind in the trees, or the distant plash of the river. But she followed the voice, didn't she? And it led her on an unknown path through the garden of boulders. And there in the darkness was a harder darkness, blacker than nothing. But from this nothing came a welcome exhalation of warm air. And the voice.

She was so cold, so afraid, wasn't she? She had nowhere on earth to go, she saw that now. She had made no plan other than escape, and now she knew that wasn't enough. Maybe this warm breath that swirled around her, filled with whispers, was a path to oblivion, but it was a warm oblivion, and she would take it.

The darkness closed over her. The sounds of the world were swallowed, and she knew she was no longer under the canopy of trees but in a cave, dank and close. The path descended into the earth, sometimes diverging, but whenever she had to make a choice, the voice seemed to call louder from one side, and she followed it, always descending. Many hours must have passed by the time she entered a large chamber where the echoes of dripping water rang like glass. She was cold and hungry. Her feet ached, and her arm was numb from carrying her bag. Suddenly, she knew she was not alone. Two by two, little points of red light appeared in the darkness. Eyes. Hundreds of pairs, staring and blinking.

She was afraid, of course, but she was also too tired to be afraid. And they had led her away from danger, hadn't they? So, she asked, "What do you want with me?"

And then there was a new light, a beacon that glowed far down another tunnel. It was pure and white, and she turned from the staring, red eyes and followed it.

Time lost all meaning as she walked down and down, stumbling after the beacon despite her mortal fatigue. And then Sanjani was outside, back in the forest. But this wasn't the acre of trees in River's Edge Park. This was a real forest, tall and deep. She walked the path beneath the comforting silence of the trees and emerged into a meadow. Behind and above her, like a startling dream vision, were the towers of the City. Before her, a stone bridge crossed a stream, and beyond that, rising above the tress in the curling mists of the morning, was a circus tent. The sound of a distant calliope accompanied her as she crossed the bridge into a new life.

CHAPTER 29

Barnabas followed Wickram across the postage-stamp front garden and out through the little gap in the knee-high stone fence. His family home sat at the end of a narrow road, at the top of a small hill. Ranging down the hill on both sides of the road were a series of small cottages painted in bright colours.

Wickram said, "Most of the people in the circus live in the dormitories, but some of the older denizens, the ones who brought the circus to the Valley, live here. Personally, I hate it."

"Why? Isn't it better to have your own room? And some peace and quiet?"

"No way. All my friends live together. They have a blast, and I'm stuck here with my stupid parents."

"Not last night, you weren't."

Wickram shot him a look of annoyance, but then he yelled, "Come on!" and took off the down the hill, running at full speed and howling like a wolf. Barnabas, more inclined to caution, took the slope at a reasonable lope and caught up with Wickram where the steep path met Pastoral Park's main road.

Everyone they passed on the road stared at Barnabas, smiling and waving. He reached into his pocket and pulled out the squashed clown nose.

"Don't bother, Barn," Wickram said. "We can keep a secret here in Pastoral Park. Not from each other, but from the rest of the Valley."

The boys didn't have to walk far before Wickram led them off the road to a concrete building. "Here's our school." They rounded the corner and found a group of kids standing outside, talking to a slender middle-aged Black woman, whose tight greying curls were cut close to her head. Barnabas recognized her from the performance, part of a balancing act, and he knew about half of the kids from dinner the night before.

"Wickram, you're almost on time," the older woman said. "And welcome to your friend. I'm Kalarax. I teach the older children three days a week. Maybe tomorrow you can enlighten us with some of your up-to-date City education."

Barnabas didn't know how to respond to that.

"I'm kidding. I was just telling the children that classes are cancelled today."

"Woo-hoo!" Wickram cheered and pumped a fist in the air.

"You all had a long, hard day yesterday, and anyway, you need to study for next week's exams. So, don't just spend the day swimming in the river."

After she left, the kids all huddled around Barnabas, except Graviddy, who stood a little apart, smoothing her hair and tying it into a wide plait.

"Did you like the show?" little Beaney asked. "I was one of the clowns."

"I know," Barnabas said. "It was amazing. Are you guys really bummed by how it ended?"

"It's fine, who cares?" Thumbutter said, jutting out her chin like she was the toughest cookie around.

Hulo said, "Speak for yourself. We could barely sleep."

"What will happen if Clouding gets the circus disbanded?" Bulo said.

Garlip shook his head. "Don't even say it. There's no place in a Clouding world for inverts like me. Or you, Thumbutter. You were born in Pastoral Park, you don't know."

Thumbutter shrugged. "Well, what can we do about it anyway?"

Garlip looked down at the ground, turning a stone over and over with his foot. "We just have to do our work and make the circus the best it can be."

"You…" Barnabas started to say, and they all turned to him. "You could do something, like go around to the Guilds who like you and get them to sign, you know, a petition. We're talking about your *lives* here, everything the circus has built. Sometimes you have to stand up for what's right."

They all looked at each other, embarrassed maybe, all except Graviddy, who was watching him from her place outside the circle.

"Hey, fresh fryers should be ready at the bakery," Garlip said loudly. "Anyone coming?" He left with most of the group, the others scattering in various directions. Barnabas felt like an idiot. Why couldn't he keep his mouth shut?

Wickram tapped him on the shoulder. "Barn, I got a surprise for you. We're going to the best place in the Valley."

"Flamtasmic," Beaney called from up in a tree Barnabas hadn't noticed him climb. "Can I come?"

"I dunno." Wickram appeared to consider the matter carefully. "You have studying to do and a rehearsal tonight. What would Kalarax say?"

The boy replied in high-voiced indignation, "She'd say stop being a big slizzpot and take me." He jumped down to the ground.

Wickram clutched his head in shock. "Language, child. Fine, you can come, but I need your help now. Barn, meet us at the dining hall in half an hour."

They turned and ran down the road, and Barnabas tried to remember if he knew where the dining hall was or not. He decided he'd follow the others to the bakery and ask someone for directions. Halfway down the hill, he came across Graviddy sitting under a big beech tree, reading a book.

"Hi, Graviddy," he said, immediately regretting interrupting her. She looked up, so he had to say something. "I loved watching you perform last night."

"Thank you. Dimitri counts on me to carry the show." It didn't sound like a brag, just a fact of life.

"You call him Dimitri?"

"The maestro is like a father to me. I was very interested in what you said to us, about standing up for our community."

"Sorry, I should mind my own business."

"No, maybe we need to learn a philosophy beyond blind acceptance. I hope you stay around to teach us some courage."

"Courage? Ha, if you knew me, you wouldn't think I'm…" He ran out of words and blushed furiously. "Okay, I have to go. Wickram's waiting."

Chapter 30

He found the bakery just as Garlip emerged carrying a paper bag. The boy smiled when he saw Barnabas and offered him one of the sugary, fried pastry balls, still warm from the hot oil.

"Mmm, that's good, thanks."

"Bless the Father, who teaches us to find sweetness in the world," Garlip said, and then laughed. "I'm kidding. I don't do the prayers anymore. But me and my parents were pretty devout before we joined the circus. Where are you headed?"

"Dining hall to meet Wickram. He's taking me somewhere."

"Okay, this way." They began to walk, sharing the pastries, their sugar-dusted fingers sometimes meeting at the mouth of the bag.

"So, you left your guild to come to the circus," Barnabas said. "Were you in Clouding?"

"Forming, actually, but the plastics sub-guild is very religious. Deviating from the true path is not allowed. So, when it became clear I was going to turn out like this, my parents applied to move to Pastoral Park. They're engineers. They build apparatuses for the circus now."

"They left because you're…what did you say? Inverted?"

He stopped walking and looked Barnabas in the eye. "An invert, yeah. Homosexualist, quire." He threw the terms at Barnabas as if daring him to say something nasty.

"I get it. Up in the City, we say 'gay.' Or 'queer.' You must have been glad to leave."

"I was furious! I believed in the whole thing—Father Glory, Mother Mercy, the Celestial City. And I felt terrible that they were moving just to protect me."

"The Celestial…you mean the City? My City?"

"No. Well, that's part of it. Come on, I'll show you."

He led Barnabas to the dining hall where another cart with two mules was parked out front. Garlip took him around the corner to the mural painted on the long stucco wall.

"Oh, I saw this yesterday," Barnabas said. "Sanjani said you made it." They sat on the grassy slope opposite the mural.

"This is the schematic of the Great Plan. My parents stopped praying when we moved here. Gave it all up. But that just made me determined to be the best little acolyte in the world. So, I started working on the mural."

"It's beautiful."

Garlip tilted his head, considering his work. "It's okay. The perspective sucks, and I didn't know *anything* about colour theory back then. Look. Down at the bottom is the Valley, right?"

Barnabas recognized the main transfer station, the churches, the hill with the Big Top. "Yeah, I see," he said.

"Then there's the City on the cliff. The Temporal City, we call it. But above that, that's the real thing. The Celestial City."

The City on the cliff—Barnabas's home—occupied only a thin layer in the painting, a series of shiny towers rendered without much detail. But above that was a City perched on the clouds, bristling with so many sunbeams, it looked like bombs were going off in mid-air. Towers, bridges, parks, and walkways were suspended high above the earth, drawn in immaculate detail, sparkling new. And in the sky to either side of the buildings were portraits of Father Glory and Mother Mercy as if formed from the clouds themselves.

The image produced an odd sensation in Barnabas's heart. He felt the presence of something larger than himself, a kind of universal order, comforting and attractive.

"Amazing," he whispered. "Am I imagining it, or does Mother Mercy look a bit like Graviddy?"

Garlip frowned. "What can I say? Everyone kind of crushes on her at some point. It was confusing for a minute."

Barnabas nodded with understanding. "But what is the Celestial City?"

"Father Glory told us by building the Temporal City in our daily work, we are really building the Celestial City, brick by brick. In the Book of Precepts and Perceptions, it is written: 'Your sweating backs and straining muscles are a testament to your devotion.' When we die, we will ascend and live in the great metropolis of our creation."

"We'll build the Holy City in the sky…" Barnabas said.

"Where'd you hear that old song?"

"Falstep and Wickram." Barnabas's head was reeling. He gestured at the mural. "So, that's what you believe?"

"Not anymore." Garlip crossed his arms over his chest. "I painted and painted for weeks, barely eating, praying continuously. Everyone was worried about me, but my parents told them to just let me do it. And when I finished, I sat right here on this hill and cried."

"Because you were proud?"

"Because I didn't believe anymore. Like the last drop of faith I had went up on that wall, and there was nothing left in my veins. After that, the world was only what I could see. The Valley was the Valley and the City, the City."

Barnabas watched Garlip's profile as he examined his work, at the long eyelashes, the freckles, the full lips. He wondered what it would feel like to kiss those lips, to feel his body pressed against a boy's.

Garlip caught him looking. Like he had read Barnabas's mind, he asked. "Are you?"

"What?"

"You know. Do you like boys or girls?"

Barnabas blushed and almost went for the easy lie, but Garlip's honesty made him brave. "Maybe both, I think?" It was the first time he'd ever said that out loud.

Garlip stood, sweeping the grass off his butt, and reached down a hand to help Barnabas up. "You know," he said, "I was thinking about you all night."

Barnabas started coughing on a stray grain of powdered sugar.

Garlip shrugged. "I'm just saying if you ever want to kiss me, you can, okay?" Mercifully, Wickram and Beaney burst out the doors of the dining hall at that moment, carrying two wicker baskets.

"Hallooo, Barnabas!" Beaney called, arm waving like a puppy's tail.

"Hey, Barn!" Wickram said, running to greet him. "Ready for your adventure? We got lunch for the road. Beaney, get in the back and let Barn up on the bench."

As they drove away, Barnabas turned to wave at Garlip, but he was walking away. Barnabas dropped another barrier inside himself and decided to appreciate the beautiful view.

CHAPTER 31

Before long, the three boys had descended from the green plateau and were out on the dusty road. It was a different road than the day before. Along this stretch, massive turbines whirred inside concrete buildings. Green pipes as tall as elephants emerged from the buildings and criss-crossed the scrubland. Far ahead of them was the great cliff, the City perched on top.

They passed three low buildings, stinking sweet and sour with rot. Barnabas crinkled his nose and saw the others were doing the same.

"Sewage treatment," Beaney said, waving his hand like a fan until they'd passed.

In contrast to the bleak surroundings, Wickram was in a great mood, as if the fight with his father, as if quitting the circus where he'd grown up had never happened. He was keeping Beaney laughing hysterically, singing songs with dirty lyrics and doing a spot-on imitation of Tragidenko.

"You are all my children, *yes?* And I am loving you the way the dynamite is loving the detonator, *yes?* Like the top of my head is loving the little drop of bird shit that falls from the sky. We, my dear artistes, must be like that little shitting sparrow in everything we do."

Beaney screamed with laughter. "Now do Kalarax."

"Hey, Wickram," Barnabas said. "What's that?" To their left, down the slope from the road, was a great depression in the earth, a circle maybe a mile in diameter, shallow at the edges and deep in the centre. The ground was muddy in places and pooled with brown water elsewhere, especially toward the centre of the depression.

"Ahhh. Welcome," Wickram said with a sweeping flourish of one arm, "to Lake Lucid, the traveller's refuge, the sweetest of waters." He pulled on the reins, and the mules came to a stop.

"This used to be a lake?" Barnabas asked. "When? Dinosaur times?"

"It's been like this forever," Beaney said.

But Wickram shook his head. "No, I can just about remember my folks taking me here to swim when I was little."

Barnabas saw docks, boathouses, and other buildings that now sat deserted along what was once the shore of the lake. Two jetties thrust themselves uselessly out into the mud. Between them lay the broken bulk of a large boat. A half dozen of the fat green pipes pushed out from the muddy lakebed, running off into another of the concrete buildings, which shook with the deep thrum of the pumps inside.

The plundered lake was profoundly ugly and disheartening, like an image from an oil field in the Arctic or somewhere equally desolate.

"Where did all the water go?" Barnabas asked.

"You drank it," Wickram said, flipping a thumb toward the cliff and the City on top. "Cheers."

"Oh," Barnabas said, guilt washing over him.

"There's still groundwater under the lake, at least for a few more years."

Barnabas clearly heard Deni Jiver's voice in his head. *This story is huge, Barnabas. A full-on conspiracy. Get documentation.* He reached for his phone and started taking pictures.

"Whoa!" Wickram snapped. "You can't do that."

"What?"

"You're not allowed to take pictures. Not anywhere in the Valley."

Barnabas stared at him. "Why not?"

"It's the P&P. The Book of Precepts and Perceptions. Wait, let me remember… 'To steal light is to steal from the thing itself.'"

"But what does that mean? How do you steal light?"

Wickram pointed to a lone, thirsty-looking willow on the shore of the dry lake. "It means that if you take a picture of, say, that tree, you diminish the tree. If you just take one, you would hardly notice. But say you take a hundred pictures and share them with everybody. Then they don't need to come here and see the real tree anymore. They wouldn't care or even know if someone cut it down."

"Or maybe they ban photography," Barnabas said, "to hide evidence of the Valley from people in the City."

"Whatever," Wickram said with a yawn. "When we get where we're going, you'll forget all about this muddy bowl. Yah, mules!" He shook the reins, and the cart lurched into motion. Barnabas looked across the lakebed and saw another green area on the far shore, a small forest with a mansion sitting in front of it. *Some fancy person lives there,* he thought. *Or once did.*

Back on the main road, Beaney handed out sandwiches from the basket and passed around a bottle of actual raspberry soda. As they drew nearer to the cliff, Barnabas stared up at his home—so close, but completely inaccessible. He found Wickram's binoculars under the seat and trained them on the shining skyscrapers of the Tower District looming above them. While the rest of the buildings showed a blank, windowless face, Delphic Tower had a single set of windows that faced the Valley on its uppermost floor. Barnabas guessed it was the mayor's residence, the luxurious suite where every mayor had lived in the past fifty years. Obviously, the mayors knew about the Valley, and now it was Arthur Tuppletaub who had that one-of-a-kind view.

The road took a left turn, and they drove along the protective fence that marked the edge of the Tumbles. A continuous rain of dirt and rocks, along with a torrent of toaster ovens, canned produce, and premium-sized bags of dog kibble hit the ground, raising great plumes of dust.

Suddenly, Wickram called, "Hey! Hey! Shift your eyeballs front-wise, Barn. We're here."

The cart was approaching a huge sign that straddled the road on wooden posts. Barnabas read it as Wickram spoke the words out loud with almost religious fervour: "Presenting a Fabulous Feast of Fallen Finery! A Cavernous Cache of Cascaded Curiosities! Welcome to THE DROP SHOP!!"

CHAPTER 32

Wickram turned the cart right, and they rode down a long driveway toward a large warehouse built right up against the safety fence of the Tumbles. The windowless building with its grey metal walls wasn't anywhere near as big as the transfer station where he'd arrived the previous day, but something closed and secretive about it made Barnabas nervous.

"This is the best place in the Valley, Barn," Wickram said. "The Drop Shop has *everything*. Well, you're from the City, so maybe not so skull-cracking for you, but it's my little oasis in this cultural desert." He tied the mules to a wooden fence, opened the battered steel door, and led them inside.

Barnabas had been expecting the interior of the building to be as drab as the outside, so he wasn't prepared for the tsunami of light, colour, and sound that hit him. The crazy array of lighting included stark fluorescents, homey table lamps, tacky tavern lanterns, neon teeth advertising a dentist's clinic, and rotating disco spotlights in bright primary colours. Multiple marching band recordings clashed in bright discord, an operatic tenor keening loudly over their bombast.

The Drop Shop was something between a dollar store, an antiques emporium, and a funhouse. Dozens of bicycles hung from chains on the ceiling, some of them with their pedals and wheels turning eerily on hidden motors. At one end were home appliances, dismantled by their fall down the cliff and rebuilt Frankenstein-style. Every variety of art hung from the walls, from posters of pop stars to oil landscapes in gold frames.

Aisles of shelves were filled with books, tools, games, medical supplies, garden gnomes, and gaudy gowns. Beaney was standing on a step stool, rummaging through a box of action figures, while Wickram ran up and down the aisles, pulling down merchandise and shouting, "Oh my God! It lights up when you shake out the salt," and "Look, a golf magazine with a 3D hologram cover."

A voice as cloying as toffee spoke right into Barnabas's ear. "What are you looking for, young man? *It falls from the skies, a brand-new surprise.*" He turned in alarm to find himself facing a middle-aged woman in inch-thick makeup and a mountainous hairdo so stiff and shiny, it might have been plastic. Her mile-wide smile seemed to contain too many shiny white teeth. Their gleam competed with the glitter of the costume jewellery pinned across the chest of her blue coveralls.

"Uh, no thanks. Don't need anything now."

"Everyone needs something, young man. Wouldn't you look just fine in this?" She pulled an old bowler hat off a shelf and plunked it on his head. "*It falls from the skies, a cunning disguise.*"

Annoyed, Barnabas removed the hat and tried to hand it back to her, but she was staring upward, hands raised. "The bounty of the City. Things fall over the edge every day, and my Georgie goes out to collect them. Risks his life in the Tumbles, he does, just to keep our little business going. *It falls from the skies, our wondrous supplies.*"

Barnabas looked around at all the merchandise on display and the piles of boxes still unpacked. Everything had fallen down the cliff, each object lost to someone from the City. He walked over to Wickram, who was thumbing through a pile of old paperbacks, lost from backpacks or back pockets, living a lonely life on the streets before finally falling into the Tumbles.

"Check it out, Barn," Wickram said. "*Molly Malolly and the Haunted Bride.* My mom loves this series." A handwritten sticker on the battered book read "11 farthings AS IS."

"How much is a farthing?" Barnabas asked Wickram.

"Pocket change is standardized at twenty farthings per work shift. And people sometimes gather for the food depot. Like, we can sell them a basket of chanterelles for around fifty farthings."

Just then, the whole building shook. A great door in the side of the warehouse slid open with a wrenching shriek of metal on metal. The man who dragged it open stood dramatically silhouetted in a big square of sunlight. With a grunt, he pushed a huge flatbed trolley ahead of him. It was covered with more junk, and both he and the cart were sending up great clouds of dust as he entered.

"It's my Georgie," the shopkeeper shouted in delight. "Back again from the Front."

Now that he was inside, he seemed less impressive than he had a minute before—a middle-aged man in soiled coveralls and thick black goggles, grey with dust and sweating profusely under a badly scuffed football helmet. He huffed and puffed with the effort of sliding the giant door shut again. It slammed into place with a resounding bang.

"Thank the Lord you weren't killed, my love," the woman said, throwing her meaty arms around his torso. "It sounded like the whole world was coming down out there today. Oh, and I need you to fix the compressor on the fridge." She turned to the boys. "He's so clever with his tools."

"Unhand me, woman," the man said with brusque rebuke. "I can hardly breathe as it is." He tossed the helmet and goggles to the floor, wiping his eyes on his dirty sleeve. When he raised his head, Barnabas jumped back, startled.

"Glower," he gasped.

CHAPTER 33

"Yeah, of course Glower," said Wickram. "George Glower, the owner of the Drop Shop. Why? Is he famous up in the City, too?"

Barnabas didn't answer. He knew it was vital he not be recognized as a resident of the City, and Glower was the only one who could do that. Barnabas was still holding the old bowler hat. He put it on, pulling the brim low, and skittered into an aisle of farming equipment to peer out at the dusty man through a scrim of chicken wire.

The shopkeeper approached the trolley and began sorting through the objects. "A good haul, was it? Ooh, Georgie, a hair dryer. And a pair of roller skates. Oh, just one. Don't make no never mind. I'll sell it for top dollar, don't you worry."

"None of that garbage matters, Greta," Glower answered. "Look at this." He lifted a long black box off the trolley and blew the dust from its surface. It was made of dense matte metal with a red logo sunk into it. Maybe it held a rare bottle of wine or an antique revolver. Glower opened it carefully to reveal two lines of little blue pyramids and one orange cube. He removed one of the pyramids and turned it slowly in his hand, examining it with intense concentration.

The man's husky growl was full of awe. "You see? I've been looking for something like this. It's a laser communication system. If I boost the signal, I can use it for remote triggering of the—" He stopped abruptly. Wickram was waiting nearby like a good dog hoping for a treat.

"Hi, Mr. Glower. Did you find any more issues of *Shredd*? The guitar magazine? You know I buy them the minute you get them in."

Glower looked suspicious. He quickly replaced the blue pyramid in the box and slammed the lid shut. "What? What do you want from me?" But then he seemed to collect himself. "Oh yes, you're Tragidenko's boy, right? No. No *Shredds*. Only a bundle of *Amateur Sociologist* magazines and some real estate fliers. Get them out of here, Greta," he hissed at the shopkeeper. "And lock the doors. I have work to do."

"But Georgie, we're supposed to be open until seven today."

"Get them out!"

Greta turned to Wickram, her look of annoyance visible for just a second before she turned her fifty-megawatt smile back on. "Sorry, love, no *Sledds* today. But look at what you've found! Molly Malolly, is it? Oooh, the adventures you'll dream up after you read that fine volume." She began shepherding Wickram toward the cash, pulling Beaney from a display of Halloween masks as she passed him. The boy clutched his action figure and staggered after her. "And what a price I'm going to give you on that lovely doll. You'll mistake me for an angel." She pulled them toward the front counter with its ornate, brass cash register.

Barnabas watched all this from his hiding place, knowing he didn't have long until Greta figured out one of her customers was still on the loose. Glower, meanwhile, was fingering the contents of the black box with growing excitement.

"I could move the whole timetable up. Do it next week. The bastards..." His voice became inaudible as he moved toward a black metal door at the back of the warehouse. He punched in a code on a digital pad, and from behind the wall came a loud clunk and the whir of gears. A light above turned from red to green as the heavy door opened smoothly to reveal a totally different kind of space—uncluttered, orderly, with long, shiny work benches and bright lighting. It was a workshop of some kind, full of half-assembled machines and blueprints pinned to the walls. Glower entered and the door slid closed behind him.

Wickram and Beaney were up at the cash, and as Barnabas headed their way, he passed the battered trolley loaded with its bounty from the Tumbles. A glint of light amid the debris made him slow and then stop. He gasped and ran to the trolley. As he pulled the object loose, he dislodged a pile of tin cookie boxes, and they clattered loudly to the ground. Barnabas didn't care. He was holding something he thought he'd lost forever: the diaboriku!

"What are you doing, boy?" called Greta, running to him from the front of the store. "Those items haven't been catalogued. Come back tomorrow if you want to purchase—"

Barnabas tightened his hand on the diaboriku. "This is mine. I dropped it yesterday in the..." He couldn't tell her without admitting he was from the City and that he crossed the Frontier illegally. He might end up in Doomlock, and his hosts at Pastoral Park would be in deep trouble for hiding him.

Greta's cheeks reddened. "It's not yours, you greedy little boy. That is legal property of the Drop Shop." Like a snake striking at its prey, she shot out a hand to grab the device. But Barnabas was faster. He pulled his prized possession against his chest, just avoiding the red-lacquered nails.

"No!" Barnabas replied sharply. "It's mine." He knew he sounded like a two-year-old, but he could neither explain nor accept defeat.

Wickram and Beaney were running his way. Wickram yelled, "Barn, man, not cool. If it fell into the Tumbles, it belongs to Mr. Glower."

Barnabas dodged around Greta and ran up to Wickram, whispering, "I dropped it in the City yesterday. It must have rolled right over the edge of the cliff. No one else even has one. It *has* to be mine."

Wickram shook his head. "The Guild Council granted Mr. Glower salvage rights to anything he finds in the Tumbles."

Greta advanced on him. "That's right, you miserable thief. *It falls from the skies, I don't apologize.* Those toffy bastards in the City are like careless children. They spend and spend, always coveting the next purchase. Meanwhile, their precious little treasures slip from their pudgy fingers. Whoosh! Over the edge! Then they're *mine*." She gave a harsh laugh. "You want that shiny toy, child? You can trade it tomorrow for a fistful of farthings."

Barnabas had put Wickram between himself and the advancing shopkeeper. He was calculating whether he could run from the Drop Shop with the diaboriku. But where would he go? Wouldn't the shopkeeper call the Aqua Guard? He heard a grinding of gears behind him and spun around to find George Glower in the door of his pristine workshop, looming over him, staring in fury at the drama.

"Why am I being disturbed? I thought I told you to get rid of these people."

"He stole that whatchamahoozis right off your cart, Georgie!" Greta shouted, but there was fear under her anger.

Hearing a little gasp behind Glower, Barnabas peered around the man, spotting a kid with tousled hair. Galt-Stomper.

"Don't I know you?" the boy murmured. But before he could answer, Glower stuck out his hand toward Barnabas.

"Give. It. To. Me." Angry veins stood out in his temple. Barnabas dropped the diaboriku into the big sweating palm and backed away.

"Are you finished disturbing me?" He was addressing them all but looking in particular at Greta.

It was Wickram who answered in a pinched voice. "Yessir."

"If this thief is the kind of companion you bring to my store, perhaps I will have to bar you."

Wickram's face paled. "P-please no, sir," he stuttered. "Won't happen again. I swear."

A minute later, the three boys were outside, blinking in the sunshine.

Wickram turned on Barnabas. "Dungbuggies, Barn! You almost got me banned from the Drop Shop."

"But my diaboriku…"

Suddenly, the door of the store flew open again, and Barnabas yelped liked a cartoon hound. Glower stepped out, carrying a large sheet of stiff paper that flapped in the breeze. With quick, assured movements, he taped the sign up before retreating inside, the heavy door slamming shut behind him.

Hand-lettered in bold, block print, the sign read: "The Drop Shop will be closed until further notice."

CHAPTER 34

Barnabas hated being angry. If he was that kind of person, he could be angry all the time. He could be mad at his father the way Thelonius was. He could be mad at his mother, who used to be fun and spontaneous and now filled their lives with stress and schedules. Then there was the way Principal Rolan-Gong had believed the mayor without even asking Barnabas for his side of the story. But what was the point? No one liked angry people. And did their anger ever change the injustice of the world?

As they returned to Pastoral Park, Barnabas chose to sit in the back of the cart, turned away from the boys up front. They were taking a different route, supposedly a shortcut. This new road offered a view of yet another giant factory building spewing smoke, followed by a brain-battering ride along a dirt path full of ruts and potholes. Wickram was babbling ceaselessly, and Barnabas wasn't sure how much more he could take.

"How could he do it?" Wickram asked. "Mr. Glower would never close the Drop Shop. For one thing, I would die." They hit a pothole, and Barnabas accidentally bit his tongue. Wickram's voice switched abruptly from misery to enthusiasm. "Hey, everybody ready for some music?" He started to pound a beat on the bench between his legs. Wickram's brain was like one of Deni's old vinyl records. If you bumped against the record player, it would jump to some other random track.

In a high, strained voice, he sang, "'Beauty's in the eye! When you behold her!' Hey, Barn! Do you know that song? It's by Big Mouth Grouper. I love them. When's their new album coming out?"

Barnabas turned and shouted, "It's not. They broke up, okay? The lead singer is doing commercials for car insurance now." Wickram and Beaney spun around in surprise. "It's just not fair," Barnabas screamed at them. "The diaboriku is mine. Yesterday I didn't even know this stupid Valley existed, and now there's some random rule that I can't even have what's mine. I mean, I *lost* it and then I *found* it again, but now I can't *have* it! It's *bullshit!*" He punctuated the word by punching the side of the cart. Pain flared across his knuckles.

The wind was rising, the sky filling with dark, forbidding clouds. Barnabas looked up at the City, wishing he was there and that he could just forget everything that had happened in the last twenty-four hours: the mayor and Mr. Klevver, the Aqua Guard and Clouding Guild. And why stop there? He wished Thelonius had never sent him the diaboriku in the first place. Cal Kabaway could make it work no problem, but he couldn't, and it just made him feel stupid, like he was a disappointment to his brother. He realized Wickram and Beaney were staring at him, worried, and Barnabas turned away in shame.

The minute they got back to Pastoral Park, Beaney ran off to rehearsal, and Wickram drove the cart up to the stables.

"Really?" he asked. "Big Mouth Grouper broke up? That drags the mud *utter*. I wanted to see them perform at the Manhammer Audiodome someday."

"Well, maybe they'll do a reunion tour in a few years." Looking down, Barnabas saw the bowler hat at his feet. He picked it up and dusted it off. "I think I accidentally stole this."

Wickram laughed. "Accidentally, you say."

"Seriously. I was still wearing it when that Greta woman kicked us out. I keep stealing stuff. What's wrong with me?"

"You're definitely a bad influence on a pure boy like me."

They returned the cart and headed back along the dusty road. Wickram said, "This feels so weird. I haven't missed a rehearsal or a performance since I was six. And now I'm free as a bird!" He stretched out his arms and ran in circles like a swooping hawk.

They showered in the solar-heated bathhouse and then returned to Wickram's house, where they traded their road-dusty clothes for fresh ones. Wickram supplied Barnabas with a bright tie-dyed shirt he'd have never chosen for himself. There was still an hour until dinner, so they hung out in Wickram's room reading old magazines. Wickram picked up his guitar to play for Barnabas, but after thirty seconds, a loud peal of brass and cymbal rose from the Big Top, where the rehearsal was going on without him. He stopped to peek out the window, letting loose a tiny sigh.

Barnabas wore the bowler hat to dinner. In a town full of circus performers, he figured he had the right to some flamboyance. Furthermore, wearing the stolen item felt like revenge against Glower and Greta for stealing the diaboriku. Sanjani waved at them as they walked toward the kids' table.

Barnabas waved back with a smile, but Wickram muttered, "Shit, I can't do this," and ran from the dining hall.

"Hey, Wick, where are you going?" shouted Hulo, but he didn't stop.

"That was weird," Bulo said.

"Now that he's quit the circus, he thinks he's too good for us," said Thumbutter, chowing down on her stew with enthusiasm. Barnabas was hungry too, and he was glad to see a plate of hot food waiting for him. Or maybe it was Wickram's he was eating. No one stopped him.

"Hey," he said to Garlip, who sat down next to him. They grinned at each other until it became a contest.

"Give up," Garlip said. "I can do this all night."

Bulo said, "I think Wick's depressed that we're all getting ready for a new show and he's not."

"He's going do a delve and wallow for a whole month, you'll see," Hulo added.

"He didn't act depressed today," Barnabas told them. "We were at the Drop Shop. He said he feels free."

"That's just a mask," Garlip said. "Graviddy! Go talk to your boyfriend, he's sliding drain-down." Graviddy was sitting by herself at another table, reading a book.

"Leave her alone," Hulo said. "She's getting in the zone for tonight's rehearsal."

"The zone…" Garlip rolled his eyes. He grabbed Barnabas's bowler hat and dropped it on his own head, doing a series of fashion poses.

"Didn't you already rehearse this afternoon?" Barnabas asked.

"After last night's disaster, the maestro is working us extra hard," Thumbutter said.

When dinner was through, they all left together. There was still an hour before sunset, but the dark clouds were conspiring to dispel the daylight. The circus kids headed for the Big Top, Garlip still wearing the bowler hat, but Barnabas couldn't decide whether to follow them or hunt for Wickram. Was he in Falstep's cottage, stealing his booze again? Maybe if he kept Wickram company, he could keep him from getting drunk and getting in trouble. The wind was shaking the trees up, and the air felt chill with imminent rain. Barnabas wished he was wearing more than a T-shirt.

Suddenly, out of the gathering darkness, the white horse reared up in front of him. Barnabas leaped back as the horse's rider brought it to a halt.

"Halloo, Barnabas," Graviddy said, sitting tall and straight in the saddle. "I hear you found something for sale at the Drop Shop that belongs to you."

She was like a magical vision, towering above him with her preternatural poise. "Did-did Wickram tell you?" he stammered.

"No, Beaney. Anyway, I agree with you. No matter what agreement that old crocodile Glower has with the Guild Council, that round thingy is yours, and we need to get it back." The horse pawed the ground restlessly, and Graviddy stilled it with a small shake of the reins.

"But the Drop Shop is closed," Barnabas said. "Until further notice."

The wind lifted her shining black hair, and she reached back to tie it with an elastic. "I was thinking about what you said to us. Sometimes you have to stand up for what's right." She stretched a hand down to Barnabas. "Climb on up."

CHAPTER 35

It wasn't his first time on a horse. Barnabas had spent hours at summer camp, miserably circling a corral on a pony, clouded by flies and wishing he was in his bunk reading comic books. But this wasn't the same thing at all. He was galloping along on a huge, white stallion, his arms wrapped tightly around the waist of a beautiful girl while the wind howled around them, making the sparse trees that lined the road dance and sway. The ground seemed a long way down, taunting him with threats of calamitous injury.

Barnabas peeked out from behind Graviddy's back and looked up at the City. It was a bright ball of light high up on the cliff, with the Tower District cutting a dark silhouette in the foreground. In Delphic Tower, a light in the mayor's apartment snapped on, like the distant beam from a lighthouse. He imagined Tuppletaub in there, practising his smile in front of a mirror.

Graviddy rode them past the Forming works, the road illuminated by powerful lights on high poles. Giant machines, under the supervision of the evening shift, roared tirelessly. What would those workers think if they looked up and saw the white horse fly by?

As they left the factory area and plunged back into the darkness, Barnabas called over the wind. "I think it's going to rain. Like any minute."

"Don't worry, we're almost there."

"Aren't you missing rehearsal? Are you even supposed to take the horse like this?"

"Are you supposed to be in the Valley at all?" Her defiant spirit made him smile.

When they reached the turn-off to the Drop Shop, they climbed down from the horse. Barnabas could hear it breathing heavily in the stillness of the night. Pulling a flashlight from her pack, Graviddy led the horse down the embankment where the drooping branches of a willow tree hid it from anyone passing on the road. She fed it an apple from her bag, talking in quiet, soothing tones, the way Wickram had with the mules. A low rumble of thunder sounded in the distance.

"I wish Wickram was here," Barnabas said. "The Drop Shop is kind of his place."

Graviddy laughed. "Exactly. He'd never approve of us stealing from them." She shone the flashlight into her bag, checking its contents. "Wickram has very strange loyalties—Falstep, Glower…The one he should be listening to is his father."

"Oh?"

"I'm not just quoting Precepts and Perceptions. 'Follow the path through the woods your parents blazed before you' and all that balderdung. I don't care about the P&P. No, it's just Dimitri knows Wickram is a flamtasmic composer, and he wants to give him the chance." She said this with great conviction.

Barnabas saw a light on the road. "Look," he said. It was a truck, its engine noise growing steadily as it approached. They ducked behind a bush.

When the truck got closer, Barnabas recognized the banks of lights and the massive grill, like a set of teeth clenched in anger.

"That's Carminn!" he whispered urgently, and Graviddy nodded, her eyes wide with surprise. The truck was right above them now. It turned sharply and headed down the driveway toward the Drop Shop, which stood dark except for a single bulb glowing above the front door. Carminn parked and headed inside.

Graviddy stood up. "This is getting interesting." They scrambled up the embankment and began jogging down the long driveway. Graviddy ran easily, head held high, but Barnabas was hunched over like a spy, looking all around for eyes in the night. Somewhere in the Tumbles, there was a shattering crash like a sideboard full of grandma's best dishes had met its sad fate. Barnabas cringed.

They passed Carminn's parked truck and ducked around the corner of the building.

"We need to get up on the roof," Graviddy whispered.

He was sweating and panting from the run, and she wasn't, which was kind of embarrassing. "I saw a ladder on the wall this afternoon," he said, leading them along the side of the building until they reached the base of the ladder, bolted to the wall.

"Let me get my flashlight," she said, but then a flash of lightning lit up the entire valley for a second. They had seen enough to get their bearings, and Graviddy began to climb. As Barnabas followed, the thunder arrived. At the top, he grabbed Graviddy's outstretched hand and scrambled over the eavestrough onto the roof.

"Okay?" she whispered.

"Yeah, are we there?"

As if in answer to his question, another flash of lightning erased the night. In that brief moment of illumination, Barnabas saw a raised hatch up near the apex of the sloping roof. The thunder came more quickly this time. Then out of nowhere, Graviddy said, "He thinks his music is useless if he's not singing in front of 20,000 rubes up in the City."

"Wait. Who are we talking about?"

"Wickram. He thinks he needs to be a superstar up in your Manjammer Drone or else he's an utter failure."

"Manhammer Dome," Barnabas corrected, and the lightning flashed again. In the brief moment of illumination, her face was full of doubt. She looked less goddess and more human than usual. "I thought you didn't like Wickram. But you do, don't you?" Maybe she would have replied, but the thunder arrived sooner and louder than ever.

"We better hurry," she said. "Before we get hit by lightning."

The slope of the roof was gentle, but every step made the steel surface creak and pop, and they were obliged to creep forward on hands and knees. Luckily, the hatch wasn't locked. Graviddy went in first, stepping onto the ladder inside. Barnabas followed, carefully lowering the hatch above him. This was it. They were committed.

CHAPTER 36

Every light in the Drop Shop was on. Barnabas and Graviddy stood on a narrow walkway that ran under the peak of the roof, the entire length of the building. The rain began to fall in earnest, drumming loudly on the steel above them.

"Excellent!" Graviddy said. "They won't be able to hear us with all that racket."

Barnabas stood on tiptoe to peer over the wall of the walkway. They were above the store part of the building. George Glower and Carminn stood in one of the wide aisles, talking with grave enthusiasm. The drumming on the roof was good cover, but it also prevented him from hearing their conversation.

Greta's voice, though, was more than capable of cutting through the noise. "Oh, that's delightful. You two just catch up on school days or what have you while I do all the back-break!" She was taking merchandise from the shelves and packing box after box. Strands of her heavily lacquered hair were standing up like charmed snakes, and sweat was pouring down her forehead, leaving long furrows in her thick makeup.

"It's madness, Georgie!" she screamed, though Glower didn't appear to be listening. "You give me four days' notice to pack up all our treasures? You're mad to close the shop. I'm going to have to abandon two-thirds of the inventory. Thousands of farthings left behind for ruination and devastation." Galt-Stomper ran past her, carrying a little folding table. "Boy! You stay and help me with the bundling and the twining."

But Galt-Stomper, his face its usual mask of fear and determination, didn't even slow down. He ran right through into Glower's secret workshop, whose big mechanical door stood open. Graviddy and Barnabas crept back along the walkway until they were over the workshop. Barnabas peered down at the precision measuring tools on the worktables, at metal lathes, welding equipment, and a dozen devices he could not name. On one table, a set of plans lay open, its curling edges weighed down by whatever tools were at hand.

Down at one end of the room, Galt-Stomper was setting up two chairs and the folding table across from what appeared to be a diorama of the City. It was a detailed, beautiful piece of work, and the boy was now up a stepladder focussing lights on it, like they were getting ready for a show. With that complete, Galt-Stomper ran back out of the workshop. The walkway shook as the workshop's hydraulic door slid shut with a decisive *clunk*.

Graviddy tapped Barnabas on the shoulder and pointed down. "Is that it?" There, sitting casually on a table, was the diaboriku.

"Oh my God!"

Graviddy bent down and pulled a bunch of shiny white material out of her bag. Barnabas recognized the silks from her performance. With great care, she tied the material to the handrail of the walkway. She pulled out a container of powder and applied it liberally to her hands. "Rosin, so my grip doesn't slip."

"You're going to climb down and get the diaboriku?"

"I'm going to do a full three-and-over fall to a leg swing. Then when I have it, I'll—"

"Why don't we just use that ladder at the end of the walkway?" He pointed, and Graviddy swore some obscure Valley swear. But it didn't matter since at that moment, the workshop door opened, and Glower and Carminn walked in.

The hammering of rain on the roof had grown lighter, and Barnabas could hear Glower say, "Greta! We're starting."

She appeared in the door, wiping her brow with a polka dot handkerchief. "As if I have time for your little pantomime."

"You need to see this," he insisted, and she threw up her hands in exasperation. "Galt-Stomper, you too. Get in here."

The boy arrived instantly, trying to negotiate a safe path around Greta, but she grabbed him by the shoulder with her sharp nails and said, "Oh no, Georgie. If you want to waste my time in here, this little grub needs to move all those boxes to the loading dock." She sent Galt-Stomper back into the shop with a kick in the pants.

Glower showed Carminn around, and Greta drifted along behind them, bored, hips swinging to some melody in her head. Barnabas strained to hear the conversation, but only caught curious snatches.

"...she won't tell a soul..."

"...won't matter after it's done...a whole new order..."

"...now is the time for resolve...ruthless and bloody...the Father will forgive..."

Glower brought the two women over to the open set of plans on the worktable and gestured with excited sweeps of his hand.

"I don't like this," Barnabas whispered to Graviddy.

"I know. We'll never get your toy now."

"No, I mean what are they up to? Why is Carminn here, and why are they packing up the Drop Shop?" He looked down the walkway to the ladder. Did he dare?

"Where are you going?"

"I've got to hear what Glower's telling them." Barnabas's stomach was tightening with fear, but he grabbed the top of the ladder and gave it a shake. It held solid and made almost no noise. He put his feet on the rungs.

"What if they turn around and see you?"

"They have their backs to me. I can do this!" He wasn't sure where this confidence was coming from, considering he could practically see his pounding heart tenting the front of Wickram's tie-dyed T-shirt. But he couldn't shake the feeling something big was going on.

He climbed down as quickly as he could without making too much noise. Glancing over his shoulder, he saw the trio still bent over the plans, although Greta was tapping her foot impatiently. All he could do was pray they would give him another minute.

CHAPTER 37

Barnabas was halfway down the ladder, and already he could hear Glower, Carminn, and Greta more clearly:

"There hasn't been a day I didn't...revenge for all the...inflicted on me."

"I understand, Glower. The Father demands...take action in his name."

"Will this take much longer, Georgie?"

Infuriatingly, the ladder ended six feet above the floor. How could he possibly jump the distance silently? The answer came a moment later in the form of another lightning flash. Barnabas only had to wait a few seconds for the great *Ka-Boom!* to shake the building, and in that moment, he jumped. He hit the ground and rolled, finding shelter behind one of the worktables.

From this vantage, Barnabas had a better view of the diorama. There was the cliff, and at the top of it, the buildings of the Tower District, each one crafted with care in wood, painted with no little attention to detail. The scale was impressive; the highest of the buildings stood two feet tall. Beyond them, the rest of the City was just a suggestion of architecture, with a bunch of green modelling clay in the back standing in for Riverside Park. The diorama's broad base was skirted by black fabric that hung to the floor like curtains over whatever table must be holding it up.

It was time to start documenting all this, but when he reached for his phone, he remembered he had left it in his backpack, back in Wickram's bedroom.

"But I don't understand," Carminn asked in her guttural voice. "You told me we were still weeks away, and now you want to do it on Tuesday?"

"Because of what I found in the Tumbles—a find so fortuitous it almost makes me believe your Father Glory intervened."

Carminn drew herself up and crossed her arms on her breast. "You can no more accomplish your aims without the Father than you can without me."

Greta sneered. "Georgie doesn't need you at all, you frumpy old elephant."

"Enough, Greta," Glower snarled. "Both of you, follow me."

To Barnabas's horror, they began walking his way. He scuttled like a crab out from under the table, dodging the legs of several stools. Squatting low, he ran and dived headfirst through the black skirt that hid the base of the diorama. He smoothed the curtains closed behind him and tried to pant as quietly as he could. Peeking out, he saw Glower holding the black box he'd found in the Tumbles. He pulled out one of the little blue pyramids and handed it to Carminn.

Greta leaned in for a better look. "Ooh, a lovely cerulean, that is."

Carminn turned the pyramid over in her rough, plump hand. "What is it?"

Glower said, "A laser communication system. This is the control node." He removed the orange cube and placed it on the table.

Impatiently, Carminn dropped the pyramid beside the cube. "We don't need to communicate with anyone. We need to tear them screaming from the sky."

"Oi! Easy on the merchandise, girlie!" Greta snarled.

Glower snatched up the little pyramid and put it back in the box. "You don't understand, Madam Speaker." A dirty edge of glee had entered his voice. "I'm going to use them as remote triggers, signalling from the one place in the City where I have line of sight on every building in the Tower District. Take your seats, and I'll show you."

Barnabas pulled himself back and smoothed the black curtain closed.

Turning upward, he saw a faint light entering his little dark cave. He realized the diorama wasn't on a table after all. The legs were attached to the model itself and he could see the whole of the underside. Getting up on his knees, he found he could look out from behind the diorama's cliff face, a painted mesh material. It looked solid from outside, but from where Barnabas crouched, it was a window. In front of him, maybe six feet away, sat Carminn and Greta, Carminn's wide frame all but eclipsing the dainty wrought iron chair. Glower picked up a remote control from the folding table and stood behind them. All three were staring at Barnabas, but they could not see him.

"Is all this arts and crafts necessary?" Carminn asked.

Greta gave the diorama an approving nod. "I think it's lovely, Georgie. We should put it right by the cash register. A real *objet d'art.*"

Glower ignored them. His eyes were wide, and he was licking his lips like a dog anticipating a bone. "It's important," he said, "to visualize a project as clearly as possible before you begin. When those great City fathers were planning their metropolis, they too commissioned intricate models." Barnabas felt goose bumps rising on his arms.

Glower pushed a button on the remote, and the lights in the rest of the workshop dimmed, leaving only the spotlights that shone down on the diorama.

His voice was growing feverish. "Those architects of the past planned the construction of the City with infinite care. Can we do any less for its *destruction?*" Glower raised the remote, and right above Barnabas's head, there was a sharp *bang!* that scared him so badly he almost screamed. A piece of the diorama disconnected itself, and he saw one of the tower models falling into the Valley.

He dropped to the floor, covering his ears with both hands as the next explosion came, and the next and the next. One by one, the towers of the City diorama fell into the Valley. His nostrils burned with powder smoke, and his ears rang painfully. Lying on the floor, knees curled up to his chest, Barnabas looked up at the holes above him where the towers had stood. Through the ringing in his ears, he heard Glower laughing. And then Carminn joined in, howling as the lightning flashed and thunder shook the Drop Shop.

Chapter 38

Barnabas felt like he was going to throw up. The immensity of the horror was too much to take in. That maniac Glower was actually plotting to blow up the Tower District and crash the buildings into the Tumbles along with all the people who lived and worked in them. Barnabas wanted to scream, but people willing to do something so terrible wouldn't hesitate to kill a witness. And he had more than his personal safety to think about. He was the only one who knew, the only one who could tell the world to stop them.

Despite his terror, he made himself concentrate, trying to take in every word they were saying.

"Georgie," Greta cried. "Are you mad? We have a good business here. Why would you do such a lunatic thing?"

Carminn and Glower took no notice of her. Carminn said, "But even with these new triggers, isn't Tuesday too soon to be ready?"

Glower laughed again, "That's the beauty of it. With the laser trigger, it's so simple. I'll need to work fast, but don't forget I have complete access to all of the towers, and I've been preparing for months."

"I could allocate more explosives if you—"

"Don't question my calculations," he barked. "Everything stands ready."

Carminn grew agitated. "But maybe *I* need more time. I'm only working with a handful of people inside Clouding, and this will be a major operation. After the fall, we'll have only a short window to assert control of the guilds and—"

"What you do after the day of reckoning is entirely your affair. As long as I'm exempt from prosecution, I am content to let you rule over your little kingdom."

That's when Greta made herself heard. "Not so fast. Georgie and I have the rights to everything that falls into the Tumbles. *Everything.* When those towers come down, it will be the greatest windfall of our lives, and *he* may not care what happens afterward, but I do. *We have a contract.*"

Carminn's tone was contemptuous. "You have a contract with the Guild Council. After Tuesday, the Guild Council will cease to exist, and Clouding Guild will be in charge."

"Oh no, no, no, no, no. You and your people honour our contract or Georgie isn't making his pretty fireworks for you."

"Greta, please…"

"Shut it, George. This time you listen to me. I want your blood oath on this, you sanctimonious cow."

"You ridiculous market-stall harpy! We are trying to establish a Holy Order for the majesty of Father Glory, and you just want to keep on selling your blasphemies and pornographies. Fine," Carminn spat. "You have my oath. Now, Glower, you're leaving for the City tomorrow?"

"Yes, at 1130 hours. Make arrangements."

Their voices grew quieter. Barnabas got back on his knees and peered out as the trio exited into the shop. He didn't hesitate. He pushed himself out from under the diorama, ran across the room, and jumped up to the ladder, pulling a foot up to catch the lowest rung, and then climbing quickly. He didn't give a thought to the noise he might be making. He needed to get out of this place and tell people what he knew. There was so little time. In a few short hours, it would be Saturday, and three days later…*boom!*

At the top of the ladder, Graviddy helped him up onto the catwalk.

"What was that all about?" she demanded. "I couldn't hear a crumping thing!"

"But you saw?"

"Of course. Major pyrotechnics."

Barnabas went up on tiptoe and peered down at the destruction. The model towers lay on the floor, scorched black. It was only a cheap model, but knowing what he knew, it looked sickeningly real.

"Glower's going to blow up the towers and crash them into the Valley."

Graviddy started to say something but could only manage a groan.

"We have to go," Barnabas said, feeling truly terrified for the first time in their night of adventure. He began walking shakily toward the hatch in the roof.

"Wait," Graviddy called after him. "Go look down into the shop."

"We have to leave!"

"Do it! Where are they?"

"Th-they're all down by the front door. Carminn is leaving. Wait! Glower is heading back toward the workshop!"

"How long until he gets there?"

"What are you going to…?"

"How many seconds?"

"I don't know. Ten!" He turned to her and saw that she had wrapped her silks around herself, like she was a caterpillar halfway through spinning a cocoon.

A look of calm focus fell over her features. She put her hands on the railing of the walkway and pulled herself up and over the side. Barnabas stretched up to see, horrified as she spun down into the workshop, the silk unravelling layer by layer. And at the bottom of her fall, she swung upside-down in a graceful arc, one ankle wrapped in the silks, arm stretching down to scoop the diaboriku off the table.

As the hydraulic door slid open, Graviddy, nimble as a monkey, climbed her silks, collecting the material as she went. As suddenly as she had leaped, she was back on the walkway, a smile on her sweat-shiny face.

She handed Barnabas his precious sphere. "Okay. Now we can leave."

CHAPTER 39

The rain beat down on them as they raced through the night on the white horse. The steady downpour had soaked them to the skin so far back down the road, Barnabas could only suppose it was now soaking them to the soul. He held tight to Graviddy, as deep in his belly, something awful was growing—a great, green worm born of shock and despair eating away at his sanity.

In his mind, he could see the towers in flames, tumbling down the cliff into the Valley with all the people in those glorious buildings killed, and everyone else in the City traumatized. He imagined his mother in that terrible tomorrow, afraid to leave the apartment like she had been in the months after his dad moved out.

And what was Graviddy feeling? Carminn, the Valley's new dictator, would surely break up the circus. She might send all the acrobats and clowns down into the mines, Tragidenko and Falstep chained together, breaking rocks in a quarry. He imagined Wickram red-faced in front of a smelting furnace, his guitar tossed into the heart of the inferno for fuel.

Barnabas was so lost in his misery, he didn't realize they were back in Pastoral Park until they were galloping around the Big Top and into the wide square in front of the dining hall. A dozen people ran out from the building to intercept them. Barnabas recognized Sanjani, Whistlewort, and Kalarax among the faces as he and Graviddy were all but pulled from their mount. Most of their distress was, for now, aimed entirely at her, and Barnabas stepped back into the shadows.

"Where have you been?"

"This horse is not your personal pet, youngster."

"We were flattened with worry for you."

"Was this the tourist's idea?" said Whistlewort. *The tourist.* That meant him, Barnabas realized.

Graviddy stood her ground, hands across her chest. "This is a lot of teeth-cracking for nothing. I can take care of myself."

And as Barnabas waited, cold and damp, the green worm of despair in his belly seemed to swell and climb up his throat until he had to scream. "He's setting explosives in the City! He's going to blow up the towers and crash them down into the Valley!"

The whole group turned to him. The rain ran down his face and off his chin so only Barnabas knew his tears were flowing. A gentle hand touched his arm. It was Garlip.

"Who's going to blow up the towers?"

"Glower! And he's doing it with Carminn." Saying it out loud should have been a relief, but right away he could hear how absurd it sounded, too huge and terrible to be possible.

The adults stood looking at each other in dumb confusion as the rain fell on their heads. Finally, Sanjani said to Graviddy, "Is this true?"

She gave Barnabas a desperate look before answering. "I was there. I saw…Well, they had this model of the City and…and they blew it up."

"But you didn't hear what they said?" Whistlewort asked.

She shook her head, and the adults all looked at each other again. "He's telling the truth!" Graviddy shouted.

Whistlewort grabbed Barnabas by the arm. "You, come with us. We need to hear the whole story. Graviddy, take that horse back to the stable, dry him well, and make sure he has food and water, then off to bed. No, Garlip, you too. All of you, back to the dorms. And hold your gossiping tongues until we know something that doesn't sound like a tall tale." He turned to Sanjani. "Where's Dimitri? Still haunting the Big Top?"

"Probably. I'll get him."

In the dining room, Barnabas saw lanterns glowing on one table along with mugs of cooling coffee and an unfinished card game. He realized the adults had spent hours waiting there for him and Graviddy. Whistlewort deposited Barnabas on one of the benches. "Don't move."

Kalarax emerged from the kitchen with a large towel which she draped over his shoulders, and someone he didn't know brought him a steaming mug of tea. Sanjani and Tragidenko entered the dining hall, and now he had seven pairs of adult eyes staring at him as he shivered and sipped his tea.

"Start from the beginning," Tragidenko said in a deep, tired voice.

But what was the beginning? Barnabas started by explaining how the diaboriku had been lost in the City and then found at the Drop Shop. Then he told them how Graviddy offered to help. From there, Barnabas tried to remember every detail of their evening, although he was having trouble putting together the exact sequence of events. It was as if the whole narrative had become scrambled in his head when the deafening explosions went off around him. He felt like an idiot. He felt like a liar.

Tragidenko, seated directly opposite him, combed his beard with his fingers throughout the recitation. When there was nothing left to say, the maestro just shook his head. "But that is madness. What would be the point of such a conflagration?"

Barnabas's voice shook as he answered. "Glower said it was revenge. I'm not sure against who."

Sanjani came to sit beside him, taking his hand in hers. "And you say you met Glower in the City? The day you came here?"

"Yes. I talked to him at Admiral Crumhorn Station, and then again outside my school." He was aware of flies buzzing at the windows, searching for a way out.

Sanjani gave him a look like she pitied him. "But Barnabas, dear, that's not possible. George Glower or anyone who moves here from the City, me included, can't get travel passes. We can never go back."

"I'm not even sure we can get *you* back up there," Whistlewort said.

Barnabas felt his throat close around a lump. The anxiety worm had returned. "But Glower was there. I saw him."

Kalarax asked, "Was he on the train with you?"

"N-no."

She continued, her voice calm and reasonable: "He could never get past the Aqua Guard at the Frontier, Barnabas. Coming or going."

"Then he came some other way."

"There *is* no other way."

Barnabas looked at Sanjani. "You asked if I came through the forest."

Sanjani shook her head forcefully. "It's not a highway. You can't just come and go. You have to be…guided." She seemed embarrassed, like it was hard for her to say these words in front of the others.

Tragidenko shook his long grey curls. "No. We cannot go to the Guild Council with this. Where is the proof? He is just a stranger—a boy we don't know. A boy who shouldn't even be here. And Carminn… Can you imagine? After the Clouders and that terrible visit? No, we would be setting ourselves up for derision and disasters." He put his hands on the table and heaved himself to his feet, causing all the lanterns and mugs to dance and sway. "Everybody go to sleep now. This is nonsense. I am sorry, young man, but no. Not possible."

He turned and swept out of the room. Sanjani patted Barnabas's arm. "Perhaps you should go sleep somewhere else tonight," she said.

"It's just, with all this, and Wickram not himself…" Barnabas felt like he had been thrown out of his shelter into the rain and wind. Sanjani wouldn't even look him in the eye. "Kalarax will find you a place at the dorms." And with that, she stood and hurried after her husband.

CHAPTER 40

Barnabas followed Kalarax out into the night. The rain was now a drizzle, the air damp and cold, and he was exhausted, defeated, and alone. But as they crossed the square, Garlip fell in beside him and then Graviddy on his other side.

As they followed the path around a small copse of apple trees, Barnabas said to Graviddy, "I'm sorry if I got you in trouble."

But Graviddy grabbed his arm and stopped him in his tracks. "No, it's me who's sorry. Please don't think I don't believe you. But the adults were all so looming and fire-eyed, and I was weak."

Looking into those beautiful eyes, Barnabas felt his misery lift. "You were fine. You were *great*."

"And you were incredibly brave." She leaned down to plant a soft kiss right on his startled lips. Before his mind could settle again in his skull, she had pulled away.

It was as close to perfect as Barnabas could imagine, until he remembered Garlip's earlier offer of a kiss and wondered if now he'd hurt *his* feelings. But when Barnabas dared a look at Garlip, Garlip was looking past him with an expression of shock. Barnabas spun around, and there was Wickram, smudgy with rain and blurry with drink, staggering toward him, fists raised.

"You little weasel! You rat!" Wickram screamed. He grabbed Barnabas by the shirt like he was going to kill him, but simultaneously leaned on him for support. The two of them staggered backward a few steps, a pair of clumsy dancers, as Wickram shouted into his ear. "Riding off with her. Kissing her. Thought you were my friend. You-you came down to the Valley to steal my girlfriend, you traitor."

Wickram tried to stand up and punch him, but it was a wild jab that half-caught Barnabas on the side of the neck and sent Wickram spinning sideways. At that moment, Hulo and Bulo ran out of the darkness like twin angels of mercy, catching Wickram before he fell over into a puddle.

"Whoa! Easy, Wick," Hulo said in a soothing sing-song. "You don't want to go hitting Barnabas, he's your friend."

"Sorry, guys," Bulo said, trying to get an arm around Wickram's neck. "We've been trying to get him home, but he keeps escaping." The girls looked like two cowboys roping a wild bronco.

Graviddy, meanwhile, had gone from tender to furious. "Great gricklicking pugglenuts, Wickram, what is this pathetic performance? Act two of the great *I Quit* drama?"

Wickram ignored her, trying to break free of the twins and get back to pummelling Barnabas.

"Wickram, honest, I would never take your girl—"

Graviddy cut him off. "Shut up, Barnabas. And you, Wickram..." She marched right up and shoved a finger into his chest. "I will ride with who I like. I will kiss who I like. Is that clear?"

Wickram stopped fighting. He slumped back against Hulo and Bulo, looking pathetic, his long hair hanging limp around his face like seaweed.

"Children!" Kalarax called out. "It's time we were all in bed." They followed their teacher through the night like a ragged parade of wounded veterans. Hulo and Bulo supported Wickram, who now seemed to be asleep on his feet. Graviddy walked alone, head down. Garlip, who had retreated into the dark, returned to Barnabas's side.

The dorms were a series of two-storey buildings of concrete, wood, and glass. The silent group passed inside through the double doors, but before Barnabas could follow, Garlip grabbed his hand and led him over to a small playground. They sat on a damp, wooden bench under a maple tree, and Barnabas dropped his face in his hands.

"Hell of a night," Garlip said to him.

"I want to cry, but I'm too tired."

Garlip put an arm over his shoulder. "At least you kissed Graviddy. I don't know anyone who's ever done that. How was it?"

Barnabas, comforted by the boy's touch, looked up at him. "It was good."

"Want to see if I can make you forget it?"

"Okay."

Barnabas had kissed Deni and also a girl named Nella at a school dance. Graviddy was the third. Kissing a boy was different, but maybe only because of what it meant about his identity, about what people might think of him. In truth, all four were different kisses, and kissing Garlip wasn't about kissing *a boy*, it was about kissing Garlip. The kiss was firm and sliding, daring and playful. Barnabas tightened his arms around Garlip's broad back and felt his sadness and cold melt away in a rush of lust.

Then a bony finger tapped Barnabas's shoulder, and he almost jumped into the tree. He spun around to stare up into Whistlewort's weather-beaten face.

"You'll need proof," the old man said in a low, cracked voice, eyes bright in the dark night.

"Wh-what?"

"Your story is crazy as a fever dream, but you got no reason to make it up. Who knows what madness goes on in Glower's head? Wandering around in the Tumbles all day, just daring Father Glory to squash him like horsefly. But Carminn? I know exactly what's cooking in that pot—lust for power, hot and spicy as a rabbit ragout."

Barnabas's heart was pounding. "How can we stop them? Maestro Tragidenko said—"

"Dimitri's right. Pastoral Park can't be advocating for you. You need to make the Guild Council take action. But no one's gonna believe as much as a goat raisin that comes out o' your mouth unless you get some crackin' solid proof."

"But how do I do that? I don't know anything about the Valley."

"Looks like you already got yourself some friends. You all gonna help the lad, Garlip?"

Garlip nodded. "Yes, sir, we will."

"Good. Now go to sleep. You'll need all your strength if you want to save the City."

CHAPTER 41

George Glower heard Carminn's truck roar off into the night and cursed her under his breath. The Speaker of Clouding was like so many fools he had known, full of delusions about their great destinies, when in fact, they were born to further his.

Glower realized Greta was speaking. "I have to prepare," he said, cutting her off mid-sentence. He could tell she was hurt, but that was merely an academic curiosity, like observing the behaviour of a strange insect in his yard.

When he was alone in the quiet of his workshop, he wondered idly where Galt-Stomper was. *Gone back to whatever hole he hides in,* George supposed. He didn't know what would happen to Greta or the boy after Tuesday, but he wasn't really worried. They were, for all their faults, useful helpers. Still, George could not be expected to take care of everyone. Who had ever taken care of him?

The acrid smell of explosives still hung in the air. Though his demonstration had gone flawlessly, he felt strangely empty. What if he felt just as empty when the real thing was done? But no, that was impossible. Tuesday—just three days away—would finally bring him the victory that had been denied eight years ago. His heart beat faster with anticipation, and he suddenly felt faint. Slumping forward, he caught himself on the worktable.

He felt faint and slumped forward to place his hands on the folding table. He had swept past the reporters waiting outside his campaign headquarters, but their voices still echoed in his ear.

"George! George! Over here, George!" Like so many seagulls on a pier.

"The results show your opponent surging in early returns."

"Are you going to concede the election?"

"Would you comment on allegations of campaign finance violations?"

Would he comment? Lower himself to their level? Never.

Under his splayed hands on the table, his own face looked up at him a thousand times from a thousand flyers—flyers suddenly rendered obsolete. The slogan read A Tradition That Built the Past, A Vision to Build the Future and his name over and over in confident block letters.

He gave a terrible moan, and a campaign functionary in no-nonsense navy blue ran forward to slide an arm under his. He thought he recognized her as somebody significant.

"George, we'll have the text of your concession speech ready in five minutes. Please hold it together until then."

Hold it together? But that was the problem exactly. It had all fallen apart, fragmented into a million loose bits as if one minute he had been driving a superb automobile on the highway when it had suddenly disassembled into an endless inventory of screws, flanges, belts, microchips, LEDs, carbon-steel lattices, precision performance parts, and redundant safety measures, all stretched across a mile of blacktop, while he flew unprotected through the air, tumbling end over end into oblivion.

He lurched sideways, vomiting prodigiously into a garbage bin. The remains of a thousand campaign lunches, pancake breakfasts, and booster backyard barbecues exploded from him, raining down onto yet more campaign literature. Vision! Focus! Giving YOU a voice at City Hall!

He was drenched in sweat, hugging the rim of the bin, strangers with his name on their T-shirts running to him with water and paper towels, talking, talking more meaningless words. It was their fault. The election had been his for the taking. But these slack-jawed fools, wallowing in their incompetence like a dog rolls in filth, had stolen it from him.

He'd had enough.

George could dimly hear their shouts as he left the building through the back door and ran out into a dark alleyway, past stinking restaurant dumpsters, rats scuttling at his approach. He came to the main street, full of action and light on this sweltering summer night. He hated all these fools with their loud voices and their pointless revels. The City, once so glorious, was sinking into a cesspool, and they didn't care. He alone could have rescued them, and they didn't care.

He ran across the street heedlessly, a delivery truck nearly ending his story. Maybe that would have been better. No. He was not the one who should be destroyed. He imagined the City emptied of these fools. Without them, it would still gleam bright with promise, burble with steam-driven genius. And he would walk the empty streets as Master, without all the idiot naysayers and vote-stealers. Then he would finally get some real work done!

Either that, or he could tear it to the ground and stand laughing on its ruins.

Revolted by the howling crowds, George left the main street and returned to the warren of empty laneways good citizens know instinctively to avoid. But he had no fear. He was a survivor, a scuttling rat.

And he was hungry. No, that wasn't it. He was tired. No, not exactly. He had to…get there. Where? Oh yes. The end of the line. Also, rock bottom. He became aware he was shouting. "I'm sorry! It isn't my fault! Don't punish…" He slapped both hands across his treacherous mouth, but the sound of his voice seemed to echo on. He was under a bridge, a mighty arc of steel spanning one of the dirty trickles that fed the great river. Garbage choked the stream and garbage lined the concrete slope of the embankment. He dropped his hands from his mouth, but immediately screamed again, the sound exploding from him as the vomit had. When the echoes died away, he thought he heard a snickering voice.

"I'm not afraid of you!" *he shouted into the night, and he was proud of the hauteur of this pronouncement. He felt his sense of control returning. The night was hot and unbearably humid. Sweat soaked his shirt. The voice returned, speaking all but inaudibly in its chittering whisper. And with the voice came a breeze, deliciously cool, that called him into the shadows under the bridge.*

George followed the voices down into the underworld. And it was all right, wasn't it? There was nothing for him above. And as the narrow tunnel steepened, and a true chill entered his bones, he wondered if he was dying, walking willingly from life into oblivion. The voices snickered again. Points of red light began to appear in the darkness—red eyes, hundreds of them, watching him, waiting.

"Do you want to hear my acceptance speech?" he asked them, and it seemed they did. "Citizens!" he proclaimed. "You have granted me a great honour, to carry on my family's tradition of service and leadership. Tonight, when you tuck your children into their beds, then lay your heads upon your pillows, I want you to dream. Dream of growth, dream of a future for your city that surpasses even the glory of its past.

"And I will hear your dreams, and they will become my dreams. Or perhaps it is my dreams you have been dreaming all along. Perhaps I am already in your homes. That noise you hear in the night that awakens you, gasping, out of sleep—maybe it's me. Haha, a-hahaha! But do not worry. I am your friend. I am your father. I will lead you into the light."

And even as George said the word, a light appeared to his left. It was just a faint glimmer, but his heart gladdened. He walked to the light and found himself in another tunnel, descending at a gentle grade. And the light bobbed on ahead, beckoning him with a promise of salvation. But I don't want salvation, *he told the light.* I want to tear the City to the ground and stand laughing on the ruins! Still, there was no sense in turning back now, so he stumbled forward and emerged into a forest deep and green, and the promise of another day.*

Part III

SATURDAY

CHAPTER 42

"Over the edge…falling," Barnabas groaned, grasping for handholds in the cliff face, straggly bushes that tore loose at his touch…

"Barnabas!" Garlip said, shaking him, and he jerked awake, sitting up, his heart pounding. "Bad dream?"

"I guess, I don't really remember." A chase, a gun, a tower on fire. He put his feet down on the scuffed hardwood floor and was embarrassed to find himself in just his underwear. "What time is it?" he asked, pulling the covers around him. He was on the lower level of a bunk bed. Garlip's bed, covered in a hurricane of brightly coloured blankets and pillows, was on the other side of the small room.

Garlip was dressed in a white pirate shirt and loose blue pants that ended mid-calf, with an old-time explorer's hat on his head. "It's eight thirty. I let you sleep as long as I could."

Barnabas nodded and winced. His neck was sore where Wickram had punched him. Despite the sunshine pouring through the window, misery was descending on him. It started small, with the idea that Wickram hated him now. Then he remembered how the adults all thought he was a liar. This was followed by the fact that he might not be able to get home for months. Only then, when he had warmed up to epic hopelessness, did he dare to remember the worst thing of all: Glower and Carminn's plan to knock down the towers. Again, he heard the explosions going off around him, saw in his mind Delphic Tower burning, tumbling down the cliff to crash into the Tumbles. Whistlewort said he needed to get proof of their plan. But how? The task seemed impossible.

Then Garlip was standing in front of him, holding something. "My hat!" Barnabas said, smiling despite himself as he took the stolen bowler. Somehow, this one stupid thing blew away the dark clouds on his heart. "You're amazing, but what I really need is my phone."

Garlip opened a drawer in the dresser by his bed and pulled out

Barnabas's backpack. "Your wish is our command. Hulo and Bulo already biked over to the maestro's house and got your stuff."

Barnabas jumped up and took the bag from him, digging through it until he had his phone. "You're amazing!" he said again, grinning at Garlip, and became aware again of his near nakedness. He turned back to the bunkbed to gather his clothes and found himself face-to-face with Wickram, asleep and drooling on the top bunk. Wickram slowly opened his eyes, and the two boys stared at each other. Wickram mumbled something inaudible, which might have been "sorry," but might also have been "porridge," and closed his eyes again.

Barnabas dressed and pocketed his phone. He decided to leave the hat behind. He'd be worthy of wearing something so fine *after* he found his proof. He followed Garlip out to the playground where Hulo and Bulo were waiting for them. The twins were dressed in matching denim shorts, bright, short-sleeved tunics, kneepads, goggles, and old-fashioned leather aviator helmets. Barnabas thought they looked like exotic insects.

Hulo said, "You missed breakfast."

"So we brought you this," Bulo continued. She pulled a fresh cinnamon bun out of a paper bag and handed it to him. Barnabas ate greedily, not realizing until he started just how hungry he was.

"So, what are we doing?" he asked as flour and sugar gave him life.

Hulo said, "Heading out to find proof of Glower and Carminn's plan." She jumped up to grab the bar of the jungle gym and began doing pull-ups.

Barnabas felt a weight lift off his chest. "You mean you believe me?"

"If Whistlewort says it's true, it must be," said Bulo, jumping up to join her sister, the two moving up and down like pistons in an engine.

Garlip snorted. "Who cares about the old mulemonger? I believed you from the start."

The girls jumped down and led the group around the end of the dorm building where four bicycles leaned against the wall. Bulo said, "Whistlewort offered us a mule cart, but we figured we'd make better time if we borrowed these from our family. Barnabas, we got you one we outgrew a few years ago."

He thanked them, though he didn't appreciate the reminder of just how small he was here in the Valley. The four of them rode experimental circuits around the adjoining field, ending up as if by mutual agreement in a conspiratorial circle. The sky was dotted with clouds and the breeze stiff, but the sun was strong and promised a good day.

Garlip said, "Okay, City boy. Where to?"

"Huh? I have no idea."

"Back to the Drop Shop?" Hulo suggested.

Barnabas thought about this. "No, there's no way to sneak up on the place in daylight. Besides, they're packing everything up. Won't be any evidence left."

"Did Carminn and Glower say anything that might be a clue?" asked Bulo.

Barnabas thought some more. "Glower said something about leaving at eleven thirty today. Carminn said she would make the arrangements. What do you think that means? Is there a train going to the City this morning?"

"Nope, not on Saturday," Bulo said.

"Besides," Hulo added, "Glower can't get a travel permit to cross the Frontier."

Garlip bit off a corner of fingernail. "If Carminn offered to make these mysterious *arrangements*, then it must be something over at Clouding Town. That's where we should start."

"I guess you're right," Barnabas said. Having encountered Clouders a few times already, he wasn't thrilled with the idea.

"A plan is born," said Garlip.

"Let's ride!" the twins shouted in unison, but then Hulo said, "But fast and quiet. We're not supposed to be leaving Pastoral Park."

"Or taking the bikes," Bulo added.

Chapter 43

Flying down the long, winding hill from Pastoral Park on a ridiculously effortless bicycle was, for Barnabas, somewhere between ultimate freedom and fundamental terror. Despite their insistence on making a quiet getaway, Hulo and Bulo were whooping like howler monkeys, weaving in and around each other, while Barnabas was hanging on for dear life. He could all too easily imagine hitting a pothole and flying over his handlebars to a messy death. But at the same time, he didn't want to pump his brakes the whole way down like a loser and end up at the bottom ten minutes after the others.

Then Hulo was at his side. "Unclench, guy. It's more dangerous to ride all tense like that. Drop your shoulders, open your chest, and look up. That's it. Feel the road through your wheels. Breathe. Good." And then Hulo pumped her legs like a charging rabbit and pulled ahead, swinging her feet up onto the handlebars in a terrifying show of nonchalance as she swerved in front of her sister.

With this bit of professional advice under his belt, Barnabas actually enjoyed the final leg of the descent. He wasn't even the last to the bottom. Garlip, he saw, was still far behind him, and Barnabas stopped at the bottom to wait. Garlip rolled up a minute later, looking less than thrilled.

"That was exciting," Barnabas said.

Garlip rolled his eyes. "Sometimes the performers forget that not everyone in the circus is a suicidal daredevil exhibitionist."

They rode down the road holding hands as they caught up with the twins. For the first time in days, Barnabas felt like his life wasn't totally hopeless. He had an actual *gang*. And they were all heading off to get the proof he needed to save the City.

"We'll take the most direct route to Clouding Town," said Hulo as they rode.

"Okay," Barnabas agreed.

Bulo said, "Even though it doesn't smell the best."

The most direct route took them past high mountains of garbage, one after the other as far as Barnabas could see. The smell came in waves: chemical, biological, sour, and cloying. The kids batted at flies as they rode, and truck after truck passed them, turning off into one of countless trash yards to deposit yet more waste for the mountains. Barnabas saw large processing plants where garbage rode wide conveyor belts to be sorted, but he didn't see how they would ever get ahead of the City's refuse, which just kept arriving. He thought about the shiny promise of products that fuelled the dreams of the Citizens. Automated delivery vans and drone units pulled up to every apartment every day with boxes of new clothes, gadgets, toys, and tools, all stuffed into the City's hungry consumer mouth. And simultaneously, out the other end shot the discarded refuse of goods tossed aside because they were built to break in a year, because they'd gone out of fashion or had been "improved upon" with one more pointless feature. And the result was mountains of waste. Wasted plastic, wasted textiles, and wasted dreams.

The gang rode on, leaving the garbage fields behind, heading straight for the cliff. In its shadow, they came to the home of Clouding Guild, which produced the steam that provided the City with power and heat. Clouding Town consisted of short, unadorned housing blocks and communal buildings all built from the same rust-coloured brick. Dominating the town like the Big Top dominated Pastoral Park stood an imposing, red brick church with two tall spires. Behind the church, right up against the cliff face, was a huge industrial building that spewed smoke into the sky. Dozens of steam pipes emerged from the top of the plant and snaked their way up the cliff to the City.

Barnabas, Garlip, and the twins were anything but inconspicuous as they rode through the streets of Clouding Town. The denizens that passed them were either dressed in loose grey clothing or in work clothes, from simple coveralls to versions of the masked monsters Barnabas had seen on the subway. More than once, massive dogs wearing leather tool harnesses barked savagely at the riders.

"Where do we start?" Hulo asked.

"Everything at Clouding starts with a prayer," Garlip said, "so I guess we better go offer our respects."

They left their bikes in the courtyard in front of the great church and climbed the wide steps that led to its massive front doors. An image of Father Glory was embossed in the shiny steel panels on the doors. The deity's hands were raised in fists, holding bunches of lightning bolts the way a child clutches wildflowers. He didn't look happy with the work of his earthly followers.

"Where's Mother Mercy?" Barnabas asked.

Garlip shook his head. "The Clouders dropped her ages ago. It's all about the Father for them."

Barnabas liked the place less and less. "Are we even allowed to be here? It's obvious we're not from Clouding."

"Doesn't matter," said Garlip, cutting through their little worried clump and marching confidently up to the doors. "All worshippers are welcome. My family used to come here on all the important festivals."

"Lucky you," said Hulo, flexing and releasing her fists nervously.

"Oh hush," Garlip said, smiling. He seemed perversely happy to be here. "Check this out," he said, and pulled down a lever beside the doors. With a great hiss and a cloud of steam, they parted majestically. The group walked inside through the dissipating cloud.

CHAPTER 44

They found themselves in a large foyer at the back of the sanctuary. Garlip explained what they were looking at. "The entrance to the Clouding steamworks is behind the church. You're supposed to offer prayer before beginning your shift. See? You leave your gear and your dogs in that holding area, and then proceed into the sanctuary."

The huge hall with its high-vaulted ceiling ate up Garlip's voice, and Barnabas had to lean in close to hear him. And while it was nice to feel the heat coming off his body, Barnabas felt like a hundred disapproving eyes were staring at them, judging their homosexual proximity. Suddenly the air was shaken by massive organ chords that sounded like the musical equivalent of the Valley's great factories, powerful but not beautiful.

"The service is starting," Garlip shouted over the cacophony. "Just follow me and do what I do." They walked behind him into the sanctuary, in a line like ducklings, and down the central aisle between the rows of pews. Huge paintings of the different guilds lined the walls, the painted workers kneeling, reaching hands up to the Celestial City, which hung shining in the sky.

But the most impressive part of the sanctuary was up front. The sections of the stage were circling slowly in steam-powered, clockwork motion. The apse rose and fell as if floating on an ocean. Above it all stood another majestic incarnation of Father Glory supporting the whole world in his raised hands. From beneath the floor, figures of working men and women rose through little doors in the stage to dig in the earth, stoke the furnaces, and haul ore. Steam burst out in deafening exhalations from vents throughout the diorama, including from Father Glory's nose and ears, leaving the air distinctly humid.

Halfway to the front, Garlip stopped and lowered his head. He brought his closed right fist to his chest and then up to his forehead, saluting the churning spectacle at the front. The twins and Barnabas did the same in clumsy unison and then followed Garlip into one of the rows of pews.

The organ's spray of dark notes thickened into a single sustained chord. With one more loud exhalation of steam, the rotating floor of the stage brought a priestly figure forward to his place at the pulpit. The music quieted to a low undercurrent, and he began the service.

Barnabas checked the time on his phone. 10:37. He whispered to Garlip, "How long will the service take? If this is where Glower is coming, he's probably already here."

"Just twenty minutes. They're total fanatics, but they don't let it slow down their production schedule."

Barnabas was barely listening to the priest. He caught something about loving the sweat of your brow and easing the ache in your back, but mostly he was peering through lingering wisps of sacramental steam into the dim corridors that flanked the sanctuary, hoping for a glimpse of...

"There!" he said a bit too loud, drawing annoyed glances from the worshippers sitting nearby. He lowered his voice. "That's Carminn, isn't it? Just walking past those pillars there." He pointed.

Hulo squinted. "Yes."

"Looks like she's in a hurry," Bulo said.

"Let's go!" Barnabas got to his feet.

Garlip hissed at them in alarm. "No, we can't leave in the middle of the service. Everyone will notice."

But Barnabas was already hurrying back to the centre aisle. They couldn't afford to lose Carminn. At the back of the sanctuary, he turned and headed down the corridor where he had seen the Speaker. And there she was, just disappearing around a corner, carrying something the shape of a small hard drive or an old cigarette case that swung on the end of a long chain. The rest of his gang caught up with him, and just as he waved at them to follow Carminn, they heard a voice behind them:

"Well, Father bless me, if it isn't Tragidenko's Flying Circus."

CHAPTER 45

Simultaneously, Hulo said, "No, that's not us," and Bulo said, "So what? We're allowed to be here."

All of a sudden, Barnabas recognized the young Clouder who had stopped them. "You're Sensash. You were with the Clouding contingent that came to the circus. The only one who enjoyed the show."

Sensash put a finger to his lips. "You better follow me."

Garlip crossed his arms on his chest. "You're arresting us? You haven't got the authority to charge anyone from another—"

He raised his hands in supplication. "I'm not your problem. But others won't appreciate your visit."

It was all Barnabas could do to stop himself running after Carminn, but he didn't feel like he had a choice. Sensash led them down a hallway beside the sanctuary, nervously peering ahead and then back over his shoulder. His nerves were contagious, and the kids instinctively pulled themselves in to a tight knot behind him. Sensash took a bright silver key from his pocket, undid a small door, and swung it open.

"This way," he said. "The last of you close the door behind us."

Inside was a short landing and then a set of metal spiral stairs that reverberated with the sound of them descending—descending into the dark once Garlip closed the hall door. At the bottom, Sensash turned on the bright work lights that hung from the ceiling. It was an industrial room, high ceilinged and filled with giant gears and pistons. Large tanks with quivering meters hissed quietly with the power of the steam inside. When Barnabas saw the familiar figures of the worker puppets, maybe three-quarters life size, he realized they were under the stage of the sanctuary. This was the mechanical room that made all the steam-powered platforms and animatronics above do their magic.

"Don't touch anything," Sensash said, "especially the pressure tanks. They'll burn you. We don't have long before the next service begins, but this is the most private place I can think of. Please sit." He took what seemed to be the only chair, so Barnabas and the twins sat on the floor in front of him, like it was preschool story time. Garlip remained standing, looking suspicious. Like the rest of the Clouders, Sensash's body under his loose grey clothes was broad and solid. But his face was surprisingly delicate, his pale skin bordered by copper-red hair, with a thin nose and gentle blue eyes that looked at each of them in turn, curious and without malice.

"So, yes, I'm Sensash, the youngest member of Clouding's Convention of Elders. I inherited the post when my father died in January."

"I'm sorry," said Hulo and Bulo in unison.

"Thank you. So, what do you want in Clouding Town? You're obviously not here to pray."

Barnabas considered his options and just how little time there was, and he decided to tell Sensash everything he knew about Glower and Carminn's plans.

Sensash sat back in his chair, shocked. "Why would Carminn do such a thing?"

"Something about...the Guild Council...?"

Garlip spoke up. "Come on, Sensash. I could see what she was like when she came to Pastoral Park. And you know her better than we do. Carminn wants an excuse to take over the Valley, make everyone into believers, chop Mother Mercy out of the sacred family and, you know, end *laughter* forever."

Sensash stood and paced the room in obvious agitation. Barnabas wondered if they should maybe just run away now before he called Carminn or the Aqua Guard and had them arrested. But then Sensash stopped. He stared into the corner of the room and said, "It's terrible." Silence for a long-held breath. "But possible." He turned to look at Barnabas. "You're not from the Valley, are you?"

"No. How can you tell?"

"You don't fit in. Your size obviously, but the way you talk, the way you move." He shook his head, clearly trying to decide their fate. "I ask again, what do you want here at Clouding?"

"To find proof for the Guild Council, so they can stop Glower and Carminn."

"And what can I do to help?"

Barnabas sighed with relief. "Glower said he's going to the City this morning at eleven thirty. Carminn said she would make the arrangements, but I don't know what that means."

"There is no way up to the City from the Clouding steam works."

Hulo leaned forward. "Yeah, but Carminn's here. And she looked kinda purposeful."

Barnabas said, "She had this box on a chain."

"Sounds like a switching key," Sensash said.

Just then, a loud ticking commenced. With a hiss of steam, a big gear behind them began to turn. Great cantilevered arms in the ceiling started churning as, one floor above, pieces of the sanctuary sprang into action. Swiftly, piece by piece, the room around them came to life, louder and louder.

Sensash already had to shout over the noise. "Quickly, get out of here!" Instead of running for the spiral stairs, he headed to a small door at the back of the room. The other four tried to reach Sensash, but each found themselves shunted along a different treacherous path. Steam shot up from the floor, separating Hulo and Bulo. A pair of worker puppets jerked into motion in front of Garlip, swinging their pickaxes which, though made for show, looked like they could easily impale someone. He ducked and rolled out of the way, scampering on all fours to join Sensash.

Barnabas, trying to avoid being ground like sausage between two enormous, interlocking gears, climbed up on a platform that suddenly began to rise toward the ceiling, where hot steam was jetting out of nozzles.

"Help!" he shouted, and then he watched in wonder as Hulo made of a cup of her hands and Bulo, running to place her foot into the cup, launched into the air and up onto the platform. Wrapping her arms around Barnabas, she slid them both off the far end of the platform and they plummeted back toward the floor, right to where her sister had run. Hulo took their momentum and rolled the three of them across a narrow strip of unobstructed floor, ending up in a winded heap at Sensash and Garlip's feet by the open door.

"Wow," Sensash said. "Okay, this way."

Beyond the door was a corridor, its ceiling so low everyone but Barnabas had to duck. Still, he had a strong and immediate dislike for this tight, dark space. As they followed Sensash deeper into the shadows, Barnabas felt crushed and queasy, as if the walls were pressing in on him. He had to stop, curl into a squat, and bury his face in his hands.

Garlip crouched in front of him. "What's wrong? Do you feel sick?"

"I don't know. Give me a minute."

"I don't think we have the time." He grabbed Barnabas's hand and helped him to his feet. "Let's keep going."

They reached a chamber which was an intersection for many underground corridors. Barnabas felt immediately better under its high ceiling. In the middle of the chamber was a ladder climbing straight up to a hatch in the ceiling.

"That's the switching depot up there," Sensash said, "but we're right in the middle of a busy shift. I'll go first and see if there's a way to sneak you in." He hopped onto the ladder and climbed quickly. At the top, he spun a big wheel, like on a waterproof door in a submarine. Steam vented from two ports, and Sensash pushed the round hatch upward and peered out.

He called back down. "This is too strange. There's no one there. No one at all."

Bulo headed for the ladder. "Then let's go."

"No," Barnabas said. "Stay down here and let me do this alone." He put his hands on the ladder.

"Are you crazy?" Garlip said, grabbing Barnabas's arm. "What if you get caught?"

"What can they do to me? Send me back to the City?"

"Or disappear you in Doomlock!"

This idea made Barnabas feel queasy again. "But if you get caught, the circus will be in trouble." Before he could lose his nerve, he shook off Garlip's hand and started up the ladder.

Barnabas and Sensash climbed out into the switching depot, where they crouched behind a workstation crowded with switches and levers. They were in a vast space with a vaulted ceiling many stories over their heads. Steam ducts came together on the far wall and rose in parallel, like the pipes of a huge organ. Through the large, dirty windows in the roof, Barnabas could see the pipes strapped to the cliff face, climbing toward the City. Dozens more workstations filled the depot, presumably controlling the passage of steam. The place looked like a control room at NASA, but eerily deserted.

"What do we do now?" Barnabas whispered.

"I don't know. Wait for Carminn, I guess. And Glower if he shows." Barnabas pulled out his phone and checked the time. 11:05.

"What's that?" Sensash asked.

"You know, my phone." But Sensash didn't know. "It's also a camera." He snapped a few pics of the deserted switching depot and showed them to the young Clouder, only then remembering that photography was illegal in the Valley.

But Sensash just smiled in appreciation. "Clever."

"Sensash, go down and keep the others safe. I'll join you as soon as I'm done."

Sensash nodded. "You're a brave kid, Barnabas of the City." And with that, he climbed back underground.

CHAPTER 46

Barnabas, alone now in the echoing chamber, silent but for the quiet ticking of machines and the gentle hiss of steam, felt his heart pound in his chest. *You're a brave kid,* Sensash had said. Just like Graviddy had. Deep down, he still didn't quite believe it, but at least he knew he could fake brave when he needed to.

But there was no more time for contemplation, because at that moment, Carminn entered the switching depot with George Glower at her side. Instead of his usual coveralls, Glower wore a brown suit, a powder blue shirt, and a pale yellow tie. His dress shoes needed a shine, but they were pretty decent. Clashing with his professional attire, he wore an enormous khaki backpack, complete with a sleeping bag rolled up at the top as if he was going camping. Barnabas snapped three, four, five pictures, hoping some would be sharp enough, even without a flash.

"Where are your workers?" Glower asked, sounding tense.

"I cancelled the shift. But don't make a habit of these daytime trips. It's suspicious." Barnabas hopped and skittered from hiding place to hiding place, keeping up with Carminn and Glower as they crossed the floor. He tucked himself behind a bank of lockers as the pair walked up a short staircase to a landing where one of the biggest steam pipes began its climb up to the City. On the side of the pipe was a nearly invisible door which Carminn opened with a long, narrow key.

Glower entered, flicking on a light inside. Barnabas could see a tiny room inside the pipe with a single small bench. It looked like a space capsule. He zoomed his camera in on the door and began snapping pictures.

"Everything's on schedule," Glower said, leaning out the door of the capsule. "You need to be ready on Tuesday. Everything will happen at 1430 hours."

He slammed the door, and Carminn hurried down the steps to take her position behind the closest workstation. She took out the little box Sensash called the switching key and fitted it into the panel. She pushed buttons and spun knobs, and the big pipe began to vibrate. When a red light on the panel turned on, Carminn threw over a large lever. Hissing steam vented from two small nozzles in the rumbling pipe, and a loud clattering sound erupted, then quickly diminished. Carminn looked upward through the rooftop window. Barnabas suddenly understood. The capsule containing George Glower had just shot up, like a cannonball in a steam-powered cannon, through the pipe and up to the City. That was Glower's secret route—a private steam-powered express elevator.

Barnabas raised the phone and took picture after picture, though he saw nothing new to capture. He hoped he had enough evidence to convince the Guild Council of his story. Then his responsibility would be over, and it would be up to them to save the City.

CHAPTER 47

The last of the day was vanishing behind the trees as Barnabas, alongside Whistlewort, Sanjani, and Tragidenko, crossed the dry lakebed of Lake Lucid in Pastoral Park's most luxurious mule cart. Barnabas and his friends had returned with enough evidence to convince the maestro to contact the Guild Council. Now Barnabas was on his way to testify at an emergency session. For the first time since he'd discovered the terrible plot, he felt a surge of hope. Soon the appropriate authorities would know about Glower and Carminn's plans, and they would stop them.

Because of the gravity of the occasion, the circus folk were all dressed up in a manner they called formal. Tragidenko, in a hunter green suit and orange cravat, still looked like he was about to introduce the arrival of the clowns. Whistlewort wore a long yellow coat and pointy leather boots that made Barnabas think of a jazz musician from the Forties, while Sanjani's dress was printed with enormous, blood-red poppy flowers and bright yellow bees. For Barnabas, the star witness, they had provided a suit of mauve velvet and a thickly ruffled shirt. He felt more like he was playing a young lord in a costume drama than speaking before the Valley's Unified Guild Council.

The Council building was a huge, historic mansion overlooking the former Lake Lucid, and it must have had a hell of a view back when the lake had water in it. A clerk met them at the door and brought them into a high foyer. They were led to a wooden bench just outside the great oak doors of the Hall of Deliberations and told to wait until they were called. The doors were flanked by stiff, unsmiling Aqua Guards holding ceremonial spears. Inside, they could hear the voices of the Council, already in session.

Barnabas looked around at the fancy woodwork and huge landscape paintings. "This place looks like it used to be the home of some fancy people."

Sanjani nodded. "Yes, it was the residence of Father Glory and Mother Mercy." Barnabas was startled by this revelation. *Were they real people? Not just symbols and statues?*

Whistlewort stood and began pacing up and down on the parquet floor. "I don't like that they started without us."

"This will not be ending well," the maestro muttered.

Barnabas fought the urge to apologize for all the trouble he was causing. For five minutes, the only sounds were muffled voices from behind the oak doors and the ceaseless tap-tapping of Whistlewort's hard-soled boots as he paced up and down. Then came the sound of shouting and commotion from inside the hall. The two Aqua Guards in the foyer dropped into a defensive posture, gripping their spears like they might be more than ceremonial. The double doors flew open, and out burst Carminn, seething with rage, three more Aquas following her.

"What is this idiocy?" she shouted. "I have been a member of this Council for fifteen years."

An immaculately dressed older man ran out after her. His long, grey hair fell over the shoulders of his elegant black coat, and his open hands were working the air as if he could smooth out her anger from a distance. "Carminn, please, there have been allegations made. I'm sure they *can't* be true. But—"

She was marching swiftly toward the exit. "I don't care what nonsense you get up to, Borborik. You're wasting my time and I'm leaving."

Two of the Aqua Guard circled around to stand between her and the exit. "Madam Speaker," one said in a clear, cold voice. "I'm afraid we're under orders to hold you until Council finishes its deliberations."

"Hold me?" she growled in disbelief. The other three guards were around her now, brandishing truncheons instead of the ornamental spears.

The grey-haired man wrung his hands. "No, no, not *hold*. We just need you to stay—"

"I'm not a dog."

"Stay here for a little while."

Carminn didn't look scared; she looked dangerous. She turned to stare at the four visitors from Pastoral Park in their bright clothing. "What are these libertines doing here? What lies are they spreading about me?" And then, "Who is that *boy*? I don't know that boy." Goosebumps rose on Barnabas's skin.

One of the Aquas stepped closer. "Madam Councillor. If you will please follow me to one of the side offices. I'm sure you'll be comfortable there."

She made them wait for ten tension-filled seconds before saying, "Fine," a single syllable that seemed to convey as much threat as forbearance.

When she was gone, Borborik, the elegant, grey-haired man, wiped his brow and sighed. As he re-entered the Hall of Deliberations, he nodded at Tragidenko and said to one of the Aqua, "Give us two minutes, then bring them in."

CHAPTER 48

Barnabas and the circus cohort were escorted through the double doors and told to sit on another long bench at the back. The Hall of Deliberations, spacious and richly appointed with marble lintels and crown mouldings edged in gold leaf, might once have been the ballroom of the mansion. The council members sat in a semicircle behind small, old-fashioned desks of dark wood. Borborik sat in the centre, his desk on a raised platform. Above him was a fresco of Father Glory and Mother Mercy watching a geyser of water shoot skyward from an industrial pipe. There was an empty desk which must have been Carminn's. Barnabas recognized the other two Clouding councillors from their visit to the circus.

"Welcome, young man, I am President Borborik of the Unified Guild Council. You may address me as Your Eminence." His voice, though authoritative, had a gentleness to it, and Barnabas let himself hope his case would be heard with open ears. "Please step forward and stand at the testimonial." He indicated a little platform with a lectern.

Sanjani put a hand on Barnabas's shoulder and whispered, "Just speak the truth. Those who speak the truth are always heard." He stepped up to the testimonial, but the lectern, built for people of Valley stature, came up to his chin.

Borborik pulled out a sheet of paper from his desk and cleared his throat. "This is the statement of Maestro Tragidenko of Pastoral Park, which I took down telephonically earlier today." He cleared his throat. "Young Barnabas Bopwright, who stands before you, infiltrated George Glower's emporium, the Drop Shop, just before midnight last night in the company of a young performer from Tragidenko's Circus of Humanity. Their goal was to retrieve an object which young Bopwright believes is his property. While at the establishment, the young man claims to have witnessed a demonstration and overheard a plan to explode charges in the City's Tower District—"

Every member of Council reacted to this, crying out in disbelief or repeating the shocking words to each other for confirmation. Amid the hubbub, Barnabas heard one councillor say, "…never trusted Glower. He's from the City."

Borborik raised his hands in the air. "Please, if I may continue: to explode charges in the City's Tower District this coming Tuesday, and cause some or all of the skyscrapers to topple down the great cliff and into the Tumbles.

"Putting aside for the moment the issues of trespassing and illegal entry, young Bopwright's story, while incredible, does require us to investigate, especially as his account has been brought to us by Maestro Tragidenko, who is a friend of this council."

One of the Clouding councillors, a man with a sharply pointed auburn goatee, spoke up. "Why was the Clouding Speaker removed from these proceedings?"

Borborik dropped his head and shuffled the papers on his desk as if the answer might be hiding among them. "Councillor Fayrbrin, the reason for Carminn's removal will become clear when we hear from our witness." He looked across at Barnabas, standing at the testimonial. "Young Bopwright, we would like to ask you some questions."

"Um, sure, Your Eminence," Barnabas replied, surprised at how the echo of his voice returned to him, sounding higher and more childish than it had felt leaving his throat.

Borborik asked, "Was Glower alone at the Drop Shop when you saw his demonstration?"

"Well, no, the other person who works there, Greta, she was around. And this kid, Galt-Stomper, was in and out of the room." Barnabas felt more than a little reluctant to go on because he knew his next words would not go down so well. "And, yeah, so was Carminn."

Councillor Fayrbrin burst out, "Carminn? Speaker Carminn of Clouding Guild?"

Barnabas turned to look at the man, whose goatee was pointed directly at his heart like a weapon. "Um, yes, sir. She was there. And she knew all about the plan."

"Councillor," said Borborik. "I will address the witness. If you have any questions, you may ask them through me."

Fayrbrin squinted his eyes at the Guild President. "Yes, Your Eminence. I am *curious* about the origin of the witness's strange name. Is Pastoral Park now reverting to the City custom of given and family names?"

There was no hiding it, so Barnabas spoke up. "I'm from the City."

Again, the room descended into noisy chaos. Fayrbrin leaped to his feet. "Eminence, Speaker Carminn was right. We are wasting our Saturday night here. Some interloper has flouted our laws and infiltrated the Valley surreptitiously with malicious intent. Once here, he has committed acts of trespassing and theft, and now he brings outrageous accusations against one of our most esteemed and unassailable denizens. It is this Bopwright who needs to be on trial, not my Guild and Speaker."

Another councillor called out, "How did he cross the Frontier?"

"What is Pastoral Park's role in hiding this fugitive?" shouted yet another.

President Borborik picked up a gavel and banged it on the desk. "Councillors, I must be allowed to run these proceedings. There are indeed many irregularities here, and they will be addressed. But first, young Bopwright, tell me, do you have any proof to back up your assertions?"

"Well, yeah!" Barnabas dug into his pants pocket and pulled out his phone, excited to finally present his evidence. "I'm just glad I still had charge, 'cause it's getting low, but here!" He turned the phone out toward the councillors with one of his pictures on it.

Everyone in the room leaned forward. One of the councillors put on a pair of wire-rimmed glasses and said, "What is it?"

"I took some pictures at the Clouding steam plant of Glower and Carminn. See?"

Fayrbrin was on his feet again. "Your Eminence, this is a disgrace. The scripture forbids photographic images. Not only is this boy slandering one of our finest denizens, he has desecrated our Holy Steam Works with his device."

The other Clouding delegate pounded on the table. "Mr. President, I move these disgraceful pictures be destroyed immediately, and the witness be remanded into custody in Doomlock. And send Tragidenko there, too! He has been aiding and abetting this inveterate invader to evade the law."

From the back of the room, Whistlewort shouted, "You idiots. At least look at what the boy risked his tail to bring you!"

The councillor with the glasses conferred with her neighbours. "Forming Guild is in favour of this evidence being admitted. We want to see the pictures."

This led to a shouting match between different factions. Barnabas, clutching the phone against his breast, sensed a lot of old resentments were being aired. It was like the kind of fights his mom and dad had on the rare occasions they met up now, supposedly about something small like what time to pick Barnabas up, but really about all the years of hurt.

The president again banged his gavel. "My dear councillors. Might it not be possible to separate the illegality of the picture-taking from the potential good the pictures could do in helping us determine what might be transpiring? Let us put it to a vote."

The result of the vote was terrifyingly close—seven to six in favour of seeing the pictures. Barnabas realized not only was the fate of the City in the Council's hand, so was his. He might end up in Doomlock, a place whose very name promised endless misery.

The president called for a projector, and soon Barnabas's pictures were being beamed onto a large screen. "Uh, I know it's hard to see, but this is the switching depot at Clouding. Uh, and that's Carminn there with Glower."

"Could be anyone," Fayrbrin muttered.

"No, you can see—wait—in this next picture. That's them."

The room was silent again. The president exchanged glances with several councillors before turning to Barnabas. "Is there more?"

"Yes, and this part is important." He skipped ahead, trying to find the pictures he needed. In the middle of the phone, ominous words appeared in bold red letters: "Low Battery!" Barnabas tapped the warning, and it went away. "Here, look. It's a kind of elevator. The steam sends it up to the City. See? That's Glower sitting inside."

A councillor who had not spoken before turned to the two representatives from Clouding and asked, "Is this true? Is there such means of transport?"

Fayrbrin was startled, all his former bluster gone. "We know nothing of such a means."

The other Clouding representative stammered, "We will, of course, look for this anomaly. Immediately."

The president wiped his brow with a handkerchief. "The witness will kindly step down."

A surge of desperation ran through Barnabas's chest. "Wait! What are you going to do about this? You can see I'm telling the truth."

The president picked up his gavel and banged it three times, the sound echoing like a gunshot off the walls. "The witness will be seated. Now!"

Sanjani came forward and led Barnabas back to the bench. "Don't worry, dear," she whispered. Whistlewort patted his back, and Tragidenko squeezed his shoulder.

The president turned to the clerk. "Bring in the next witness."

CHAPTER 49

Barnabas had no idea who this next witness might be until he heard a familiar strident voice out in the foyer. "Take your interfering fingers off my body, you brute. I can move on my own. You'll catch more flies with honey, remember that." Greta entered. The buttons of her pink knit sweater were misaligned, and she wore a kerchief over her dishevelled hair, strands of which stuck out from under the fabric like cold, hard spaghetti.

She took her place at the testimonial, her chin raised defiantly despite the terror in her eyes.

Borborik said, "You were apprehended driving away from the Drop Shop with a fully laden truck of your merchandise. Why has the Drop Shop closed down?"

"We're doing inventory. And giving the floors a good wash down. You wouldn't believe the filth people track across my floors. I say to Mr. Glower, I do, 'Georgie! People are animals,' and he always tells me—"

"Where is George Glower?" Borborik interrupted. "There are allegations he has illegally left the Valley, perhaps not for the first time."

"My George? Illegal? The idea! The service that man does for the Valley is incalculable. Just *try* and calculate it. You can't count that high."

"Then where is he?"

"I'm sure I couldn't say. On a spiritual retreat, mayhap?" She examined the purple polish on her long nails.

"That boy there"—the president pointed at Barnabas with his gavel—"claims this coming Tuesday, George Glower will commit extreme and mortal sabotage. He says you know about this plan."

Greta twisted around and glared at Barnabas. "That boy," she thundered, "is a liar and a sneaky little sneak thief! Got no respect for the ways of our Valley, he has."

"And so, you stand with George Glower?"

"I do."

"Even if on Tuesday the towers crash into the Tumbles? If such a disaster occurs, we will come and take you from your cell in Doomlock and charge you as a co-conspirator. Do you still have nothing to tell us?"

Greta's supply of quick replies seemed to suddenly run out. She stood blinking for a minute before patting down the kerchief on her head. "Well, I might have heard one or two suspicious things over the last week. Nothing, you understand, definitive."

"And did these suspicions extend to Speaker Carminn of Clouding Guild?"

"Ooh, she's a bad one and have no doubt. A snake what's tempted my poor Georgie away from his honest, lucrative path into some foul abyss." She suddenly howled like a cat whose tail got stepped on. "Ohhhhh, your Eminent Worshipful Honour! Have pity on a miserable lady who's never known nought but grief!"

"Silence! The witness will be remanded into custody in Doomlock, pending the outcome of this investigation."

Greta's whining turned to a cry of fury. "You can't do that. I have a truck full of valuables parked outside. Any nefarious crook could pilfer my hard-earned treasures."

As the Aqua Guard lead her out the door, Barnabas could hear her calling, "Wait until my George hears of this. You lot will be barred from the Drop Shop for *life*, you will." Barnabas felt a cold satisfaction at her arrest. The Council finally understood who the real villains were. Now they would help.

President Borborik lowered his head, supporting it with both hands as he pored over his notes. "Council, we have some difficult decisions to make."

One councillor stood. "Eminence, we must calculate where the towers might fall and form an evacuation plan."

"Yes," said another. "And with an eye to salvaging as much valuable equipment as possible."

"If, that is, there is any truth to the boy's accusations," Borborik said.

"Yes, *if*," the councillor agreed, nodding vigorously.

"What?" Barnabas said. He sat up, looking around the room in disbelief. Could he be hearing what he thought he was hearing?

"And it begins," muttered Whistlewort.

An older, rotund man in a striped poncho stood with some difficulty. He cleared his throat and declaimed in a voice like an old Shakespearean actor, "My esteemed colleagues, while this potential pending tragedy *would be* very unfortunate, I hope it is not too early to consider the opportunities such events *might* afford the Valley. There *could* be years of rebuilding, renegotiation of the terms of our contracts with the City, emergency powers this Council could take on—"

Borborik sat up straight, putting out a hand in the man's direction. "Yes, Swarnish, I think such discussion, while valuable, might best be left to a time…to such a time…after…in case of…*if* it turns out there's any truth to the allegations." He cleared his throat, and the whole Council looked sheepish.

Barnabas leaped to his feet. "What are you talking about?" The whole room turned his way. "You know this is true. This is *happening*! How can you just sit there? You have to warn Mayor Tuppletaub immediately. I know he knows all about the Valley. His apartment looks right down on it." He had moved to the centre of the room, turning to take in the embarrassed, impassive faces, searching for any sign of acknowledgement.

A woman with short-black hair said, "Young man, we meet with the City only twice a year. Our relationship follows traditions that date back for the better part of a century."

Barnabas ran his fingers through his hair. "But this is life and death."

Fayrbrin answered coldly, "When the City needs our help, they ask for it. We don't tell them how to handle their affairs."

The two Aqua Guards in the Hall had moved to stand near Barnabas, one on either side of him. But he was too desperate to be intimidated. "Then if you won't do something, I'll warn the mayor myself. Put me back on the train and I'll do it. I don't have any *traditions* or whatever."

"No, no, not possible," said Borborik. "At this point, the existence of this conspiracy is mere conjecture. As has been pointed out, young Bopwright, you are an infiltrator in the Valley. Your motives are uncertain. Then there is the issue of your illegal photographs. A most serious matter."

"Most serious," others echoed. Barnabas turned to look back at the adults from Pastoral Park. *Help me*, he begged them with his eyes.

Borborik stood. "It is the will of this Council that you be remanded to custody in Doomlock, where you will be held until the matters of your illegal entry and illegal photography can be settled with representatives of the City at our semi-annual meeting in two months' time."

Tragidenko stood. "Mr. President, I am asking you for some excellent reconsideration. Many lives, many dreams may be at the stake. This boy meant no harm. His actions were accidental or committed for the goodness."

"Maestro," the president said, his voice growing cold. "The role of Pastoral Park in hiding the fugitive is something Council will have to investigate. You have already stuck your neck out a good deal farther than you should have."

Tragidenko sat, shaking his head. The guards moved closer to Barnabas. *If I just took off and ran, could I get out before they grabbed me?*

Just then, there was a huge crash outside and the sound of shouting. The members of Council all rose in alarm. The doors flew open, and an Aqua Guard ran in, bleeding from his forehead.

"Mr. President, Speaker Carminn has escaped. We were unable to apprehend her before she vanished into the trees."

One of the guards flanking Barnabas ran out into the hall to help, and the remaining guard grabbed him firmly by the arm.

President Borborik lowered himself into his chair, and everyone else followed suit. "I want her captured by morning. And Maestro Tragidenko, this new disaster just confirms my resolve. Young Bopwright will be kept in Doomlock not only for his transgressions, but to keep him safe from Speaker Carminn's wrath."

Barnabas looked desperately back at his companions. Sanjani was crying. *How could this have all gone so terribly wrong?*

"Take him away," said Borborik.

CHAPTER 50

When Barnabas was twelve, there had been a kid in his class named Henry who everyone said would eventually wind up in jail. Henry stole from kids; he stole from the office. He actually smoked! At twelve! The shocking idea that jail inevitably awaited the boy did not originate with the kids. It was overheard from their parents, who gossiped openly, assuming their children didn't listen to *that* kind of conversation. But the children did listen, and soon Henry was shunned by his peers. There followed more acts of vandalism and some mysterious crime so terrible his schoolmates were never told the details. And then Henry was gone—expelled or withdrawn, or perhaps already incarcerated.

Barnabas wondered now what had become of that poor, bedraggled boy who always seemed to have boogers in his nose. Maybe in a new environment, Henry had changed. Maybe whatever was going on in his life that made him so unhappy got better. But maybe once the rumours started, they stuck with you and doomed you. Doomlock.

Meanwhile, Glower was about to make his dreams of revenge come true, and Carminn would return to take over the Valley. People like that didn't wind up in jail. Henry did. Barnabas did.

It was late, maybe close to midnight. They had taken his phone away, so he couldn't be sure. Fatigue tugged at him, but he didn't want to sleep. The Aqua Guards were coming at dawn to take him from this holding cell in the Council building and escort him to the train station. He would be taken on the subway down into the dark to a tiny cell without a window, so he didn't want to waste his last glimpse of the sky, his last chance to hear the birds sing before sunrise.

There was a window high up on the wall of the cell, and standing on his cot on tiptoes, Barnabas could just peer out. There was no glass in the steel frame, just four solid, vertical bars. He looked between them at the moon as it illuminated the dry lakebed. The night mist was growing thicker, and Barnabas could almost convince himself that it was water, that the lake was still there, fresh and inviting.

After a while, he started to shiver from the cold and sat down on the bed. He pulled the scratchy blanket over his shoulders and buttoned his ruffled shirt up to the neck. How had he failed to make them understand? He replayed the events of the trial over and over in his head, but he couldn't see what he might have done differently.

Through the walls came a miserable wail, as it had come every hour since he had been locked up. "Aaaaaaoowwwwwwwwwwoooooooooooooo!" followed by "Georgie, my Georgie, why have you left me here? Don't you love me, my big pigeon? Fly down and save me! Save me from Doooomlock! AAAAOOOWWWWooooooooooo!"

Barnabas covered his ears. Why didn't the guards tell her to shut up? Worse, her cries opened the door to his own misery. Would he ever see his family and friends again? Who would even know he was locked away in the ground, in a valley no one knew existed?

He was moments from wailing into the night like Greta when he heard whispers. The sound of a twig cracking. He stood in the centre of the cell and looked up at the high window.

Quietly, but forcefully, a voice said, "Annnnnnd—*hup*!" Shuffling, grunting. A face filled the window. Even in the darkness, Barnabas recognized Thumbutter.

"Hi, Barnabas!" Her mischievous smile shone in the moonlight. "We thought maybe you wanted to get out of there."

"Yes, please," he whispered, grinning and wiping tears from his eyes with a corner of the blanket.

Someone from below handed Thumbutter a socket wrench, and she began to undo the bolts that held the bars in place. It took almost ten minutes, and Barnabas could hear strained curses from below. When she had the heavy frame loose, someone hissed, "For Glory's sake, don't drop it, girl." Barnabas watched hands from below take the frame and lower it out of sight. Thumbutter pulled herself half into the window and reached out her strong arms.

"Come on," she said. "There's not much time."

He dropped the blanket, put on the velvet jacket, and hopped up on the cot. She pulled him through the narrow window, and only then did he see what was happening. Thumbutter was at the top of a pyramid of men and women, all sweating with the exertion of the long pose. He was passed down the face of the pyramid with disconcerting ease as if they had been practising The Amazing Pyramid Jail-Break! for months. As soon as he hit the ground, the pyramid disassembled around him in a series of leaps, thumps, and grunts.

Whistlewort stood to one side in his customary patched work clothes. "Well done. Now, get yourselves back to Pastoral Park. Don't all travel together. It'll draw too much attention." He placed a strong, bony hand on Barnabas's shoulder. "Sorry you had to go through that." He reached into his pocket and handed Barnabas his cell phone.

"They let you have it?"

"Well, yeah, if you call me lifting it from the clerk's pocket 'letting me have it.'"

"Hey!" came a loud whisper from above. It was Greta, peering through the bars of the neighbouring room. Her kerchief was gone, and her hair was wild as a gorgon's. "You get me out of here, or I'm going to scream blue murder, draw the guard right quick."

Whistlewort laughed up at her. "Sorry, honey. They were so worked up about Carminn, they only left one guard on duty here. And now he's tied up in the basement."

She let loose her miserable wail again and screamed into the night. "And what am I supposed to do?"

"Rot in Doomlock, I guess," the old man replied breezily, turning away. "Come on, Barnabas. We only have a few hours until they realize you're gone. Lots to do."

"Wait, boy!" cried Greta. "Please, you're going to the City, ain'tcha? Gonna see my Georgie?"

He didn't know what to think. The woman wasn't as evil as Glower. On the other hand, she had done everything she could in the Council meeting to get him in worse trouble. But she looked so miserable, all he could say was, "Yes, I think so."

"Just let him know his darlin' Greta is deep in the deep, in deep, deep trouble, and she's counting on him. I was always there for him, you know. His help-meet. He won't let me moulder away. Never."

"I'll tell him," Barnabas promised.

"Come on," said Whistlewort. "We gotta move."

CHAPTER 51

A fine chestnut horse was waiting around the side of the mansion. Before he and Whistlewort rode off, Barnabas thought he saw movement, a large shadow in the trees flanking the mansion. And it was watching him. Then Whistlewort shook the reins, and they were off.

A crowd awaited them in the main square of Pastoral Park, and everyone pushed close to Barnabas, demanding to hear juicy details of the evening's events. But Sanjani slid through the crowd and put her arm over his shoulder.

"You will have to talk to Barnabas later. Time is short, and we have much to do."

Sanjani led him back to the little house at the top of the hill. She hurried inside to light a lantern, and as Barnabas closed the door, he noticed Falstep sitting on the garden fence, silhouetted in the moonlight.

"Have something to eat," Sanjani told Barnabas, motioning him to the table, placing a plate of chickpeas and cheese and a basket of bread in front of him. "I'll be right back." She hurried up the stairs as he dug into the food. The lantern in front of him was the only light, leaving the rest of the room in shadow. When a voice spoke up in the dark, he almost choked on a chickpea.

"I'm heartbreakingly sorry, young man," Tragidenko said. Squinting into the dimness, Barnabas could just see him slumped on the couch like a pile of laundry. "Last night, I was an unforgivable coward. But now, you are reminding me what it is to be brave."

"But maestro," Barnabas said. "Pastoral Park is in danger because of me."

He shook his head and gave a mighty yawn. "No, Barnabas, this is not on you, though much burden falls on your shoulders. We will do all we can to help you save the City, yes?"

"What do we do next? Maestro?" But the only response was a rising snore.

Sanjani came back downstairs, and much to Barnabas's surprise, Wickram was with her. They sat across from Barnabas, Sanjani reaching over to take his hand, Wickram staring down at the table.

"At dawn," Sanjani said, "the Aqua Guard will return to the Guild House and find you gone. They will guess that Pastoral Park freed you, and they will make their way here. That means we had better be on the move within three hours."

"Where are we going?" Barnabas asked.

"The City, of course. Obviously, you can't take the train, and Glower and Carminn's secret steam elevator will be shut down by now. The only way, as you suggested last night, is through the woods."

The way she said it sent a chill through him. "Is that how you came to the Valley? Is it dangerous?"

"Perhaps. There were strangers who helped me in my passage through the earth. Hopefully, they will help us again on the return journey."

"Wait, are you coming with me?" A wave of relief washed through him.

"I never thought I would return to the City, but I have no choice. Glower must be stopped." She turned to Wickram. "Pickle? Do you have something to say to Barnabas?"

Barnabas said, "You don't have to."

At the same time, Wickram looked up at him and muttered, "Sorry."

"It's okay," Barnabas told him. "You heard about everything? Glower? Carminn? The towers?"

"Yeah," Wickram replied, running one of his long guitar-picking fingernails down a groove in the tabletop. "I can't believe Glower would do that. Totally guts me. Guild Council really won't do anything about it?"

"Nope. They just want to throw me in Doomlock. But I'm going to the City to stop him. Me and your mom."

"Wickram," Sanjani said, "I want you to accompany us."

Wickram sat up straight, a head higher than everyone else at the table. "What are you talking about?"

Sanjani went to the door and opened it. "Please, come in."

Falstep entered, swiping his cap off and looking around. "Been a while since I was here. Not much has changed."

"Well, things are changing quickly now," she said, taking her seat. Falstep sat down beside Barnabas, across from Wickram, who looked more than a little suspicious.

Sanjani steepled her fingers on the table. "Pickle, your friend needs your help to stop Glower and save the City. But there's something else.

It was me who sent Falstep to the City last Tuesday. I asked him to visit a school for the performing arts. He has arranged an audition for you. I hoped you could travel legally, but now the very future of Pastoral Park is in doubt, and there will be no favours for Dimitri Tragidenko's son. You must leave with me and Barnabas tonight."

Wickram started bouncing his foot on the floor like he was a jackrabbit. "That's crazy. I can't go to the City. Not now."

Falstep said, "I thought going to the City was your biggest dream."

Wickram shot him an angry glare. "You heard her—the circus is in trouble. Don't you think I have any loyalty?"

"Gee, that's funny." Falstep tossed his hat high in the air and it landed perfectly on his head. "I thought you just quit the circus."

"That's different. That's because of *him*." He stabbed a finger in Tragidenko's direction, and the sleeping maestro responded with a loud snore.

Sanjani's voice was steady and calm. "Then why not get away from your father for a little while? Build a life for yourself in the City."

Wickram's eyes narrowed. "Oh, I see. You're just sick of hearing us fight. You want a bit of peace and quiet for once."

A tear escaped her eye. She sighed and stood up. "I am not helping here. Listen to what Falstep has to say and let me know your decision." Barnabas wanted to get up and follow Sanjani out the front door. This conversation was too personal for him to witness. But he missed his moment, and she was gone.

"One down, three to go," Wickram said.

Falstep snorted in amusement. "Okay, wise-bone, Sanjani's the problem, Dimitri's the problem. Let's say you woke up tomorrow, and *poof*, none of us was here anymore. No one to push you around or give a road apple what happens to you. What would you do with your life?"

"Nothing! Everything! I'd go and help out in the kitchen, or maybe join a road crew. Make myself useful." He put his chin on the table and draped his long arms across his head.

"And what about your music?" the clown asked.

Wickram's sat up again. "What about it?" He gave an angry nod in Tragidenko's direction. "I don't owe him my music. It's the best part of me, and he can't just take it and make it his."

"And so, you'll refuse to make any music at all. And then maybe get yourself good and drunk when that hurts too much."

Wickram rose to his feet and screamed down at the clown. "Getting drunk is good enough for you, O, King of Hypocrites."

Falstep jumped up on top of the table, regaining the height advantage. "And who in the name of the Fathermothering dung pile told you to act like *me*?"

Wickram collapsed back into his chair, and Falstep dropped off the table into his own chair. They both breathed hard for a minute before Falstep said, "Why don't you go see what those City rubes can teach you? You can always come back if the school licks goat stones. I know you're scared."

"I'm not scared. I don't do scared."

"Lucky you. Personally, I was crapping myself when we performed for the Clouders, but I did it anyway."

"But where would I live?" Wickram asked, suddenly sounding like a lost kid.

"You have an aunt up there. Your mom's sister."

"No way. Mom's family was terrible to her."

Falstep pulled half a cigar and a match from his breast pocket and lit up. "Nah, just the old man. Your Aunt Kareena is aces. Flirted a lot with me, so you know she's got taste."

Wickram looked drained. "I don't know what to say." He turned to Barnabas. "And I don't have any idea how to save the City."

"Me neither. But two clueless brains are better than one."

Wickram gave him a lopsided smile, "Well, I do have a clue or two." Then he looked off into the shadows, and his smile died. "You're not asleep, are you? You been listening the whole time."

Tragidenko's voice was heavy, like thick, brown ink. "Not the whole time, but I heard enough."

CHAPTER 52

Falstep jumped to his feet. "Dimitri, you know I never wanted to come between you and your kid. I wouldn't do that to you."

"Hey, don't talk about me like I'm not here."

Tragidenko heaved himself off the couch with a cascade of groans and came to sit at the end of the table. "My friend, I think no such thing. On the contrary, I thank you for taking care of my child when I could not. Now, if you would please leave us, I will see you in the morning."

Wickram looked a bit panicked. "Hey, no, you don't have to leave." But Falstep stood and went out the front door. Again, Barnabas almost followed, but there was inertia to his stillness.

Tragidenko's shoulders were hunched, his hands clasped in front of him on the table. "Wickram, you said I wanted to take your music from you. Firstly, this is not true, has never been true."

"Oh, road apples. Admit it, you want me to take over your circus when you're done. Well, I have my own life."

Anger wrinkled the maestro's brow. "Of course I want you to take over the circus. Why wouldn't I?" He ran his fingers through his thick hair and growled in frustration. "Listen, when you were born, your mother and I were so happy. We were busy making a place for the circus here in the Valley, and then suddenly you arrived, this beautiful dumpling with a smile like the sunrise. I didn't care what you did with your life as long as you thrived, wrapped in the glow of our love. But then so early I saw your creative soul, and I thought, 'Oh, yes, this one he is like me.' I was proud when I heard your beautiful voice singing out louder than the other children, so tuneful, so sure. And as you grew, I pulled you close to my side, told you my dreamings for each part of every show. 'The maestro's little assistant,' they called you."

Barnabas gave Wickram a furtive look, but the boy was again hiding behind his hair.

"Then we found you the guitar, yes? At the Drop Shop, in the first days after that madman Glower opened his store. Nothing existed for you after that but your music. You had no use for me anymore. Because I could teach you nothing about your new love."

Wickram's voice shook a bit. "So, why couldn't you take a hint? I knew what I wanted."

"Do you think I was not happy for you? I was delighted! And I wanted you to share this gift with our circus."

"*Your* circus."

The Maestro banged a big hand down on the table. "No! Not mine. Never *mine*. We are a community—a family—and we all serve the Big Top."

A tear was moving down Wickram's cheek, but his voice was defiant. "Well, I don't. I'm going to the City and maybe I won't come back."

"Then go. Be happy," said Tragidenko, but it didn't sound like a blessing. Wickram stood abruptly, and his chair tumbled to the ground. He ran out the front door.

Barnabas looked helplessly at Tragidenko and said, "I'm sorry," before he ran after Wickram. He found him in the little front garden, sitting on a bench that had been built for someone smaller, maybe for him as a little boy. He was crying, and Barnabas debated whether to say something or just let him be.

But then Graviddy stepped out of the shadows across the road. "Are you okay?"

Wickram looked up defiantly, gritting his teeth, wiping away his tears. "I'm golden. I'm cinnamon toast. So, what's up? You here to yell at me, too? I'm the official Pastoral Park punching bag?"

"No, I just wanted to say—"

"Right, that I don't own you and you can kiss anyone you like, got it." Jumping to his feet, he grabbed Barnabas by both shoulders and planted a sloppy kiss on his mouth. "Well, so can I. You and me are just two free birds, flying free in Freeville." Wickram stormed back to his bench, leaving Barnabas wiping his lips in confusion.

Graviddy rolled her eyes. She came in through the garden gate and joined Wickram on the bench. "You really are an idiot, you know that? I heard you're going to save the City with Barnabas and Sanjani, and I'm really impressed."

"Oh yeah?" he said, crossing and uncrossing his legs nervously. "Who told you that? Falstep? Maybe I said no."

"I have no doubt you're going. Maybe you don't know how brave and strong you can be, but I do. And I'll tell you what, I'm not kissing anyone else until you get back. Deal?"

"What if I'm gone for a long time?"

She gave him a quizzical look. "How long?"

"I don't know. Months. Maybe a year."

Graviddy made a show of considering this. "I think I can hold out."

Wickram pushed the hair back on his head, suddenly the coolest guy in the world. "Oh yeah? And what happens when I get back?" She jumped to her feet and vaulted elegantly over the garden fence. "I kiss you, the returning hero. I kiss you hard." And she ran off down the road, her footsteps light as a deer.

Barnabas came over and sat beside him. "Please don't kiss me again, okay?"

"Just making a point."

"Even so."

"I'm an excellent kisser. Don't complain."

They heard voices approaching and looked up to see Garlip, Hulo, Bulo, Thumbutter, and little Beany coming up the road with lanterns. Soon, they were all talking and laughing. Barnabas was glad for the company—especially Garlip's—because he was beginning to worry more and more about what would happen in the next few hours.

Sanjani, returning from her walk, asked Wickram and Barnabas, "Don't you want to get a little sleep before we go?"

Barnabas shook his head. "I don't think I could sleep anyway. If it's okay, I just want to hang out."

"Me too, Mom," said Wickram.

"Okay, but when I call you, be here and be ready."

The kids sat under the starlight and talked about the night's adventures, about the circus, and what the future held for all of them. Wickram told them about the music school, and while they peppered him with questions, Garlip led Barnabas around to the side of the house.

"Since you liked my mural, I wanted you to see my sketchbook." He opened it up and showed Barnabas all his beautiful drawings by lantern light.

There were landscapes and animal drawings, plus sketches of circus performers, the trapeze boys in their tights especially detailed. One was of Mother Mercy embracing the world like it was her baby. Garlip stared at that one in silence for a long time. "I miss believing."

"So, maybe you shouldn't have stopped."

"No, it's like missing the way you used to have naps in kindergarten. Some things are just sweet memories."

Then they kissed, at first awkwardly, and then with increasing freedom. About a minute into what was the best make-out session of Barnabas's life, Wickram came around the corner of the house.

"Oops!"

Molten embarrassment shot through Barnabas, and he pulled away from Garlip's lips. But Garlip didn't let him fully out of the embrace, and when Wickram departed, calling over his shoulder, "Back to work, gentlemen," Garlip reeled him back in. He met nervous resistance for a few seconds before Barnabas let himself go and once again fell headlong into ecstasy.

When they finally pulled back, Barnabas felt powerful, drunk with pleasure. "Do you have a boyfriend?"

"Nah, I'm busy learning my craft. I'm not looking for romance. But I'm sorry you're leaving."

The birds were singing now, and the eastern sky was edging from purple to orange when a woman ran up the road, calling, "Maestro! Maestro!" Tragidenko and Sanjani must have been awake, too, because they were out in the yard in a moment.

"Lights on the road," the messenger said. "Heading this way."

"Barnabas, Wickram," Sanjani said. "It's time."

PART IV

SUNDAY

CHAPTER 53

Sanjani and the boys hurried through the woods as the last of night evaporated. Every time Wickram's guitar bumped into a tree, the sound threatened to give them away, and Sanjani shook her head in frustration. In her plan, they were to carry only backpacks filled with essentials, but her son had insisted he couldn't audition on a borrowed guitar. She was grateful Barnabas's only demand was to wear his ridiculous bowler hat. Sanjani knew she couldn't be too strict with them. After all, she was counting on them to be adults in the coming days.

They followed the burbling creek until they reached the stone bridge. The sun had risen, and little glints of illumination were starting to penetrate the gloom of the woods. Sanjani started across, Barnabas at her heels, but then Wickram called, "Wait."

She turned and saw him standing before the bridge. "What's wrong?"

"You don't really know the way back up to the City, do you? You need to be, whatever, helped by those people underground."

"They'll help us, I'm sure."

"What if they don't?" Wickram asked.

"I don't know. But when you are given only one path, you must follow it. Once we're inside—" She stopped. Deep in the woods behind them, a light was blinking in and out behind the trees. Despair crushed her chest like a stone, but there was no time for regret. "Wickram, come. The Aqua Guard have found us." Wickram hurried across the bridge to join her and Barnabas. "Give me your backpack," she told him, crouching on the ground to transfer some of her food and water to his pack and handing some to Barnabas for his.

"Aren't you coming with us?" Barnabas asked, alarm in his voice.

"I have to stay here and keep the Guard occupied." She held up a small, worn book with a soiled cover, just visible in the dawn light. "Do you see this, Pickle?"

Wickram's eyes were wide with fear. "No, wait. Mom, listen to me—"

"No, *you* listen. In this book, I have written the name and phone number of the music school as well your Aunt Kareena's number and address." She put the book in the front pocket of Wickram's backpack and closed the strap securely over it. She couldn't hold back her tears. "Go. Run!"

Barnabas turned back to wave. "Thank you, Sanjani, for everything. We won't let you down."

"Barnabas, please don't tell them about the Valley. The circus, this world, it's all I have." And then the boys were gone, disappearing into the dark pine forest across the river that the light of day had yet to penetrate. Sanjani wiped her tears away with her sleeve and turned to wait for the Aqua Guard.

Soon, she heard heavy footsteps and saw the bushes shaking. But it wasn't the Guard who emerged from the trees. It was a woman in grey, formidable and furious. Carminn.

CHAPTER 54

She was the Speaker of Clouding Guild and proud to helm the most powerful and devout of the guilds. Carminn had a platform from which to speak great truths, and yet so many of the Valley's denizens would not listen. If Clouding Guild were in charge instead of the Guild Council, the Valley would be purer, more tranquil, and mightier. She had dedicated her life to this goal.

But now, mere days before her greatest triumph, she had been stripped of her office and hunted like an animal. It was galling. She had no doubt the situation would be rectified as long as Glower did what he'd promised. The towers would fall, and in the chaos that followed, only she and her inner circle would be ready and able to restore order. Her destiny as Prophet of the Rebuilding would be a certainty. But for that to happen, she had to stop the boy. It should have been easy. He was just a weak City rat. But Carminn saw in this Barnabas creature the tenacious grain of grit that could grind her plan to a halt. Now she was almost upon her quarry, and only the City-born wife of the abominable Tragidenko stood in her way.

"You're too late, Carminn," the woman shouted at her defiantly, standing at the foot of the bridge. "Barnabas and my son are long gone, and there's nothing you can do to stop them."

Carminn tried to remember the woman's name. *Ah, yes...*

"Sanjani, let me pass, and you will not be hurt." She moved slowly and resolutely down the path toward the bridge. Panic flickered in Sanjani's eyes, and she reached down to pick up a fallen branch, a weighty cudgel that could inflict some real damage. Carminn smiled. Motherhood had given her enemy courage beyond her stature. Carminn understood this. She had three children of her own, though she had little time to raise them. Her children might resent her for her absence, but they would someday appreciate what she had sacrificed for them. That, too, was a mother's love.

Carminn didn't slow her advance. Sanjani backed up onto the bridge, swinging the heavy branch in front of her. "Get back! You're a criminal. A murderer." Carminn kept her breath steady. She watched the rhythm of Sanjani's swings. Then, in one swift move, just as the stick changed direction at the end of a swing, Carminn leaped forward and caught it in one big hand. Sanjani cried out as Carminn wrenched the branch away from her and brought it down across her ankles, knocking her to the ground.

But this little mother was not done. With no weapon but savage anger, Sanjani tore at Carminn with her bare hands, trying to stop her crossing the bridge at all costs. Carminn lifted the frail City creature off the ground like a bundle of kindling and tossed her against the stones of the bridge. Her head connected with a sharp crack, and blood pooled on the stones beneath it where she fell. Carminn sent up a short prayer to the Father that the brave little mother not die. Then she turned her back on Sanjani and crossed to the far side of the river.

❖

Barnabas and Wickram ran the twisting path through the forest. The woods were darker here. The brilliant morning sun only just penetrated the dense canopy of pine needles as pinpoints of light in the gloom. They broke from the trees at last and found themselves before the great cliff. Cut into the stone was a cave mouth so black, it looked like an absence cut in the fabric of the world. Wickram paced the ground, his head snapping right and left as if he was expecting an attack at any minute.

"I don't know about this, man," he said.

"It's how your mom came to the Valley, Wick. It has to be okay. Do you think this is how Glower got here, too?"

Wickram ignored the question. "What if we get lost? It's not like there's going to be signs inside saying, 'This way to the City.' We could die in there."

"They'll help us. Sanjani said they would."

Wickram's voice edged closer to hysteria. "That's your plan? Hope for directions from underground demons?"

Barnabas pulled out the flashlight from his backpack and shone the beam into the interior, illuminating damp rock and a narrow, rising path. "Yup, that's my plan." After another moment, as if answering an unasked question, Wickram nodded. Together, they entered the cave.

❖

Carminn followed the forest path until she stood at a cave mouth. Before it, fresh footprints ran helter-skelter. She read in their pattern the boys' fear of the road ahead. Those fears were not unfounded. The fetid smell and the chill, damp air that emanated from the cave seemed like a warning. She thought she heard whispering inside, and a seedling of terror unfurled in her own heart. "Bah!" She spat on the earth. "The Holy Father is architect and site manager. His blueprints guide my life." Unclipping a lantern from her tool belt, she marched into the darkness.

Chapter 55

The air was damp and cold, and the climb a steep one. All the surfaces were slick, and the boys each fell more than once. Wickram, protecting his guitar, took the most painful falls. As they walked, the walls of the path grew closer together, the ceiling lower, until Wickram had to hunch over just to walk. He complained loudly, but Barnabas, in the lead, was in far worse shape.

He wasn't sure what was happening, but as the walls pressed closer, and the darkness consumed all but the flashlight's narrow beam, Barnabas felt a terrible sense of dread grab hold of him. He finally stopped dead, listening to his loud breathing and the pounding of his heart.

"What's wrong?" Wickram asked. "It's too soon for a break."

"I dunno. I-I feel really crappy. It's like…like the walls are going to squash us." He looked back the way they had come, but the cave's entrance was too far behind them to be seen. He was encased in rock. Buried alive.

Wickram gave him a little push. "Come on, we have a long way to go."

Barnabas nodded and pulled his bowler hat down more snugly. *I'll just have to tough it out*, he told himself. *The City is depending on us.* He began to climb the steep path again. Suddenly, he remembered feeling the same sickening unease in the narrow corridor in Clouding Guild. It was much worse deep underground. He tried to distract himself, counting his steps in batches of a hundred. But then Wickram's guitar would tap against the wall, and the echo of the strings would make Barnabas lose count. The squashing feeling immediately returned.

After what seemed a very long time, they came to an intersection, the two choices apparently identical.

"Which way do we go?" Wickram asked as Barnabas shone the light first up one, then the other.

"The one on the right is steeper," Barnabas said. "Let's go that way." *And we'll be up and out of this hell faster!*

The steep path was hard going, but Barnabas's panic was now driving him forward with determination. Then they came to another intersection. Shining the light down each of the two paths, he was overcome with doubt.

"What do we do?" He could hear the fear in his own voice.

"I dunno. Hold your flashlight down the left tunnel again. Look, isn't that another split up ahead?"

"I think you're right. Oh, God." Barnabas started doing the math. "We already made one choice. That's a fifty percent chance we're already wrong. After the next choice, we're seventy-five percent likely to be wrong and after that—"

"We're lost underground," Wickram said.

"Forever."

Panic consumed Barnabas utterly. He turned around and ran back the way they had come, falling frequently on the steep, slippery slope, but jumping to his feet each time to race downward, gripped by fear.

Wickram, shouted after him, "Slow down, Barn! Don't go all spinning dog on me!"

But Barnabas wasn't slowing down, and when he got back to the first intersection, it was all he could do to stop himself from running the rest of the way down the tunnel and back out into the forest. There had to be some other way they could get to the City. He jumped when Wickram laid a hand on his shoulder.

"Hey, hey, Barn. Easy, man. Sit down, take deep breaths."

Barnabas found himself complying, putting his head between his knees to hide from the unending darkness. If only he could catch his breath, he would scream. Wickram kept rubbing his back, talking in soothing tones, and after a minute, the sharpness of the panic receded.

"Better?" asked Wickram. "You're claustrophobic, Barn. It happens to some people in Furrowing Guild. They can't stand it down in the mines. They have to join other guilds. You didn't know you had it?"

"I was never underground like this before. Not in any caves or anything."

"Okay, well, it's good we stopped. We gotta figure out how we're going to navigate." Barnabas shone the flashlight up one tunnel and then the next, looking for anything that might help.

"Hey!" Barnabas shouted, which caused Wickram to shout in return.

"Glory! What?"

"I–I saw something that way." He shone the flashlight up the left path, the one they had originally skipped.

"What kind of something?"

Barnabas turned off the light. The darkness closed in, making his heart beat faster, but he willed himself to be calm. He turned back to where the now-invisible left path was, and he saw it again—two glowing, red lights. The way they moved together made them look like a pair of eyes! He shone the flashlight up the tunnel, but there was nothing there. Only when he shut off the beam and waited a few seconds did the red eyes return.

This time Wickram saw them too. "Holy Mother Mercy, something is lurking up there. It's them."

Barnabas whispered. "What do we do?"

"We obviously don't go up the path with the red-eyed demons."

Barnabas really wanted to agree with this logic, but he couldn't. "No, your mom said they would help us. We…" He swallowed audibly. "We have to go toward whatever that is."

Barnabas turned the flashlight on, but again, nothing was there. The incline was shallower than the first path, and they reached another intersection after a few minutes.

"Now what?" Wickram asked. Barnabas turned off the flashlight. Up the path to the right, he saw not one, but two sets of eyes. He turned on the flashlight and led Wickram that way. After a few more such choices, Barnabas was feeling confident about their system. On the other hand, the number of figures lurking in the dark grew with each turning. He had to wonder if they weren't just wilfully following some carnivorous predator straight into its lair.

"Are they even human?" Wickram asked.

"Am I the expert here?" And then the flashlight's beam began to flicker. Barnabas gave it a whack with the palm of his hand, and it stayed on for a few more seconds before failing completely. "Shit!"

"Just keep going," Wickram said.

Barnabas stumbled forward in the dark, Wickram repeatedly stepping on his heels. "Watch it."

"In case you didn't notice, it's pitch black in here."

"Put your hand on my shoulder."

Wickram did and they continued forward, feeling their way along the walls in grim silence. "How's the claustrophobia going, Barn?"

"Thanks for reminding me. I kind of want to throw up." Barnabas noticed his voice was echoing, and a draft was moving across his face. He reached in front and to the sides, but he could feel no walls. They had entered a large chamber. He made himself perfectly still and opened his senses wide, taking in small shufflings, a snort, and a smell—dank, rank, and alive. In front of him, not more than five feet away, a pair of red eyes opened. And then another to his left, and then more and more until there were tens, hundreds. In the diffuse pink light of all those eyes, Barnabas could just see the movement of furry beings.

"Krump!" Wickram breathed. "Say something."

"Hi," Barnabas called out, the echo circling all around. "We were wondering if you could show us the way up to the City."

A hand grabbed his upper arm. It had sharp nails that dug into his flesh. He only had time to say, "Wait!" before he and Wickram were hustled forward, out of the big cave and back into one of the claustrophobic tunnels. After a few minutes of this forced march, they were pushed to the ground. Wickram's guitar reverberated as it banged against the rock. Heart pounding, Barnabas circled on his hands and knees until he had determined they were in a closed cell, smooth stone all around them and a low ceiling above their heads. He couldn't even find whatever door they had been pushed through.

CHAPTER 56

Carminn climbed through the tunnels resolutely, lighting her way with an electric lantern. At intersections, she made notations on the rock wall with a piece of chalk. Were the tunnels natural or organized by a human mind, she wondered. The design seemed haphazard, but that wasn't surprising. She couldn't expect some subterranean animals to think with the same logic as a child of Father Glory. She stood at an intersection, pondering her route, when she suddenly heard a whisper.

"Who's there?" she called, repressing the nervous shiver in her breast with an iron will.

There was no answer, but she decided to walk in the direction of the whisper. Her lantern blinked on and off and abruptly died. Cursing quietly, she knelt in the tunnel. She took a small candle and dry matches from a sealed compartment of her tool belt. Only four matches. She had forgotten to replenish, a foolish mistake. She reassured herself with words of scripture: "When the darkest hour comes, a single match will reveal your destiny."

With the candle dancing on the floor of the tunnel, she opened the lantern and cleaned the battery contacts, wet with condensation. The lantern flickered again to life. The whispers grew louder and more insistent as she continued on her way.

"Yes, yes, I'm coming. If you had any decency, you would show yourselves."

But no sooner had she said that than the tunnel opened up into a wide cave. Shining her light all around, she saw a vast space with ledges and walkways of stone at different levels. The high ceiling was a gallery of dripping stalactites. Tunnel mouths opened everywhere, suggesting the whole underground world was complex as an anthill. But there was no one there.

Her lantern sputtered and died again. Suddenly the cave was alive with dozens of red eyes and the sound of shifting bodies. She was tempted to light the candle again to see who these primitives might be, but the darkness which felt so oppressive to her seemed to make them feel safer. Fine, her faith and fortitude could carry her through.

"The blessings of Father Glory upon you, great congregation!" she called. "I am Carminn, Speaker of—" She stopped. She saw no reason not to embody her new role here and now. "I am Carminn, Prophet of the Rebuilding. It is clearly the will of the Great Father that I should meet you today, at the dawn of the new age."

Carminn looked around at the blinking red eyes. Did they even comprehend her words?

"I presume you know of the City that rises over your heads, and of the millions of lost souls who walk its streets. In two days, the great towers of that city are destined to fall, as fell the giants of old. The earth will shake with their collapse, and the air will be filled with cries of anguish. Such is the will of the Holy Father. But in the wake of this tragedy, a world of purity and pious humility will be born. Do you feel the strength of Father Glory flowing in your veins? I do!"

She let forth a great moan of satisfaction. The assembled horde had grown very still. Were they listening to her revelations?

"But I am sad to inform you that here in your mighty halls, there are two unbelievers, children who would derail the Holy Engine before it can enter the Station of Grace."

Whispers, the shuffling of bodies. They *were* listening to her. "In the name of the Holy Father and his great future, I ask you to bring those deluded young men to me. I will lead them back to the Valley, where we will kneel together and pray for strength in the coming time of tribulations." It was better, she knew, to say this than speak the truth. The boys had to die, but these coarse and credulous creatures might not understand the subtleties of faith and service.

Carminn gasped when a heavy arm descended on her shoulder. She turned and stared into the creature's red eyes. It led her away, and she felt a moment's fear. But she believed in her Glory-granted powers of oratory. The Father would open their ears and grant her what she asked for.

Chapter 57

Barnabas woke confused from a troubled sleep. At first, he thought he had gone blind, but then he realized he was still in the stone cell, staring into absolute dark.

"Wickram?" he said huskily, then louder, an edge of panic in his voice. "Wickram!"

"Wha…?" Wickram snorted. There was a pause. "Oh."

Adrenaline spiked through Barnabas's body. He was trapped under a thousand tons of rock in a room with no door. The horrible grip of claustrophobia squeezed his mind and body. He groaned miserably.

Out of the thick, inky darkness, Wickram asked, "How long have we been asleep?"

"I don't know. What are we gonna do?" he whimpered, tears rolling down his cheeks. They would die here underground. The towers would fall, and Barnabas was powerless to prevent it. A stupid, embarrassing sob escaped, and he hit the ground with his fist in aggravation.

"Hey, hey, Barn, don't worry. Let's just…I dunno…take stock." Barnabas heard him moving around, and then the boy was right beside him, putting a big comforting hand on his shoulder.

"Where's your backpack?" Wickram asked, his voice remarkably gentle. "Oh, I got it." He took out fruit, bread, and water, and they ate in silence.

"So," Wickram said, as if this were a picnic under a cloud-dotted sky. "You and Garlip, huh?"

The darkness hid Barnabas's blush. "Maybe? I barely know him."

"But you liked kissing him? That's cool water. There are a bunch of inverts in the circus. It's one of the things Clouding hates."

"Doesn't bother you? About me, I mean?"

"Why would it? Means you're not actually interested in my girl."

Barnabas was going to correct him, but instead he said, "You know, you're the most confusing guy in the world."

Wickram laughed. "Flamtasmic. Do I get an award?"

"No, seriously, in the last two days, you've been this enthusiastic tour guide, then you were a jealous, drunken creep who punched me, and now you're being all…well, really nice."

"So, you're saying I should choose one personality and run with it?"

"This one's okay," he said with an unseen smile. "I like kissing Garlip. I hope we do more if we get the chance. But you're my friend."

"Same, man. Hey, I just found your little ball toy. What does it do?"

"It makes monsters."

"Oh yeah? We could use some of those to fight our way through the red-eye dudes."

"I can't figure out how to use it. Shit." The panicky tightness of the room was starting to overwhelm him again. "I have to get out of here, Wickram."

"Easy, Barn. Just lie down and relax." Wickram tuned his guitar. He started with an undulating river of arpeggiated chords, but then a melody began to take shape. Barnabas felt his panic recede a little.

"I wish my brother Thelonius was here. We need someone brave like him."

Still playing, Wickram said, "What makes him so brave?"

"Well, for one thing, he's part of this group called the Junior Sherlocks. They solve mysteries and go places you're not supposed to. A 'No Entry' sign is like an invitation to them."

"Huh."

"What?"

"Well, that sounds like you. You snuck into the Drop Shop, into the Clouding steam works…"

"That's not the same. The Drop Shop was Graviddy's idea. And I had no choice about Clouding. I needed to get proof for the Council."

"If you say so." He switched back to the soothing arpeggios.

Then he stopped playing. Barnabas looked up and saw the red eyes of a dozen lurkers, peering from a corridor where a solid wall had stood. Whispering in their hissing tongue, the lurkers retreated back down the tunnel. Barnabas sat up urgently, afraid the cell would close around them again.

"Don't go!" he cried. "Wickram, we're going to follow them. Keep playing."

Like some surreal parade, they followed the shadowed figures through the dark tunnels. Wickram brought up the rear, playing a dissonant marching song. Soon, they were back in the cool, echoing cavern.

"Play them another song."

"No, you have to talk to them."

"But it's you they want to hear."

"Barn, if you don't talk our way out, they'll just keep us as entertainment, bring me out once a day to perform. And if that happens, I hope you can tap dance or something."

"Okay, okay, I'll talk to them."

Thankfully, his claustrophobia wasn't as bad under this high ceiling, and he could gather his thoughts. A hundred or more pairs of eyes stared his way. *Well, I have their attention.*

"Hello, uh, Lurkers," he said as Wickram continued to play. "My name is Barnabas Bopwright. We're sorry to, you know, invade your home like this. It's the only way we can get back to the City. You see, someone wants to do something bad up there. And a lot of people will be hurt, and even die. I know the two of us don't look like much, but we're the only ones who can stop Glower from destroying the towers."

They had no idea what a Glower was or maybe even a tower. He was making a mess of it. Even if the Lurkers did let them go, everything else felt impossible. He wasn't any kind of hero. But then Barnabas thought about what Wickram said, that maybe he was like Thelonius after all. Okay, what did he have going for him? Not height, not muscles, not the smartest brain in the world. But he had friends and a mission. And a voice.

With more confidence, he said, "I don't know what you believe in or what's important to you. All I know is everywhere I go, I see people trying to live their lives. And everyone's worried. The kids are worried about what the world will be like when they grow up. The adults are worried what will happen to their kids. And sure, there are bullies like Glower and Carminn everywhere, but also people who are good, even if they sometimes mess stuff up."

Wickram stopped playing his song. "Barn, enough with the sermons. Just tell them what you want."

"Oh, right. Uh, so please—*please*—help us get through your tunnels so we can save the City."

The gathering of red eyes blinked out, and Barnabas's heart sank. They were gone, His words hadn't convinced them.

"Barn, look." High up the cavern wall and off to the left, in one of the many cave mouths, a light was flashing on and off.

"That's it," Barnabas breathed. "That's the way out, Wickram. Let's go." They stumbled their way up unseen paths toward the light.

CHAPTER 58

Carminn sat on a rock in the small chamber where the creatures had brought her. Presumably they were off somewhere in their labyrinthine world deciding whether to follow her or not. With nothing to do but wait, she lit her candle and got her lantern working again. That done, she ate the musty stew of grubs and pale roots the creatures had given her and washed it down with cold, clear water from a nearby pool. An hour later, the lantern died again. The moment the darkness closed in, a set of the red eyes appeared before her.

"Don't be afraid, child," Carminn said. "My Lord accepts all who are prepared to dedicate the strength of their limbs to His glorious works."

Feeling her way along the walls, she followed the creature back to the main cave. The congregation of red eyes looked down from the rocks above. She felt rough material on a rock before her and used her second to last match to again light the candle. It was a cloak of woven mosses, and on top of it lay a twisted ring of roots which she understood was a crown. She was moved by the gesture and put on the primitive vestments with a show of reverence. The red eyes stared down from the darkness, and Carminn felt a rush of motherly affection for the simple creatures.

"My children," she said, "I thank you for this honour, and I am grateful to be the one who will open your eyes to the brilliant light of Father Glory. When the towers have fallen, and the great rebuilding commences, I will send missionaries here to teach you. Your lives will at last know purpose."

Sensing it was time to show them her natural authority, Carminn let the smile drop from her face. "But now, you must help me. Bring me to the boys so I may stop their wrongheaded interference in the Holy Plan."

The creatures whispered, then the red eyes winked out two by two. Carminn sensed she was alone. From a cave mouth on the right, at the lowest level of the chamber, a light began blinking.

"That is my path?" she asked. No answer came. She tried her lantern, but it was dead. Raising her candle, she hurried to the cave mouth. Inside, she descended through a long corridor of sleek rock, her candle like the last star in a dying universe. At the first intersection, she saw another beacon winking on and off down one of the two paths. Negotiating intersection after intersection in this fashion, Carminn plunged ever deeper into the underworld.

She was almost running now, shielding the candle's flame with her other hand. How far ahead were the boys? She mustn't lose them. The taste of the stew still fouled her mouth. The fetid smell of the moss cloak and the scratch of the crown on her head grew more and more unbearable. She threw them down and hurried on, not stopping to wonder why she was descending instead of climbing.

An errant breeze blew out her candle after the seventh or eighth intersection, and she stopped dead, the only sound that of her breathing. A voice inside her said, *Sister, go no farther—this is the path of doom.* But she could not retrace her steps. She had forgotten to mark the turnings as she had when she first entered this infernal world. Fear took hold, and she made herself remember the teachings in the Book of Precepts and Perceptions: "Do not doubt the Father's path. Follow his blueprint and you will never be lost."

She descended into the darkness, hands stretched out in front of her. The ceiling grew lower, grazing the top of her head, and she was forced to crouch. Then her outstretched hands hit a wall. She felt her way to the left, but there she found another wall. The same to her right.

"I went the wrong way at the last turning," she said out loud, trying to quell her growing fear.

Carminn turned around and started forward, but somehow a sheer wall of rock was there, too. Rock walls in every direction. Feeling her way in the dark cell, she kicked into something that clattered like a pile of sticks. She stumbled and fell, scraping her arm as she landed on it. She cursed. With shaking hands, she pulled out the last of her matches and struck it, filling the tight space with the choke of sulphur.

Through watering eyes, she examined her prison, its closed surface of smooth stone. She looked down at the clattering sticks she had kicked. They weren't sticks; they were bones, the skeletons of unlucky travellers who had died here. A moan escaped her lips, and the match, its life nearly spent, burned her fingers. She dropped it to the damp floor where it sputtered out.

Carminn sat in the absolute blackness of her unintended sarcophagus, and the words of Father Glory rang in her ears. *When the darkest hour comes, a single match will reveal your destiny.*

CHAPTER 59

"I can't take this anymore," Barnabas said. They had been climbing in the darkness, following the Lurkers' beacons for what seemed hours. The terrible feeling of the walls closing in on him never let up.

Even Wickram's bottomless well of enthusiasm sounded a bit ragged. "We're almost there, Barn."

"That's what you said an hour ago." But the only way out of his claustrophobic misery was up. One step and the next, and the next…

"Hey," Wickram called. "Check it out."

"Another beacon? Must be the next intersection."

"This one's different. It's red."

Barnabas tilted back his bowler hat and looked up. Squinting into the distance, he saw the distant red, rectangular light. Despite his exhaustion, he began to run on stiff legs. Soon he was close enough to see it clearly. It was a blissfully familiar sign, emblazoned with the word EXIT.

The illuminated exit sign hung above an ordinary steel door, painted a dull industrial beige. The door would have looked utterly normal if it hadn't been fitted into a wall of rough-hewn stone at the end of a long stone tunnel. The sight was so incongruous that Barnabas laughed. He turned the shiny doorknob, and the door swung inward. Holding it open, he looked back at Wickram in bewilderment. Wickram just shrugged and walked through. They were in a nondescript hallway with beige walls and acoustic tile on the ceiling. The other doors in the hallway had signs that read B-15 and B-17. They were in the basement of a City building.

Barnabas let go of the door, and it swung closed, locking itself with a click. He turned back to read the sign on this amazing, ordinary door that led down to the secret Valley of hidden wonders. It read "No Entry."

PART V

MONDAY

CHAPTER 60

"Ground floor," said the mellifluous automated voice. "Going up." The doors slid open, and bright light from the crowded lobby poured into the elevator.

"Let's go," Barnabas said.

But Wickram hesitated. "Wait. Is that the whole trip?"

"Yeah, we went from the basement to the lobby."

Wickram began fingering the elevator buttons, smiling in surprise as they lit up under his fingers. "Does this mean there are twenty-six storeys in the building? Can we go to the top?"

Grumpy morning people were pushing into the elevator. Barnabas grabbed Wickram's arm and dragged him out into the lobby. "Come on, we're in a hurry," he said, but now he was smiling, too. The sight of people in business attire carrying briefcases and KonaBoom Coffee cups while they scrolled through their phones filled Barnabas with sweet relief. He was home.

He turned and saw Wickram stumbling behind him, muttering "Oops," and "Sorry!" every few steps, and pirouetting to avoid collisions in the onrushing crowd. The guy at the security desk was watching them suspiciously, and Barnabas steered them through the revolving doors out onto the sidewalk. He caught sight of their reflections in the building's shiny, steel siding. They were dirty, dishevelled, and slightly wild-eyed from their twenty-four hours underground.

Barnabas pulled his phone from his backpack and powered it up. The battery was down to a nerve-shredding three percent. The time was ten after eight, and he had twenty-three text messages and fourteen voicemails. Twenty-one of the texts were from his mom, and he figured the voicemails must be too. He bit his lip guiltily and decided not to think about it. He dialled Deni. Three rings, four… *Please don't go to voicemail!*

"Barnabas!" Deni screamed.

"Yeah, I'm—"

"Oh my God, your mother keeps phoning here, and I had to program both *my* moms' phones to forward her calls to me. And if she texts me during class—"

"Deni, listen!" Barnabas shouted. "This is an emergency, and I'm about to run out of charge. We're on our way to your place." He did a quick calculation in his head. "We'll be there at eight forty-five. You'll have to be late for school, sorry."

"What do you mean 'we'? What kind of emergen—" His phone died.

"Phew, that was close. Okay, Wick, we're going to—" He turned and stared at his friend, whose eyes were darting wildly from face to face as the crowd swept by him. His mouth was working silently, his arms wrapped protectively around his guitar. "Come on, Wickram," he said gently. "I think this is Greyshiver Street. We can pick up a Blue Line train on the far side of Gumber square."

"How do you…how do you get in?"

"Into what?"

"The walking, all the people! How do you step in?"

Barnabas had never thought about it before. It was just something he'd always known. "Look, put a hand on my shoulder and move when I do." They set off, but it was like pulling a wagon that didn't always turn the way you thought it would. Barnabas wished he could call a rideshare, but his phone was dead. They crossed at the lights, and as they reached the less crowded far sidewalk, he heard Wickram gasp.

What now? Barnabas turned and saw the great skyscrapers of the Tower District, sticking into the air like the splayed fingers of some mighty earth god. The boys stared in silence. The towers had always represented strength and permanence to Barnabas. Now, he could only imagine them bursting into flames, teetering and tumbling backward down the cliff.

As Barnabas navigated them down into the subway, he was unusually conscious of all his well-rehearsed City routines. After his five days in the strangeness of the Valley, they seemed like superpowers. In contrast, Wickram tripped getting on his first ever escalator. He kept stumbling into people's paths on the platform, and almost got mangled by the closing subway doors.

When they reached Deni's building, the doorman didn't recognize him at first.

"Oh, it's Barnabas. You look…um…" The man turned away tactfully. "I'll ring up to Ms. Jiver and tell her you're here."

Wickram excitedly watched the floor numbers in the elevator

change. "Remember what your mom told us before we left?" Barnabas asked him.

"Something about clean underwear?"

"No, she said don't tell anyone about the Valley. Just say you met me at one of my dad's shows."

"Your dad does shows? I don't remember you telling—"

The elevator door opened, and Deni stood before them in the hallway. She screamed, and Barnabas thought her reaction seemed a little rehearsed.

"What have you been *doing*?" she shouted. "Who in the world is *this*? And what in the name of sanity have you got on your head?"

"It's a bowler hat," Wickram said. "Cool, right?"

Barnabas did the introductions. "Wickram, Deni. Now can you let us in before anyone sees us?"

She nodded. "Yeah, you look like pickpockets from *Oliver Twist*."

As soon as they were inside, Barnabas shrugged off his backpack and collapsed into a low canvas chair in the front hall. Wickram, meanwhile, handed Barnabas his guitar and moved right into living room, looking around, exclaiming, "Wow!" and "Quality!" He leafed through thick, glossy magazines on the coffee table—esoteric journals of political thought and interior design—and then found a dimmer panel on the wall and began to play with the lights.

"I really like your dorm," he said.

Deni blinked in confusion and said to Barnabas, "Explain *that*."

"It's complicated." Barnabas let loose a huge yawn. All the hours of climbing through the domain of the Lurkers had finally caught up with him.

Wickram returned, carrying a small prehistoric fertility figurine, moulded in bright red plastic.

"What's this?" he asked, turning it slowly in his hands, examining its wide hips and heavy breasts. "You have a whole box of them."

"They were give-aways at a women's health fundraiser," Deni explained, a little flustered. "Keep it. Look, my moms will be gone all day, so you can hang out here. But I have go to school now, at least for the morning. What do you need?"

"Food," said Wickram.

"Sleep," said Barnabas. "And can we shower, Deni?"

"Yes!" Wickram shouted in agreement. "And do you have any clean clothes?"

"Oh, and a charger," Barnabas added, holding up his dead phone.

"Right," Deni answered matter-of-factly, taking his phone. "Follow." Passing the kitchen, she said, "Anything you want from the fridge, *except* the stuff in the Sigram's Deli bags—that's for a candidate's fundraiser here tonight." From the linen closet, she pulled out two big, fluffy towels and handed them to the boys. They followed her into her bedroom, where she plugged Barnabas's phone into a charge station.

"You can sleep on my bed." She wrinkled her nose at them. "I'll change the sheets later. Boys' clothes, I'm afraid, are at a premium in our household. I'll see what I can dig up at school. Anything else?"

"No. You're a life saver, Deni," Barnabas said.

"I'll be back at one, and then I need to know everything. Everything!"

As soon as she was gone, they ate ravenously and took turns enjoying long, luxurious showers. Barnabas collapsed into Deni's bed beside the already comatose Wickram, and sleep immediately dragged him down like quicksand.

CHAPTER 61

Three hours later, Barnabas snapped back to consciousness shouting the word "Glower!" He didn't know where or when he was. Somewhere nearby, he heard jazz music and the sound of a familiar laugh. The heavy grip of sleep started pulling him back under, so he forced himself to sit up. He followed a strange path of associations back to reality:

Joan Miró print on the wall…like something Deni would have… wait, she *does* have that print…oh, this is her room…this is her bed… did I have sex with Deni and I can't remember it…? No, I was sleeping with Wickram…I was *what*…? no, not like that…Lurkers…Valley… blow up the towers… "*Glower!*" he shouted again, and this time woke up all the way.

The laughter in the next room stopped and people entered the bedroom—Deni, Wickram, and then Cal Kabaway, the source of the familiar laughter.

"What did you just say?" Deni asked, sitting down in her desk chair.

Barnabas pulled the sheet up around his naked shoulders. He was not enjoying this new trend of waking up half-naked in people's beds. Wickram sat on the end of the bed and began tuning his guitar. He was dressed in a brand-new set of brown and blue sweats with a matching baseball cap bearing the old logo of the Sky High School of Youthful Enthusiasm.

"Barnabas is shouting about George Glower," he explained to Deni and Cal. "He runs the Drop Shop. It's this store full of flamtasmic haul, except that he turns out to be skull-cracked and lethal." He began practising scales, his fingers spidering up and down the fretboard.

Cal, still at the door, laughed again. "Barnabas, your friend here is really entertaining. I don't understand anything he says. Something about circuses and a steam-powered cathedral." Cal was leaning nonchalantly against the door frame like he owned the place. Barnabas, who had been coming here since he was a little kid, found this irritating "Going back to my game, Deni," Cal said, leaving the room.

"Here," Deni said, handing Barnabas a set of sweats that matched Wickram's.

"What are these?" he asked as he dressed under the sheet.

"Track team uniforms from when the school first opened."

"Our school had a track team?"

"No, they just ordered the uniforms. The team never happened. They've been sitting in boxes down in the storeroom all these years, waiting to be plundered." He dropped the sheet, and she gave him a once-over. "Score! I got your sizes right. Do you want the matching hat?"

"I'll skip it."

"Good call. So, we've been trying to get some deets on your week with your dad," she said, "but Wickram is a little hard to follow. Where exactly did you go?"

Barnabas opened his mouth to answer. He had spent the last few days wishing he could discuss everything with Deni—the Valley, Carminn, Glower and the plot to blow up the towers. He knew how happy she would be. At age fifteen, she would be a rookie journalist with the scoop of the century. But Sanjani had told him not to tell anyone about the Valley.

The jazz record was still playing in the next room—some woman singing in a bluesy moan, and a tenor saxophone answering her, which he was sure must have been Brownbag Bopwright himself.

"Well," he said, "Dad played three different cities. We saw the sights, caught up with each other. I was shy around him at first, but it was special. Dad-son time. I'm sure you would have got more out of the music than me, but—"

"Oh, the music was brilliant," Wickram said, getting into the spirit. "I didn't know the trumpet could make sounds like that."

"Saxophone," Barnabas said quickly.

Wickram nodded. "Right, what I meant." The relentless scales were getting annoying.

Deni's face dissolved into a dewy look. "You are just so lucky. But what does it have to do with Wickram's circus and red-eyed people underground?"

"Ignore him," Barnabas said, giving him a sharp look. "He just has an amazing imagination. Wickram's here in the City to audition for a music school."

Deni's expression shifted from dewy fan into curious journalist. "But you said there was an emergency. And what's a 'glower'?"

"George Glower," Wickram said.

"Oh yeah. We met this George Glower guy on tour. He's friends with the mayor and wants us to bring him a message. Something important about the election." Barnabas's current and only plan was to get to Mayor Tuppletaub and tell him what Carminn and Glower were up to.

Deni screwed up her lips. "Are you sure this Glower isn't just another figment of guitar boy's imagination?"

Barnabas scrambled out of bed and retrieved his phone. "I have pictures of him. This is Glower in the steam works at Clouding…um, it's sort of a branch of the municipal steam works. Never mind. What's important is—"

"That's not George Glower," she said.

Barnabas froze in confusion. "What? Yes, it is. I took this picture." Wickram stopped playing.

Deni snatched the phone from his hand and flipped through the pictures. "No, I know this man. He was here in this apartment when I was just a kid. This was even before he ran for Mayor. Mom-Morgan was setting up a foundation, and she thought he would be useful for fundraising. You know, given his name."

"His name is George Glower," Barnabas said.

"No, it's George Glorvanious."

Barnabas's brain did a backflip. "Glorvanious? As in Lawrence Glorvanious, the great mayor?"

"Lawrence's great-grandson, yeah. Hold on." Deni turned to the laptop on her desk and did a search. "Here. In the *City Courier*, seven… no eight years ago. 'Glorvanious Campaign Collapses after Last-Minute Surge by Rival Dudley.' If I remember correctly, George was the favourite in the mayoral race, but there was some scandal in the last week of the campaign—illegal donations or something—and he tanked on Election Day. I was eight. That was when I got interested in municipal politics."

Barnabas looked over her shoulder at the screen. Beneath the headline was a picture of the person he knew as Glower, only younger and dressed in a suit and tie. The weirdest thing was the smile plastered across his face. It was hard to imagine George Glower of the Drop Shop ever smiling. Although now that Barnabas looked more closely, the smile was more like some uncanny special effect—mirthless and cold, manufactured for the camera.

"Oh my God," Barnabas said, peering over at Wickram. "It's him."

"That's not all," Deni continued. "The night of the election, he disappeared. His campaign staff said he was sick, acting strange. Then he was just gone. Poof! And no one has seen him since."

"That works, Barn," Wickram said. "The Drop Shop opened back when I was nine."

The sound of gunfire and screaming monsters erupted from the living room. Wickram started in fear, and Deni said, "It's just Cal. We have a new ImmersionStation 4D and Cal's on it all the time, gunning down the undead."

Wickram's eyes widened more. "The 4D? With Shatterclash Integrated Sound Intrusion?"

"Uh, I think so?"

Wickram threw his guitar onto the bed and ran for the living room. Barnabas was replaying the words "Cal's on it all the time" in his head. He'd only been in the Valley four days. How could Cal already be a fixture in Deni's house?

Deni said, "I can't believe Glorvanious is back and that you ran into him. Small world."

"It's starting to feel like it."

"Isn't it illegal to vanish like that? Maybe you should go to the police."

"No, I have to talk to the mayor. He'll know what to do with this, um, secret message."

She grabbed him by the shoulders and shook him. "Your vague vagueness is driving me crazy. Okay, give me five minutes. I have to send Calvin back to school."

Alone for the moment, Barnabas looked at himself in Deni's closet mirror. In the team track suit, he looked kind of like a lanky athlete, strong and competent. Maybe he *could* save the City, after all! Buoyed by this bit of rented confidence, he strode into the living room, just in time to see Deni, attached mouth to mouth with Cal.

CHAPTER 62

The blues singer on the record was crooning, "Black velvet nights, and my lonely life…" while Brownbag Bopwright answered her with a broken-hearted sax lick. The vinyl melancholia was punctuated by the screams of zombies and the crackle of machine gun fire from the big TV where Wickram was playing a game with clueless enthusiasm.

Barnabas felt a burning surge of humiliation, and his new-found confidence blew away like a fart in a tornado. He slunk over to the foyer to collect his backpack, but it wasn't closed right, and with one careless gesture, books, pens and the last of Sanjani's snacks spilled onto the floor. Then the diaboriku bounced out and rolled into the living room, where Calvin interrupted the ongoing kiss to put a foot on it.

"Hey," he said, bending to pick up the device. "It's your monster machine. Did you ever figure out how to work it?" He tossed it to Barnabas, who almost missed the catch.

"Of course." The lie burned his throat. "And for your information, I *also* kissed someone this weekend. Two people."

Shut up, idiot, he chided himself. And it didn't help when Wickram shouted over his game, "Three, actually." Barnabas's face grew hot.

"Impressed," said Cal, breezing past him on his way out the door. He called out, "Keep fighting, Wickram."

"I keep dying!"

"And good luck with your top-secret emergency, Barnabas. Bye, baby," he said to Deni, slamming the door on his way out, something Barnabas would never have done. He stared at his oldest friend, who was busy putting the jazz record away, deliberately not catching his eye.

"'Bye, baby'? *Baby?*" Barnabas said in an icy voice. He started re-packing his bag with quick, angry movements. "Seriously, Deni, I've been gone four days. When did all this happen?"

"Well, if you really want to know, it was your fault. Or, I mean, I have you to thank for helping me find *true love*." He followed her into the kitchen, where she poured them glasses of orange juice. "The day you left, Barnabas, I was such a mess because of the interview. And Calvin took me to the coffee shop and got me a Kona float with organic vanilla bean ice cream. He just really *listened*, you know? He has a sensitive soul. That's because he's known a lot of pain in his life."

"I'll get my mom to set up a charity for him."

"Wait, are you mad because you know Cal is—?"

"No. Of course not," he snapped. "Listen, Deni, I have to get an important message to Mayor Tuppletaub."

She instantly forgot all the Cal drama. "Barnabas, you need to tell me everything about *everything*, right now."

"I can't. I promised."

"Hmm, too bad you're being so difficult. Because I know exactly where Tuppletaub's going to be this afternoon."

"Wait, really?"

"The Executive Committee of City Council is meeting at three. Last session before the election."

"How do you know that?"

"Mom-Morgan is working for the utilities chief on his re-election campaign. Look at that printout on the wall behind you. That's his schedule for the whole week."

Barnabas examined the busy grid. Executive Committee: 1500 hours. The utilities chief, he noted, was also fully booked on Wednesday, and Barnabas could only think how all those meetings would be abruptly cancelled if Glower—no, Glorvanious—succeeded in his Tuesday plans.

"So," Deni said, slurping her juice, not taking her eyes off him. "You need to get into that meeting to bring Tuppletaub a crucial message from his unlikely friend, George Glorvanious, who vanished mysteriously eight years ago but reappeared at one of your dad's gigs. Have I got that right? Is it a message about *secret subways*?"

"You heard the mayor. There are no secret subways."

She actually wagged her finger at him. "Fine, I'll let you get away with that for now, but after you talk to Tuppletaub, Mr. Bopwright, you will tell me everything you learned. *And* about these three people you kissed."

"Deal. But how will you get me into the meeting?"

She flipped a thumb in the direction of the living room where the war against the zombies continued. "Is he really good on that guitar?"

"Really, really good."

"Exec Committee sometimes starts their meeting with local entertainment. They're trying to look like they care about the arts. Mom-Morgan could talk them into a little concert by one of the City's young prodigies before they tackle gridlock strategies."

"Oh my God, you're a genius." He jumped forward and hugged her.

"But after…"

"I'll tell you everything, I promise."

A sound like a nuclear explosion demolishing a city came from the living room, followed by a horrible cry from Wickram. "Oh, no, I died again."

"And him," Deni said, pinching the bridge of her nose. "You'll explain him."

Chapter 63

They took the Green Line subway to City Hall Station and exited up to the Civic Plaza, right at the feet of a huge statue.

"Whoa, who's that?" Wickram asked.

"Lawrence Glorvanious," Barnabas told him. "The mayor who dreamed up the City. And if I have this figured out, the one who secretly set up the Valley as the place that does the City's dirty work."

It was an impressive sculpture in bronze. The great mayor, four times life-sized, wore a stylish suit and a miner's helmet with a big headlight. Leaning on a shovel, he stared off into a prosperous future. At his feet was a miniature of the new City as it would soon be built. A plaque on the base read: "We are ever grateful."

"Glorvanious...," Wickram said. "That's a name I'm hearing a lot today. He looks like Father Glory." Barnabas considered this. It was true. "Listen, Barn, this is one of the songs I'm auditioning with." He dropped his baseball hat to the ground, shook out his hair and tuned up his guitar. "It's called 'The Father's Promise.'" He began playing a beautiful anthem, and a woman passing by dropped some coins into this hat. Wickram stopped in surprise and bent to examine the money. "Hey, they like me in the City. Maybe I'll be playing the Manhammer Audiodome sooner than I thought."

At the far end of the Civic Plaza's expanse of black paving stones stood City Hall, a twenty-two-storey pyramid of dark green glass whose top five floors, right up to the pointed peak, were encased in pink marble. Barnabas and Wickram entered the massive lobby and walked up to the raised reception counter.

"Can I help you?" said the man behind the counter. He had the worn-out, bored look of someone counting the minutes till the day was over.

Barnabas cleared his throat. "Uh, yes. We're performing today for the Executive Council meeting."

The man turned to his screen and typed something. "Names?"

"I'm Barnabas Bopwright. And this is Wickram."

"Wickram what?"

Wickram said, "What do you mean 'Wickram what?'"

"You got to give me *both* your names, kid. That's how it works after kindergarten."

"I don't have—"

"Tragidenko," Barnabas said quickly. "Wickram Tragidenko."

"That," Wickram said in an offended tone, "is not my name."

The man typed, and Barnabas turned around. "Will you please be cool? I'm already freaking out."

"Not my name!"

"That's how it is in the City. You'll need a last name for the music school, too."

The printer on the reception desk began to whine, and the man pulled two squares of paper from it and handed them to the boys. "Peel off the backing and wear these the whole time you're in the building." He said into the headset, "Ms. Doublegrey, your performers are here."

A minute later, Barnabas saw a woman heading their way across the lobby. Everything about her, from hair to heels said *super professional, don't mess with me*. Ms. Doublegrey locked eyes with Barnabas, her gaze wavering for just the quarter second it took to check his name tag. "Barnabas Bopwright, welcome to City Hall. And Wickram Tragidenko, your guitar has so much character."

"Just Wickram," he said tersely.

"Noted. I love your school tracksuits. Very retro." She was looking Barnabas in the eye again, and she seemed to recognize something. Pulling out her phone, she swiped through several screens before looking back up at first one boy, then the other.

Barnabas was growing increasingly nervous. "You were expecting us, right?"

A wide smile full of gleaming white teeth appeared on her super-professional face. "Oh yes, I was told to look out for you. Please follow." As they walked across the lobby, she made a call. "Ms. Coomlaudy? They're here. Yes, *them*. Yes, ma'am, we'll be right up." Barnabas wanted to pull Wickram aside and discuss the woman's strange behaviour, but Wickram looked perfectly confident, staring up with awe at the glittering steel mobile that hung from the lobby's ceiling. *Maybe I'm just being paranoid*, Barnabas thought.

Ms. Doublegrey used a key card to call a private elevator. She pressed the button for the seventeenth and highest floor, and they shot skyward.

"So Wickram plays the guitar," she said. "What about you, Barnabas?"

Wickram said, "He sings and dances."

Barnabas's eyes went wide.

"Good, good," Ms. Doublegrey said. "Listen, there's someone who needs to hear you before you can perform for the committee." The elevator doors opened, and they followed her down a carpeted corridor. They passed a set of double doors with a gold embossed sign that read Executive Council. Barnabas peered inside at the empty table and chairs that awaited the arrival of the mayor and his top councillors. But Ms. Doublegrey passed the chamber and carried on down the corridor. Two burly security guards appeared and fell in behind them. Barnabas looked at Wickram, but he was bouncing along obliviously, checking out pictures of long-gone City councillors that lined the wall.

When they reached a large steel door, Ms. Doublegrey opened it with her key card and ushered the boys through. Inside was a stairwell circling its way up, and in the middle an old-fashioned caged elevator shaft like the ones Barnabas had seen in old movies. Ms. Doublegrey pushed the call button, and the elevator descended noisily and majestically from above. She pulled open the metal gate and motioned them inside. The large guards followed them in, forcing the boys up against the metal cage wall.

"Go to the top floor and wait," she announced. She was all business now, her smile gone, as if surgically removed.

The elevator rose slowly, grinding along its tracks. Barnabas peered through the cage walls at the strange scene around them. This part of City Hall could not have been more different from the rest of the airy, modern building. In the windowless rooms beyond the elevator, a small army of sallow, harried clerks sat at dozens of old-fashioned wooden desks, filing, stamping, and stapling stacks of paper as if the digital age had never arrived. As the elevator ascended to the tip of the pyramid, each floor grew smaller than the one before, adding to the sense of airless density. Barnabas felt his claustrophobia itching behind his eyes.

The elevator finally came to a clanging halt. The guards pulled open the gate, and the boys stepped out into a room without desks, without clerks, lit by overhead windows. The square room had sloping walls that rose to meet each other in a point, some thirty feet overhead. They were at the very pinnacle of the pyramid.

CHAPTER 64

One of the guards rode the noisy elevator back down while the other stood in silence to the side of the elevator shaft, face a blank. The beautifully appointed room seemed to be frozen in the distant past. Each corner had one of a set of matching chairs, elegantly curved and richly upholstered. The walls were lined with shelves of old leather-bound books that smelled like history. Barnabas took down one enormous tome, laid it on the carpet, and opened it up to reveal architectural blueprints for the City.

Wickram tapped him on the shoulder. "Hey, Barn, can I borrow your phone for a minute?" Caught up in this glimpse of history, Barnabas handed him the phone absently, and Wickram asked, "How do I work it?"

Sighing, Barnabas took it back. "Who are you calling?"

"The music school." He pulled out the worn blue notebook Sanjani had given him in the forest. "Here's the number."

As Wickram talked excitedly into the phone, Barnabas thumbed through the pages, finding original plans for the Jumble Market and River's Edge Park, complete with pencil annotations in the margins. He returned the blueprints to their place and walked solemnly along the rows of books, a finger trailing along the spines, until he found a series of dark blue volumes, each with a date range. He picked up *March to August, 1916* and opened it randomly.

"Can I hold what?" Wickram asked behind him. "Oh, yeah, I can wait. Hey, Barn, it's playing music!"

The handwriting in dark blue ink was spiky and deeply slanted but still legible.

May 14. It has been nearly four years since my son left to live in Scraptown, tasked with gathering the workers who will be the secret of our new City's success. When he left, Florian was still a frail and fresh-faced boy of eighteen. Imagine a father's shock at meeting the solid, moustachioed man in his own well-appointed offices.

Barnabas gasped. He was holding the personal diary of Lawrence Glorvanious.

But it is not just an administrative office. No, my son has built a church and installed himself as spiritual leader! Father Glory, his sycophantic followers call him. He's just a foolish boy, I wanted to shout at them. Always with his head in the clouds! But so sincere was their devotion, I had to hold back my mockery and go along with the charade throughout my visit. And the shocks did not end there. Florian has married some low creature of Scraptown named Julianna, known to the credulous flock as Mother Mercy. With this revelation, I nearly gave my temper free rein. A Glorvanious marrying beneath his station? Disaster!

Barnabas pressed the open book against his chest, taking this in. Father Glory was another Glorvanious. The son of the Great Mayor himself! All the mysteries he'd been uncovering this week were a big family drama, one that went on to affect millions of lives. Barnabas sat on the floor and dived back into the diary.

But Florian's followers are nothing like I imagined. Men and women both, many of them not even white, all treated as equals under his church's laws. How can this be anything but folly? Yet it must be said, they are formidable group! Tall and strong and devoted. Perhaps my son is the true genius here. How better to galvanize a generational workforce than through the spiritual pantomime of religion? One thing bothers me. Does Florian actually believe he is their MESSIAH, or is it an elaborate ruse? I didn't find the nerve to ask. I suppose it doesn't matter. Still, I find myself unaccountably sad. Some part of me, I confess, mourns the loss of the boy I knew.

"Hi," Wickram was saying, "Yeah, I'm supposed to have an audition. No, I didn't apply in line—*online*, whatever."

Barnabas skipped forward a few pages.

But with war coming, I told Florian that now must be time. I won't have this amazing workforce lost to the bloody fields of France. To make my point, I borrowed from my son's religious rhetoric: it is time for Father Glory to lead his people into the peaceful Valley, the

Promised Land, where they will disappear and yet remain ever-present.

Wickram was now pacing with excitement. "Yes, my friend Falstep came to your school last week. That's right, the little guy in the cap. He said that to you? Well, then you must be really beautiful. No, I don't have a phone number for him."

With a distant clang and grind, the elevator began moving up toward them again. Barnabas jumped to his feet, heart pounding. *I know too much*, he thought. *Me and my stupid curiosity.*

He waved at Wickram, who was grinning into the phone. "Okay, thanks, I'll see you Wednesday." He handed Barnabas back the phone as the elevator rose before them like mechanical doom.

"Wick, I think we're in trouble."

"No, everything's flamtasmic. Are you worried about the performance? Just sing whatever you like, and I'll make it work."

The elevator door opened.

Chapter 65

*A*n old woman emerged from the elevator, much shorter even than Barnabas, followed by two equally wizened old men, one with pure white hair, the other bald and leaning heavily on a walker, wheezing with each step. In contrast to them, the woman came into the room with a confident stride that belied her age. Dressed in an elegant pantsuit with a long black jacket, she had sharp blue eyes above a nose curved like a hawk's. Her silver hair was pulled back tight on her head, and her face, the skin like pale crêpe paper, was not made up other than the bright red lipstick drawn with precision across her thin lips.

"Barnabas Bopwright," she said in a voice like cracking twigs in a forest. "You have travelled far."

Barnabas could barely breathe. "J-just from Golden Pear Station."

The old woman grunted, although he couldn't tell if it was amusement or annoyance. She looked at the great mayor's diary, which he held against his chest. "I see the artefacts in this room interest you. That's a point in your favour." Her thin red lips twisted in a wry smile. "Do you understand what this collection is, young man?"

Barnabas replaced the diary on the shelf. "I think it must be Lawrence Glorvanious's personal library."

"Exactly. A treasure of incalculable wealth. We will never let go of the past, for it will never let go of us. As you saw coming up here in the elevator, we are still processing its bottomless legacy of paperwork."

The man with white hair said, "Your name is Bopwright? Are you, by any chance, related to Brownbag Bopwright?"

"He's my dad."

The man raised one heavy eyebrow a millimetre. "A sublime player. He is the true heir of Sonny Rollins."

The old woman waved away this triviality. "We have things to discuss," she said, and she and her colleagues sat in three of the fancy chairs. "I am Summer Coomlaudy, but in this place, you may address me as Prime Prelate. I have held this position for more than fifty years, and I am only the third to have done so since the days of Mayor Glorvanious. My colleagues and I represent this City in dealings with the Valley. Most importantly, it is we who meet with representatives of the Valley's Guild Council on a twice-yearly basis." She leaned forward. "I see you know what I am talking about."

Barnabas asked, "How do you know who we are?"

"We were warned by President Borborik that you had escaped custody and were likely on your way. Wickram, you were born in the Valley, but you, young Bopwright, were a clever interloper. We cannot afford to have people like you endangering the grand plan."

Barnabas's throat closed up in fear, but Wickram said, "Well, we're here because of Glower's grand plan."

"Glower? What is that?" said the white-haired man.

Barnabas found his voice. "He means Glorvanious. George Glorvanious left the Valley two days ago. He's planning to—"

"I'm sorry," the Prime Prelate interrupted. "Did you say George Glorvanious? Are you suggesting he has been in the Valley since his disappearance?"

"Yes, ma'am. We came here today to talk to the mayor. Mayor Tuppletaub knows Glorvanious, and I figure maybe he can stop him in time."

The bald man spoke in a high, breathless voice. "Stop him from what?"

Barnabas couldn't believe his ears. "You mean, the Guild Council told you to watch out for us, but didn't tell you about Glower's plan?"

So Barnabas told them. About his late-night trip to the Drop Shop. About Carminn and Glower and the steam elevator, and about the Guild Council, who refused to do anything to stop them. Barnabas was expecting the three old people to gasp in shock at the Council's inaction. They would pound their frail fists in disbelief and instantly order a phalanx of police and soldiers to descend on the towers and defuse the explosives, to take to the streets with a team of dogs and roust Glower/Glorvanious from whatever spider hole he had crawled into.

Instead, they laughed.

Summer Coomlaudy, a cruel light shining in her eyes, said, "While I am surprised that the most unimpressive of the Glorvanious clan found his way to the Valley, I'm not surprised to hear that his hateful little heart has come up with such an elaborate and futile scheme."

"Futile? It looked pretty real to me. And it's happening tomorrow. He said so."

The white-haired man, still chuckling, said, "Mr. Glorvanious has been away too long. He has no knowledge of our marvellous

GateKeeper system. GateKeeper protects the glorious Tower District from all tampering. Without access codes to the tower buildings—a different code for each, with three levels of encrypted redundancy—there is no way he has been able to infiltrate, much less sabotage *anything.*"

"GateKeeper is without equal and without flaw," the bald man wheezed. "The protocols are considered foolproof ninety-seven times out of ninety-eight with only a one percent hypothetical failure rate."

Summer Coomlaudy chuckled. "Little George's attempt at terror will be no more effective than his mayoral campaign. I expect him to vanish again in humiliation."

"You mean, you're not going to do anything either?"

She waved this idea away. "You need to trust your elders, young man. It's our job to protect the City, and we're better qualified than you are."

CHAPTER 66

Summer Coomlaudy and her colleagues rose creakily to their feet. She patted Barnabas on the head on her way to the elevator.

"We will find poor George and make sure he's not planning any mischief. Are you boys hungry? Wait here, and I'll have Ms. Doublegrey bring you sandwiches." She gestured to the guard, who opened the elevator's metal gate. "Roast beef or peanut butter?"

Something was wrong. Barnabas managed to put on a guileless smile. "The roast beef sounds great! Wick?"

Wickram nodded enthusiastically. "Sure, either. Both."

"Wonderful," said Ms. Coomlaudy and turned to the security guard. "Come with us." The guard squeezed himself into the elevator, and it descended with squeak and clank.

Barnabas took a deep breath and let it out slowly. "Let's get out of here," he said. "Fast."

"But Ms. Doublegrey is bringing sandwiches. That makes this a paying gig, Barn."

"Wickram, they're not going to bring us sandwiches. They're going to arrest us or hold us without trial or something."

"You're skull-cracked, Barn. They were nice."

"No, think about it. They're not going to do anything to stop Glower. It's their job to keep the Valley a secret, and as far as they're concerned, *we're* the real threat." The cool blue fear that had been rising in him changed to hot red anger. "Dammit. This is how I almost ended up in Doomlock. What is wrong with these adults?"

Wickram picked up Barnabas's discarded fear. "What do we do?"

"Run. Coomlaudy thinks we're just stupid kids, waiting here for our sandwiches. Come on, we're going down the stairs."

"We'll be seen."

"We'll be fast."

Barnabas pulled on his backpack, and Wickram shouldered his guitar. They began running down the staircase that circled round the elevator shaft. A few of the pale clerks looked up momentarily from their work as the boys ran past, but they didn't seem too interested. The clanking elevator began making its way back up, sliding right past them as they flew down the stairs. In it was Ms. Doublegrey and a security guard. She looked shocked to see them, but reacted quickly, shouting an alarm into her phone.

"Hurry!" Barnabas yelled.

"You were utter right!" Wickram yelled back. "She did *not* have any sandwiches with her."

They reached the bottom of the staircase. Barnabas was scared they would need a key card to get out of the stairwell, but it was a crash door, and the boys crashed through it. The double doors of the Executive Committee meeting room were closed as they ran past, and Barnabas slammed to a halt.

"Hi," he said breathlessly to a guard outside. "I'm interviewing the mayor for my school's politics podcast. When will he be done in there?"

Without looking up from his phone, the guard replied, "The mayor called in sick. Sorry, kid." Then he seemed to get interested. "What's your name, anyway?"

"Thanks, never mind," Barnabas said before the man could squint down at this name tag. He and Wickram ran around the corner in search of the main public elevators. The doors were just opening, and the boys dived in, jostling a cluster of annoyed clerks and couriers, and annoying them again when they pushed themselves out into the lobby.

Maybe it was his imagination, but Barnabas noticed there more guards than before, all moving around with great purpose. He pulled Wickram behind a large potted tree.

"That tour group is going to pass us," Barnabas said, peering out between the frilly leaves. "And we're going to join them. Keep your guitar low and out of sight."

Hiding in the middle of the tourists like two sardines in a vast school, they circled the lobby while the guide recited the official, Valley-free history of the City all over again. When the school of tourists swung as close to an exit as they were likely to get, Barnabas grabbed Wickram and pulled him through the revolving doors into the sunlight. They dashed across the Civic Plaza, and Wickram waved up at Father Glory's father as they ran past. They didn't stop running until they were two blocks away in a little scrap of park, separated from the sidewalk by a line of waist-high bushes.

Panting, holding his side, Wickram gasped, "I-I can't believe we got out of there."

Barnabas, lying back in the grass, allowed himself to enjoy a moment of triumph. "I'm not good at sports, but I know how to run away."

"I still wish we could have waited for the sandwich."

Barnabas pulled out his phone and texted Deni. *Hungry. Can we come back to your place?*

His phone instantly rang, and Deni screamed into his ear, "Ohmygod, Barnabas! Your mom!"

He sat up, alarmed. "What about her?"

"She's on her way here. She said it's high time you came home and discussed whatever problem it is you're having."

"Crap. What are me and Wickram supposed to do now?"

"Forget about you. What am I going to say to her when she gets here?"

Barnabas rubbed his forehead. He could either go home and placate his mom or else stop Glower from blowing up the whole Tower District. It wasn't even a choice. "You'll just have to figure something out. The mayor wasn't at City Hall."

"Did you tell anyone about Glorvanious?"

"Yeah, and they didn't believe he was dangerous."

"Is he?" She sounded excited.

"Never mind. I've got to go to the mayor's apartment at Delphic Tower—sneak in somehow." He thought about the GateKeeper system, and his heart sank. Glorvanious might be smart enough to defeat the high-tech security, but Barnabas was no engineer.

He could hear Deni tapping her teeth with her pencil, which meant she was coming up with a plan. "Where are you? Exactly?" she asked.

"Little park. Corner of Quarter-round and Charles."

"Okay, don't move. He'll be there in fifteen minutes."

"Who will?" But she had already hung up. Immediately, his phone rang. *Mom.* He shut off his phone and began to pace the sparse grass. All his problems seemed to be tangled together into one invincible knot. He spotted two policemen coming along the sidewalk and ducked down again behind the line of bushes.

"We shouldn't have given our real names at City Hall, Wick. Every cop in town is probably looking for us."

Wickram had returned to his usual state of calm. "Did you notice Glorvanious's statue? There was something on the hat. Some blue thing."

"What kind of blue thing?"

"Just a small blue thing. Hey, Barn, I forgot to tell you. I got my audition slot. Nine a.m., Wednesday."

Barnabas stared at him. "Wickram, in all likelihood, Glower is going to blow up the whole Tower District tomorrow. There won't be any auditions or *anything* Wednesday."

"Nah, you're going to stop Glower," Wickram said with a maddening smile. "I'm utter certain."

Barnabas was dumbfounded by this show of confidence. He didn't know what to do with the emotions he was feeling. There was something of gratitude in it, almost love, like he felt for his brother, Thelonius. But there was also a hideous certainty he was going to let Wickram and everyone else down. He turned away, afraid he was going to cry.

Five minutes later, a cab pulled up to the curb behind them and honked. Barnabas peered over the bushes and then jumped to his feet in surprise as Cal Kabaway stepped out of the cab and held the door for them. "Come on, guys, get in."

CHAPTER 67

"This is flamtasmic," Wickram said about his first ever taxi ride as they cruised down Bulwark Boulevard. His eyes darted back and forth between the passing City views and the commercials on the little monitor in the back of the seat.

Barnabas, stuck in the middle of the back seat between Cal and Wickram, was quietly fuming. How could Deni have done this to him? "Where are we going, Calvin?"

"My place. You and Wickram can spend the night." He sounded pretty enthused at the idea.

Of all the people he might choose to spend this last pre-disaster night with, Cal was pretty low on Barnabas's list. "Look, it's really nice of you, but I need to find a way to get to Mayor Tuppletaub. If I don't, things are going to get really bad tomorrow."

"Then you're in luck. I happen to live in Delphic Tower, two floors below the mayor's residence."

Barnabas was dubious. He knew the boy's family had money, but an apartment in Delphic Tower? Yet ten minutes later the cab was driving through the fancy avenues of the Tower District with its manicured landscaping and pulling to a stop in the driveway of one of the City's most exclusive residential buildings. Barnabas and Wickram climbed out, rubbernecking skyward, in awe of the majestic building.

Delphic Tower, built in the 1940s, had been modernized and renovated many times, but still carried its air of last-century opulence. Right from the start, the uppermost penthouse on the fiftieth floor had been set aside as the mayor's residence.

Barnabas suddenly imagined the explosions—hundreds of windows blowing out, smoke and flames billowing forth, and the chorus of screams from within as Delphic Tower and all its neighbours toppled backward over the cliff. He shuddered.

The uniformed guard opened the door for them with a respectful nod at Cal. At the back of the foyer was a wall of thick, probably bulletproof glass that could only be crossed at one heavily secured, automated gate with a card reader beside it. Etched on the glass was the word GateKeeper. Cal had them sign in at the security desk.

"Use a fake name," Barnabas whispered to Wickram, and soon they were passing through the GateKeeper perimeter and riding the elevator up to the forty-eighth floor. Cal held open the apartment door for them and flicked on a bank of light switches beside the door. It was an enormous place, with walls more than fifteen feet high and floor-to-ceiling, south-facing windows through which Barnabas could see the sun glowing low in the western sky. The hardwood floors were dark brown, and the walls the purest flat white. Chrome accents glittered here and there.

Cal stowed his schoolbag in the hall closet. "Please leave your shoes here. There are slippers in that box if you want them."

"This is where you live?" Wickram asked. He kicked off his shoes and ran for the windows. "Hey, I can see the Manhammer Audiodome!"

Barnabas was amazed at not just the palatial scale of the apartment, but by the fact that it was almost entirely empty. The only furniture was a huge U-shaped sofa unit in the centre of the sunken living room area, facing the biggest wall-mounted television Barnabas had ever seen. But there were no paintings on the walls, no family photos, no bookshelves or memorabilia—no evidence of home life of any kind. Every sound echoed coldly in the cavernous space.

"Let's get dinner taken care of," Cal said, "and then I'll give you the grand tour."

They joined Wickram in the living room, and each boy took his own wing of the vast couch. Cal reached into a cardboard box on the coffee table and handed out a set of restaurant menus. They weren't the little photocopied kind that you find in your mailbox, either. They were real leather-bound menus.

"Pick whatever you like," Cal said. "It's all good, and they deliver pretty fast, considering it's fine dining."

The prices made Barnabas's eyes go wide, but Wickram and Cal were already throwing out suggestions to each other for what was shaping up to be a huge and expensive feast. Cal pulled out his phone to place the order, talking to the restaurant in a loud, confident voice. The voice of wealth, Barnabas thought.

When Cal hung up, Wickram asked, "Where's the rest of your family?"

"Oh, it's just me and my father. He's usually away on business. Argentina now, I think. Come on, let me show you around."

They started with the picture windows, staring out at the amazing view. Barnabas thought he could maybe see the building where he lived, but he wasn't sure. He remembered that in the whole of the Tower District, the only windows facing the Valley were in the mayor's residence. He craned his neck upward, but he couldn't see any of the fiftieth floor from where they stood.

In an alcove to the side of the living room was a table covered in DJ equipment—turntables, headphones, stacks of vinyl records, a jungle of cables running through meters and processors, and behind them, a set of monstrous speakers. It was like the system had been lifted straight out of a huge club and transplanted here.

"This is my dad's hobby," Cal said. Wickram, mouth hanging slack with wonder, reached for the mixing board, and Cal grabbed his arm. "No! Don't touch anything. I'm not allowed to mess with any of the gear. And he remembers every setting."

Barnabas and Wickram exchanged looks. "Are there any other rules we should know about?" Barnabas asked.

"Well, we can't go in his room, but he keeps it locked anyway."

The next stop was the kitchen, large and elegantly dressed in black marble. But the giant steel fridge contained only a couple of milk cartons and a few withered fruits. The cupboards held bags of plantain chips and three unexceptional brands of cereal.

Even Cal's bedroom had a half-lived-in quality. A South American football poster was on the wall and a couple of schoolbooks on the unmade bed, as if Cal and his father were afraid to commit to the place, like they might have to decamp in a hurry.

"Where's the toilet?" Wickram asked.

"Closest one is down the hall on the left."

When they were alone, Cal said, "Can we talk for a second?" For the first time, Barnabas heard something vulnerable in the boy's voice. "Listen, I know you don't want me to be with Deni—"

"Wait. I never said that, Cal."

"I have to ask, is it because I'm trans?"

Barnabas needed a second to assess his feelings. "No. I mean it, seriously no. When I look at you, all I see is a guy. If I acted weird, it's because I thought you were maybe a *better* guy than me. Cooler, more confident." Cal looked embarrassed, and Barnabas said, "Sorry."

"No, I was the one who asked. Hey, it means a lot that you just see me as a guy when you look at me." His usual smirk returned. "The cool, confident part is a bonus."

They were standing beside Cal's open closet doors. Barnabas saw a lot of casual boys' clothing and sports gear, but at the back, half-hidden in shadow were a couple of dresses. They looked completely out of place.

Cal said, "My dad makes me wear those when we go out. It sucks."

Barnabas couldn't find words, so he just nodded. "And you don't mind me dating Deni?"

Barnabas shrugged. "I guess maybe I thought since Deni and me were best friends before, she was supposed to be my girlfriend now. But I met someone this week, and it feels different than whatever I feel for Deni. More romantic or horny or something."

"Cool. She's nice?"

"Um, *he*. Yeah, I like him." Barnabas concentrated on not looking away in embarrassment, even though he could feel he was blushing. "And if you feel like that with Deni, then that's amazing."

"She's pretty great," Cal said. "Kind of scary, but great." Wickram returned, and Cal said, "I'll meet you guys in the living room. I have to take off my binder."

When he rejoined them, Cal was wearing a baggy sweatshirt. The boys watched videos of trampoline accidents on the giant screen until the food arrived. It was maybe the best meal Barnabas had ever eaten, but Calvin seemed the most grateful.

"You're the first friends I had over since we moved here. Even Deni hasn't been."

"Why not?" Barnabas asked.

"I know why," said Wickram. "You don't want her to meet your dad."

Cal sighed. "Um, yeah, maybe."

Wickram nodded. "No, it's triple clear. I wish my dad didn't know my girlfriend. I wish he wasn't practically in love with her."

CHAPTER 68

W hen they had stuffed the last of the food down their throats, Barnabas said, "Cal, I've got to get up to the mayor's apartment and talk to him. Any ideas how I can do that?"

"Deni says he's at a big campaign dinner tonight at the Festival Hotel. Wait, his publicist is probably live-Texxing." He tapped on a keyboard, cunningly inset in the coffee table. The mayor's Texxit feed appeared as a pop-up in a corner of the big screen. "We can keep track of him, see when he's heading home."

"Okay, but when he does come home, do I just take the elevator up? Aren't there guards and everything?" *Also, I'm probably a wanted fugitive.*

"Yeah, no, you can't just barge in. But I know a way." While Wickram began sampling the desserts, Cal led Barnabas to the windowless north wall at the back of the apartment, where he put his hands on one of the smooth, white wall panels. "Help me with this. It's kind of sticky."

With no idea what they were doing, Barnabas also laid his palms on the wall, and when the two of them lifted at the same time, the sleek, modern panel slid up and off its moorings. Behind it was an older wall of inlaid wood. And in this slice of the past, barely visible, was a secret door.

"I accidentally found this when I was bouncing a basketball around. I think it was the servants' entrance back in the day." He slipped a finger into a tiny, recessed hole and, with a click, the door popped open. A gust of greasy, metallic air emerged with an eerie howl. Barnabas stepped through the door, followed by Cal, whose phone flashlight revealed a huge air shaft in the north face of the building, where a network of metal stairs and walkways traversed all fifty floors of Delphic Tower, like a hidden fire escape. Theoretically, every apartment had a similar hidden door. You could go anywhere in the building.

Wickram joined them. "Wow. This is utter spectaculous. Skull-cracked level eight."

Barnabas was breathless with excitement. "Calvin, let's go up to the mayor's residence."

"Yeah, okay." Cal was still in the entrance to the apartment, gripping the door frame tightly.

"You all right?"

"Just not so great with heights. Let's go slowly, okay?"

Barnabas felt a moment of superiority. *Who's cool now?* But then he remembered his own claustrophobia.

They climbed to the fiftieth-floor landing. Barnabas put a hand on the small doorknob but hesitated, speaking over the wind into Cal's ear. "Do you think the door is alarmed?"

"Probably not. I asked around discreetly, and I think everyone's forgotten this part of the building exists."

Barnabas took a deep breath and pulled on the knob. No alarm rang. But instead of an entrance into the apartment, he found himself staring at unfinished wood—the back of some cabinet or bookcase. He cursed in frustration, but then noticed the wood didn't go all the way to the floor. He lay down on the landing and stuck his head in for a look. On the other side was Mayor Tuppletaub's apartment—antique chairs, a Persian rug, a door on the far side of the room.

Wickram got down on all fours behind him. "You going in?"

"No. Even if there's no alarm on this door, there might be motion detectors inside. Better to wait until the mayor's home." They stood, and Barnabas closed the door.

"Okay?" Cal asked, clinging tightly to a railing with his eyes closed. "Ready to go back?"

They spent the evening getting pleasantly tipsy on cans of strong cider, watching action movies, and keeping an eye on the mayor's Texxit feed. They laughed and talked about girls, and then Cal asked Barnabas which he liked better, girls or boys.

"It's not like that. If I like a girl, then I like the girl things about her. Her softness, her, you know breasts and stuff. If it's a guy, I guess I like…" This was newer for him, harder to say. "The guy things. But maybe it's just that if I'm attracted to someone, I want, uh, whatever it is they have."

From his pocket, Wickram pulled out the little fertility goddess from Deni's apartment. "Well, I like what *she* has." He walked it down the couch arm like a fashion model.

"Give me that," Cal said, jumping to his feet. He grabbed the figurine and ran to the front door, where he dug through Barnabas's bag.

"Hey, get out of there!" Barnabas shouted, surprised to hear his words a little slurry from the cider. But Cal returned triumphantly, holding the diaboriku. He stood the fertility figurine up on the coffee table and pushed the device's big rubber buttons. A giant, faceless woman suddenly towered up over them, roaring, swinging her mammoth hips, shaking her mountainous breasts. Cal and Barnabas howled with laughter, and then laughed even harder when they saw Wickram cowering in the corner of the couch at the sight of this pendulous goddess.

Cal handed Barnabas the diaboriku. "You do one," he said. "Do Wickram's guitar." Barnabas knew it was the perfect time to admit he had never figured out how to work the device. He could have asked Cal for a lesson, but he was too embarrassed to confess his failure, so he said he needed to use the bathroom.

According to the mayor's Texxit feed, he was still partying at midnight. Cal and Wickram had fallen asleep on their respective wings of the couch, but Barnabas forced himself to stay conscious, keeping a drooping eye on the feed. Dreams began to overlay reality. The Texxit messages projected across the clouds as he peered through the small window from his airplane seat.

"Where are we going?" he asked Garlip, who was reading an in-flight magazine.

"The City in the sky. I'll show you my favourite coffee shop."

Then Barnabas was asleep, too. Outside, the glowing city enjoyed what might be its last night of peace.

PART VI

TUESDAY

CHAPTER 69

Barnabas had about five seconds to enjoy the warm, pink feeling of a good night's sleep before his eyes snapped open.

"What time is it?" he shouted.

"Sleep time," Cal groaned.

Barnabas sprang to his feet and shook him. "No, come on, we fell asleep. The mayor could be anywhere now."

Cal reached for the inset keyboard on the coffee table. The picture on the TV screen changed to a CCTV cam at the front door of the Delphic Tower.

"That's the mayor's car out front," he said sleepily. "There's his driver, waiting, having a smoke."

The clock on the CCTV display read seven fifteen a.m. "How long until he leaves, you think?" asked Barnabas.

"Anytime, I guess."

Barnabas shook Wickram's shoulder. "Wake up."

Five minutes later, the three of them were standing by the hidden door, Wickram with his guitar and Barnabas with his backpack. Cal handed them muffins, and Wickram shoved the whole thing into his mouth, making muted noises of appreciation as he chewed the enormous bolus.

"You going to school, Cal?" Barnabas asked.

"I don't know. Do you need me and Deni to help you?"

Barnabas tried to imagine the coming hours, but he had no idea what they held. "Just go. I can always text you between classes."

"So, you're going upstairs to give the mayor some message?"

"Yeah. I guess I'll just tell him what I know, and then he'll do what he has to do."

"You remember I still don't know what you're talking about?"

Barnabas opened the secret door and they stepped onto the metal walkway. Over the howl of the wind, Cal said a bit shyly, "Thanks for coming over. It was fun."

"Thanks for having us," Wickram answered, licking muffin crumbs from his upper lip.

Barnabas said, "Yeah, thanks. For everything. We should do a games night some time."

"Deni would love that."

"Yeah, or maybe it should be just the boys."

Cal grinned. "That sounds great."

Barnabas and Wickram climbed to the fiftieth-floor landing. Barnabas said, "You stay here. I'll be back soon."

"What if you're not?"

Barnabas considered this, but the alternatives were too scary. He put down his backpack on the landing. "I will be. Don't worry."

He opened the secret door of the mayor's residence and got down on the ground to peer through the gap. No movement, no sound, then suddenly a pair of feet in shiny, black dress shoes shot past, just inches away. Barnabas gasped but held still. As the shoes headed for a doorway on the far side of the room, he could see more and more of the person wearing them. It was Mayor Arthur Tuppletaub.

The mayor turned right into the hallway, and Barnabas snapped into action, giving himself no time to chicken out. He reached through the gap and pulled himself into the room. Other than the laptop and printer on the desk, he might have been transported back to the last century, like a museum display of an antique room. It was indeed a bookcase that was covering up the hidden servants' door, and he had crawled through the space under the lowest shelf.

Out in the corridor, Barnabas looked left and saw a large area that must have been the main foyer. Beyond it, the enormous apartment had another whole wing. The mayor, however, had gone to the right, and Barnabas followed, walking silently along the thick runner with its elaborate Arabian design. Across from a closed door stood an antique cabinet with a glass front. Inside the cabinet was a full set of commemorative plates, one for each mayor of the City, starting with Lawrence Glorvanious. All wore serious expressions except the last one in the series, Arthur Tuppletaub with his big salesman's grin.

Barnabas followed a noise at the end of the hall and turned right again into the mayor's sunlit bedroom. There was an open suitcase on the unmade bed, a desk covered in piles of paper, and a huge wall of closets with their accordion doors pulled open. And in the middle of it all was the skinny, panicked figure of the mayor himself. He was darting from desk to drawer to closet like a hummingbird, shoving clothes and documents willy-nilly into the suitcase. Tuppletaub looked up in that moment, saw Barnabas, and shrieked.

"Who are you? What are you doing here?" The mayor's voice

was high and tight, his thinning blond hair standing uncombed in little tufts on his oversized head. "I told the guards no one was to enter. Not even them."

"I-I told them I was your nephew," Barnabas said, impressed by his impromptu lie.

Tuppletaub examined him, but his eyes seemed deranged. "No, you're not my nephew, I'm certain of that. But you do look familiar." He resumed packing, stuffing handfuls of underwear into random spaces.

"Mr. Mayor, please. I have to talk to you. It's urgent."

"Not today. Any day but today. You have to get out. *Get out!*" He waved both arms at Barnabas like a scarecrow in a tornado. "Wait. Are you strong? Help me carry this suitcase to the foyer." He slammed the lid down and pounded on it, though it was clearly too full.

"Mr. Mayor, wait. *Stop!* I need to talk to you about George Glorvanious." And the mayor did stop.

"Glorvanious?" he whispered. His face went white, and he staggered over to sit on the bed.

Barnabas said, "You know, don't you? I told the Guild Council down in the Valley, then I told the lady at City Hall. He's going to blow up the whole Tower District."

The mayor's voice was more breath than substance. "I-I know. The Prime Prelate phoned me. Some boy told her." He looked at Barnabas accusingly. "She thought it was nonsense, of course." His hands, folded in his lap, were shaking.

Barnabas looked at the suitcase and the matching luggage already by the door. "Wait, you're leaving? *You're running away?* No! Nonono*no*! Mr. Mayor, you have to stop him."

"How? I don't know where he is. And even if I did, what am I supposed to do? Fly in the window and punch him in the nose? Hang him up in a big net in front of City Hall?"

"Call the police! Evacuate the towers!"

"I can't!"

"*Why not?*" Barnabas screamed, and the mayor cowered. He steadied himself and walked over to stand in front of Tuppletaub. As calmly as he could, he asked again, "Why not?"

The mayor closed his eyes. "Because it's my fault."

CHAPTER 70

Mayor Tuppletaub looked up at Barnabas and laughed a tired laugh. "I remember you now. You're the boy at that stupid, pretentious school. The one who asked about secret subways. Why am I cursed with people like you? I wish I didn't even know about the damned Valley."

Barnabas was growing desperate. He needed the mayor to save them, and the mayor was falling apart in front of his eyes.

"Mr. Mayor, the Prime Prelate said there's no problem because Glorvanious can't get past the GateKeeper system, but I wonder if—" He heard the mayor murmur something. "What was that, sir?"

Tuppletaub's eyes were empty of emotion, his voice flat. "I gave him the passcodes. All of them. For every tower."

Barnabas sat down heavily on the mayor's bed. "Why?" he asked in shock.

"He came to me months ago. I could barely believe it was him. George Glorvanious—missing for eight years. He said he had dirt about my opponents in the election that could assure me another term in office. For a price."

"But Glorvanious didn't want money, right? Just the passcodes." The mayor didn't bother answering. Barnabas felt like he'd cut into a beautiful, red apple only to find the insides blackened and corrupt, swimming with worms. The corruption, it was everywhere—in the Guild Council, at City Hall, in Ms. Rolan-Gong's office as she appeased the rich parents. Barnabas felt profoundly betrayed by the whole adult world.

He asked, "Didn't you wonder why he wanted to get past GateKeeper?"

"He was gone all those years. I thought maybe he had become an art thief or something. I told myself, why should I care if he rips off some billionaire? I never dreamed he was planning...that he would ever..."

They sat in dejected silence for a long minute. Barnabas even had time to think how odd it was that he should be sitting in the mayor's apartment, on the mayor's bed, sharing a problem like they were bunkmates at summer camp. The mayor stood, steady now, and forced his suitcase closed.

Barnabas asked, "What are we going to do?"

"Do? We will do what we have to. Bring that suitcase to the foyer," he commanded. Barnabas had no other plan, so he obeyed. Back in the bedroom, Barnabas watched Tuppletaub straighten his tie and put on his suit jacket. The mayor had put himself back together, though his hand shook as he ran a comb through his hair.

"I'm leaving," Tuppletaub said.

"What'll happen to me?"

"In thirty minutes, when I'm on the road, I will phone my guards and tell them to please escort you downstairs."

"And what will happen when the towers go down?"

The mayor seemed to be speaking as much to himself as to Barnabas. "The election will have to be postponed, of course. The City will be in chaos, in need of a sure hand on the wheel. It will be the defining moment of my mayoralty. My legacy."

Tuppletaub turned on his heel and marched out without saying goodbye. A minute later, Barnabas heard the door of the apartment slam. He thought it odd that Tuppletaub would leave a strange boy alone in his bedroom, but then he remembered that the bedroom would be blown up along with the rest of the building in just a few hours. Barnabas didn't know what to feel. His mind was white noise. He walked to the room's long line of windows, the one and only set that looked onto the Valley.

The morning sunlight lit up all the places he had come to know in the past week. Right below him was the Tumbles, and the big warehouse with the steel roof was the Drop Shop. There was the main transfer station where he had arrived, there the Guild Mansion, and the Clouding Cathedral. The factories continued to spew smoke, and trucks moved along the roads like lines of ants. Finally, up on its own little mountain was the green oasis of Pastoral Park. The dense canopy of the woods stood in the foreground, and beyond it, the whimsical majesty of the Big Top.

He thought of the City he had seen from Calvin's apartment, with all its vigour and verve. And here Barnabas stood, at the boundary between these worlds, knowing that soon the carefully maintained balance would collapse. He was without a plan, without hope. He wondered if he should just go back to City Hall and turn himself in, or maybe he should go down with the towers. Boom.

Then there was a noise. He tiptoed to the door and peered down the hall. A distant figure was leaving the foyer and heading into the other wing of the apartment. The man had his gun out. Despite the distance, despite how brief his glimpse, Barnabas recognized the blond bowl cut and the thick physique in the tight blue suit. It was the mayor's security man, the psychotic Mr. Klevver.

CHAPTER 71

Barnabas pulled himself back into the bedroom, his heart pounding as he tried to comprehend the situation. It hadn't been thirty minutes. The mayor must have betrayed him. Suddenly Barnabas wasn't ready to go down with the towers or go off politely to jail. He had to stop Glower, and it wasn't going to happen if he was blown up or shot. He dared another look down the hallway. The coast was clear. Running as fast as he could, he dived into the study where he'd arrived and pulled himself against the wall to the right of the open door.

Barnabas listened for Klevver's approach, but a persistent howling made it hard to hear. He realized the noise was coming from the secret stairwell through the open door behind the bookcase. It was time to get out, but he was too scared to move. Why hadn't he just run straight for his exit while he had the chance? Now he was frozen, afraid to cross the big, open room and crawl under the bookcase.

Over the howl of the wind, he could hear a door creak and another slam. Klevver was checking the apartment, room by room. There wasn't much time. *Go,* Barnabas told himself. *Just go!*

"Meow! Here, mousey-mousey," Klevver called.

"Just do it, just do it. Now, now," Barnabas whispered to his frozen feet. Abruptly, the hidden door behind the bookcase, his only escape, caught a sudden gust and slammed shut. The howling wind stopped, leaving a terrible, revealing silence in its wake. Barnabas wanted to scream. Klevver, he knew, had heard the slam. The killer was coming. To the right of the door was a red leather armchair. Without thinking twice, Barnabas dived across the study's open doorway and hid himself behind it. Just as he pulled himself down and out of sight, Mr. Klevver entered the room.

"Ooh," cooed Klevver. "Is the little mousie in *here?* Come out, come out. Mr. Kitty is hungry." Klevver held the gun in both hands, his arms straight, pointing it around the room like a searchlight. "Meeeeeeoowwwww!"

While Klevver checked in a closet, Barnabas crawled from behind the armchair and scrambled out into the hall. Now what? He couldn't just leave through the front door of the apartment because the mayor's guards were waiting on the other side. Or had they left with their boss? Barnabas couldn't be sure. The only certainty was to get back into the study and exit the way he had entered.

Klevver would be finished searching the study any second. Barnabas surveyed his surroundings, hoping for an idea. Down the corridor, the door across from the cabinet of memorial plates now stood open. Peering inside, he saw it was a walk-in linen closet, shelves full of sheets and towels. Barnabas had an idea. He slipped inside, pulling the phone from his pocket. He chose the loudest song in his library and set an alarm for one minute. Then he tossed the phone onto the highest shelf in the deepest corner of the little room and ran back into the hall, hiding himself behind the antique cabinet.

No minute in human history had ever passed so slowly. And yet when the alarm went off, Barnabas almost screamed, like he hadn't been expecting it.

"*I DON' WANNA BE ANOTHA BROK'NHEARTED BABY F'YOU!*" wailed Agranda Latté from inside the linen room.

Barnabas strained to hear movement over the song, but Klevver must have been moving silently as a panther. And then, there he was, close enough to touch, following his outstretched gun into the linen closet.

"Oh, little mouse, you squeaky sneak," Klevver said in a sing-song as he vanished inside. "Gonna bite into your flesh and hear you shriek."

Now! Barnabas moved. He slammed the door of the linen closet, dashed back to the side of the cabinet, and pulled it away from the wall with all his strength. For a second it didn't move, but then it began to tip off balance, accelerating as it went, the glass doors flying open, priceless porcelain spilling out and smashing. The cabinet hit the door of the linen closet and pinned it closed.

"*Yes!*" Barnabas screamed.

"*No!*" he heard Klevver howl as he threw himself against the door, which shook on its frame with each blow.

Barnabas scrambled over the cabinet and ran for the study. He slid across the floor, diving headfirst under the bookcase and pushing at the closed door behind it. The door rattled a little in its frame, but the latch held. He knew that, up above him, was a little hole with a hidden lever like the one in Cal's apartment, but with the bookcase pushed right against the door, he couldn't reach it. Putting his mouth close to the wall, he yelled, "Wickram! Open the door. Do you hear me?" He pounded on the wood but got no response.

A gunshot. Another. He had never heard a gun in real life, and he was shocked by how loud it was. He imagined Klevver breaking free, flying into the study in a rage and seeing him under the bookcase, butt and legs extended back into the room, twitching like a trout on the dock. Barnabas pulled himself back out and turned around, this time pushing his feet against the hidden door. Bracing himself on the edge of the bookcase, he gave the door a solid, two-footed kick.

Another volley of gunfire from the hall followed by the sound of splintering wood. Barnabas screamed, "Come on! Come on!" as he kicked harder, coiling his legs to his chest up and smashing at the door again and again. With a wrenching, antique crack, the latch broke, and the hidden door flew open. Barnabas pulled himself through the gap and scrambled to his feet on the metal landing. He threw the door closed and leaned against it, his heart pounding so loudly, his ears buzzed.

Barnabas imagined Klevver in the study, cursing and turning over the furniture in a rage. But Klevver, he prayed, didn't know about the hidden door. After a full minute of panting tension, Barnabas picked up his backpack off the walkway and started looking for Wickram. Like lava in a volcano, anger rose in him as he descended the stairs.

He found Wickram a few flights down, playing his guitar with great concentration. The wind through the airshaft was loud enough to muffle the sound of the instrument until Barnabas was almost on top of him.

"Where were you?" Barnabas screamed, bursting into tears.

CHAPTER 72

"Sorry?" Wickram asked in confusion.

Barnabas glared at him, awash in fury and humiliation. He wanted to scream, to hit Wickram. Instead, he ran down the stairs faster and faster, his clanging footfalls ringing like cathedral bells on the metal stairs, Barnabas propelled himself down dozens of floors. *Slow down, slow down*, he begged himself, thinking how ironic it would be to trip and die like this, but he couldn't slow down.

Despite Barnabas's head start, long-legged Wickram soon caught up with him, and they thundered downward together. When they reached the tenth floor, Barnabas out of breath, dizzy, thighs aching, looked up and saw Glower's handiwork.

"Noooo," he moaned.

Wickram was doubled over beside him, panting. "Wh-what?" He straightened up and saw it too. "Uh-oh. That doesn't look good."

• Wrapped around the huge upright girders that supported the whole north side of the building were plastic bags filled with something that looked like heavy white clay. They were explosives, Barnabas realized, supplied to Glower by Carminn. Red wires ran from each bag, gathering together into a dense network. Barnabas descended the stairs slowly now, as if in a trance. At each floor, more explosives were set, more wires joining the network, until they finally came together in a metal box on the seventh floor. A blue wire emerged from the other side and disappeared through the front wall of the hidden north face. Where did it lead? To a trigger? Barnabas remembered the little blue pyramids from the demonstration at the Drop Shop.

His horror was palpable. Until he saw this actual evidence of Glower's plan, he'd held on to a kernel of comforting doubt, like maybe if he failed, it wouldn't be quite so bad. But now he could see Glower had been rigging explosives and triggers in Delphic Tower, and probably in every other building in the Tower District. Suddenly, it was all sickeningly real.

In a panic, Barnabas grabbed the blue wire and tore it loose from the switching box. Only then did he remember all the bomb-defusing scenes in movies. One wrong wire cut in the wrong order triggered the detonation. His limbs failed him. He dropped to all fours and threw up his small breakfast. But there was no explosion, only the sad moaning of the wind. Barnabas became aware of Wickram's feet beside him, and when he could, he let his friend help him to his feet.

"You'll be okay," Wickram said, still holding his hand in a firm, warm grip.

They descended together to the ground floor where they found a door in the north wall. Beside it was a sign, hand-lettered in old-fashioned curly script: "Tradesmen—always lock the door behind you when exiting." They had to lean their shoulders into the door to open it, pushing against a heap of leaves and debris the years had piled up outside.

A covered walkway ran behind the building, and they hurried along it, leaving their footprints in fifty years of accumulated dust, until they came to another door. It opened into a wide alleyway, and Barnabas saw they were back in the known world. They walked past Delphic Tower's loading dock and out onto the sidewalk in front of the building.

Barnabas said, "Ha!"

"What?"

"We never signed out. We just defeated GateKeeper." Barnabas was still shaky from his ordeal, but this small victory was satisfying. He held out a fist to bump, and Wickram high-fived it.

Surveying the face of the building, Barnabas counted seven floors up and followed along the line of balconies until he saw the blue pyramid that would receive the detonation signal. If only he had known, he could have told the Prime Prelate to look for the pyramids on every tower. But maybe it would have made no difference. They all believed GateKeeper was infallible, and he was just a kid with a story.

A security guard from Delphic Tower yelled from the front door, "Can I help you?"

With palpable disgust, Barnabas called back, "Even if you could, you probably wouldn't." He returned to the sidewalk and said to Wickram, "Follow me."

They surveyed the front of each tower—the Neverlander, Greatest Hiltz, and all—until they spotted all the blue pyramids. Every tower was wired.

They sat at a picnic bench in a little park across the road. Rich children played on the slides and swings, and their nannies chatted.

"So, I guess the mayor didn't offer to fix everything?" Wickram asked.

"He ran away. Probably out of town by now. He's planning to return after the disaster and shed some tears at a press conference." Hopelessness washed over him, but Wickram just nodded.

"Okay, then we'll have to find Glower ourselves. Where do you think he is?"

"I don't know. He could be anywhere!" Barnabas thought of the view from Cal's window. Anywhere was a big place.

Wickram grabbed his shoulders and shook him. "Come on, Barn. You've been spying on the slizzy lizard for days. Didn't you hear anything useful?"

Barnabas chewed his lip. If he was really going to be a Junior Sherlock, now was the time to step up. He thought of Glower meeting Galt-Stomper in the subway, but they never mentioned the towers. What about when he first went to the Drop Shop with Wickram and Beaney? No. If there was anything, it must have been the dark and stormy night when he and Graviddy took their ride on the white horse, the night he learned of the terrible plan.

"It was raining," he said, putting himself back in that night. "Glower was showing Carminn the triggering system."

"Those little blue pyramids?"

"Exactly. They're triggers. The orange cube sends a signal, and the blue pyramids receive it." Barnabas struggled to remember.

The memory rose shining out of a dark shadow. "Glower talked about the one place in the City where he had line of sight on every building in the Tower District."

"That's it, Barn," Wickram said. "There's only one place that fits the description."

"Where?" Barnabas asked, his heart quickening.

"The Manhammer Audiodome."

CHAPTER 73

"Excuse me, could I borrow your phone for just a second?" Barnabas, standing at the subway entrance, had picked the woman with the most "mom" energy. He tried to look as needy and trustworthy as possible, but she still seemed suspicious.

"Where's your phone?"

"It's at the store getting new glass."

He could feel he was about to lose her, when Wickram jumped forward. "Please, ma'am, his grandmother's really sick." And that did it.

Barnabas and Wickram turned their backs on her and huddled over the phone. Barnabas brought up a browser window. "There's a baseball game at one thirty at the Dome. Glower told Carminn the towers were going down at two thirty. We have to get tickets to the game."

The woman said, "I thought you were calling your grandmother"

Wickram turned and nodded sadly. "She loves baseball. It might be the last game she ever sees."

"Damn," Barnabas said. "Sold out. Not that I can afford tickets anyway." He knew what he had to do, but the idea made his stomach lurch. He dialled, saying to the phone's owner as it rang, "I'm just going to call Grandma real quick and...oh! Uh, hi. Yeah, it's me."

Soon they were stepping out of the elevator into the loud reception area of K97, Hit-Digit Radio. The walls and furniture were a riot of aggressive colour choices plastered over with oversized photographs of grinning on-air personalities and the biggest pop stars of the moment. Something about the atmosphere seemed fake and desperate, like someone had ordered a kit labelled Instant Top 40 Station.

Sam was already waiting for them. The look on his face was one Barnabas hadn't seen before, a knot in his features that might be holding back any emotion from fury to grief.

"Hi," Barnabas said nervously before Sam lunged forward and pulled Barnabas into a bear hug.

"Oh my God, we were so worried about you," his stepfather breathed into his hair. He pushed Barnabas back, holding him at arm's length and looking him up and down with such intensity that Barnabas blushed. "Are you all right? Your mother is frantic. She went to Deni's last night, but you weren't there."

"I'm sorry. I'm fine."

Still gripping one of Barnabas's shoulders, Sam sat down with him on a fuchsia couch. He noticed Wickram for the first time. "You're his friend?"

"Wickram is visiting from out of town," Barnabas explained, "and I remembered that the station has seats for ball games. Do you have anything left for this afternoon? Wickram loves baseball."

Wickram raised a fist. "Touchdown!"

Sam said, "Wickram, would you mind excusing us a minute? I need to talk to my son."

Barnabas almost did the automatic "stepson" correction but managed to hold his tongue. Wickram crossed to the other end of the reception area and sat in a canary yellow armchair.

Sam's eyes were deep set and surrounded by wrinkles. But out of this fractured background, his personality shone through, bright and warm. "You can skip another day of school if you have to, but your mother and I need you to come home right now."

"Sam, listen—"

"I know you got into trouble last week with the mayor and Ms. Rolan-Gong, but we won't let anything bad happen to you. You have to trust us."

"I can't come home now. There's something I need to do, and it has to be today."

Sam's voice edged into annoyance. "You can take your friend to a baseball game some other time."

"It's not that. And it's not about school. I can't tell you what it is, but it's important."

Sam sighed. "Barnabas, I'm sorry, I know I'm not your father, but you're forcing my hand. I can't just let you go away again. I care about you too much."

Guilt and frustration warred in him. "Look, Sam, am I a bad kid? When do you ever have to worry about me? Just this once, I'm asking—"

"You've been gone who knows where for almost a week. You had Deni lying to the school for you, covering up heaven knows what. How do I know you're not in terrible trouble, making a mistake you won't be able to come back from?"

Barnabas turned away from the intensity of those eyes. He wished he could tell Sam everything, not be so alone in this terrible situation. But every adult he'd confided in had betrayed him.

He took a deep breath and willed himself to sound mature. "Sam, I know it looks like I'm in trouble, but I'm not. I'm trying to do some good. You know I respect you, Sam, and I'm really happy you and Mom ended up together. But now, please, you have to trust me with my mission. It's almost over. I just need this afternoon." Barnabas watched the struggle in his stepfather's face.

Sam sighed. "And this important mission involves going to a baseball game?"

"Sort of, yeah."

His stepfather pulled the tickets from his jacket pocket and handed them over, along with two twenty-dollar bills and a pair of binoculars from the reception desk. "You'll need these. They call them VIP seats, but they're way out in right field."

"Thanks, Sam."

"Barnabas, I'm trusting you not to screw up."

"I know, me too."

"And don't tell your mother we saw each other, or I'll have to move to Deni's with you."

CHAPTER 74

Gumm Hill was a geological oddity. It stood alone, jutting up a hundred metres above the surrounding neighbourhoods with nearly vertical walls. When the Great Mayor, Lawrence Glorvanious, presided over the opening of Gumm Hill Stadium on the site, he promised the Gumm family the name would endure through the ages. Ninety years later, Manhammer Audio made an irresistible offer to City Council. Some outraged citizens refused to use the new name, but the forces of apathy and advertising soon won the day, and now everyone called it the Manhammer Audiodome.

Whatever it was called, approaching the stadium was one of the great rides in the City. Ticketholders and tour groups were transported up to the plateau from the parking lots and subway station in spacious, glass-sided cable cars that afforded magnificent views of the City. As the boys rode up, Wickram's eyes were wide, like a religious zealot making the pilgrimage of a lifetime.

"I can't believe we're here," he said. "The Manhammer Audiodome is where Grubbyboy recorded his infamous live album *Crood Criminal*."

They were more than an hour early for the game, but Barnabas didn't want to take a chance of missing Glower's arrival. When they got off the cable car, he left Wickram sitting in the grass playing his guitar while he circled the huge building. When 35,000 people converged on this spot, how would he find Glower? Or maybe he was already here.

The north section of the building was the only part of the original stadium that remained, and the only part with windows. Barnabas trained his borrowed binoculars across them but saw nothing.

Circling back around the building, he found Wickram jamming with a three-piece band playing classic R&B for the crowds. Wickram broke away, high-fiving the musicians. "Hey, Barn, one of the hot dog guys has already opened up. Aren't you starving?"

Barnabas got them two dogs with everything and two drinks. The day seemed too nice to end in terror. The sun shone brightly, and everyone was in a great mood, playing hooky from work or school and otherwise trying to make this an afternoon to remember. But didn't people always say that about the time leading up to disasters? "It was such a beautiful day. We had no idea what was in store."

"You'll have to check in your guitar at the security office," the ticket taker at the VIP entrance told Wickram.

"What? Why?" Wickram protested.

"It's a security risk. You could be smuggling contraband inside."

Wickram turned his guitar over and shook it to show nothing was hidden inside, but just then, the lights overhead began to flicker.

"What the hell's going on?" the ticket taker said to someone on his headset, and the boys jumped the turnstile. They ran up the concrete ramp to a big hexagonal lobby ringed by concession stands.

"That was no way to treat VIPs," Wickram sniffed. "Hey, can you buy me a baseball bonnet?"

"You mean cap. Focus, Wick. Just keep your eyes open for Glower."

The lights were continuing to flicker, and it was making all the employees nervous. Power to every system seemed to be coming and going randomly. Elevators were taking turns going out of service, and food machines could no longer dispense their syrups and condiments.

"It has to be Glower causing this," Barnabas said. "It's too much of a coincidence."

"Ladies and gentlemen," came a cheerful announcement. "The Manhammer Audiodome apologizes for the current technical difficulties. Work crews have been dispatched, and we expect to have the problems resolved shortly."

Wickram said, "Maybe we should start searching or something."

"But search where? Every room in the entire stadium?" He didn't mean to raise his voice, but the task looked hopeless.

"Okay, don't get all skull-cracked. Let's go up to our seats."

"Sure, why not?" Barnabas said in frustration. "If we can't stop the disaster, we might as well enjoy the game."

They checked their tickets in the disorienting glow of the intermittent light and headed toward their section. The PA crackled and whined, and all the different sound cues for revving up the crowd—clapping songs, bugle calls, snippets of rock anthems—began to play back-to-back. A sizeable crowd was waiting impatiently in front of a bank of three elevators. One elevator stood open, and a dozen people were stuffed inside, stubbornly holding their ground as a security guard tried to make them exit.

"Please, the elevators are not safe to ride during these power fluctuations. Any of you that are able to take the ramps—"

"You expect us to give up our place?" shouted a man inside, firmly gripping the hand of an eight-year-old dressed head to foot in team merchandise. "We already waited ten minutes."

An electrician in an orange vest and hard hat pushed his way through the crowd to the front. The guard, relieved, said, "Here we go, folks. Shouldn't be long now." The electrician unlocked a panel on the wall and began to flip switches inside.

The angry man in the elevator yelled at him. "Do you know what I paid to be here? Fix this thing."

The electrician pushed a button, and the elevator door closed, almost cutting off the man's nose. Then the elevator closest to the electrician opened. He slipped quickly inside and turned to look out through the open doors.

"Out of service," he announced.

Wickram shouted, "Barn, it's *Glower*."

CHAPTER 75

S tuck at the back of the crowd, Barnabas was too short to see. "Don't let him get away." The boys pushed roughly through the impatient horde, but by the time they reached the front, the door had closed, and the floor numbers above it were climbing.

"*No!*" Barnabas yelled.

A bell sounded and the third elevator opened. The crowd gasped and someone screamed, "It's Agranda Latté!" Everyone pulled out their phones to take pictures of the pop star. Her makeup and hair were flawless, and she was dressed in blue latex and bare skin, like she was ready to shoot a video. Agranda Latté smiled an automatic smile and began cycling through various poses Barnabas had seen in a hundred pics of her online.

"What the hell?" yelled an older woman at the singer's side. "We're supposed to be backstage at field level."

Barnabas looked up at Wickram and said, "We're getting on." The security guards were trying to push their way to the front to protect the pop star from the screaming crowd. But Barnabas and Wickram got inside first, just as the doors closed. The elevator began to rise, but very slowly.

In front of the button panel stood a young man in a Manhammer Audio jacket with a nametag that read Oolie.

The older woman was still tearing into him. "What kind of amateur monkeys are running this place?"

Oolie couldn't talk back to her, so he took his frustration out on the boys. "This is not a public elevator."

Wickram raised his hands reassuringly. "Whoa, whoa, don't worry, buddy. Me and Barn are from K97, Hit-Digit Radio. We're here to make sure everything's going just the way Agranda needs. And maybe do a little interview?"

The star smiled. "That's really sweet of you. I'm on my way to sing the national anthem, and then maybe we can sit down and—"

The other woman shook her head. "I'm Ms. Latté's road manager. We have to be at the airport by three. Sorry. Maybe we can do a phoner from the car."

Barnabas saw Wickram hadn't even heard this. He was staring, star-struck, at the singer, who looked to Barnabas like a video come to life, but also unnervingly human.

The lights flickered ominously, and Oolie started moaning, "Oh no, oh no, oh no," like he was about to burst into tears. The elevator lurched to a halt, and Agranda tipped over on her high heels, landing in Wickram's arms.

The manager checked the time on her phone, cursing fluently and screaming at the man from Manhammer to get them moving.

"Thanks," Agranda said to Wickram as the red emergency lights came on. "You're a guitarist? I'm just learning."

"I could give you a lesson, since we're stuck here."

"No," Barnabas said, "we *can't* get stuck here. Is that one of those emergency trapdoors up on the ceiling?"

Oolie pushed the call button on the panel over and over, sweating so hard, it looked like he'd been caught in the rain. "I think so, but…" He began to quote from some manual. "In case of emergency, all passengers will stay put and wait for assistance."

Agranda's road manager screamed, "We can't *stay put. Entertainment Hourly* is here to film my client." She turned to Barnabas. "If you can get out and get us some actual help…"

Wickram was just tall enough to push the panel open and pull himself up through the little square door, legs flailing in the air. Once he was up on top of the elevator, Barnabas passed him the guitar.

"I need a boost," he said to Oolie, but Agranda's road manager was the one who lifted him to the ceiling.

"Hurry," she said. "Don't let them start the game without Agranda."

The air in the elevator shaft smelled of diesel and dust. Wickram stepped carefully off the elevator and began to climb a ladder on the wall.

"We'll get some help," Barnabas called down into the car, and then followed Wickram up the ladder. Beside a pair of closed elevator doors, the word "Field" was stenciled on the wall. Wickram pushed the big red button, and the doors opened.

The boys stepped out into chaos. They were in a wide hall, big enough to drive a truck through, full of people shouting into cell phones. The words "delays," "costs," and "unacceptable" featured prominently in their curse-laden rants. A few baseball players were going through their stretching routines while reporters interviewed them. One end of the hall was a big open portal onto the playing field of the Manhammer

Audiodome. The impatient crowd beyond buzzed like a hive of angry bees.

A sweating man in a dark suit rounded on the boys. "What the hell are you kids doing here? This is an emergency. We're fifteen minutes late. I'm having you arrested."

Wickram pointed into the elevator shaft, pulling his hair in desperation. "Hurry! Agranda Latté's trapped. They're running out of air."

A group of concerned officials quickly formed and peered down into the shaft, arguing with each other. Barnabas and Wickram ran toward the field entrance. The crowd noise was a palpable force. Most of the fans were already in their seats and more than ready for the game to start. The giant SuperScreen read "Sorry for the delay."

"This is amazing," Wickram breathed. And under better circumstances, Barnabas would have agreed.

He began scanning the stadium with the binoculars. "Just let me find him before it's too late," he whispered. It was almost a prayer, sent up to Father Glory or Mother Mercy, or maybe to his mom, dad, and friends—everyone who needed him to succeed.

And then his prayers were answered. If Glower hadn't been wearing the orange vest and hard hat, Barnabas would have missed him, but there he was, directly across the field beside one of the team mascots. Glower peered around, then unlocked a door in the outfield fence and slipped inside.

"Wickram, we can't lose him," Barnabas shouted and took off straight across the field.

He heard Wickram calling, "Barn, wait," but it had all come down to *now*. Overhead, the dome was open, the sun shining merrily—a perfect day for a game. Wickram quickly caught up with him, and together they powered across the field. The restless crowd had begun to clap, and Barnabas realized the applause was for them.

In the centre of the field stood a microphone, and as they passed, Wickram said, "Wait a sec, Barn." Barnabas skidded to a halt in confusion and looked back at Wickram. In the distance, five, maybe six security guys were leaving the backstage corridor and racing toward them.

"Wickram! We can't stay here."

Wickram stood still, staring back at the thousands of faces turned their way. "Barn, let me distract them. You run."

"What are you talking about?" The men were getting closer.

Wickram smiled at him, like everything was just fine. "Run, dummy," he said. "Glower's getting away."

So Barnabas ran. And as he ran, Wickram's voice filled the stadium.

"Uh, hi, ladies and gentlemen. Due to circumstances beyond comprehension, Agranda Latté has been delayed, so, uh, here's the national anthem."

Barnabas turned to look at the SuperScreen, and there was Wickram, sixty feet tall, lowering the microphone to his guitar. As cool as ice cream, he gave his instrument a quick tune and launched into a short, instrumental version of the anthem.

Barnabas reached Glower's door just as Wickram played his final notes. Something hit the mic with a stadium-filling thud. Barnabas turned and saw the security men pulling Wickram away. With his one free hand, he gave the crowd a friendly wave. They cheered back and then booed as the security men took away his guitar and roughly pulled his arms behind his back. Up on the SuperScreen, a car ad was playing.

There wasn't much time. Three guards were running his way. Still panting heavily, he tried the door, but it was locked. Obviously. Why hadn't he expected that? He began pounding on its metal surface, shouting, "Hey, hello! Please open up! It's an emergency!"

The guards were getting closer, shouting to him. He thought about running, but where would he go? Around the perimeter of the stadium until they cut him off? A camera was above the door, and he waved frantically at its dispassionate eye, screaming, "*Please! He's going to blow up the towers if you don't let me in! Hurry!*" To his astonishment, the door buzzed. Barnabas tried it and found it was unlocked. With the security guards almost upon him, he dived inside and pulled the door shut. A second later, the men on the outside were shaking the handle, banging their fists on the door. Barnabas stood still, holding his breath until he was sure they didn't have the key.

A tinny voice spoke from a speaker on the wall. "Turn to your left and take the first staircase. I'm waiting for you on the fourth floor, third door on your right." So Barnabas began to walk, though the cold, metallic taste of fear was now filling his mouth. He knew that voice. It was George Glower.

CHAPTER 76

Only as he climbed the stairs did Barnabas realize he had no plan. He had never had one beyond finding Glower and "stopping" him. He felt sick with adrenaline, his heart pounding, and every instinct telling him to run in the other direction. But if Glower was on schedule, there were only forty minutes left to derail his plan. *Derail his plan?* Barnabas almost laughed, almost puked. Glower had been setting this plot in motion for months, maybe for years. He was meticulous and driven. Barnabas, on the other hand, had no plan.

As he marched to his death, Barnabas was at least able to appreciate his surroundings. The honey-coloured varnish on the mouldings was flaking away, and the plaster ceiling was mottled with water stains, but the old wing of the stadium had a hundred times more personality than the concrete and plastic of the new. Barnabas admired the fading team emblems in the scuffed hardwood and the brass signs on the doors that read "Photostat" and "Radio Room." The long halls were deserted. It was just him and Glower, hiding in history.

On the fourth floor, the door on the right also had a brass sign, "Archives and Memorabilia." He could still run away. Hadn't he done enough? He was just a kid. He had told multiple authorities, including *the mayor of the freaking City*, and they hadn't stepped up. Then Barnabas thought of Wickram being dragged away by the guards. His fearless friend had accompanied him through the bowels of the earth and let himself get arrested so Barnabas could get to this place. Didn't he owe it to Wickram to try? He opened the door.

A musty smell of old newsprint hit his nose, and he sneezed twice. He rubbed his watery eyes and found himself staring at George Glower. The man was on his feet, bent over a laptop on an old wooden table in front of the large double windows.

"I'll be with you in a minute," Glower said without concern. "Close the door."

The room was full of trophies from decades past, stacked by the dozens on old bookshelves and around Glower on the big worktable. Some were tall and ornate, but most were modest: Most Valuable Fielder and Chimney Cigarettes Player of the Season. There were framed newspaper pages on the wall, the stock yellowed, bold headlines muted by the dusty glass: "The Championship Is Ours!" and "Hail the Conquering Heroes!"

To the left of the door was a wooden statue of Lawrence Glorvanious, half the size of a real man. It took a few seconds for Barnabas to recognize it as an exact duplicate of the giant statue in front of City Hall. The Great Mayor looked off into the future, the buildings and boulevards he had dreamed into existence clustered around his feet.

"The artist's preliminary model," Glower said and quoted the inscription on the base. "We are ever grateful."

Barnabas turned and found Glower pointing a gun at him. Barnabas had never seen an actual gun before today, but now he'd been threatened by two of them in the space of a few hours.

"You keep appearing," Glower said, deadly calm. "Over and over this past week. At Crumhorn station, outside the school, in the Drop Shop, surprisingly. And yet you're too young to be anyone's agent. Who are you?"

Barnabas had to clear his throat painfully before his voice would work. "I-I'm Barnabas Bopwright." Through the windows behind Glower, Barnabas could see the whole of the Tower District in the distance, gleaming in the sun.

"And you've been following me?"

"Not at first. It was just a coincidence."

"But now you're on a mission to stop me. I've been watching you since you entered the stadium." Glower nodded toward the shifting quilt of surveillance feeds on the laptop's screen. "You and the circus man's son are here to prevent my moment of triumph."

"I guess." There was no point in denying it.

"It's almost time. You might as well watch." Glower reached out a hand. "Phone."

"I-I lost it," Barnabas said, wishing he'd found a way to stop Klevver without sacrificing the phone. Barnabas cursed his lack of foresight. *No plan, no plan.*

"Sit down against the wall beside that pipe," Barnabas did as he was told, placing his backpack on the floor beside him. He was beside the model statue, in the shadow of the Great Mayor's confident chin as Glower secured his right wrist to the pipe with a plastic cable tie.

He remembered Wickram's absurd faith in him. Even five minutes ago, Barnabas himself had imagined finding a crack in Glower's plan which he would exploit to defeat the evil man. *Barnabas Bopwright, the young saviour of the City!* the headlines would proclaim. But instead, here he sat with an impotent front row seat to the disaster. He had no weapon, no means of communication. He had nothing, *was* nothing. Shame suffused his heart.

Glower locked the door before returning to the worktable. Lines of code had replaced the security cams on his laptop, and the man typed in little bursts each time a prompt appeared.

Out of nowhere, Glower asked, "Bopwright? Is your father Harold Bopwright?"

"Uh, yeah. Do you know his music?"

"Music? No. He painted my apartment once. His procedures were sloppy."

Barnabas remembered his dad had done house painting when gigs were scarce. "Why are you hacking the stadium's systems? Don't you just need line of sight to operate the triggers?"

"First of all, I needed to control the movement of security in the stadium. But most importantly, I will be broadcasting the destruction of the towers live to the SuperScreen. I want 35,000 witnesses who will scream and then pour out of the building, spreading terror in their wake. I want everyone in the City paralyzed with fear. I want them to question their privilege and remember their place." Glower said all this with great satisfaction, like he'd already succeeded.

Barnabas pulled against the plastic tie holding him but only hurt his wrist. He kicked the pipe again and again, but it was firmly attached to the wall. Glower picked up the gun and spun around.

"Stop that, boy, you're distracting me."

CHAPTER 77

"You're a dick," Barnabas yelled, staring down the gun, determined not to let his fear show. The petty insult had no effect. Glower just put the weapon down and turned back to his work. He opened the black box Barnabas had seen in the back room of the Drop Shop and removed the orange cube, placing it on the table in front of him.

"Why do you have to do this?" Barnabas asked. "People are going to die! Doesn't that bother you?"

Glower pushed a button on the orange cube. It beeped three times and then two times more, and a line of lights flashed across its surface.

Barnabas thought Glower hadn't heard him, but then he answered. "Why *should* it bother me? It won't really bother anyone, except insofar as they fear they will be next. Self-interest is the only principle that governs people's actions. Any show of concern for others is just a pretty social lie." The answer hit Barnabas like a slap. It couldn't be true. People cared about more than themselves, didn't they?

Glower emptied a box of Go, Team! buttons onto the floor and used it as a stand for the orange cube. It stood before the window, ready to send its message of death to the blue pyramids in each tower.

"Now, Bopwright, I have a question for you. Before you left the Valley, you must have sought help. Who did you tell about my plan?"

Barnabas didn't answer. He wouldn't help Glower justify his actions. Glower picked up an old glass paperweight from the desk and threw it at Barnabas, who cried out and batted it away painfully with his free arm. A sick wave of terror flowed over him, and he pulled at the tie holding his wrist.

Glower asked again, his voice as calm as before. "Who did you tell?"

"The Guild Council," Barnabas shouted back, gritting his teeth to stop himself from crying.

"And they sent you packing, right? I'm surprised they didn't stick you in Doomlock and throw away the key. You're dangerous to them. If they know about my plan, they become responsible for stopping me." He reached across the desk, unlatched the big windows, and pushed them open. The noises of the City entered the room, the familiar hubbub of everyone just going about their business, certain the future was safe and secure. Barnabas could also hear the closer buzz of the stadium crowd. Someone must have hit a runner home because a cheer rose up like a single joyous roar of a great animal, blissfully ignorant of the predator at its back.

The sound seemed to give Glower a jolt of excitement. "The Guild Council knew people were going to die. Why were *they* not bothered?" He sneered. "So, then you got back to the City somehow. You're a resourceful boy, apparently. Who did you tell once you were here?"

"I'm not playing this game," Barnabas answered, humiliated by the fearful quaver in his voice.

Glower abruptly lost his cool. Face darkened in fury, he picked up a large trophy with the golden figure of a batter on top and raised his arm to throw it. Barnabas cowered, covering his face. "Stop! Okay! I told these old people at City Hall, the ones who know about the Valley. Then I told the mayor."

Glower laughed and put the trophy down. "Wonderful. And tell me, son of the sloppy painter, did the upcoming deaths of all those innocents in the towers bother *any* of these illustrious people?"

"I don't know," Barnabas answered, and then more quietly, "I guess not."

Eyes glittering, Glower brought his face close, like he really needed Barnabas to understand. "That's how people are, Bopwright, don't you see? I wanted to save them. I offered to be their mayor and give them a better future, but they spat in my face. They're not worth saving, and the sooner you learn that, son, the less disappointment you'll know." They stared at each other for a moment before Glower said, "Running out of time," and returned to his laptop.

But his calm, methodical shell was crumbling. His fingers chattered recklessly on the keyboard, and he cursed under his breath, pulling scraps of paper from his pocket in search of important notes. The screen changed from lines of code to a video feed of the statue of Lawrence Glorvanious in front of City Hall. The camera was mounted high on a building across the street. Barnabas could see people walking past the statue. A flock of pigeons swooped by in front of the camera. *What does the statue have to do with anything?* he wondered with growing dread.

As if in answer, Glower said, "A little message to my family." A giggle bubbled out of him, and he hit a key with a flourish.

Barnabas heard the stadium crowd react with a surprised swell. "What was that?" he asked.

"I put the image of the statue up on the SuperScreen instead of the usual meaningless garbage."

So, it's really starting. With the hijacking of the SuperScreen, the authorities would know something serious was going on.

Barnabas felt a cold wave of fear. "What are you going to do?" Glower ignored him. He swivelled his chair and adjusted the orange cube. Then Barnabas remembered what Wickram had said about seeing something blue on the statue's hat. Was it one of the blue pyramids?

"Wait..." Barnabas said, but in that moment, Glower pushed a single key on his laptop, and the cube beeped three times. On the screen, Barnabas saw a flash of light, and the huge statue of Lawrence Glorvanious exploded, scattering shards of dust and debris across the plaza. There was no microphone, so he couldn't hear the explosion, but the crowd in the stadium cried out as one—the great animal roaring in terror.

Chapter 78

Barnabas was cold with shock. Through the window he could just see a column of smoke rising in the distance. "Oh my God, oh my God," he breathed.

Glower sprung to his feet and slammed his hand down on the table. "Boom!" He turned and strode toward Barnabas, who curled himself into a ball. But it wasn't him the man was after. Glower bent over and screamed into the face of the half-sized statue, the wooden miniature of the bronze he had just destroyed. "How do you like *that*, Great-grandfather? Did you think you were immortal? Boom. Up in flames. You made all your pretty, perfect plans, Lawrence, but I will undo them all!"

He lurched back to the desk. His hands were shaking now, and moons of sweat stained his underarms and back. Glower attached a video camera to his laptop and stood it on a mini tripod in the open window, the image appearing on his screen. He adjusted the zoom and focus until he had a clear shot of the whole Tower District. He typed on his keyboard, and Barnabas knew from the rising roar of the crowd that the image had appeared on the SuperScreen.

Authoritative voices were shouting outside now, sirens screaming in the distance.

An old analog clock on the wall was still dutifully counting out the hours and minutes. It read two twenty-five. Barnabas's mouth was dry, but he had to speak. "Mr. Glower…Glorvanious…Please listen." The man paid no attention. He was checking connections, making sure everything was ready for the final act of the show, but Barnabas continued. "I know the people in charge didn't care, but they're not everyone. All the people at Pastoral Park, they helped me escape, Sanjani got me and Wickram out of the Valley so I could save the City. The Lurkers underground helped us get back here. And my stepdad believed in me even though he had no reason to."

Glower shifted the camera slightly, double-checking the image on his laptop.

Barnabas pressed on: "I get it. People were jerks to you. I know about the jerks winning and the good people being ignored. The point is, most people are just trying to have a good life, despite the jerks. But if you hurt them—"

Glower snapped his head around. "They're the ones I hate the most. Come on, think. I see you're not stupid. Those are exactly the brainless sheep who could have had me as their mayor, their shepherd. But they squandered their chance. Better to slaughter them and start again."

With a wide sweep of his arms, he cleared the trophies off the table. They came crashing to the floor, one of them bouncing smartly into Barnabas's leg. He cried out in pain as Glower threw back his head and sang the City anthem in a brusque, coarse baritone:

> *Hail to the future, sprung from the land!*
> *Hail to the roads built by spirit and hand!*
> *A world where our children can prosper and play,*
> *In this fair, golden city rising skyward today!*

From outside the open window, someone shouted, "Who's there? This is the police, show yourself!"

Barnabas didn't hesitate, he screamed in a raw, frenzied voice. "He's up here! Stop him, he's here!"

Glower dove across the room and, with a great backhand sweep, struck Barnabas across the face. "Shut up!" Barnabas's head smacked against the pipe with a nauseating thump, and he saw stars. Through the tears in his eyes, he looked up into Glower's face, twisted in fury, teeth showing, sweat pouring from his brow. He brandished the gun in one shaking hand and said, "I won't give you another chance, boy."

The police called up through a megaphone. "Come to the window with your hands raised. We need to see your hands. You have thirty seconds to comply."

Glower leaned across the table and stuck his head out the window. "It's too late. You're finished." He pulled himself back in and turned to Barnabas. "I don't blame you for trying. I don't. Someday you'll understand that I was right." He raised a finger above his keyboard. "Delphic Tower first. Are you home, Tuppletaub? I hope so."

The finger struck and the orange cube beeped. Barnabas buried his head in his backpack, moaning in terror. He braced himself for the explosion, wondering if he would hear it this far away.

"What?" Glower said. "What what what?" He was incredulous, furious. Barnabas opened his eyes and relief washed over him. Delphic Tower was still standing. Of course it was. Barnabas had torn out all the wires that connected the trigger to the explosives. But the other buildings were still wired and set to blow. In a second, Glower would recover and try those. Barnabas had to do something.

The police outside spoke again. "Approach the window with your hands visible. This is your last warning." Glower began to swear, a long stream of curses.

Barnabas realized he might as easily get shot by the police as by Glower. He sat up in alarm and his bag tipped over. Something rolled out, and he kicked out his leg to stop it. With a shaking hand, he reached out and took hold of the diaboriku.

This singular object, which had tried so hard to escape him, now sat contentedly in his palm, awaiting orders. Barnabas knew exactly how he could use it to stop Glower, if only he could work the damned thing. Even last night he could have asked Cal to teach him. Cursing his arrogance, he began to punch manically at the buttons to no effect.

He had to calm down and focus—a deep breath, a slow release. He pushed the buttons methodically, and quickly realized he was just repeating things he'd already tried. He forced himself to breathe, to clear the panic from his mind. What if, he thought, I hold one button like a function key while I press the others? The big red button was the obvious choice, and if he was right, there were only a few permutations to try. The first sequence did nothing, ditto the second, but with the third, the machine buzzed in his hand, and its lights came on. Barnabas felt like his chest would explode with excitement. He had done it. The diaboriku was activating.

CHAPTER 79

George could not understand what had gone wrong. Delphic Tower should now have been a smouldering pile of wreckage at the bottom of the great cliff. He searched his perfect memory, reviewing each connection he had made, looking for any possible error. There were none.

Focus! Let it go, move on. The next logical step would be to bring down a different tower. But the plan had called for Delphic first. He willed his mind to be flexible, but it was not. *The plan is the plan is the plan is the—* He smacked himself in the head. *Stop it!* His mind was not behaving. *Focus!*

"Approach the window with your hands visible," blared the idiotic megaphone outside. George had a childish desire to hurl trophies and mascot toys at them. But no, he didn't have much time. The police would soon find their way in, and everything would be lost. All right then, another tower. He checked that the video feed was still up on the SuperScreen. Thirty-five thousand pairs of eyes were watching. He could almost feel their viscous weight.

See me, he said to them in his mind. *See what I have done. I could still be your mayor. Fall to your knees and beg for my leadership.*

A huge shadow rose above him, darkening the table and all his gear. *The police?* He grabbed his gun and turned. What he faced was terrible, incomprehensible. It rose higher and higher until its undulating grey locks brushed the ceiling like the tentacles of an octopus. It was Lawrence Glorvanious, returned from the dead to demand an explanation. The hand that stretched from the torn sleeve of the mayor's time-worn wool suit was raw and bloody, the chipped nails like claws. The hand clutched spasmodically at the air, closer and closer, like it wanted to choke the life from him.

The Great Mayor cried out, "I sweated and fought and dreamed the City into existence. I am grace and glory, and the people still speak my name in awe. And who are you?"

George tried to speak, but his voice was a hoarse, meaningless rasp.

"You are a failure...a *shopkeeper.* I will destroy you rather than suffer you to live another moment."

George shot the gun, once, twice, three times into the advancing figure who was steam and earth, power and rectitude. But the giant only roared, fire erupting from its nose and ears.

"I tried!" George screamed in a childish, humiliating voice. "Please, give me another chance. I promise I'll win."

"You have destroyed the family name!" the ghost bellowed. George scrambled up on the worktable to get away. Emerging from the ghost's other sleeve, where his hand should have been, was a ceremonial shovel of shining gold, the blade sharpened to a lethal edge. The ghost-mayor swung it at George, who backed up until he suddenly hit the emptiness of the tall, open windows. He slipped backward into the warm afternoon, a single hand and the heel of one shoe the only things holding him in place. The brilliant sunlight blinded him.

The monster Glorvanious spat out its final curse: "Better you had never been born." And George lost his grip, tumbling headfirst toward the pavement, and death opened its generous arms to greet him.

CHAPTER 80

Barnabas was curled on the floor, shivering uncontrollably when the door was kicked in. Police in black armour poured into the tiny room, shouting and trampling over all the bits of history. They shot questions at him. *Who was that man? How did you get here? Are there any more terrorists?* Easy questions, but his brain was just not accessible. Circuit overload, system shutdown.

Then a woman in an Aqua Guard uniform was there kneeling before him, speaking calmly as she cut the tie holding his wrist. "I'm Lieutenant Blenbooly, Aqua Guard Frontier Deployment. I'll get you out of here."

She left him sitting in a chair in the corridor while she negotiated his release with the officer in charge. Barnabas was still holding the diaboriku, and he tried to make sense of what had happened. The device had projected its monstrous hologram of Lawrence Glorvanious based on the wooden statue, just like Barnabas planned. But when Glower began shooting, Barnabas had dropped the toy in panic. The projection had vanished, but Glower acted like the monster was still there. Not only that, he was answering back as if the hologram were speaking to him. But it wasn't. The diaboriku was just making its usual tinny monster noises.

Over and over in his head, Barnabas saw Glower disappearing backward through the open window. The sound of that terrible crack on the pavement below echoed in his ear.

Lieutenant Blenbooly returned and sat beside him. "You ready to go, Barnabas?"

"My backpack..." he said, voice shaky, and she went to collect it. The armoured police were everywhere, and their shouts and thundering footsteps made Barnabas cringe. He and Blenbooly were challenged at every conceivable checkpoint, but each time she calmly produced some document—a stamped sheet of paper on heavy stock—and they were allowed to pass.

Out in the stadium, the crowd was being evacuated in a well-rehearsed emergency procedure. Blenbooly led Barnabas around the perimeter of the field and knocked at another metal door in the fence. A second Aqua Guard answered and let them into a room. Wickram was inside, perfectly cheerful and finishing off the last bites of another hot dog.

He ran to Barnabas. "Hey, did you see me on the big screen? Did you hear me play?"

Barnabas looked at the happy face stained with mustard and felt his own smile return. It was the moment he finally believed the danger was over. "Yeah. You were amazing."

"I utterly was. Ha! And now I'm not the skinniest bit scared for tomorrow's audition."

Lieutenant Blenbooly approached with the other Aqua Guard. "Boys, this is Sergeant Trallergott. We all have to leave. Now." They travelled down through the bowels of the stadium to a basement garage where they climbed into an unmarked, aqua-coloured SUV. Soon they were driving down an eerily deserted Grand Avenue filled with military personnel and emergency vehicles that blazed past, sirens screaming.

"Nothing else blew up other than the statue?"

Blenbooly smiled at him. "Thanks to you."

Barnabas had dreamed of being a hero, of hearing just this kind of compliment. But he didn't know how to take it now. He turned away and stared out the window. His beloved City looked temporary and fragile. And worse than that, what had been the best City in the world was tainted for him by generations of secrets and lies, and by the exploitation of the Valley.

The SUV took them to Admiral Crumhorn Station, where the boys were escorted into a windowless room. The two Aqua Guards were joined by City officials who made Barnabas and Wickram relate everything they knew about Glower and his plan for two endless hours. Barnabas felt like his sanity was slipping. There was a scary moment at the end when it seemed they would not be released, even when Blenbooly showed her magic document. But after some impressive threats about the wrath of higher-ups, the locked doors opened. Odd that Barnabas was now relying on the Aqua Guard to protect him after days spent avoiding them.

When Deni opened the door of her apartment and saw Barnabas, her brow quirked in concern. *Just how bad do I look?* he wondered. Without a word, she pulled him inside and into an enormous hug. Deni looked over his shoulder at Wickram and the Aqua Guards and asked, "Are you, um, all coming in?"

"Just Barnabas and Wickram, ma'am," said Trallergott, and Wickram pushed past the hugging pair.

"Hey, Deni," he said. "I'm going to do a reconnaissance of the fridge."

Barnabas said to the guards, "Uh, thanks?"

"Our pleasure," Blenbooly said. "We'll be in touch soon," and then they were gone.

Deni led him to the living room couch. "And of course, you'll tell me later who those two were. Mom-Amy is on her way home. The whole City's shutting down for the day. You were there, weren't you? In the middle of everything?"

"Yeah," was all he could say. "Mind if I lie down a bit?" He stretched out, and Deni got him a blanket. It only took a minute for the couch to pull him down into its warm embrace, the peaceful darkness taking him away.

Chapter 81

"Barnabas, wake up, dear." He climbed up a long dark tunnel into wakefulness and saw Deni's Mom-Amy sitting on the edge of the couch, her grey braids tied in a bun on her head. "Deni told me you want to spend the night, but first you have to talk to your poor mother." She handed him a phone. He looked up at Deni, who shrugged, which meant *don't blame me*.

"Hello, Mom?"

"Bar…?" was as far as she got before she started sobbing.

"Mom, don't. I'm fine." He didn't know what else to say, and just listened to her cry for a minute, feeling like a terrible son.

His mother finally pulled herself together. "I know, I'm ridiculous. But have you been listening to the news? They say that madman Glorvanious was going to blow up the whole Tower District."

"I-I heard that, too."

"I didn't know where you were. And whether he was taking care of you at a time like this."

"No, I'm great. There's no—wait. Whether *who* was taking care of me?"

"Oh, Barnabas, I'm not a fool. I know you've been with your father for the last five days."

"My father." He looked over at Deni, who raised both hands, palms up, which meant *I never told her, I swear on my Kurly Kuties collectibles.* Somehow, his mom and Deni had jumped to the same wild conclusion. That was the effect Brownbag Bopwright had on the people who loved him.

"You could have told me, Barnie-lamb," his mother said. "Did you think I wouldn't let you go?"

He realized it was easier to just go with her story. "It meant missing school, Mom, so yeah, you might not have let me."

"I'm not the monster you think I am, Barnabas," she shouted unexpectedly. "I want you to have a relationship with your father."

"Mom! Did I *say* you were a—"

"Just please, promise me you won't go live with him," she said, and started crying again.

The conversation had steered so deep into the unbearable, Barnabas was close to ripping his own ears off just to escape. "Okay. I won't go live with him. I promise."

"I mean, this was basically kidnapping. You tell him that for me."

"Mom, I'm not with him. I'm back at Deni's, right? And I'll see you tomorrow—right after school."

Amy took the phone and left the room, chatting earnestly with Barnabas's mom about Glorvanious and mental health and security.

Barnabas felt like truth and lies had been thrown together into a juicer and smoothied. Deni appeared with a mug of a steaming cocoa.

"Thanks," he said, and they sat in silence as he blew and sipped. When he was ready, he began. "Glorvanious has been hiding out ever since the election eight years ago. I met him while I was away, found out about his plot and tried to warn everyone, including the mayor. But they wouldn't listen. I did what I had to."

"Later, when things calm down and you're feeling, you know, better, can I interview you? Exclusive? It would be really good for us."

Barnabas smiled. He couldn't help it. All he wanted was for things to be normal, and there was nothing more normal than Deni Jiver and her ambition, and her promise to bring her best friend along for the ride. "Sure," he said.

"Just one more thing, and then I'll leave you alone."

Barnabas nodded.

"If it weren't for you, would the towers be gone now?"

"It wasn't just me. There was a whole bunch of people, including you and Cal. So yeah, if it wasn't for us…" They both sat in silence, feeling the weight of this fact settle on their shoulders.

Deni's Mom-Morgan came home later from City Hall which, she reported, was a chaotic scene of denial and finger-pointing. The two parents and three kids sat down for a big meal. Maybe to spare Barnabas and Wickram more trauma, they stuck to safe subjects of conversation, and in this warm family atmosphere, Barnabas began to feel better. After dinner, Wickram performed the pieces he was going to play at his audition, and they all told him how beautiful it sounded. Still, Barnabas could see he was nervous.

Deni and her moms turned on the news at ten, and Barnabas watched it standing in the doorway of the guest bedroom in case he felt the need to duck out. The bomb squads had evacuated all the towers and were now removing the explosives. Mayor Tuppletaub appeared on screen, asking for calm heads in this time of tribulation. He said his administration was launching an investigation into the failure of the GateKeeper System. The election would proceed on schedule.

These words of reassurance, which made Barnabas feel ill, were followed by a profile on the life of George Glorvanious, including theories about where he had been for the past eight years. Already an urban myth was emerging that he'd been holed up all that time in the Memorabilia Room of the Manhammer Audiodome, a hermit slowly crafting his revenge.

Glower's face stared out at him from the screen, and Barnabas could still hear the cold, logical voice in his head. "Self-interest is the only principle that governs people's actions. Any appearance of concern is a lie."

He went into the bedroom, where Wickram was already in bed, reading a big coffee table book about famous jazz musicians. Barnabas stripped to his T-shirt and boxers and climbed into bed, pulling the blankets over his head and murmuring goodnight to his friend.

"You still awake, Barn?" Wickram said after a minute. "I wanted to say thanks. Everything was going to hell in my life before you showed up last week. And now look—the City's safe and maybe I'm gonna move here."

Barnabas pulled his head free of the blankets. "It wasn't just me, Wick."

"Well, obviously. If I hadn't been there, this whole enterprise would have been fizz in a slizzpot." He grinned. "Just think how proud they're gonna be of us back in Pastoral Park."

Barnabas thought about the circus people, about Sanjani and Garlip, and he thought about Cal and Deni and Wickram. Then he thought about Glower—a man with no companions but his dreams of revenge, and he realized how rich his own life was in comparison.

PART VII

WEDNESDAY

CHAPTER 82

The next morning, Barnabas sat in a plastic chair outside a room marked Ensemble B in the Dieter Wieder Academy of Music. Wickram had been inside for more than fifteen minutes.

Music filled the building, like a glorious soup of voices, horns, drums, and strings. Students, singly and in little clusters, passed by him, carrying instruments, reading scores, and laughing and flirting with each other. This was the first time in almost a week Barnabas had been alone with his thoughts, and he decided to do an experiment. Which of these young musicians was he attracted to? There was a girl with big brown eyes, whose breasts and hips and every other part seemed to dance when she laughed, and a boy with dreads and nerdy wire rim glasses whose long brown fingers played against his taut stomach like it was a piano keyboard.

Barnabas let himself feel the lust, let himself imagine being naked with these people and being in relationships with them. What would that life be like? How would it feel to say, "I'm Barnabas Bopwright, bisexual," like it was a secret agent introduction? Further experimentation would be required.

He went back down the hall to talk to the secretary in the office. "Will the audition take much longer?"

"Your friend's still in there? That's a good sign." She looked around to make sure they were alone. "So, that little guy who set up the audition—Falstep, right?—Do you know him pretty well? Is he a serious guy or a player?"

"He's actually pretty funny."

"That's not what I meant."

"He doesn't live in the City, but if I see him, I'll tell him you said hi."

"Do that. Oh, look, they're done."

Barnabas turned to see tall Wickram bend to shake the hand of a stooped man with long, unkempt grey hair.

Wickram walked past Barnabas like he didn't even see him, but then called over his shoulder, "Let's get out of here." Without a word of explanation, he turned and ran down the hall and out the front doors of the school. By the time Barnabas caught up, Wickram was at the far end of the patchy lawn, standing on a picnic table with a stunned look on his face, hugging his instrument.

Breathless, Barnabas looked up at his friend. "What happened?"

Wickram, wide-eyed, replied, "I'm in!"

"Really?"

Wickram jumped down from the table and hugged Barnabas awkwardly with the guitar between them. "It's not official. They have to inform me when they tell the other applicants, but Mr. Gileppsy—he's the head of composition—told me to go ahead and move to the City." They began jumping around like the ground was a trampoline.

"Follow me," Barnabas said. "I'm buying us celebratory ice cream."

But when they got to the gate of the school, they found Lieutenant Blenbooly and Sergeant Trallergott waiting for them.

Blenbooly removed her hat. "Wickram, Barnabas, we're instructed to escort you back across the Frontier."

Wickram's face grew red. "No, I'm staying here in the City and going to this school." He looked around like he was going to bolt.

Trallergott reached for his nightstick, but Blenbooly put a hand out to stop him. "Guild Council already knows about your audition. I'm pretty sure they're going to grant you an open travel permit. But if you want to leave now, we won't try and stop you. Just remember that will mean you can never return to the Valley, so I suggest you come with us."

Barnabas said, "And what about me? Are you taking me to Doomlock? That was the plan before."

"President Borborik of the Guild Council has asked to speak with you. Following your interview, you will spend the night in Pastoral Park and return to the City on the morning train. I've been told to assure you your presence is entirely voluntary, though it would be appreciated."

Barnabas looked from one to the other. "It's hard to trust you, frankly, but let's go."

CHAPTER 83

"Hang on tight!" Wickram shouted over the wind. Barnabas didn't need to be told. They were in the open back of an Aqua Guard transport truck, racing away from the Valley's train station at high speed. Hardly any time passed before the truck was bumping up the steep winding road to Pastoral Park. Barnabas realized the whole Valley wasn't actually that big when you travelled by truck instead of mule cart. They screeched to a halt in the parking lot, sending up a shower of gravel. Wickram immediately leaped over the edge of the truck bed and ran toward his father, who was standing in front of the Big Top. Maestro Tragidenko threw his arms open, and his son fell right into them, accepting a surprisingly long hug.

Barnabas started to climb down from the truck when Blenbooly stuck her head out the passenger window. "Stay where you are, please. We're taking you right to the Guild Council building." Before he could respond, the immense form of Dimitri Tragidenko crossed the parking lot and climbed up into the back of the truck with him.

"I am accompanying the young man," he told Blenbooly, who looked like she was about to object. But Tragidenko had already clicked his seat belt in place. "He is my guest in the Valley, yes? And his parents—even if they do not know this—are counting on me to keep him safe. We go now," he announced as if he was in charge of the operation. Barnabas hid his smile.

They hardly spoke as the truck drove at the same terrifying speed along the road around Lake Lucid. At one point, Tragidenko squinted up at the cloudy sky and shouted, "It will rain later. Hopefully we are back by then, dining deliciously at Pastoral Park."

When they entered the Hall of Deliberations, Barnabas was surprised to find the room empty of councillors. Only President Borborik, on his raised platform, and one councilwoman Barnabas remembered from his last visit were in their chairs. A clerk led

Tragidenko to the benches at the back of the hall, while Barnabas was ushered forward.

"Welcome back, young Bopwright," said the president as he approached. "This is Councillor Ix-Navim of Forming Guild. She is Chief Liaison to the City. We requested your presence here so we might ask you some questions and discuss your future." This sounded ominous, and Barnabas sat down in a chair in front of them.

From the back of the room, Tragidenko called out in his best ringmaster's voice. "And I will be back here. Watching."

Ix-Navim pushed her glasses up on her nose and studied a sheaf of papers. "This is the statement you gave yesterday following the incident at the Manhammer Audiodome." She looked up at Barnabas. "First of all, on behalf of the Guild Council and the denizens of the Valley, we thank you for your bravery." President Borborik nodded in agreement.

Barnabas felt himself blushing. "Um, I'm just really glad it worked out. Can I ask something? Did you ever catch Carminn?"

"The former Speaker of Clouding Guild remains a fugitive," said the President.

"Aren't you afraid that she'll try to do the same as Glower?"

"No. Her followers have been arrested and her steam elevator deactivated. Glower would not have been able to accomplish as much as he did without his knowledge of the City and his association with the mayor. Carminn has no such advantages. We will find her eventually and bring her to justice."

This unresolved threat lodged itself in Barnabas's chest. For many years, it would wake him at night, along with the feeling that his apartment was tumbling off a high cliff into the abyss.

Borborik cleared his throat. "In retrospect, the Council might have reacted with too much caution when you brought us your concerns. We were caught off guard by the severity of your news."

Barnabas wanted to say *You tried to throw me in jail instead of stopping Glower. I guess you could call that "caution."* But he kept his mouth shut.

Ix-Navim said, "You have our eternal gratitude, and we offer you free passage out of the Valley tomorrow. Our trust is rarely earned so quickly, but you have demonstrated exceptional character for one so young."

"Thanks. Then could you please give Wickram an open travel permit so he can go school in the City? Without him, Glower would have succeeded."

Borborik nodded. "So granted."

Barnabas turned to make sure Tragidenko heard the good news, and just then, the doors of the Council chamber opened again. An old woman with a cane entered and walked down the aisle with steely resolution. It was Summer Coomlaudy, the Prime Prelate.

Chapter 84

Summer Coomlaudy climbed the platform carefully and took a seat beside President Borborik. The president and Councillor Ix-Navim stood and didn't sit again until she was seated.

Without acknowledging her colleagues, Coomlaudy looked down at Barnabas. "Mr. Bopwright, I had not thought we would meet again, much less here in the Valley, but these have been days of exceptional circumstance." He wasn't sure if he was supposed to answer, so he only nodded. "We believe you have a bright future, and we wish to help you fulfill it."

Barnabas sat up straighter in his chair. "What do you mean?" Pause. "Ma'am?"

She smiled. "The system of secrecy put in place by Lawrence Glorvanious and his associates all those years ago has been a great success."

Ix-Navim, her hand waving in the air like an orchestra conductor, said, "It has brought prosperity to the City and allowed the Valley to fulfill its holy role undisturbed."

"Just so," said the Prime Prelate, dryly.

"Ahhhrrrrmm-hemmm," said Tragidenko, and Barnabas turned to look at him.

President Borborik frowned. "Maestro, is something wrong?"

"No, no! Just clearing my throat." He returned the president's stare.

"As I was saying," Coomlaudy continued, "in order to maintain the balance, we need to have a very small number of bright and capable people in charge of relations between the two realms—our triumvirate in the City and my two esteemed colleagues here."

"What does this have to do with me?" Barnabas asked warily, like he was talking to a telemarketer.

Now Borborik smiled, but it didn't make Barnabas any less wary.

"It has everything to do with you," he said. "We hope you will consider a life path that would someday put you in our unique company."

The Prime Prelate said, "There are specific courses in civics and City planning at some fine institutions that we would like you to consider following high school. We can guarantee you admission to these elite programs and help you with tuition. We know your parents might not be in a position to afford such schools."

How do you know that? he wanted to ask.

"We see how competitive your world has become," said President Borborik. "You probably won't get a better offer than this." It sounded vaguely like a put-down. Did they know about his less-than-stellar grades, just as they seemed to know his family's finances?

Summer Coomlaudy leaned forward, smile fading, eyes pinning him to the back of his chair like an insect she was mounting for her collection. "Of course, this opportunity would require a lot from you, primarily your ability to keep a *secret*." She paused and let the word sink in. "And that secrecy would have to begin now. Do you understand?"

Three sets of eyes bored into him. "Oh," Barnabas mumbled, "Yeah, of course. I wasn't going to tell anyone about...the Valley or... Glower or...whatever." Summer Coomlaudy leaned back in her seat, nodding.

President Borborik, too, nodded gravely. "I'm glad to hear that, young Bopwright. Telling anyone—*anyone*—would not do *anyone* any good. Including yourself."

Ix-Navim joined the company of nodders. "Exactly. Think of your bright future."

"Aaaaaa-hrrrmmmm-hemmrrr," Tragidenko growled.

The Prime Prelate banged her cane on the desk in front of her. "Who *is* that man, Borborik? Is he unwell?"

"What is it now, Dimitri?"

Tragidenko rose and walked to the front, his heavy footsteps echoing in the empty hall. "Oh, nothing," he said. "I must have dropped off into a lovely little slumber. Your words startled me back to reality." He was standing behind Barnabas's chair now, and the boy felt a big warm hand fall on his shoulder. "So, perhaps you are done thanking this brave young man for his work of valour, and I might take him back to Pastoral Park. A feast is awaiting us, and you know how it disappoints the chefs if their culinary marvels dry out in the oven, yes?"

There was a long pause. Borborik looked down at Barnabas and said, "Just as long as the boy understands everything we have said here."

"Sure," Barnabas answered. "Thank you. I'll think about it. All of it." He got to his feet and followed Tragidenko toward the door.

Just before they exited, the president called out, "Maestro! While we recognize the circumstances that led Pastoral Park to break so many laws in the past days, we feel this would be a good time to review the role of the circus in the Valley."

Tragidenko turned and took a deep, audible inhale. "Thirty years ago, at a time of flagging morale, the Council invited the circus to join the Valley. We dedicated ourselves to our task of bringing joy to the hardworking denizens. In all these years, we have not wavered. I look forward to hearing just what role you now wish us to play. Come, Barnabas."

Again, they rode in the back of the truck in silence, both lost in thought, until Tragidenko bent low to speak over the roar of wind and engine.

"I hate this noisy transport. Give me instead the musical clip-clop of our dear mules, with the occasional aromatic *plop* behind for counterpoint, yes?"

"I guess this is faster."

"Faster, yes. So, what do you think of the offer made by our esteemed councillors?"

"It was a pretty generous, the tuition and everything. My mom will be over the moon, but I'll have to make up a story to explain it to her."

"Secrets…I am thinking they are ugly little bunnies. They spend all their time just making more ugly little secrets."

"But sometimes they're necessary, right? President Borborik's right, isn't he? The system has been a huge success, and part of that is keeping the existence of the Valley secret."

"Yes, but how long before another Carminn or Glower wishes to change the balance? If not for the secret, would their plan have had a chance? Those bunnies, I am thinking, grow uglier with time."

"Are you saying that I *shouldn't* keep the secret?"

"Look out there. Lake Lucid used to be so beautiful. I suppose if no one speaks of what was lost, the next generation can live in blissful ignorance. Is such a secret, then, a blindfold or a kindness?" Tragidenko threw his hands in the air. "Who am I to tell you what to do? You are the boy who saved the City. Do what your heart tells you."

"My heart is confused."

Tragidenko smiled. "To really listen to your heart is like learning to juggle. It takes many hours of quiet persistence and a belief that the result is worth the effort."

The truck began to climb the hill to Pastoral Park.

CHAPTER 85

Barnabas and Tragidenko scrambled down from the truck in front of the Big Top. Lieutenant Blenbooly rolled down her window and said, "Barnabas, you have a seven a.m. train tomorrow. I'll meet you here at six fifteen. Be ready."

"Sure," Barnabas said, turning his back on her. Just a couple of hours ago, he would have said *Yes, ma'am*, but he was getting fed up with all the so-called authorities telling him what to do.

As he and Tragidenko rounded the Big Top, Wickram intercepted them, his face set in angry mode. "When were you thinking of telling me about Mom?"

Tragidenko was immediately on the defensive. "Barnabas and I were in a rush. They were waiting for us at the Guild Hall. The president himself."

"And that was more important than your wife's concussion?"

They were standing nose to nose now. "It was not breaking news. Your mother has been in bed two days. The doctor says she will be fine." He poked a finger into Wickram's chest. "While you were playing around in the City, I was sitting by her poor side, spooning excellent broths into her, made by my own hands."

Barnabas interrupted them, concerned. "What happened to Sanjani?"

"It was Carminn," Wickram said. "She was there at the bridge after we crossed. They fought, and Mom's head got knocked open."

Barnabas was speechless. He couldn't imagine small, fragile Sanjani going up against the power of Carminn.

"Come on, Barn," Wickram said. The anger had fallen from his face, leaving only his concern. "She wants to see you."

Sanjani, her head artfully bandaged, sat up in bed when they arrived. Wickram immediately pushed an extra pillow behind her back. "Pickle, stop acting like I'm about to die. Dr. Starbrott says I will be fine in a day or two."

"I was so dumb," Wickram whined miserably. "I should have realized Carminn was coming after us."

"We were all improvising that day. Now hush." She smiled warmly at them. "Look at my brave boys. You saved the City. I knew you would." She put one hand on Wickram's shoulder and the other on Barnabas's hand. "Did you meet my sister?"

"There wasn't time," Wickram said.

Barnabas said, "I'll call her when I get home, let her know Wickram is moving to the City."

Wickram crossed his arms over his chest. "Maybe I won't go. After all, Mom, Carminn's still on the loose. She might come after you."

"Oh, for heaven's sake, Wickram. Are you planning to lock me in the house and stand guard? Of course you're going."

Soon, he and Barnabas were walking down the steep lane away from the house. Wickram said, "Do you think she'll be okay, Barn? 'Cause I really want to go." The words came out in a breathy rush. "To the music school. To the City." He looked around at the streets of Pastoral Park. "I never noticed just how krumping *small* this place is."

They turned into the central square just as the sun slipped below the low ceiling of dark clouds that had hidden it all afternoon. Soon it would set, but for this brief time, the world was tinted in reds and golds. And in that magical light, Barnabas saw the dining hall, decorated in spectacular fashion. On the roof was a reproduction in cardboard of the buildings of the Tower District. Across the front of the building hung bright red letters that proclaimed "Bravo to Barnabas and Wickram!!"

CHAPTER 86

Barnabas mostly found the celebratory dinner embarrassing, with people raising toasts to him and making speeches. Wickram was bummed because everyone was there except Graviddy.

"She's still rehearsing," Hulo said.

The clowns came over to the kids' table and Falstep shoved a bunch of flowers at Barnabas. "Congrats, Platypus."

Barnabas leaned away. "Are these going to squirt me with water or something?"

"Of course not," Falstep said, shocked. "But they are a hat." He plopped the arrangement gracelessly on Barnabas's head, and sure enough, the colourful blooms were built around a little cap. "You have to wear that all evening, or you will offend the entire clown community."

The clowns all left except Beaney. "Someone wants to say hi, Barnabas," he said with a grin and stepped aside to reveal a familiar face.

Barnabas gave a happy cry. "Galt-Stomper!"

Glower and Greta's little assistant stuck out a shy hand. "Nice to meet you again, sir."

"Stomper didn't have anywhere to go after the Drop Shop closed," Beany said, "so we invited him to join the circus."

Galt-Stomper looked worried. "They say I have to learn to juggle, sir. I don't know if I can."

Barnabas remembered Tragidenko's words. "It takes many hours of quiet persistence, and the belief that the result will be worth the effort."

Just before dessert was served, the door of the dining hall flew open, and everyone turned to see Graviddy enter like a queen. Unlike the rest of the community, she was dressed in performance clothes—a shining white tunic with gold ruffles at the sleeve, glittering pants, and black boots. Her hair seemed lifted by its own private wind as she strode over to Wickram and planted a long, passionate kiss on his grateful mouth.

When the kiss finally ended, Graviddy took Wickram by the hand and led him back out the doors. Barnabas thought he looked as scared as he was excited. The rest of the kids jumped up, Garlip taking Barnabas's hand, and they followed the couple into the night. On her way out, Thumbutter grabbed a bottle of elderberry wine from one of the adults' tables.

Soon, the gang was tramping through the forest, lighting their way with kerosene lamps that cast looming shadows on the canopy of trees.

Garlip said, "I think it's going to rain."

"Stop worrying," said Thumbutter, clearing their path with a big branch.

They sat down by the river, not far from the stone bridge, and Barnabas told them the long version of their adventures in the City, including the dark details of the end of the man they knew as George Glower. They sat quietly, passing the wine bottle around the circle and feeling the weight of the tale, safe in each other's company in the enclosing darkness of the forest.

It wasn't long before Wickram and Graviddy joined them, emerging from the trees, pressed together in their own aura of warmth. Barnabas felt a little jealous of their intimacy, but then Garlip slipped his arm around Barnabas's waist, and the situation seemed more promising.

Garlip said, "Wouldn't it be flamtasmic if we did a set like this forest for one of the shows? The whole back wall could be a giant tree, and the performers would swing from branches and fly out between leaves."

"A lot of sight-line problems," Hulo said.

"And really tricky to light," Bulo added.

"Well, it's tricky if we just use kerosene and reflectors," Graviddy said, "but if we had electric lights..."

Thumbutter's booming voice echoed through the woods. "That can't happen, Graviddy. No electricity, remember? It's one of the—what do you call it?—founding principles."

Graviddy tossed her hair. "Maybe it's time for a change. In a few years, we'll be the ones making the decisions around here."

The discussion devolved into a fight between Graviddy and Thumbutter, with Hulo and Bulo alternately supporting both sides.

Garlip, who had also remained a neutral spectator, whispered in Barnabas's ear, "Want to go for a walk? I know a nice spot by the river."

Garlip was wearing a cape like Sherlock Holmes which he spread on the mossy bank so they could lay together. It was sweet and thrilling to kiss Garlip and pull his body close, hands exploring his dimensions.

There was so much more Barnabas imagined doing with him, but it was enough for now. It was great, in fact.

"You're going to become an amazing lover," Garlip sighed. "I can tell."

The idea seemed laughable to Barnabas, but stranger things had already happened. So, he just said, "Thank you."

As the group marched home, Graviddy started singing a beautiful song that had been the theme of a show years earlier. The melody was both sad and joyous, and the others joined her in flawless three-part harmony. The words were about falling backward with your eyes closed, trusting that your friends would be there to catch you. Barnabas smiled, but then suddenly the image of Glower's final moments filled his mind—backlit in the window of the Memorabilia Room, teetering above the fatal drop and falling backward into nothing.

As they reached the village, the rain began, at first lightly, and then falling in sheets, making them scream with laughter and break into a run. At the crossroads, Hulo, Bulo, Graviddy, Thumbbutter, and Garlip ran toward the dorm, shouting "Goodnight" and "See you in the morning." But when he and Wickram reached the house, Barnabas remembered this wasn't true. He wouldn't see them in the morning. He wondered if he'd ever see them again.

CONCLUSION

THE FOLLOWING WEEK

CHAPTER 87

It took days before Barnabas felt the tension release. He constantly looked over his shoulder as he walked the City streets, checking if maybe black limos were trailing him, or if Klevver was standing behind a bus shelter pointing a gun his way.

He was with Deni in the cafeteria a week after his return when his phone rang. "Hi, Mom. Yes, of course I'm coming home after school. Straight home, I promise. Yeah? Okay. She's right here, hold on." He put his hand over the phone and said to Deni, "Mom's doing a big dinner extravaganza tonight. She told me to ask you over. Feel free to say no."

"Sounds fun. I have an Italian lesson after school, but I can be there by six forty-five."

He thought about asking his mom if Cal could come, too, but then he had an idea. Once he'd thought it, it wouldn't go away. It needed to be just Deni.

At six that evening, he opened a VidChat with Thelonius.

His brother was getting ready for his workday, wet hair combed back, blowing the steam off his breakfast ramen. "Is everyone in the City still freaking out?"

"They're more excited than scared. New conspiracy theories every hour."

"Ha! Nothing stops the City."

Barnabas flopped back on his bed, tossing the diaboriku from hand to hand. *Juggling 101.* "So when are you coming home?"

"My mom and I are skiing in Nagano in January, so maybe I'll spend Christmas with you guys."

"Christmas? Flamtasmic!"

"Flam-*whatnow*?"

Barnabas smirked. "Just something we say. What about Dad? Maybe he can come for Christmas, too."

"He'll probably be playing in the house band on some Caribbean cruise."

"But if we ask him now…"

Thelonius's eyes grew hard. "Don't let Brownbag too deep in your heart, Buster. He has a habit of breaking them." The air seemed to thicken with sadness, and Thelonius changed the subject. "You figure out how to use the diaboriku yet?"

"Of course. It's easy."

"Well, show it off to your friends while you have the chance. They're going to release them in the West next fall. Monsters everywhere."

Monsters everywhere. Barnabas was back again in the Memorabilia Room, and Glower was on the window ledge, facing off against the monsters of his past. And then he was gone.

Barnabas tossed the diaboriku back onto the bed and sat up. "Oh yeah, I'm a Junior Sherlock now."

"Shut up! Really? What was your rookie mission?"

"I can't tell you. But it was utter sweet."

"Oooh, big secret."

Secrets, secrets. "Lony, what if…what if I told you I was bisexual?"

"Uh, is that something you're likely to tell me?"

"Yeah, I just might."

"Then I'd say it was cool."

Barnabas smiled with relief. He felt tears in his eyes and turned away from the screen, as if he'd just noticed something interesting out the window.

Deni rang the doorbell right at six forty-five, and Barnabas and his mother collided in the hall.

His mother pushed ahead, getting to the door first. "Do you mind if I play hostess in my own home?"

"You're just trying to impress her because you want her parents as contacts."

As his mom took her jacket and school bag, Deni said, "The new place looks great, Carol. Last time I was here, everything was still in boxes."

"Oh, it's so small. No room for any visionary design, like in your beautiful apartment."

Barnabas rolled his eyes.

He watched Deni during dinner, trying to make up his mind whether to go through with his plan. He caught Sam giving him sideways looks. His stepfather knew Barnabas had a big secret, but he wouldn't make him tell. *Secrets, secrets,* everyone keeping *secrets.* Meanwhile, the conversation flowed on around him.

"The mobilization was huge," Sam told them. "Over ten thousand police and firefighters at key spots around the City."

Carol touched her breast. "So much bravery. The mayor should have a parade for those people."

Where's my parade? Barnabas wanted to shout. "Can I be excused for a minute?" he said.

He hurried to his room and closed the door behind him, leaning against it while he tried to organize his thoughts. He crossed to the window and looked out. Night had fallen, and the City stood around him, a great organism of steel and flesh, its lights outshining the stars above. Barnabas knew the City—its people, its streets, its history. But he hadn't known the truth. He looked down at the crowds pushing along under the streetlamps and thought about how they were kept in ignorance. So much had been chosen for them by men named Glorvanious and their followers. If the people of the City knew the truth, would they have made the same choices?

And who am I to choose for them? Barnabas Bopwright, age fifteen years and five months, asked himself. And the answer came to him. *I'm the one who was given the choice.* And maybe, in the end, that kind of randomness was the true engine of history.

Deni knocked on the door. "Can I come in?" Barnabas snapped on the lights guiltily like he had been doing something wrong and opened the door. "Sam says we should come out for dessert in fifteen minutes. I think they're lighting it on fire."

"Oh, God. We should escape while we still can."

"That's a new poster, right?" She walked over to examine the lone climber atop the snowy peak. "Dramatic. What does it mean to you?"

"Ugh, that is such a teacher question. I guess something about rugged individualism. Conquering your mountain alone."

"Yeah, but he's not alone."

"What do you mean?"

"Duh, there's a photographer there with him. They climbed the mountain together."

This had never occurred to Barnabas. He stared at the poster, and it was suddenly a whole different story than he had thought. He shrugged. "Maybe I'm not a rugged individualist after all."

"Mmm. What are you, then?"

A sudden certainty, like a bold ray of sunshine, pierced the fog of his doubt. "I'm Barnabas, the Bunny Killer."

She laughed. "What?"

He was excited now. "What time do you have to be home?"

"I don't know. It doesn't matter. Why?"

"I've got a story to tell you."

He could see she was trying to control herself, not let her imagination get the better of her. Still, she was a little breathless as she asked, "Good story?"

"The best you ever heard," he said, beginning at the beginning.

About the Author

J. Marshall Freeman is a writer of fiction and poetry. He is the author of the young adult fantasy novel *The Dubious Gift of Dragon Blood* (2020) and one of three authors in the YA novella collection *Three Left Turns to Nowhere* (2022). He has appeared as a featured poet, and is the author of the poetry chapbook *Arthropoda* (2020). Freeman is two-time winner of the Saints+Sinners Fiction Contest (2017 and 2019). He lives in Toronto with his husband.

For more information and to contact the author, please visit jmarshallfreeman.com.

Young Adult Titles from Bold Strokes Books

Barnabas Bopwright Saves the City by J. Marshall Freeman. When he uncovers a terror plot to destroy the city he loves, 15-year-old Barnabas Bopwright realizes it's up to him to save his home and bring deadly secrets into the light before it's too late. (978-1-63679-152-4)

Take Her Down by Lauren Emily Whalen. Stakes are cutthroat, scheming is creative, and loyalty is ever-changing in this queer, female-driven YA retelling of Shakespeare's *Julius Caesar*. (978-1-63679-089-3)

Boy at the Window by Lauren Melissa Ellzey. Daniel Kim struggles to hold on to reality while haunted by both his very-present past and his never-present parents. Jiwon Yoon may be the only one who can break Daniel free. (978-1-63679-092-3)

Three Left Turns to Nowhere by Jeffrey Ricker, J. Marshall Freeman & 'Nathan Burgoine. Three strangers heading to a convention in Toronto are stranded in rural Ontario, where a small town with a subtle kind of magic leads each to discover what he's been searching for. (978-1-63679-050-3)

#shedeservedit by Greg Herren. When his gay best friend, and high school football star, is murdered, Alex Wheeler is a suspect and must find the truth to clear himself. (978-1-63555-996-5)

The Infinite Summer by Morgan Lee Miller. While spending the summer with her dad in a small beach town, Remi Brenner falls for Harper Hebert and accidentally finds herself tangled up in an intense restaurant rivalry between her famous stepmom and her first love. (978-1-63555-969-9)

Bury Me in Shadows by Greg Herren. College student Jake Chapman is forced to spend the summer at his dying grandmother's home and soon finds danger from long-buried family secrets. (978-1-63555-993-4)

I Am Chris by R Kent. There's one saving grace to losing everything and moving away. Nobody knows her as Chrissy Taylor. Now Chris can live who he truly is. (978-1-63555-904-0)

The Dubious Gift of Dragon Blood by J. Marshall Freeman. One day Crispin is a lonely high school student—the next he is fighting a war in a land ruled by dragons, his otherworldly boyfriend at his side. (978-1-63555-725-1)

Jellicle Girl by Stevie Mikayne. One dark summer night, Beth and Jackie go out to the canoe dock. Two years later, Beth is still carrying the weight of what happened to Jackie. (978-1-63555-691-9)

All the Worlds Between Us by Morgan Lee Miller. High school senior Quinn Hughes discovers that a broken friendship is actually a door propped open for an unexpected romance. (978-1-63555-457-1)

Exit Plans for Teenage Freaks by 'Nathan Burgoine. Cole always has a plan—especially for escaping his small-town reputation as "that kid who was kidnapped when he was four"—but when he teleports to a museum, it's time to face facts: it's possible he's a total freak after all. (978-1-163555-098-6)

Rocks and Stars by Sam Ledel. Kyle's struggle to own who she is and what she really wants may end up landing her on the bench and without the woman of her dreams. (978-1-63555-156-3)

Two Winters by Lauren Emily Whalen. A modern YA retelling of Shakespeare's *The Winter's Tale* about birth, death, Catholic school, improv comedy, and the healing nature of time. (978-1-63679-019-0)